REVIEWS FOR CLEOPATRA

'Enchanting, smart, and subversive – this is El-Arifi's masterpiece'
R.F. KUANG

'Saara El-Arifi's lush world-building and lyrical prose invest Cleopatra with a humanity, dignity, power and independence that burn brightly on every page. Her deep love and vast knowledge of her subject shine through, and we see Cleopatra's fascinating life portrayed on her own terms, as readers have never encountered her before'
JENNIFER SAINT

'With this unflinching take on her life and legacy, El-Arifi raises Cleopatra from the sands of time, greets her with profound compassion, and liberates her from the judgement of men, granting her dignity and humanity. An extraordinary achievement'
SAMANTHA SHANNON

'A sensational work in historical writing: Cleopatra as she is meant to be told'
HANNAH KANER

'So vividly immersive you feel you are physically present with Cleopatra, watching events unfold'
ELODIE HARPER

'Searing, masterful... this novel establishes Saara as the voice of a generation – bringing to dazzling life stories that have been obscured by the sands of time'
AMY MCCULLOCH

'Saara El-Arifi seamlessly blends rigorous research with sparkling imagination, bringing to life a Cleopatra broken free from the reductive roles men have forced upon her throughout history'
A.S. WEBB

'A compassionate, beautiful and lustrous insight into Cleopatra. Saara El-Arifi is a master of her craft'
TASHA SURI

'Vividly realised and skillfully unravelled, Cleopatra is as insightful as it is engrossing. A sorely needed new light'
KAT DUNN

Also by Saara El-Arifi

The Final Strife
The Battle Drum
The Ending Fire
Faebound
Cursebound

CLEOPATRA

SAARA EL-ARIFI

b
THE BOROUGH PRESS

The Borough Press
An imprint of HarperCollins*Publishers* Ltd
1 London Bridge Street
London SE1 9GF

www.harpercollins.co.uk

HarperCollins*Publishers*
Macken House, 39/40 Mayor Street Upper,
Dublin 1, D01 C9W8, Ireland

First published by HarperCollins*Publishers* 2026

1

Copyright © Saara El-Arifi 2026
Internal illustrations © Sophie Dunster 2026

Saara El-Arifi asserts the moral right to
be identified as the author of this work

A catalogue record for this book is available from the British Library

HB ISBN: 978-0-00-869721-1
TPB ISBN: 978-0-00-869722-8

This novel is entirely a work of fiction. The names, characters and incidents portrayed in it are the work of the author's imagination. Any resemblance to actual persons, living or dead, events or localities is entirely coincidental.

Set in Scala Pro

Printed and bound in the UK by
CPI Group (UK) Ltd, Croydon CR0 4YY

All rights reserved. No part of this publication may be reproduced, stored in a retrieval system, or transmitted, in any form or by any means, electronic, mechanical, photocopying, recording or otherwise, without the prior written permission of the publishers.

Without limiting the author's and publisher's exclusive rights, any unauthorised use of this publication to train generative artificial intelligence (AI) technologies is expressly prohibited. HarperCollins also exercise their rights under Article 4(3) of the Digital Single Market Directive 2019/790 and expressly reserve this publication from the text and data mining exception.

This book is produced from independently certified FSC™ paper
to ensure responsible forest management.
For more information visit: www.harpercollins.co.uk/green

*For my mother, Karen El-Arifi,
who taught me what it was to be
a mother, wife and friend*

AUTHOR'S NOTE

Ginestho [Let it be done]
— Cleopatra

A papyrus signed in Ancient Greek, believed by
some archaeologists to be written by Cleopatra. If so,
it is the sole surviving entry of the Pharaoh's voice
in her own history.

This is a true story. As true as any other biography of Cleopatra VII. Despite her being one of the most famous women in classical antiquity, we know very little about the life she led. The historians we have relied upon to tell her tale lived centuries after her death. Plutarch – most likely Shakespeare's predominant source for *Antony and Cleopatra* – captures one of the fullest accounts of her history in *Life of Antonius* and *Life of Caesar*, though his sources included his great-grandfather – who had never met the queen – and a deserter of Antonius's army, Dellius. Mentions from her contemporaries are fleeting and rarely substantial. The men whose words were preserved, such as Cicero, often originated from Rome, and their opinions were shaped by the propaganda of the Roman Republic. Her legend is only referenced in relation to Antonius and Caesar; too significant to ignore, too unpalatable to warrant her own narrative.

Therefore we must always be wary of absolutes when it comes to Cleopatra. No one can say for certainty who her mother was, or who she loved and was loved by. As a result, every choice I have made in this novel intertwines intention and interpretation.

A note on naming: some names I have represented as their transliterations, such as Marcus Antonius, and for others I have retained the modern familiar – the goddess Isis rather than the goddess Aset. In the same vein I have bucked against historical consistency for ease of recognition; for example, Plutarch mentions that Cleopatra spoke the tongue of the 'Arabian people' which was likely at that time Aramaic, but for familiarity I have referenced Arabic. I have also played God when it comes to dates and timelines – simply too much happens in Cleopatra's life to represent it all on the page. And then there are the events I have conjured from my imagination – that does not mean they bear any less truth. Cleopatra's myth has permeated collective memory. Her story lives in the minds of many, far beyond what history has provided.

I sought Cleopatra's voice in the dust between tomes. And from that ancient stillness, she spoke back.

This novel is not history, it is memory.

PROLOGUE

You know my name, but you do not know me.

Your poets have sung about my tainted crown, your bards have spoken on my infinite variety.

For millennia you have tried to pull straight the threads of my life to see the tapestry whole. But those threads are unruly, curling away from you to obscure the truth.

Besides, I have ever favoured carpets over tapestries, as you well know.

You have tried to parse the tones of my skin and sift through the crimson rubies of my blood, upon which you weighed my worth.

There are those of you who seek my bones. But my roots lie deep beneath the dirt and soil of every woman who has drawn breath.

Like the blue veins that flutter under the translucent skin of your wrist, I am the Nile of your body and the surging waters of your heart.

I was a pharaoh once, a wife twice, a mother more than thrice.

I have ever been what people sought to find. Some called me Queen, lover, Mama. Others called me witch, villain, whore. Each archetype is a brick that has raised me up like the great pyramids, further and further away from my humanity until I have become nothing more than a myth.

It is hard to know me at such a great distance.

My image shimmers behind the sand-filled haze of Egypt's sunset. Am I a mirage? Or the water you seek?

You know my name, but you do not know me.
I am Cleopatra. This is not the story of how I died.
But how I lived.

PART ONE
THE WITCH

'[She] had the power to subjugate the hearts
of all she met'
Cassius Dio, *Roman History*

'The noble ruin of her magic'*
William Shakespeare, *Antony and Cleopatra*

'The contact of her presence . . . and the character that
attended all she said or did, was something bewitching'
Plutarch, *Life of Antonius*

* To be ruinous and noble, both! Sometimes, when I stand very still,
I hear the whispers of each rendition on the wind. From children
reciting lines on rickety stages, to wizened elders savouring the bard's
words like aged wine. Though no matter their age or experience, all
players know not of what – or whom – they speak.

CHAPTER ONE
51 BCE

I bit into the flesh of the fig, its skin warmed by the heat of the sun.

Charmion watched me through half-lidded eyes as I chewed. The wind tousled her linen dress and tugged the collar to reveal the sun-touched glow of her skin.

For all the years of my life, Charmion had been my companion and handmaiden. Her mother had been my nursemaid. And so, we were forever bonded by the milk that had strengthened us as babes. At eighteen years of age our eyes still sparkled with possibility, but our cheeks had slimmed from the plumpness of youth.

Though there were some remarkable moments in the years prior, my story for you starts here. The day I became Pharaoh.

The crunching of the fig's seeds in my mouth were the only sound between us.

Then Charmion spoke, her voice solemn. 'You cannot deny the inevitable.'

I placed the half-eaten fruit on the ground between us. With my other hand I lifted the playing sticks and clenched them in my fist.

'I do not think your win is inevitable.'

We spoke to each other in Arabic, one of the nine languages we had been schooled in. Though we used both Egyptian and Greek in court, Arabic was just for us.

It had all started when a travelling hakawati had passed through

Alexandria from the great city of Gaza. I was eleven years old and had already developed a fondness for stories.

I begged my father to invite the storyteller to the palace. For three nights the hakawati took up residence in the temple. And for all three nights that was where Charmion and I stayed. His tales filled us with wonder, so much so that I requested to keep him.

'I am not yours to shelve like an ornament or trinket,' the hakawati said. The guards by the temple entrance bristled but I paid them no heed.

'Why not?' I asked with genuine curiosity. I had not yet found something I could not make my own. I was a Ptolemy. My blood was lit with the spark of divinity.

The hakawati smiled politely, far more conscious of the guards at his back than I. 'Would you ask a fish to stop swimming?'

I thought about it. The truth was, yes, I would if I wanted to eat it, but that wasn't the answer I thought he was looking for. 'No.'

'Would you ask a hippo to stop smiling?'

'Never.'

'Then you cannot ask a hakawati to stop travelling. It is in our nature. Without it, we will run out of stories. And without stories I would have nothing to tell.'

Tears sprang to my eyes. That sounded very dire indeed.

The hakawati saw my distress and kneeled on the ground beside me. 'Do not worry, there is another way to keep a part of me here. Tell my stories, again and again.'

My smile returned. I could do that.

For years Charmion and I had repeated the hakawati's tales, every story blossoming into something new with each retelling. It was then that Arabic became the language between us.

I looked at Charmion now. The sincerity of her expression had melted away into something more playful.

'Look at the markers – you may as well concede,' she said.

I stood up with the pretence that I needed a better vantage

point to view the senet board. I was cunning that way, always performing something or another. Manipulative, the unkind would go on to claim, but I did not see it that way.

From the moment my first cry rattled from my chest, I was taught to be something more than I was. I wanted to be a babe, but I had been born a pharaoh's daughter. So they wiped the birthing ichor from my skin and swaddled me in gold-trimmed cloth. My cries were silenced by a polished amber stone, a poor replacement for a mother's teat.

Despite being too young to remember the stone's weight, sometimes I still imagined it lying heavy against my tongue. It tripped my words and filled out my cheeks, especially when I chose to be bold.

'C-concede? I will not.'

We were playing on the balcony in the lighthouse, my place of serenity and solace. Close enough to the god Re to feel his gaze beating against my brow, and far enough away from my duties at the palace. Even with the furnace above us radiating heat, it was preferable to the burning of many eyes wherever I went. Sometimes, if the wind blew east, the smoke would wind its way to my bedroom window, seasoning my sleep with embers and ash.

The board game lay on the ground between us. Charmion was the better player, but I was too proud to admit it. Instead, I began each game with the same foolish hope that one day I'd best her.

I rolled the playing sticks in my hand in frustration. 'Amun's wrath,' I cursed as a splinter pierced my palm.

'Are you well?' Charmion asked with concern. A light sheen of sweat glistened above her top lip.

I took the opportunity to brandish my hand towards her. But instead of displaying my wound, I surged forward and thrust the playing sticks over the balcony.

Charmion's eyes met mine, one dark eyebrow quirked. 'So, you *do* concede?'

'Never,' I said with a grin.

Charmion laughed and together we peered over the balcony's edge.

Alexandria lay before me. The city had neither the beauty of Rome nor the grandeur of Babylon. No, Alexandria was not a city to be admired, it was far more than that. It lived and breathed like a beast.

Sailors called to one another across the harbour, the cacophony of many languages resonating throughout the city like a pack of wolves yipping and howling in the hunt. Though we were far above the docks, I could smell the brackish char of eels being cooked over fire. Boats undulated on the waves along the expanse of the coast, their many-coloured sails glittering like scales on a sea snake.

To the south, the Heptastadion causeway connected the lighthouse's isle to the mainland. Beyond that, the awnings of market stalls lined the streets and though I couldn't see them, I imagined the traders gesturing emphatically to their customers.

You could not separate the citizens from the city's heartbeat; they were one and the same. Asiatic, Parthian, Greek, Egyptian; no matter their origin, the silt of the Nile Delta thickened their blood. It brought a wildness to the city, tamed only by the pharaohs who ruled over it – my family.

Soon to be me.

But I was not sure I had the fortitude to bridle the people of Egypt.

My doubts were not new, though they had grown more prominent since my father's affliction. He did not have much time left before departing this world for the next.

As he got sicker and sicker, I became tormented by dreams of my own reflection; like the facets of a jewel, each side a different version of the pharaoh I was to be. One was cruel and callous, another gracious and gentle. Every echo of my being was a stranger to me, and I would awaken bathed in a chilling sweat, haunted by the outlanders in my mind.

I was not ready to be Pharaoh. Though I wonder if I ever would have reached true readiness. Without the skill of prophecy, I was always going to be ill-prepared for the years that followed. No one could have been prepared to live the life I would go on to lead. I must forgive my younger self this flaw, if nothing else.

Charmion leaned over the balcony, her brows pinched, unaware of my dark thoughts. 'I don't think we can see what you rolled from here, so we shall presume I won.'

A sudden breeze plucked a braid from the knot above my head. Charmion immediately moved to tuck it back into my diadem.

Her fingers grazed the mark on the back of my neck. Black, as if drawn in kohl, the three-stepped shape of the throne ran from the edge of my hairline to the top of my back. It marked me as chosen of the goddess Isis.

I shivered from her touch and Charmion drew away.

'If we cannot see the sticks, then we will never know. So we must call it a draw,' I teased her.

Charmion laughed, tossing her head back until her curling hair crested the tips of her shoulder blades. 'Every time you do not win it must be a draw.'

'I am a Ptolemy; we were not born to lose.' Though I smiled, my words felt a little bitter. Like the rind of a pomegranate, the reminder of the duties that awaited me tainted the sweetness of the day.

Charmion heard the footsteps first. 'Someone comes.'

'Who knew we were here?' I asked with a flash of annoyance.

'I do not know. But since your father has been bound to his bed, I have long suspected Pothinus has been watching you.'

I felt my lips twist at the eunuch's name. He lingered in my father's shadow like a crocodile amongst the reeds of the riverbank.

For the last ten years he had been a tutor to my younger brother. But since the onset of my father's illness, his interest in teaching had seemed to wane. Instead, he turned to politicking, circling my father in the murky shallows of the throne room.

I tightened my gold belt where I had loosened it from sitting on the ground. Charmion tutted behind me and moved to help.

She twisted the metal links until the belt bound my ribs like armour. I dusted away the sand that clung to the weave of my skirts and waited for the newcomer to present themselves.

The slapping of sandals on stone slowed as the servant approached.

He entered the balcony, his eyes averted, and then kneeled prostrate on the ground. 'Cleopatra, chosen by the goddess Isis, second daughter to Ptolemy, twelfth of his name,' he said, breathless from the long staircase.

The goddess's name pricked at a raw wound in my mind.

Chosen by Isis but not yet gifted with her power. I dismissed the familiar disappointment and replied, 'Yes?'

'You are needed at the palace.' The messenger's shoulders slumped as if his life's purpose was complete. Perhaps it was.

'*Death courts the Ptolemy name,*' my mother had once said.

I was little more than eight years old when she spoke those words to me. A man lay dying at my feet, his blood pooling between my small toes. I wriggled them, watching the blood ripple. I remember thinking how plain the knife at his throat was, no gold or silver embellishments.

My thoughts were those of an eight-year-old: *If I were to kill myself, I'd be sure to do it with something finer than copper.*

Though, as you know, it was poison in the end.

'Why did he kill himself, Mama?' I asked as the guards removed the servant's body from the throne room.

She stood next to me, the hem of her priest robe now soiled with blood. The eyes she turned to me were sorrowful, like those of the heifers blessed by the goddess Hathor. 'He could fathom no greater honour than serving a pharaoh's daughter. There was nothing else to accomplish in this life that could eclipse it.'

He was the first servant to end their life after speaking with me.

And in a few decades, Charmion would be the last.

I turned to the messenger, shaking away thoughts of my mother and death. 'What has happened that I am needed in the palace so urgently?'

He quivered and didn't immediately answer. When he eventually mustered the strength to speak, his voice was a croak. 'Your father. He has departed this life into the next.'

Charmion's quick inhalation sounded like the hiss of a snake. I didn't hear anything after that.

My eyes stung with the cinder of grief. Each breath came slow and laboured as if smoke choked my throat.

Father is dead.

Though I had known this was coming, nothing prepares you for the loss of all the unclaimed moments yet to pass.

I lifted my gaze to the top of the lighthouse where a statue of my ancestor crested the cylindrical tower just below the furnace.

The lifeless eyes of Ptolemy I, the founder of my dynasty, stared back at me. Sōter, he was called – *saviour*. Hundreds of years separated the two of us, and there was little to be seen of me in his Macedonian features. His chiselled alabaster chin dipped towards the mainland, looking over the empire he had come to rule.

'Sōter, welcome my father to the field of reeds,' I murmured quietly to myself.

Heavy tears blurred his image into that of my father. His brow became wider, his jaw softer. Even his stomach grew prouder.

My father had been prone to indulgence. His love of festivities was one of the many things that set us apart. I saw the frivolities of my status as a burden, he saw them as a joy.

'We must live like gods to honour the gods, daughter,' he would rumble. 'It reminds our people that we reign above them. You will understand more when you are Pharaoh.'

Pharaoh. It had been a far-off thing to conceive of back then. Now, the title set my heart stuttering behind my ribs.

Sōter's face wavered once more before my unshed tears. The alabaster distorted until I looked into one of the many faces of my dreams.

Is this a premonition of the future?

I tried to parse the vision I was seeing: was she wise? Was she merciless?

I had not the plays and sonnets and books that told me of my future demise. Though worry not, a demise you will still have.

I had the one thing we all have: time. And only that would reveal to me the pharaoh I was to become.

During our descent from the lighthouse, the sun had set. The god Re's journey through the clouds had tarnished the sky from gold to a deep orange.

I picked my way down the cragged shoreline where the waves lapped at the rocks.

'What are you doing?' Charmion asked.

'It's quicker to swim to the palace from here. I cannot waste time taking a litter across the Heptastadion.'

'Cleo.' It was the nickname Charmion only used beneath the softness of our sheets.

'Cleopatra,' I corrected her with irritation. *Glory of thy father.*

As I began to remove my clothing, I wondered if I was quite fulfilling my name's meaning in that moment.

Charmion sighed behind me before her fingers joined mine at the knot of my dress. She rested her hand there for a moment as she said, 'All will be well. Osiris will grant him passage to the next realm.'

I felt some of the tension inside me loosen slightly as the layers of my clothing fell to the ground like petals. Charmion soothed me in a way that no other person could.

I turned and reached for her cheek. 'I know, because you are by my side.'

Charmion leaned into my touch and brought three fingers up to her lips in turn. 'One for the past and the happy years well spent, one for the present and the patience we extend, one for the future and the love that never ends.'

She recited the prayer we had composed as children. I felt the words give me strength.

We had been each other's first lover, and for years that's all we were. But then our love shifted, it grew outward, beyond our bodies into something more potent than the ecstasy of pleasure. Our friendship was celestial, greater than the two parts of us.

I turned away from her. I now wore nothing but my diadem, a single gold band that met in the middle of my forehead to form a rearing cobra. Charmion reached to remove it and I shook my head. 'Secure it with my braids. When I arrive, they must see me as Queen.'

Once Charmion had finished weaving my hair around my diadem, I instructed her to make her way to the palace. Though she too could swim – we'd run off enough times to the Nile for her to learn – I knew she didn't like it.

'I will not leave you—'

'Go,' I commanded. Then, more quietly, I said, 'This is my favourite dress, I do not want the seawater to harm its fibres.'

Charmion's lashes fluttered. She heard the lie and saw the mercy in it. 'I will be sure to have it washed and ready for you later tonight.'

Her shadow stretched across the shoreline as she walked away. The further she got, the hotter my breath felt in my mouth, until I shouted, 'I-I can't do it, I can't be queen!'

'You can!' she called back.

Dread curdled my stomach. 'Do you remember when Father asked me to lead the Ptolemaia procession?' I said. It had been the first festival after I turned fourteen and Father had wished to present me as the future Pharaoh of Egypt.

'I remember.'

'Do you? Do you recall how I tripped and fell in front of the whole of Alexandria? All I had to do was lead the dancers. And I couldn't even do that.'

'Walking does prove difficult for some people.'

'This isn't funny, Charmion. I was never a good pharaoh's daughter – how can I expect to be a good pharaoh?'

Charmion pointed to the ground. 'Look.'

I followed her line of sight.

There, scattered between rocks and sand, were the throwing sticks.

'You won after all,' she said, smiling.

The odds had been so small. But by the angle at which the sticks had fallen, I knew she was right. The gods had guided my hand.

The dread within my belly eased.

'A Ptolemy never loses,' I repeated softly. This time the words held hope.

'I will see you at the palace,' Charmion said.

I turned back to the ocean with triumph in my heart.

The water was warm and refreshing as I lowered myself into the churning waves. It was late shemu season and the air was hot and dry. Though I preferred the rain and milder weather of akhet, I was glad for the warmth now.

My braids floated on the surface of the water for a moment as I dipped beneath the froth of waves. I opened my eyes. The seawater was clear, despite the swirling currents. I wondered what it must be like to be able to breathe beneath the water like my younger brother. Blessed by the god Sobek, Lord of the Waters, he had received his gift as a babe.

At first his nursemaid had screamed as his fat little legs kicked him out of her grip and into the depth of the baths.

Guards were called, which in turn drew mine and Charmion's own curiosity. I still remember the envy that coursed through my veins at his laughing face as he surfaced, perfectly fine. My father had called for three days of feasting.

The goddess Isis was yet to awaken my gift. Some thought it would never arrive. Others whispered that it was too weak to show. That I was tainted, unworthy of the throne.

I did not require a very great power. My own father's blessing had been modest. As an acolyte to the god Ihy, he could play any instrument with flawless beauty. His preference had been the flute.

My lungs began to burn, and I kicked myself back to the surface. I reached my arms out in quick, even strokes, parting the waves with my hands.

Now I will never hear Father's sweet music again.

The waves licked at my tears, but I didn't stop swimming until I reached the shoreline of the palace.

When my feet struck sand, I stood.

The beach soon turned to the white tiled ground of Antirhodos. The small island looked out over the city of Alexandria to the south and the harbour to the west.

The isle boasted its own necropolis, menagerie, cistern and cultivated gardens. It was a city that I called my home, but it didn't seem large to me. I had stood upon every rock and climbed every tree. There was no place on this earth that I loved more.

Antirhodos was too beautiful to survive the test of time; unlike my myth, which is a gnarly thing.

I heard it said that all the birds from the island flew away the day before the earthquake struck the palace.

But that happened many hundreds of years from now. Long after I had died.

On the pathway beside me, two servants had wrapped cloth around the bark of a palm tree and were swaying the trunk back and forth. Another was collecting the dates that fell into a woven basket.

They stopped as they saw me, clad in nothing but my crown.

All will be well. Charmion's words came to me, and I straightened.

There was a thud as the basket fell to the ground and the servants threw themselves down beside the spilled dates.

I cleared my throat to ensure it rang out without a warble. 'Lower.'

The servants pressed themselves further into the dirt. I reached for one of the strewn fruits and chewed on it slowly. My hand was still wet from the seawater, seasoning the sweetness of the date.

'Have a basket of these sent to my rooms,' I said with the same tenor of authority.

'Yes, Pharaoh's Daughter,' the three said in unison.

'Just Pharaoh,' I corrected them.

I wiped the sticky residue of the date on the cloth that still bound the trunk of the palm tree. My hands trembled like I had seen my father's do when he had used his godtouched power.

I had no such divinity surging through me. But I did have power of my own.

And now was the time to wield it.

CHAPTER TWO
51 BCE

I stalked past the stone sphinxes that flanked the entranceway to the palace. Basins filled with lotus flowers lined the hallway. The heat of the afternoon had turned their sweet scent sour, wilting and bruising their leaves.

From that day on, even the freshest of lotus flowers brought back that smell of decay, carrying my mind to this moment: legs slick with seawater, cold granite beneath my feet, the throne of Egypt ahead of me.

I left wet marks on the tiles as I made my way to the heart of the palace. I was careful not to slip. Pothinus would take advantage of any weakness to soil my reputation – a mere fall could burgeon into a rumour that I was born with a scorpion tail to bring poison to the heart of Egypt.

No, I would not let him tarnish my rule.

Father would not want that. At the thought of him, my steps faltered but I did not fall. Shock had not yet given way to the full extent of my grief.

There was a sound in the corridor ahead of me and I looked up to see an ibis in flight. Its white wings were tipped black as if it had flown through ink.

The ibis flew low enough that for a moment I thought it might strike me, its curved beak angled down as if to peck at my scalp.

Ibis are not aggressive birds, but this one shrieked and cawed as it flew by.

A giggle fluttered through the corridor like the rustling of palm fronds.

'Arsinoe!' I called my younger sister's name with mock annoyance.

For where Qar flew, Arsinoe was not far behind.

The ibis had come to her on her seventh birthday. Since then, she had become bonded with the creature as only one blessed by the god Thoth could. As the scribe of the gods, he had granted her the language of the birds.

I tried not to be jealous when I watched them, heads together. It was difficult, when once it had been my brow against hers as we spoke our secrets to each other.

It is not just sound, it is more than that, she said to me once when she caught me trying to parse Qar's chitters. *What more is it?* I asked. But she only shrugged.

Arsinoe appeared at the end of the hallway. Though her laugh still lingered on her lips, I could see her eyes were red from crying. I opened my arms to her, and she ran to embrace me.

At fourteen, she was four years my junior, though she was taller than me by at least a palm's width. She wore her curling hair in a twist at the side of her neck. The knot pressed into my throat as she held me.

We stood together for a little while before she said, 'Where are your clothes?'

I released her. 'Charmion has them. I swam from the lighthouse.'

'So you *were* at the lighthouse.'

'Did you tell Pothinus to find me there?'

Arsinoe tilted her head to the side. 'Yes, he asked, and I thought you would want to know . . . about . . .' Her words stuttered to a stop and her eyes filled with tears.

'Where is he?'

'They have laid him out in Ihy's temple.'

I had suspected that I would find him there. The temple would soon become his tomb. 'Let us go together.'

I looped my arm in hers with the pretence that I was lending her strength. But the truth was, it was I who needed hers.

We walked through the palace gardens towards the necropolis where Ihy's temple rose up from the earth. As we approached the entrance, something scuttled across my feet and I jumped back.

'Quell.' Arsinoe's voice rang out loud and clear. The command was for Qar and the ibis was quick to carry it out. He swooped down, his long beak snapping the neck of the rat before dropping the carcass at Arsinoe's feet.

She picked it up as if it were no more than a fallen leaf and threw the dead thing towards the sea.

I watched her casually dispose of the rodent and my stomach roiled. I would like to say that my father's death made me more sensitive to the sight of a corpse, no matter how small, but the truth was death had always unnerved me.

I see the irony in that now.

We reached the entranceway to my father's tomb, marked by red granite pillars. The cool stone grazed my leg as we passed, and for a moment I stood between two hard things: my sister and the pillar.

'*You are too soft.*' My father's words came to me like the unwelcome cloud of dust from behind an old chest. Musty and best ignored.

'I am as the gods will it,' I had retorted in response.

Father's fever had been high, and his words looser than usual. It was rare he picked at the flaws of my character so deeply.

'Soft and powerless,' he had insisted.

'I am not.'

And then, like a serrated knife drawn back against my skin, he said, 'I should have dealt with you like I did Berenice.' He had not spoken her name in many years.

'Do not say these things, Father; you cannot mean them.'

'Did you say something, sister?' Arsinoe's question brought me back to the present.

I shook my head, releasing the last plume of dust from the memory.

'No, I am fine.'

Rushlight flickered in clay pots around the temple. The warm smell of the burning tallow thawed the cold that had crept into my bones.

Shadows shifted as the priests of the temple moved to the far corners of the room to grant Arsinoe and me privacy. I cannot say I was ever truly comfortable under the gaze of the priesthood. Even my mother, who was one of the few people who truly loved me as a child, seemed to see the entirety of my shortcomings through the eyes of her god.

I rubbed at the Isis mark on the back of my neck. The skin there was smooth as though unblemished, and I often asked Charmion to hold up a polished mirror so I could see Isis's sigil. Every time, I let out a sigh of relief to see the mark still there.

I took the last few steps towards my father's body. He lay upon a stone slab, cloaked in a linen robe. His hands were clasped across a stomach that had, in bygone days, been plump and full of laughter. Cheeks that had once budded with smiles were now emaciated and wan.

'You will smile once more in the great beyond.' My throat was hoarse and the words came out as a rasp.

In four days, my father's body would be taken by the priests for purification before being interred in this temple seventy days from now. His body would be hollowed out, the fragile cage of his chest pulled apart to replace the vital organs with myrrh and cassia.

I placed my hand on the soft skin below his throat. Soon the flesh there would be marred with stitching, the skin drawn taut to keep the aromatics within.

He was a shadow of the great man he had been two years

earlier. But day by day, season by season, Osiris had beckoned for him to cross into the afterlife.

'The only other body I have ever seen was Berenice's.'

I started at Arsinoe's voice, having forgotten she was there. 'You were so young, I did not think you could remember.'

She turned her cold brown eyes to mine. 'It is hard to forget the bloodied neck of one's sister.'

I grimaced. I was twelve when my father had killed my older sibling. You see, I was never meant to lead Egypt. Berenice was the one destined to follow my father's legacy.

'She would have been made Pharaoh today,' I said.

If Berenice was still alive, I would not have to take the throne. I felt a wave of guilt as I realised my wish for my sister's resurrection was rooted in my misgivings towards ruling Egypt.

Arsinoe snorted. 'She was never going to be Pharaoh, not with the divine power gifted to her.'

When Berenice had been born, she had been marked with the swirl of a snake on the back of her calf. There had been much celebrating, as Hapy of the Nile was a generous god, and when a Ptolemy was marked by him the harvest was always plentiful.

But the soothsayer who had read the signs of Berenice's mark had been wrong. It was not the blessing of Hapy but the snake of Apep, the Lord of Chaos.

Instead of a bountiful yield, the crops dwindled year on year and Father claimed Berenice's power was wilting the plants. My older sister always denied her gift was to blame, but when a swarm of locusts ravaged the fields on her fifteenth birthday, she could no longer hide the truth of it.

Her feud with Father had incited a civil war, but the throne would not be taken from him easily. For as joyful as my father was, he was equally ruthless. He had Berenice's throat cut in her sleep.

A day and a night I spent weeping amongst her bloodied sheets.

As I looked down on my father's expressionless face, I recalled what he had said that day after he had lifted me from Berenice's cold bed: 'We are Egypt, and Egypt is us. Sometimes we must sacrifice what we hold dear. But Egypt must live. Always.'

Sacrifice was a new concept to me back then. I did not know what it was like to lose something I held so dear. Berenice had to die so Father could reign in peace.

And now the cycle continued. 'Father, I will ensure that Egypt lives. Always.'

Arsinoe was still watching me, and I reached for her hand once more.

'Come, sister,' I said. 'It is time for me to take my throne.'

I wish I could say that I intended to make the scene I did, but the truth is I had entirely forgotten that I was naked. I strode into the court with a singular purpose, to begin my rule as Pharaoh.

But as I reached the bottom of the dais, my feet felt laden with honey. Every step was harder than the last. I paused when it became too much.

The throne is three steps away. Three short steps.

They may have been short steps, but in my mind, each one might as well have been the height of a pyramid. Impossible to scale. I pressed my knees together to stop them from buckling.

Father was right, I am too weak for this. I cannot even rise to the throne.

Tears pooled in my eyes and I blinked them away in frustration. The thought of my father's disappointment was more potent than my grief.

I may not want this, but I do it for him. For Egypt.

With a battle cry in my throat, I raised my foot. And when it struck the tiles, I felt my father's approval from the realm beyond. The final steps came more easily.

I reached towards the armrests of the throne and clutched the gold lions that adorned their surface. I looked up and my father's face stared back at me. Small tiles of marble and coloured glass inlaid carefully into the back of the chair made up his features.

Depictions of four women surrounded his image, each identified by their crowns.

My mother, his second wife, was among them, wearing a religious cowl fashioned in black stone. In her arms she held a young baby whose eyes were made from carnelian studs. My fingers caressed the warm orange stones before I lowered myself onto my father's throne.

To my left was another, equally decorated chair that was occupied by my brother. It had once belonged to my father's first wife, Cleopatra V, Berenice's mother.

Six Cleopatras had come before me. Aunts, mothers, even sister-wives. So many of your historians have trailed their fingers through the tributaries of my ancestors' river, parting the water for any sign of my name – Κλεοπάτρα. Somewhere along the way, Cleopatra VI was lost in the currents.

Let me tell you of her now.

The babe with carnelians for eyes was yet another sister that no longer lived. Though her body had been born in this life, her spirit had been summoned by Osiris, and she did not take her first breath.

And so there had been yet another destined to lead Egypt before me. Was there any wonder I was reluctant to rule? The shadows of my siblings' souls stretched from the field of reeds to darken my thoughts.

I leaned back in the throne and felt the carnelians press into my skin.

My brother sighed with relief upon seeing me take my seat next to him. Though we were both chosen by the gods to rule, until my brother came of age at fourteen my word would be absolute. His small chest was laden with gold and jewels. He tried to smile at me, but his headdress wobbled precariously and his young face – made for grinning – turned stoic once more.

My other brother, the younger, stood surrounded by his nursemaids. At seven years old he still insisted on a retinue of servants to sate his appetite for breastmilk. His eyes lazily met Arsinoe's as she went to stand by him before drifting to mine with the lack of interest that could only be mustered by someone unburdened by the weight of inheriting a kingdom.

The table in the centre of the room was covered with papyrus scrolls pinned down by the fingers of ambitious advisors of the court. All searching for their name within my father's will.

Pothinus stood at the head of the procession, his slicked hair a shining beacon. The tree gum he used smelled foul, like fish left out in the sun, and I tried not to gag as a swift breeze carried the aroma around the room.

'Pharaoh!' Pothinus's voice came out as a shriek. 'My queen, this is not appropriate.'

I frowned, wondering what he meant, and then I realised that the throne was colder than it should have been. For there was no fabric between my legs and the gold.

Panic seized me. This was not proper. But what could I do now? It had taken so much effort to reach the throne, I could not bear to ascend it again. So I did what I had learned to do. I performed.

'Not appropriate?' I said. 'Who among mortals dares question the blood of a god?'

Pothinus's thin lips flapped but no words came out.

No longer was I the daughter of Ptolemy XII. Now I was his ruler, his pharaoh. His god.

I gripped the armrests of the chair tighter and sent a silent prayer to Isis: *Light your divinity within me, great one. Let me be your vessel as I rule.*

There had been three known blessings by the goddess Isis in the last few hundred years of the Ptolemy dynasty. Each had manifested different traits of her legend.

Isis was a talented healer, having brought her love, Osiris, back from the dead. So, two of my ancestors could heal with varying success. She was also known as a great mother, granting one of my forebears the strength to carry five children in her womb.

I did not wish for my gift to manifest this way, but I would sacrifice my body to my growing stomach if that was the blessing I received. It was far better than being powerless.

No Ptolemy had ever ruled without the gods' divine sanction. I would be the first, so I needed to secure my authority in other ways. 'Is this how you greet a pharaoh?' I said to the room.

The beginnings of a storm thundered across Pothinus's features. But then his face shifted into a sickly smile.

'May the gods bless your reign, Queen of the Two Lands, Cleopatra Thea VII,' the eunuch said as he bowed.

'Cleopatra Thea *Philopator*,' I announced my new name to the room – *father-loving*. A tribute to my father, and a gentle reminder of my legacy.

Pothinus's smirk was slight. Too slight to call out.

I pointed to the scrolls. 'Is that my father's will?'

'Yes, Pharaoh – would you like me to read it to you?' Pothinus asked.

'No, I think eighteen years of schooling have prepared me enough for this moment.'

My brother snickered beside me, causing his crown to topple to the floor. Pothinus flashed him an angry glance.

'Oh no,' my brother whispered. He fumbled off the throne, his hands shaking as he reached for the fallen coronet.

I stood and laid a hand on his shoulder. 'Do not worry, Mikro Theos.' *Little god.* The name echoed my own secondary title, Thea – *goddess* in my ancestors' tongue. Though my brother reigned now as Ptolemy XIII, my father had always called him Theos, a reminder that as the eldest-born son, he was destined to be Pharaoh.

His eyes shimmered in distress. He was so young back then. Oblivious to the horrors of his future.

I smiled at him. 'Perhaps Pothinus could take you back to your rooms. It has been a hard day.'

Someone muttered darkly. Though my hearing was sharp, I didn't catch who it was.

Theos nodded, his mouth turning down with misery. 'I have

been sitting on the throne for half the day. I would like to go now.'

'Half a day, you say. On your own up here?'

Though Pothinus had known I was at the lighthouse, he had not called for me until the day was nearly over.

All expression had fled Pothinus's face.

I sharpened my voice on my internal whetstone. 'Take my brother to his chambers. I will continue with the reading of the will.'

Theos slumped, grateful for my intervention.

As Pothinus began to lead my brother from the room, his eyes flickered to mine briefly.

If only I had known back then that the flame in his eyes wasn't just a mere spark, but a blazing coal ready to ignite those around me. Maybe things would have turned out differently if I'd known how Egypt would burn in the inferno of his betrayal.

CHAPTER THREE
51 BCE

I stood outside the entrance of my father's tomb. Seventy days had passed so quickly.

'You were a great king, but a greater father,' I whispered. My throat was dry, as were my eyes. By then, I had cried enough to flood the Nile. I had nothing left.

The priests prostrated themselves across the temple steps behind me, their low prayers reverberating in my chest.

'Many are the cries of your subjects here on earth. Osiris, King of Death, King of Eternity. May your judgement be swift and your favour true. Chief of Pharaohs, accept this new king into your realm,' they chanted as one.

I stepped towards the tomb, breaking away from my sister and brothers. Mikro Theos was sniffling and Arsinoe held her hand out for him to clasp. The sympathetic action was at odds with her stoic expression. I had not seen her cry since the day Father died.

Qar circled the blue sky above us, his shadow weaving around my feet as I walked through the entrance of the temple.

The antechamber was full of offerings to Osiris and supplies my father might need in the field of reeds. Woven baskets filled with dried fish were stacked in rows beside barrels of palm nuts and pomegranates. A golden chest held a collection of gleaming yellow lemons, a gift from our allies in Rome. Then there was the treasure twinkling amongst the food: beaded necklaces and gold armour, painted rings and marble statues. And finally, likely to be valued the most by my father, clay pots overflowing with wine.

I walked past these riches to the main chamber where my father's body lay within a black granite sarcophagus. I kneeled on the ground by his feet and reached into my sleeve for the tribute I had placed there. The wooden flute was small but finely carved, and I'd had my father's name engraved on its body in hieroglyphics.

'May your song never end.' I placed the flute on the tomb floor. Each tile was flecked with gold leaf.

I pressed my forehead to the ground and said, 'Egypt is safe in my hands. I will look after her, for she is me.'

I kneeled there for some time, feeling the silent heartbeat of my country underneath my skin.

After I rose, I beckoned my siblings forward. Each held their own final tribute to our father.

Both Theos and Ptolemy held scarabs painted gold, amulets to ease our father's passing. They murmured their own quiet addresses before quickly leaving. The air in the chamber was hot and stifling, so I did not chastise them for their haste.

My sister lingered, withdrawing her own gift for our father. To my surprise it was a bronze-headed arrow, fletched with white feathers that I assumed were Qar's.

'I will always strike true, Father. Just like you taught me,' she said as she placed the arrow beside the flute.

Arsinoe was a keen hunter, a skill Father had nurtured. My sister saw me watching her and nodded before retreating.

I stood beside the sarcophagus and watched the shadows stretch as midday approached.

'Pharaoh.'

Black spots danced across my vision as I focused in on the administrator.

'It is time to seal the tomb,' he said, his voice like grinding stone.

I imagined for a moment how it would feel to be locked in. Relief, because no longer would I be required to play the part of Queen. Regret, because I knew that being Pharaoh wasn't entirely a player's performance.

'*We are not like the common man,*' Father had once said. '*We may bleed and die like them, but when we bleed, so too does our land. And we never die, not truly. For there is always another Ptolemy to take our place.*'

My father's lesson hadn't been meant as a threat, but with my siblings at my back, I would be remiss not to acknowledge how easily the throne could change hands. It had happened enough times in my family's past.

Egypt is mine. I was surprised by my own conviction, but there was something potent in the air beyond the sweltering heat. Facing death, the thing I feared more than anything in the world, urged me to cling on to life.

'Pharaoh?' the administrator said again uncertainly. 'We are sealing the tomb now.'

I nodded and followed him towards the temple entrance.

It took twelve men to slide the granite door across the opening.

Hands touched my waist and I looked down to find young Ptolemy pulling on my dress.

'Is it time for the feast?'

I laughed. His callous words would have been celebrated by my father.

'Yes, it is time for the feast.'

I had invited all the governors of Egypt to celebrate my father's journey to the afterlife. Their ships filled the palace harbour while their voices filled the great hall.

The dining table was overflowing with food served on fine gold platters. Servants weaved between my guests, their faces adorned with copper jackal masks in honour of Anubis, the guide of the dead. Sharp ears, studded with lapis, rose up above their heads.

My father had always enjoyed dressing up the palace workers. Like they were pieces on a senet board to be cast and played with.

'And me? Do you wish for me to wear this mask too?' Charmion had asked earlier that night. Though she didn't show it, I could feel her disapproval as I ordered the servants to change their garb.

'I am not my father,' I replied quietly. 'I only wish to honour him with a feast he would have thrown himself.'

When she did not respond, I continued, 'No, you are not required to wear it.'

Charmion reached for one of the masks laid out across the bottom of the throne. 'But I am a servant, and by your command, all servants must wear this . . . uniform.'

My cheeks grew hot. At the time I had thought it was anger, but now, looking back, I recognise the feeling as shame. 'Then wear it,' I snapped. 'But I have given you the choice.'

'Choice,' she repeated before picking up the mask and leaving.

I watched her now from across the room. She stood with her hands clasped by her waist, waiting to be called should I need her.

But I could not see her expression beneath the jackal's coppery snarl.

I turned back to my plate, picking at the roast pigeon.

It was my first time hosting the ruling elite, and I found myself wishing the evening away.

My brother and I sat apart from the main diners on an ivory table set on a dais.

'Eat something,' I encouraged Theos, who had sat twisting his hands in his lap all evening. He was just as unhappy as I was, though less versed in hiding it.

'I am not very hungry.'

'Listen to your sister. She protects your wellbeing,' Pothinus said from a stool by my feet. Though my brother ruled by my side, the eunuch, to my chagrin, had been named Theos's regent in my father's will. It incensed me further to see Theos follow

Pothinus's command and not mine as he took some food from his plate and began to eat.

The lyre player began a sweet melody and I paused to listen. Hailing from Thebes, she had been a favourite of my father's. It reminded me of the task I had assigned to Pothinus.

'Did I not send you to retrieve the latest tax report from Thebes?' I asked the regent.

'The tablet awaits you in your chambers, Pharaoh.'

It was a shame he was so effective in his role, or I would have had cause to put greater distance between myself and his foul-smelling hair.

'Can I see the report?' Theos asked with his mouth full.

'No need, brother.'

He deserves a semblance of a childhood, I thought as he went back to his meal, his appetite clearly revived.

'And this tax report, Pothinus, were the taxes short like the others?'

'Yes, Pharaoh. But I must advise against doing anything indiscreet. The Governor of Thebes was a good friend to your father.'

'Do you know what my father valued more than friendship? Money.'

Pothinus's lips pressed into a line.

'Bring him to me,' I said.

The regent was still unused to the strength of my obstinacy, and so he opened his mouth to disagree, but I cut him off. 'Go.'

Pothinus rose from his stool slowly, making his displeasure known. I could have dismissed him for such insolence, but the truth was, I was too scared to. Though I had been trained to take over the ruling of Egypt, Pothinus had been closer to the day-to-day activities that kept the country prosperous.

I watched as he made his way across the room and approached the Governor of Thebes. The man was of my father's age, though he wore his years more proudly in the lines of his face and the greying of his hair.

He rose from the dining table and followed Pothinus to the dais. He bowed low by my feet.

'Pharaoh. My thanks for this wonderful celebration. May your father find peace in the realm of the dead.'

I inclined my head, acknowledging his blessings.

'A feast full of splendour and elegance, just like our gracious queen,' he continued. A speck of oily food clung to the corner of his lip and I found myself dabbing an imaginary fragment from my own mouth.

'My father deserved no less.'

'Of course. He was truly chosen by the gods to have such a generous daughter.'

'Generosity comes at a price, would you not say?'

His eyes crinkled. 'Yes, that is true.'

'I have noticed that during the last few years of my father's reign, your tithe to the crown has lessened considerably.'

'My queen?'

'Your taxes, Governor. They are short.'

'But Pharaoh, your father and I had an agreement. Half of my taxes would be paid in wine.'

'Wine?' I said doubtfully, though the deal sounded very much like something Father would do.

'The finest of my batches have always been sent to the palace; I believe we are sampling some of them tonight.'

I looked to Pothinus, who nodded. And though his expression did not change, I felt the smugness ripple around him like a mirage.

He knew. Not once in all our conversations of Thebes did the eunuch mention my father's dealings with the governor.

Was this my first hint of his betrayal? Or do I grant my past self too much clemency? No, I have promised you truth, so let me bare it – I was ignorant of Pothinus's motives.

'And the shortfall from the taxes you take from your people, where does that go?' I asked the governor.

He looked abashed. 'The vineyards require maintenance, Pharaoh.'

His coffers, then.

'I had believed your father's word would hold true in the afterlife. If this is not so, then I will be happy to—'

'No,' I said, my breath fluttering in my chest. I would not go back on my father's word. I couldn't; it was sacrilege. 'Let my father's arrangement stand.'

I waved a shaking hand at Pothinus and he led the governor away.

When I brought my cup to my lips, I found the wine tasted more sour than it had before.

'How many others had arrangements with my father?' I asked Pothinus coolly when he returned.

Pothinus's expression did not change as he listed five more instances of undocumented dealings with my father. I listened, identifying each of the governors dining at the table below me. All were indulging themselves heartily in food and drink.

Food and drink they had bartered with to tighten their fists around their coin. *My* coin. But if the corruption had been sanctioned by my father, who was I to question it?

Pothinus saw me looking. 'Shall I bring them up to the dais?'

'No. I think I will excuse myself for some fresh air.'

I had hoped to leave unnoticed, but when I stood from my chair, the whole room stood with me. I had had little enough freedom as a pharaoh's daughter, but now as Pharaoh I was shackled to the land and people in a way I was unaccustomed to.

A cadre of guards followed me as I walked through the dining hall. Governors fell prostrate at my feet as I passed.

I fixed my eyes on the strip of night sky I could see through the doorway. I did not stop walking until the sea breeze tousled the gold beads on my dress, making them chime.

'Leave me a moment,' I said to the guards at my back.

Ahmose, the leader of my personal guard, stepped forward. 'But Pharaoh—'

'I will be fine,' I reassured him. 'I know you cannot leave me entirely, but please watch me from the palace doors. Let me pretend that I am alone.'

Ahmose's eyes softened. He had been by my side since we were both young. My father had personally selected him from the gymnasium after he'd seen him win a wrestling tournament.

'As you wish, Pharaoh.' He thrust a fist in the air and the rest of the guards stepped back in unison. He nodded once in my direction before turning on his heel and leading them away.

I removed my woven sandals and sank my toes deep into the sand, looking across the ocean where the reflection of Alexandria shimmered on the waves.

'I do not know how to rule,' I admitted.

The ocean offered no judgement.

I knew *some* aspects of how to rule; my schooling had barely digressed from trade, taxes and agriculture. But I had very little skill in diplomacy.

I was wretched. 'How am I to reign in your shadow, Father? Without a gift from Isis to aid me?'

A sound startled me and I turned, expecting it to be one of the palace cats. But the mewl had come from a woman. She clutched a hand to her mouth before sinking into the sand at my feet.

'Pharaoh, my apologies, I was just taking some air before my next performance. I did not realise you were here.'

It was the lyre player.

'Rise, musician.' I was irritated that my meditations had been interrupted, and worried about how much she had heard.

'Allow me to retreat and leave you to your solitude.'

I was about to agree when a thought occurred to me. 'You are from Thebes, correct?'

'Yes, Pharaoh.' She had got to her feet as commanded but would not meet my eye, her dark hair covering most of her face.

'The governor, does he manage the city well?'

She hesitated, then said in a rush, 'Very well, Pharaoh. Very well indeed.'

'Speak plain. My reports only tell me so much.'

She parted her hair and finally looked at me. I expected her gaze to be as timid as her demeanour, but her eyes were dark with fury. And I was about to learn the cause.

'He has increased taxes every akhet season for the last five years. Famine spreads across the land. Your people are dying, Pharaoh.'

I flinched.

My coin, but also *my* people.

'Thank you for your honesty, lyre player. Please, let my scribes know you have spoken to me. You may return to my court at any time. You are a courtier now.'

Her eyes widened and she lowered herself to the ground once more.

I thought I would never get used to the excessive bowing. But, of course, I did.

'Pharaoh, if it is not too presumptuous, allow me to say one more thing,' she said.

'Speak.'

'Do not chase shadows. Make your own light.'

So she had heard me after all. Her sage words stayed with me after she had gone.

I would never be my father, who led with charm. My talents lay elsewhere. I could not deny my father his faults, though they were harder to see when my grief was still so fresh.

But if I were to lead Egypt, I had to do it my way.

And I had to lead Egypt. For I loved her.

You speak of my many lovers but few of you acknowledge my first, and perhaps my only true love.

Egypt.

When I was a child, my father took me out on a small rowing boat. It was a series of unusual occurrences; first to have a pharaoh conduct such manual labour, and second for me to be alone with my father. There was always someone with us: a soldier, a scribe, Charmion. But that day he requested my presence alone.

He rowed us east, to the delta.

I looked back at the city through the glittering sea spray – *the gift of the Nile*. Words written some three hundred and fifty years prior by Herodotus, known only to the foolish among you as 'the father of history'. History is not *fathered*, it is cultivated, ever-growing, ever-changing, and most importantly it is pruned and trimmed by those who uncover it from the shade.

Though I handled them with less reverence than your contemporaries, I had read Herodotus's words, and I spoke them now.

'A gift, yes, but a responsibility also,' my father replied. He pointed to the sea beneath us. 'This is where the Nile meets the sea. Can you see the two currents? One blue, one brown?'

I had never seen anything like it and was mesmerised by the dancing eddies of the fresh water swirling commingled with the ocean. I didn't notice the blade until it cut through my wrist.

I jerked back, frightened. For as I said before, my father's charm came hand in hand with his cruelty.

But when I looked down, I saw the cut was shallow.

'Add your blood to the water, let Egypt know who will come to lead her,' he commanded.

I trailed my hand in the ocean and felt the sting of the saltwater in my wound and the silt of the Nile on my skin.

'When it is your turn to lead, blood will know blood,' he said.

Now, though it had been many years, this memory came back to me with clarity.

I walked to the water's edge and touched my hand to its surface.

'Blood will know blood.'

I sent a message to the kitchens before returning to the dining hall.

The governors partook in my hospitality until dawn. When the feast ended, my brother and I walked through the hall arm in arm, the servants following in a procession. The beaded tails stitched onto the backs of their skirts twirled as they walked. They howled and raised their hands to the sky as I had instructed them to. I should have been proud of the sight, but I felt as though the glittering eyes behind the copper masks judged me harshly. I could not pick out Charmion among the twisting limbs.

Theos leaned heavily against my shoulder. It had been a long night for both of us.

'Stop here a moment, brother,' I said as we drew level with the Governor of Thebes.

At my indication, three labourers brought in a crate of wine, still in clay pots. They set them at the governor's feet.

'Pharaoh?' he asked.

'This is the last of your wine from the palace storeroom. I expect your taxes to be adjusted accordingly. And, governor: stabilise your city. If I hear of another increase in taxes, I will personally see that you are removed from your position.'

I tugged on my brother's arm to guide him on. Though the governor's shocked expression was satisfying, I had exerted my courage and felt my knees begin to falter. It was time for bed.

'Pharaoh, that was ill-advised,' Pothinus whispered to my left. 'You have made an enemy here tonight.'

'I will not stand for corruption, Pothinus. Egypt is my country to rule.'

The lyre player caught my gaze on my way out of the door, and I saw her eyes shimmer with tears.

'I may have made an enemy, but I have also gained more allies. The story will spread tonight, and the other governors whose taxes have been lacking will rectify the issue – lest they suffer the same embarrassment. A success, I think.'

I did not wait for the eunuch to reply before turning towards the sleeping quarters of the palace.

The servants accompanied my brother and I all the way to the doors of our chambers. Before dismissing them, I said, 'Thank you for your service tonight. As a boon for all you have given to me and my father before me, keep the masks as a token of my gratitude.'

There were gasps. The copper and lapis were enough for each of them to live comfortably for a few years at least.

'Tonight, I wished to honour my father. But I am not him. I do not wish for the pageantry of this evening to be repeated. Honour and dignity can be held in both hands.'

Oh, so righteous I was back then. In the years to follow, I came to recognise that spectacle was political. It became a tool in a chest of few tricks that I could rely upon. But I wasn't always that way. That is why I preserve my original intentions here, noble as they were.

I bade goodnight to my brother before entering my bedchamber.

'That was well done,' Charmion said, following me in.

I embraced her. 'I know who I want to be now.'

'And who is that?'

'Not my father's daughter. But me. Cleopatra,' I said. 'Though Pothinus will think me half-witted when he wakes to find the servants have fled.'

'I do not think they will leave. You have earned their loyalty.'

The next day I would discover she was right. Many of the servants who'd received bounty that day stayed for the entirety of my reign. Some even refused to leave when Octavian ransacked the palace. They died along with me. Loyalty is a revered virtue of the dead.

'They'll tell stories of you in years to come,' Charmion continued.

Centuries. Millennia.

'I hope so.'

I did not understand what it was I wished for. I hoped to become a legend, but I forgot what all stories must have: a monster.

I could not have known that monster would be me.

CHAPTER FOUR
49 BCE

The next two years passed quickly. Once I realised I did not have to replicate my father's reign, I found I enjoyed ruling Egypt.

First, I cut away the rotted roots of the court, ridding the local councils of corruption. Next, I improved upon the trade routes, increasing levies on imports, which bolstered the economy.

The only true strife the country had suffered from was the unseasonal weather. Akhet had come and gone and the Nile had not flooded.

But even that, I prided myself in navigating deftly. I anticipated the drought by constructing new aqueducts in the larger cities.

The two years had proven I was a just and capable leader. I was Egypt's sun, and she blossomed beneath my light.

'The new temple is impressive, is it not?' I said to Charmion in Arabic.

We stood on the west side of the island between the buildings of the royal necropolis. The setting sun burnished the temples in a copper glow. Despite the time of day, the air was filled with the pounding of diorite hammers.

I looked over the site that was soon to be Isis's temple. Large blocks of granite were being dragged across the newly turned soil by teams of workers. A white haze shimmered around them as those with tools ground the granite into smaller bricks.

'The temple is exquisite,' Charmion said.

Pothinus sighed beside us as his language ability was limited to Greek alone.

I had learned to tolerate his presence, if not his odour. Though he disagreed with how I handled the ruling class, he too had come to accept my rule.

Accept, not *respect*. A nuance I only learned to distinguish later in my life.

I beckoned over the lead stonemason. 'I've been told you are the greatest of builders.'

'Yes, Pharaoh.' Dust had settled into the creases of his wide face, streaking his dark skin. 'My ancestors' hands placed the bricks that raised the pyramids from the earth. My blood is mortar, my bones are stone.'

'Will the main structure be ready by the year's end?'

'No, Pharaoh. We will need another season, maybe more.'

'I will send you more workers. Pothinus, please arrange it.'

I felt, rather than saw, the regent's disapproval beside me. The construction of Isis's temple had been one of the first tasks I had ordered as Pharaoh. The building would one day be my tomb, and though its construction might have seemed premature, I was hoping the gift would draw the goddess's attention, for I was still without my divine power.

I spared no expense, utilising the royal coffers that had grown lighter during my father's reign to send for red granite from Upper Egypt.

The bones of my ancestors warmed the ground beneath my feet. Many of the temples were large enough to house the remains of pharaoh, spouse and siblings – though the latter two were often one and the same.*

---

* Philadelphoi – sibling lovers – was a title bestowed on many of my forebears. Though the concept of marriage was not as you understand it today. It was not just political, it was protective. Many unions were not consummated, though those that were only reflected the gods Osiris and Isis, whose coupling resulted in the divine being, Horus.

To my right lay the resting place of Ptolemy VIII. As the second child, he hadn't been destined for the throne. Though unlike me, he had fought for it, assassinating his nephew to clear the line of succession.

The tomb of his mother, the first Cleopatra of my dynasty, stood in its shadow. Though smaller, the sealed door was decorated with an intricate sea-shell mosaic depicting the Syrian hills of her birthplace. The iridescent tiles glowed in the sunlight, drawing me to this quiet corner of the necropolis.

Some of the shells were cracked, the pattern too distinctive to be coincidence. I wondered whether someone in the past had taken an axe to it when war had broken out against Syria.

Battles and assassinations. Patricide and betrayal. So few of my ancestors died peacefully.

When I'd been a child, I and the young servants of the palace had traded stories of their deaths like currency. How could I have known that the myth of my death would outlast them all?

'The temple will be larger than any other on the island,' Charmion remarked.

'Yes. Smaller only than Ptolemy Sōter's.'

Built for the god Serapis, Sōter's tomb stood in the centre of the temple district on the mainland. It was large enough to see even with the sea that separated us. Its columns rose up from the earth like great teeth. The doorway was guarded by a statue of Serapis holding a sceptre to the sky.

'All I ask now is that Isis blesses me like Serapis did Sōter,' I said solemnly. My ancestor was the first to be bestowed with the power of the gods.

'Isis has not forgotten you,' Charmion said.

'What if she has? No Ptolemy has been presented their gifts so late in life.' I was aware that I sounded wounded, but I knew not how to staunch the bleeding. Isis's neglect was a lesion on my soul.

'What of Arsinoe II, whose god Heh granted her the lifetime of two men? She did not know of her power until long past your age.'

I listened, but Charmion's words did nothing to alleviate the pain I felt.

'Besides,' she continued, 'the temple is large enough to draw the gaze of every god. Perhaps there is even space for me within its walls.'

Oh, my dear Charmion, you knew your future even then.

'Pharaoh,' Pothinus interjected. It seemed we had stretched his patience too thin. 'I received your suggested reforms regarding the country's coinage, and I am concerned about the monetary value of bronze.'

'Pothinus, my treatises are not suggestions. They are law.'

'But if you devalue the bronze in circulation, it lessens the value of the Roman coin in which we do our trade. The nobles will revolt—'

'The nobles are just a droplet among the sea of people in Egypt. I am here to guide the tides of all citizens. By standardising the value of bronze, we may discomfit the nobles in the short term, but our economy will prosper. Is that all you wished to discuss? Because I am not willing to debate it.'

Pothinus looked like he had swallowed sour grapes, but he did not argue. As I turned away, he said, 'There is another matter we must consider. We have received word from Rome.'

I dragged my gaze back to the regent's face. 'Tell me, what do our allies want now? More gold? My father gave them enough.'

'Julius Caesar has quelled Pompey's rebellion at Pharsalus, and the traitor has fled. Caesar believes that he may come to Egypt. We must be vigilant.'

The politics of Rome were abstract things to me then, inconsequential, bordering on dull.

Pothinus read my expression well.

'My queen, we do not want to bring down Caesar's wrath on Egypt. It is clear his legions are sufficiently well trained to collect victories as easily as grains of sand. If Pompey comes to our shores – which he may, given his former friendship with your father – we must kill him or risk making an enemy of the greatest empire in the world.'

'*Egypt* is the greatest empire in the world,' I said sharply.

Pothinus recoiled from the edge in my tone. I had spent two years distilling the poison in my voice and knew when to administer a strong dose. I was a proficient alchemist, as you well know.

'I will not become involved in the petty politics of the men of Rome. Their squabbles are many. Who is to say Julius Caesar will remain in favour with the Roman senate? No blood will be spilled in his name.'

Only mine.

Pothinus's nostrils flared white. 'We must be prepared for Pompey's arrival—'

'Enough.' My voice startled a bird from an acacia tree. It flew away in a blur of black and white that was suspiciously familiar.

'I have made up my mind on this matter, Pothinus. Egypt requires my full attention.' I strode away from him at a brisk pace, a clear dismissal. Charmion followed a few steps behind me.

One of my braids swung free from its weave, the weight of its gold beads pulling it taut at my chest. I tucked it back behind my crown, brushing my fingers on the ibis feathers threaded into the gold – a gift from Arsinoe.

My sister appeared ahead of me as if summoned by my thoughts.

'Where are you going?' she asked. Qar sat preening himself on her shoulder.

'Did you send Qar to overhear my meetings again, Arsinoe?'

Her grin was confirmation enough.

'Was your schooling today that dull?' I asked dryly.

'It was. I am not sure why I am still expected to attend lessons. Sixteen years is quite enough, I think.'

I tended to agree, but keeping Arsinoe busy meant keeping her out of trouble. She had a fascination with all things political and I did not wish for another of my siblings to become entangled with the dangers of the court.

'So, where *are* you going?' Arsinoe pressed.

'I thought I would go to the library for a time.'

Her shoulders slumped.

'Would you like to come with me?' I added. The previous two years had seen us spend less and less time together than we had before.

She brightened. 'I would appreciate some time away from Antirhodos.'

I understood the feeling; the island, though close enough to the mainland to see the people on it, could sometimes feel isolating.

'Let us go, then.'

If the lighthouse was where I went for solace, then the Library of Alexandria was my haven.

It was a place of wonder and magic. The bones of the goddess Seshat had been ground into the walls of the building, imbuing the library with her divinity.

Thick columns thrust up from the tiled ground on either side of the grand doorway. People bowed as I passed. My guards flanked me, and Arsinoe found herself pushed backwards by the tightening of the officers' ranks.

'I need protection too,' I thought I heard her mutter.

We walked through the corridors towards the courtyard where the tree of knowledge grew up from the Egyptian soil.

The seven-branched tree was the most extraordinary feature of the library. Its leaves were a deep brown, almost black, like the ochre used in our inks. The bark was smooth and chalk white. But it was the blossoms that still filled me with awe.

The buds were large, bigger than my two hands cupped together. And when the flower burst forth, the petals would unfurl as scrolls, each one filled with new knowledge bestowed by the sanctity of Seshat.

No one knew how many of the library's scrolls had come from the tree of knowledge, but the number was in the many thousands.

I pressed my hand to the bark as we passed, and murmured a prayer.

'Hail, all-knowing goddess of words and ink, patron of mathematics and astrology. Thank you for your inner sight. May your power live on.'

The sun shone down on the tree through the circular opening in the roof. At night the courtyard was filled with scholars mapping the stars across the sky. And then there was the rare moment when a bud would bloom under moonlight.

'Mother, where are you going?'

I was young, I do not remember the age exactly, as memories of my mother have dulled since her death. But I do recall the excitement in her eyes as she said, 'The tree will flower beneath the moon.'

I did not truly know what she meant, as I had been to the library only a handful of times. Words didn't interest me as much as the mewl of a lion cub or a nest at the top of a tree. But I so rarely saw such vibrancy in my mother's expression and I begged to join her. She led an unhappy life, plucked from the priesthood as a young woman and thrust among the wild dogs of the Pharaoh's court.

She led me to the library's courtyard, where a small group had gathered. They made way for the Pharaoh's wife and daughter.

'Sit, child. And look up.' I did as Mother bade. It didn't take long.

The flower peeled open, and I found myself gasping along with the crowd. The moonlight turned the petals translucent, so I could see the words of the scroll as if etched in silver. When the paper unravelled – softer than a papyrus – it floated down, landing on the bridge of my nose.

Kissed by the tree of knowledge, Mother had said.

From that moment I was enamoured by the written word. If I

had not been born a Ptolemy, I would have become a scholar. I carried that longing in me throughout my life, never fully satisfied by the fate the gods had bestowed on my shoulders,

Arsinoe sighed somewhere behind me. I had lingered in my memories for too long.

I patted the bark once more before continuing on.

The stacks hummed with the quiet murmurs of those at study. Few people looked up from their work as I passed, despite the guards that followed me.

It was one of the rare occasions where I could move through Alexandria largely unnoticed. I slowed my pace and listened in on a couple of scholars.

'Aristarchus's hypotheses are far superior to those of Aristotle. They will be the foundations of future astrologists.'

'You cannot mean what you say. His work is primitive – the sun a fixed star? No, I repeat, you cannot mean what you say . . .'

On I drifted, absorbing the animated debates that brought the library to life.

'Cleopatra's power is yet to manifest.'

I faltered as I heard my name. The guards at my back were forced to make an abrupt stop, causing Arsinoe to trip. She swore but I was too distracted to chastise her.

I moved towards the voice that had invoked my name, careful to hide my presence behind the rows of papyrus scrolls.

'I have heard tales that she isn't a Ptolemy at all, that the priestess found her by the banks of the Nile and brought her to Auletes. It is why the gods punish us by halting the rain. Have you noticed the Nile has not flooded since her coronation?'

So many blasphemies in so few breaths. I felt my throat blaze with fury.

My mother had passed to the next realm bringing my youngest brother into the world, and denying my legitimacy was an insult to the way she lived and died. Auletes – *flute player* – was a sacrilegious nickname bestowed on my father, stripping him of the power of his title of Pharaoh.

And the final piece of libel they directed at my character was the wrath of the gods. It was those words that cooled my rage into fear. Until that moment I had only considered the personal burden of my lack of divine magic. Yet here was a citizen of *my* country, attributing the weather to my shortcomings – a rumour powerful enough to unseat me from the throne.

I peered through the shelves to assign the face to the voice. The man was young, too young to be speaking words with such dangerous repercussions.

Arsinoe pushed her way through my guards to stand beside me. 'You should kill him. He speaks treason.'

Her voice carried through the dusty shelves, past the ink-covered scrolls, to the ears of the heretic.

He looked up and our eyes locked through the hollow centre of a scroll. If I thought I had felt fear before, it was nothing like what crossed this man's features. His lips thinned to pale brown, his cheeks growing sallow, and the black centres of his eyes grew to the size of a tetradrachm coin.

I had a choice: have my guards execute him and end the rumour before it spread, or continue on my way.

I have said before that I did not relish killing. My father would say it was a weakness, and time has granted me the wisdom to understand his reasoning.

'Why ever would I execute him? I heard nothing and no one,' I said softly.

I watched as my mercy took effect, returning blood to his skin. He rose from the table he shared with his companion and knelt on the ground in front of the stacks. I could no longer see him beneath the shelves, but I felt the impact of my clemency.

Arsinoe scowled beside me. 'He will repeat those words for others to hear.'

I turned away from her. 'It is impossible to contain a story once it is spoken. Especially here of all places, where Seshat's blood is the ink we read, her veins the stacks, her skin papyrus.'

I continued through the library to a quieter section where a desk was set into the corner. Only one person moved amongst the notes and scrolls of my work.

'Archibios, how do you fare?' I said.

The librarian startled before smiling and bowing low. The fingers that he clasped by his belt were tipped with ink and paint. His dark skin was glossy from sweat. There was little breeze in this part of the library.

'Pharaoh, I wasn't sure you would return today,' he said. His Greek was heavy with the tones of the east; he originally hailed from Damascus before the library had lured him here.

I was grateful that Seshat's will had brought him to my city.

'It was a busy morning, but I thought I would spend some of my day here.'

I dismissed my guards to the far corners of the room. Sometimes their presence was suffocating.

Arsinoe moved towards the desk and began to look through the jars and bottles that were stacked behind it.

'Careful!' both Archibios and I cried.

'This smells foul,' she said.

I gently removed the vial from her hand and placed it back on the rack. 'That is a healing balm I have been working on.'

My work was another attempt at eliciting my god's attention. Given Isis's healing attributes hadn't come to me naturally, I thought that if I exercised the skill, I might yet summon the power in it. I had requested that Archibios train me in all he knew.

'Can you teach me?' Arsinoe asked.

I was surprised. Arsinoe had already proved her lack of interest in scholarly matters. She had mastered the Egyptian and Greek languages, but that was all.

I was delighted to show her my recent projects, but she quickly grew bored.

'I'm hungry,' she said with the petulance of a girl half her age. 'I saw the cooks stuffing a goose with dates to roast. I should like to eat it fresh from the fire.'

I had always been bewildered by Arsinoe's penchant for poultry despite her connection to Qar. The ibis hadn't joined us on the journey to the library and I wondered whether Arsinoe's true woe was that she missed him.

The voyage back to the palace felt longer than usual. Perhaps because I felt more tension in my shoulders than I had on the way there.

The rowing boat moved through the waves towards Antirhodos, the guards cutting through the ocean with their oars. I recalled the scholar's words from earlier: 'Have you noticed the Nile has not flooded since her coronation?'

What if the gods are punishing Egypt for my shortcomings? What if Isis has deemed me unworthy of the throne?

Arsinoe's voice drew me back from my thoughts.

'There's another boat there that is not one of ours.' She pointed.

I peered closer. Arsinoe was right. Moored at one end of the harbour was a sailing boat with a hull far wider than anything we used.

'Pharaoh? What would you like us to do?' Ahmose asked.

A man was standing at the end of the pier, looking up at the palace. He wore leather armour and a kind of red sash I had seen only once before, on a Roman general. Though opulent, the fabric was threadbare and battle-torn. His hair was unkempt, and his skin blood-streaked.

There was no doubt in my mind that this was the Pompey that Pothinus had spoken of that morning.

'I will go ahead,' I said to Ahmose.

'Cleopatra, what are you doing?' Charmion hissed.

'I will be fine, Charmion.' If I said it, it must be true.

Should I send my guards to kill him and gain Rome's favour? What I knew of Caesar had painted an impressive figure in my mind, and strengthening Egypt's relations with him could only be a good thing.

Ahmose followed close behind as I approached the man.

Pompey turned at the sound of our footsteps, and I was surprised to see a smile on his lips.

'Pharaoh—'

There was a blur of white feathers and the distinctive caw of an ibis as Qar appeared in the sky above. He dived for Pompey, striking him in the eye.

I heard Charmion shriek behind me as blood and fluid burst from Pompey's face. I flicked my wrist at my guards to intervene, but Arsinoe reached Pompey before them.

She held a sabre, and with one quick thrust she buried it in Pompey's neck.

As Pompey collapsed bleeding at her feet, his dying breath rattling in his throat, Arsinoe began to cry.

I swallowed my surprise and went to comfort my sister.

'Why did you do that, Arsinoe?'

'I heard what Pothinus said . . . that Pompey had to die.'

I sighed. 'This was not your burden to carry.'

'I wanted to help,' she cried, her sobs growing stronger.

Pothinus and Theos arrived a breath later.

Theos looked down at the body with interest. 'He does not smell yet,' he declared.

'No, not yet,' I confirmed.

Pothinus's expression was triumphant. 'Well done, Arsinoe.'

I ignored him and guided my sister to Charmion's open arms.

'Take her to the baths,' I said to her. 'It will help ease her shock.'

I ordered for the body of Pompey to be taken away.

'Wait,' Pothinus said. 'First, we should take his head. Theos, you must do it. A gift for Caesar.'

Pothinus withdrew a blade and pressed the hilt into my brother's hands.

Theos looked glad of the task, until the sabre struck bone and he retched.

'Press down harder,' Pothinus insisted.

And I let him. I did not want to admit how my own stomach roiled to merely hear the slicing of flesh, let alone to think of being the one to cause it.

When it was done, Theos dropped the blade and ran to the sea to empty his stomach, and I averted my gaze as the body and head, now separate, were taken away.

The sabre Arsinoe had used lay on the ground.

Where did this dagger come from?

As I went to retrieve it, I thought for a moment my eyes were twisting the truth. For there wasn't one sabre but two.

The blade Arsinoe had used and the one Pothinus had given Theos were identical, clearly made by the same craftsman. Arsinoe had been gifted the blade by Pothinus.

I looked at the eunuch sidelong, and for the first time I began to sense the danger that was to come.

CHAPTER FIVE
49 BCE

From the moment Pompey died, Egypt began to bleed.

A few days after his execution, I journeyed through the city in my litter. Charmion dozed next to me, lulled by the footfalls of the servants carrying us.

A slice of sunlight parted the heavy curtains that separated me from my citizens. I danced my fingers through the beam and watched as my gold nail overlays glittered. My hands, which had been so often prone to tremors in the days after I took the throne, had started to quiver once again. Pompey's death had rattled me, and I knew it would not be long before Caesar arrived to claim his enemy's remains. My father had spent many years allying himself with the Romans, but I sensed Caesar was a hungry man and I did not wish Egypt to fall into the maw of his ambition.

'Pharaoh! Pharaoh! Pharaoh!' my citizens cried as we passed.

I didn't like travelling by litter, preferring to feel Egypt's soil beneath my feet. But to cross the breadth of the city it proved a necessity.

Every seventh day I made this same journey. I wanted my people to know me as their queen. My father had created distance between himself and his people in the belief that this fortified his divinity. But what greater blessing could there be than the presence of a living god? So I hallowed the city streets, often throwing coins and food to the crowds that followed my procession.

I looked through the gap in the curtains and watched as we drew closer to the city's walls, thick slabs of limestone stacked high above the litter, cleaving the blue sky. Ornate carvings of wheat and lotus flowers twined along an arch that parted the walls. The entrance, known as the Moon Gate, led to the villages that surrounded the Nile Delta.

I sighed as I tugged on a memory from my childhood. When I splayed my toes on the rough carpet of the litter, instead of wool I felt the grit of hot stones. The patter of my calloused young feet reverberated in my ears and the hair at my neck prickled as if tangled by the wind of my memories.

'*Be careful!*' Charmion cried, too fearful to join me in my adventure on the city's walls.

But I paid her no heed and dashed along the top of the Moon Gate with a freedom I would never feel again. I had been merely a pharaoh's daughter back then – the second daughter at that – and had little regard for the people that lived on either side of the city wall.

Now I was surrounded by guards, all armed with spears and daggers. Some of the blades bore signs of blood. It wasn't uncommon for citizens to lose all sense of reason in my presence.

I looked out at the crowds, which were thinning as we drew closer to the end of Canopic Street, the main thoroughfare of the city. In fact, something was drawing the hordes *away*.

I leaned further out of the litter and saw the source of the commotion.

'Ahmose,' I called, quietly so as not to wake Charmion.

The litter stopped and Ahmose appeared at the window's edge. Sweat seeped from behind his skull cap and gathered in the seams of his guard linens. 'Yes, Pharaoh?'

'I wish to walk among the people.'

Shortly after Ahmose dipped away, the litter was lowered to the ground. The motion woke Charmion. 'Are we at the harbour?'

'No, we're at the city walls.'

'Why have we stopped?' She stifled a yawn. Since Pompey's

beheading she had suffered from night terrors. Charmion, sensitive to any changes in the waters of the world, felt the ripples caused by Pompey's death. I should have heeded her fears.

But I didn't, and so I offered her my hand. 'Come with me and you will see.'

She gripped me tightly and I led her out onto the street.

The crowds parted as I neared, dropping to the ground. My guards closed ranks around me and Charmion leaned close. I could not wait for the surprise to be revealed to her.

'The Queen, the Queen is here.' Whispers swirled and faded like smoke on the breeze. A hush fell upon the people until only one voice remained.

'And so Re retires to the sky each night, sailing his boat through the stars above— Oh!' The hakawati saw me, and his words guttered out. His knees struck the dirt and he lowered his grey-topped head to the ground.

'Great Holiness, forgive me, I did not see you approach.' He had abandoned the ethereal tone of his storytelling, and I found his natural voice unpleasantly nasal.

'Rise, elder. I wished only to listen.'

He stood slowly, his dark eyes troubled. 'You would like me to tell a story, Pharaoh?'

'You are a hakawati, are you not?'

'I am.'

'Then speak.'

His lip wobbled at my command. But he did as I bade, projecting his voice with verve. 'The Pharaoh asks for a gift, the most precious of all gifts. A story. But what tale will satisfy a queen?'

I looked to Charmion. She stood with her lips slightly parted, her eyes twinkling with pleasure. This was the gift the hakawati was truly giving me.

I brought our clasped hands to my lips and kissed her fingers, and she smiled but did not look away from the storyteller.

'Not just a queen, but a Ptolemy?' the hakawati continued.

'There is only one tale worthy of such divine ears. The story of our saviour, Sōter, the first Ptolemy to bless our land, and deliver us into peacetime.'

I knew the tale well; the legend of my ancestor's deeds was performed at every festival. I tried to hide my disappointment, determined to enjoy the moment despite the chosen material.

'In a land not far from here, in a time not long from now, there was a great king, known to us as Alexander. He hailed from Macedonia to liberate Egypt from the Achaemenid Empire. But the gods called to him, and so he passed into the beyond, to rule beside Osiris.'

The hakawati let out a piercing wail that stole a beat of my heart. 'Oh, what there was! Oh, what there wasn't! Egypt mourned his passing. For who would herald our land, and shepherd our people?

'Alexander in his greatness bestowed the land to a worthy adviser: General Ptolemy, who sailed to us in our need.

'But Ptolemy knew little of how to rule Egypt. Without a pharaoh steering the oars of the ship, Egypt would soon be torn asunder. And so, he turned his face from Mount Olympus and looked to the Egyptian sky. For nine days and nine nights he prayed to the gods of Egypt, begging for acceptance and guidance.'

The hakawati sank to the floor, prostrate. His hands reached towards my feet as he acted out my ancestor's prayers – as though *I* were the gods he prayed to.

My guards tightened the circle around me, but I waved them away.

The old man was just a storyteller. What harm could stories do?

When the hakawati looked up from his play-acting, his eyes locked with mine. He rose from the ground, stepping closer to me, and said, 'But the gods were silent.' I saw a glimmer of something malicious in his gaze. Whether it was for me or for the fictional god, I did not know.

'Oh, what they had! Oh, what they hadn't!'

Those of us closest to the hakawati started at his sudden loud cry. A tittering of laughs followed.

'But our benevolent king did not concede. "I must know Egypt to rule it," Ptolemy said. And so, he began to read. A year he spent collecting scrolls and reading books. From the seeds of his collection, the Library of Alexandria would come to grow. Once he learned all he could, he prayed again, hoping he was now worthy of the gods' blessing. But again, they were silent.

'Oh, what they did! Oh, what they didn't! Ptolemy was not ready to surrender to the whims of mortals. Perhaps I must know the people of Egypt to rule them, he thought.

'And so he walked the Nile, meeting everyone he could. Once he came to love his citizens, he prayed again, hoping he was now worthy of the gods' blessing. But again, they were silent.

'Oh, what there were! Oh, what there weren't! I have come to know the living, and perhaps I now must know the dead, he concluded. And so he walked the valleys and tombs of those who had come before.

'Once he came to respect Egypt's ancestors, he prayed again, hoping now he was worthy of the gods' blessing.'

The crowd was silent, enraptured by the hakawati's words. I, too, was taken with the tale, despite its familiarity.

'This time, a god spoke back.' Though the hakawati whispered, his voice carried. '"Ptolemy!" the god cried. "We have heard, and seen, and felt your plight. You are Egypt's rightful keeper. Not only shall you be blessed, but your descendants too, hereafter. Each will be bestowed with a kernel of a god's power. I, Serapis, will be the first to bless you."

'And with divine brightness, Ptolemy's hands began to shine. "We name you Ptolemy Sōter; go now, and reap your reward." Ptolemy ruled Egypt with hands touched by the gods. The buildings he raised took half the time to construct, aided by Serapis's power. The serapeum, gymnasium, lighthouse and library are just some of his divine feats.'

The hakawati stepped close enough that I could smell the fish on his breath.

'And we stand now in the presence of one so blessed. A descendant of the legend who built Egypt from the rubble of war.' His hand went to his waist as he bowed towards me.

'Will the very same gods save you now, Pharaoh?'

With remarkable speed, the hakawati withdrew an ivory blade from his robes and lunged towards me.

In that instant the spell of his story, which had slowly bound me with its threads, broke. I blinked, seeing a premonition of my death beneath my eyelids; my blood misting across the crowd like sea spray, my heart stopping, my eyelids fluttering. They would gasp, as loudly as they had for the hakawati's tale. For that's all I would be.

A story.

A legend.

My death, the ultimate plot point.

A premonition indeed.

But as you and I know, I did not die that day.

Charmion proved quicker than the guards on either side of me. She pulled me behind her in time for the blade to strike.

Something warm struck my face. I brought my fingers to it and drew them back.

Charmion's blood.

I stood agape over my handmaiden's body. The hakawati had been restrained, and I heard his cries as though they came from the end of a tunnel.

'The gods have forsaken you. You are powerless and not fit to rule. Only your blood shall purge Egypt of your evil—' His shouting ended in a gurgle, so Ahmose must have swiftly sliced his throat – I didn't see it, though. The tunnel had darkened around me so only Charmion was visible.

I collapsed beside her. 'My heart?'

Charmion looked at me and tried to smile. It came out as a wince.

'You are wounded?' I was yet to fully comprehend what had happened.

'I am.' Her voice sounded wet.

I turned her on her side. Blood seeped from an open gash in her cheek. I could see the gleam of her teeth.

My schooling came back to me in that moment. 'Fetch me a needle and thread!'

Charmion whimpered. 'You will be well again soon, Charmion,' I assured her.

I ignored the blood that spilled from her mouth as I cradled her face. Soon my hands were slick with it.

'Pharaoh.' Ahmose thrust forward the needle. He and Charmion were close, I knew, but from the worry in his eyes, they were closer than even I had realised.

'Take her hand,' I commanded him. 'She will need to grip it.'

Charmion's eyes rolled in her head like those of a horse ready to bolt. I placed a hand on her hair.

'I will be quick.'

But I wasn't. I had learned the text on how to stitch together skin but had never implemented it until now. My hands shook so vigorously that the scar that went on to form was forever crooked.

All three of us were sweating by the end.

'Bring the litter,' I said hoarsely to Ahmose.

Tears and blood streaked Charmion's face, and I gathered her into my arms.

She mumbled something against my chest, but the stitches prevented her mouth from much movement.

I leaned down to hear.

'Will I be ugly?' she whispered.

I pressed a gentle kiss to her cheek. 'Never. The scar will be a symbol of your fealty to me. And there is nothing more beautiful than loyalty. We are forever bound in skin and thread.'

The stillness of the crowd was unnerving as they silently moved to let the litter through. The air was no longer charged with the silence of anticipation. The story had come to an unhappy conclusion and it left them wanting.

The guards lifted Charmion to the litter.

'Wait,' she murmured.

'What is it?'

She pointed to something behind me.

I looked back, my face growing warm with fury as I saw the body of the hakawati. His blood wasn't enough to sate my anger.

'His soul will not reach the field of reeds,' I reassured her, my voice fierce.

But Charmion was still pointing.

Then I saw it, gleaming against the dirt that had grown dark with the hakawati's blood – the ivory dagger.

'Ahmose. Bring it to me.'

He handed it to me hilt first. And as he did, he spoke quietly in my ear. 'I do not think this was an opportune attack, Pharaoh. I believe this was planned. He knew you journeyed this way.'

The hakawati's final words came back to me with clarity: 'You are powerless and not fit to rule.'

First the scholar and now this. Isis, grant me your favour so I may prove the non-believers wrong.

But no divine light struck me or glowed from my hands. So I had to make do with what I had. 'Bring my lions to the gymnasium. Draw in a crowd. Then feed his body to my beasts.'

Though vengeance surged in my veins, I was sickened by the thought of the hakawati's ravaged body. I still could not stomach violence. I am not sure when I grew numb to the fear of gore and pain. Perhaps you will recognise the moment in the pages to come.

I took the dagger from Ahmose's hand and wiped the bloodied edge against the hem of my dress. I made to pass it to Charmion. 'This is your treasure now, Charmion.'

She flinched as she replied, her words stretching the stitches, 'It is yours. I am your shield. Let this be your blade.'

I had held tears back until this moment, but now hot droplets fell onto my cheek. I dashed them away and tucked the dagger into the folds of my dress as I climbed into the litter.

Charmion leaned heavily against me. This time the movement of the litter did not lull her to sleep.

Thud. Thud. Thud.

Each footfall felt like the beat of a heart.

A heart that beats still.

CHAPTER SIX
48 BCE

'he Buchis bull at Hermonthis has died.'

I looked up from my plate to find Pothinus standing in the doorway of my dining chamber. His linen robe was streaked with fresh sweat, as if he had run here from the throne room.

Theos, who sat next to me, almost dropped his goblet. 'So soon?' he whispered.

It had only been three years since my father and I had attended the enthronement of the Buchis bull. The animal was the embodiment of the god Montu, a powerful and important symbol to the people of his cult. It was the last royal ceremony my father had participated in before he died.

'Have they begun the funerary rites?' I asked calmly, despite my breath becoming shallower. This was yet another bad omen.

It had been a season since the hakawati had attempted to strike me down. The story had spread like a plague of boils across the city, growing more bulbous and putrid with each retelling. I had attempted to temper it by seeding the rumour that my power had manifested as the ability to heal. The needle and thread were nowhere to be found in the tale I had planted amongst the hakawati I hired – and vetted – across the city.

No, Charmion's scar was a gift from *godtouched* hands.

To reinforce the deception, I made public my work in the library, publishing two books on the healing properties of different plants. I thought my efforts were working, but I was not scrupulous enough to see that the outbreak of hearsay was being spread from behind the walls of the palace.

Pothinus brought out a small cloth to wipe his forehead. 'Yes, the bull was interred before the message reached me. I suggest you prepare to travel to Hermonthis immediately, as the cult leaders will be waiting for you to choose the next bull.'

Servants moved in and out of the dining chamber, replenishing platters of food: roasted boar, stuffed eels, stewed lentils. My youngest brother, now ten years of age, had finally been weaned from his nursemaids and was the only one partaking in every dish.

There were differences between him and Theos beyond the three years in age. Where the younger Ptolemy's eyes sparkled with naivety, Theos's watered with concern. Where the younger Ptolemy ignored the smears of food on his face, Theos worried at the corners of his lips with a linen cloth. They were mirrors of each other in looks, but the weight of the crown had compressed Theos, making his belly sink inwards and his shoulders dip so that his eyes often faced the ground.

I tried to protect him from news like this, but his childhood had been fleeting.

Arsinoe seemed wholly unaffected by the death of the gods' vessel. Always quick to voice her thoughts, she said, 'Is it not curious that the bull died so soon? The people of Egypt will find cause to blame you, Cleopatra.' She lounged in a chair to my right. In her hand she held a half-consumed duck leg, the grease running down her wrist.

'The bull must have been maltreated. I will be sure to question the priesthood on their guardianship of the sacred beast,' I said.

Arsinoe nodded and wiped her hand on the underskirts of her dress. 'I can go in your stead, if it pleases you. There are many things for you to do here, and I would not mind travelling to Hermonthis for the festivities.'

As much as I wanted to concede, I knew how important my

attendance would be. If I did not partake in the service, it would be seen as a slight against an important religious cult.

But Arsinoe was right, Alexandria also needed me. The lack of rain had caused a famine in the southern parts of the country. Taxes needed to be carefully balanced to increase imports. And selfishly, I would miss my work in the library. My research consumed every spare moment I had. What had started as a way to garner Isis's attention had become a passion, ever since I had put needle to skin to sew Charmion back together. I now knew how to heal an infection of the flesh and the mind. I could brew a tincture to ease an earache, or a balm to soothe a sore stomach.

'It is a long journey. Two weeks, even if the wind is swift,' Arsinoe added.

Pothinus saw my hesitation. 'Perhaps the King should remain in Alexandria. It is true what your sister claims: Alexandria needs a monarch in these troubled times. Should Theos stay, you will then be able to undertake this pilgrimage in the name of the gods.'

It was clear Pothinus had heard the rumours too. And despite my dislike of him, his reasoning was sensible.

'Yes, you are right. I will travel to Hermonthis alone. Mikro Theos, you remain here.'

My brother frowned. 'I would like to go as well. I have never seen the Buchis bull.'

I reached over and patted his arm. 'One of us must stay, for Alexandria must have a ruler.'

'Why not *you*, sister?' he asked.

Pothinus and I exchanged a glance. We both knew the power of a royal tour, and it was my reputation that needed rebuilding.

'If you stay here, I will make sure you are given more time away from the court to go swimming,' I said, and Theos's eyes lit up.

'Thank you.'

Theos was merely a figurehead for mine and Pothinus's rule, and if I could grant him an opportunity of solace, I would.

Pothinus turned to leave but I waved him back.

'Any news from Rome?' Caesar had yet to call for Pompey's remains.

Theos leaned forward in his chair, his eyes brightening. 'Yes, does he know it was I who slayed his enemy?'

The younger Ptolemy snorted. 'You? It was our sister who brought him down.'

'Be quiet, brother,' Theos replied.

'I cannot hear you, for your lizard tongue twists your words.' Ptolemy's insults often invoked Theos's god, the crocodile-headed Sobek, who granted him the ability to breathe beneath water.

'Death-monger,' Theos shot back.

Ptolemy's god power had come to him the previous season. Blessed by the god Anubis, he had the ability to foretell one's death. He had simply looked up one day and said to one of our courtiers, *'You will die tonight.'*

The courtier laughed it off as a youthful jest, for he had been in prime health. But to everyone's surprise, his heart had failed that night. It was then that we discovered Ptolemy's ability – and its limitations. He could only predict a person's death the day it occurred.

I often wondered if he had known about his own demise before it happened. But forgive me, I have skipped forward through the years. There are many more deaths before his.

'Enough,' I barked at them, and the two boys fell silent. I beckoned once more for Pothinus to answer my question.

'No, we are yet to hear from Rome,' he answered quickly.

I had interpreted his agitation as haste to leave the den of squabbling Ptolemies. But how was I to know that the muscle feathering along his jaw denoted a lie?

Arsinoe sighed, drawing all eyes to her, as was her intention. 'Sister, can I at least accompany you?'

Pothinus nodded. 'I think that would be agreeable.'

To make it seem like the decision had not been guided by

Pothinus, I thought on it for a moment. Arsinoe looked between me and Pothinus expectantly. She had spent more and more time with him in recent days, and I always preferred to keep her close. 'Yes, let us show Egypt the might of the Ptolemy women. We leave at dawn.'

I stood from my chair, all appetite having fled. 'Charmion?'

She appeared behind me.

'Yes, Pharaoh?'

'Attend me. We have some preparations to make.'

Charmion paced the length of my bedchamber. 'Are we really going to Hermonthis tomorrow?'

I placed my hands on her shoulders, stopping her incessant patrolling. 'Yes.'

Her full lips turned downwards. 'It is impossible to have the royal barge prepared in such a short amount of time.'

'The god Re crosses the sky each night without such worry. We will be fine.'

She stopped short of rolling her eyes at me. 'Re has less jewellery than you. Eiras! Make ready the Pharaoh's wardrobe. Ahmose, prepare the royal guards for a voyage. Heba, inform the cooks of the Queen's plans.' Her orders echoed down the corridor as she wove together the threads of the journey to come.

I waited until I couldn't hear Charmion any more before crossing the room and withdrawing a bundle of clothes from beneath the sheets of my bed. I undressed quickly, my sheath dress falling to the ground by my feet until I wore nothing but the ivory dagger – the weapon once destined to kill me. It hung on a gold chain, the blade bound in leather. I had not been parted with it since the hakawati had attacked me.

We never managed to trace who had sent the storyteller to kill me, though I was not short on enemies amongst the nobility. Some I had humiliated when uncovering their corruption, others

I had brought to order with increased taxes. It was in their interests to have me killed. More of my ancestors had died by an assassin's blade than from old age.

I stood in front of a mirror made of polished gold and removed the braids from my hair. Charmion had woven the tresses into a knot at the back of my neck. I unravelled them, the soft curls retaining the kink of the weave as they fell down my back.

My hair told my family history. The rushlight illuminated the few locks of dark copper amongst the black, passed down to me by my Macedonian ancestors. The curls were a gift from my Egyptian mother, the texture a legacy of my Syrian grandmother.

I ran my hands through the strands of my heritage, loosening the oil used to style it. And I felt myself loosen too, the role of Pharaoh slipping away.

I pulled on the dress I had retrieved. The cloth was a little threadbare but functional. The pockets, however, were lined with sheep's leather, thick enough to protect the jars I carried there. I removed my sandals and walked barefoot towards a plinth that stood against the northern wall of the room.

Charmion's task had distracted my guards and maids, so my bedchamber was empty. Satisfied I was alone, I pushed the stonework away from the wall.

It should have been a job for many more arms than mine, but the plinth was deceptively hollow, and as it came away from the wall it revealed a narrow set of steps. The air smelled of sea salt and wet earth.

Charmion and I were the only two alive who knew of the tunnel that led to my room. It had once been used to access the cistern that held water beneath the palace. But following an earthquake half a century earlier, some of the tunnels had collapsed, and some were forgotten completely – like the one that led to my chambers.

I walked the length of it without a torch, feeling my way through the darkness until I reached a section where the walls grew tight around me. Then, using my bare feet to feel the pathway, I ducked and crawled until I felt the familiar surface of the stone I was looking for. With a push, it moved and I was able to climb through a small hole. The air grew sweeter and cooler as I entered the cistern. Through small openings in the ceiling, the moon cast a dappled silver light on the water's surface. The holes, used to feed the cistern with rainwater, were set into the gardens above me.

Irrigation tunnels snaked away from the pool, feeding the palace water system. I caught my reflection in the water – the image of a plain commoner, not a pharaoh.

I smiled at myself, relishing the freedom of my guise, before ducking down another tunnel that had collapsed years before. I moved through it like it was a puzzle, shifting and replacing the pieces of rock and stone that I knew would grant me freedom. Eventually the walls opened out to a stairway. I ascended into a small cave of ruins where an old part of the palace had been lost to the sea.

The tide was out; if it had not been, the cave would have been flooded and I'd have had to wait before crossing the shore towards the harbour.

The clandestine adventure had my heart racing in my throat. I had worn white to disguise myself in the twilight. If anyone caught sight of me from the palace, they would not have seen a pharaoh, but a slip of linen in the wind, hard to distinguish against the bleached shore.

Sand turned to wood beneath my feet as I crossed to Antirhodos's small harbour and walked down the pier. I was yet to be spotted. But as I boarded the small rowing boat used to cross the bay, I heard a voice behind me.

'Who dares trespass on the Pharaoh's property?'

I looked up. The figure was outlined by the full moon, his shape familiar. 'Peace, Ahmose, it is only me.'

He inhaled sharply, realising his mistake. 'My queen, I apologise, I did not recognise you.'

'That was my intention,' I said dryly.

'Are you journeying to the mainland? I can call for your escort—'

'No, I wish to go alone.'

'Alone, Pharaoh?'

Unbeknownst to him, this was not the first time I had slipped away from Antirhodos. Usually Charmion went with me, but today I needed her to remain in the palace; there was too much to be done.

'Forgive my impudence, my queen, but I do not think it wise to travel unaccompanied.'

I sat down in the boat and reached for the oars. 'I have never been wise.'

'Pharaoh . . .' Ahmose sounded pained, and I felt a little sorry for him.

'Come if you must, but I would appreciate your discretion.'

He hesitated.

'What is it?' I prompted, my patience waning.

'Will you permit me to tell Charmion? It's just that she's given each of us a long list to carry out before the morn, in preparation for the journey to Hermonthis.'

I laughed. Of course he was more fearful of Charmion than of me.

'Yes, Charmion will know of my endeavour tonight. And I'll be sure to mention you accompanied me.'

He nodded before joining me on the boat. I handed him the oars and together we set off across the short distance to the mainland.

Once we had docked the boat, I said, 'Stay a few paces behind me. I do not wish to draw attention to myself.'

Ahmose frowned but did as he was bidden, duly following me as I weaved through the streets.

Alexandria was a city that never slumbered. The night markets chimed with the sound of hands exchanging coins. The bakeries had already begun their preparations for the morning and the air was filled with the scent of warm bread.

I thought of Sōter, and how he had walked the length of the Nile, learning all he could of the people he was to rule.

'It must have been wondrous,' I spoke my musings out loud.

'What was, Pharaoh?' Ahmose said behind me.

I didn't respond at first; I was caught up in the rare joy of seeing the sights of Alexandria without the cover of a litter, or the footfalls of a dozen guards at my back.

'Sōter – his journeying across Egypt must have been an enriching experience,' I eventually replied. Then I added, more to myself, 'I long for it.'

I slowed as I moved through the heart of my city, savouring each step. My meandering took me to the poorer districts to the south. No longer could I smell fresh bread and the sea breeze; instead, the odour of stagnant water from the swamps of the Nile Delta filled my nostrils.

I stopped outside one of the mud-brick homes that lined the street.

Ahmose whispered behind me, 'My queen, I don't think you should—'

'Stay here,' I ordered.

I dipped under the door arch of the homestead, ignoring his protestations.

The room was dim, lit by a single torch to save fuel. A woman moved into the flickering light. 'Are you the healer?'

I nodded. 'I am Selene, Archibios sent me.'

The librarian was often petitioned to attend to the sick. It had been my idea to take on some of his charges covertly as the healer 'Selene'. I could no longer safely walk the streets as Pharaoh.

Though Archibios had been reluctant to be complicit in the ruse, I was his pharaoh and my word was the gods'.

'Who is it, Nilah?' Another person spoke from the bowels of the homestead. It was followed by a wet cough.

'May I?' I asked Nilah.

'Please, come, I do not think he has long.'

I strode into the darkness from where the man's voice had called out.

The home wasn't large, smaller than some of my antechambers, but it was tightly packed with their belongings. A table covered in a half-woven rug filled the centre of the room, and spools of dyed thread littered the floor. I picked my way through piles of linen until I came to a stop by the straw mattress in the corner.

My eyes adjusted to the low light and I took in my patient. He was perhaps forty-five years old, with wiry hair streaked grey. His skin was glazed with sweat, and his dark eyes were sunk deep into his skull. They were fluttering closed.

'What is his name?' I asked Nilah.

'Apollodorus.'

'Apollodorus, my name is Selene, and I am here to help,' I said calmly but firmly. Apollodorus's lips opened as if to reply, before closing again, along with his eyes.

Nilah whimpered beside me.

I pulled back the collar of his shirt and pressed the back of my hand to his chest. 'He has a fever,' I murmured. 'How long has he been like this?'

She shook her head, unsure.

'I'll need to make a poultice.' I reached into my pocket and removed a tincture of brewed willow bark. 'May I use a scrap of your linen?'

'Yes. The material is useless unless he recovers anyway.' Nilah tore a slip of material from a sheet and handed it to me.

I set to work lacing it with the potion, before pressing it to his forehead.

'He is a weaver?' I asked.

'Yes, carpets and clothing. The finest in all of Alexandria.' Nilah's chest swelled with pride before her gaze landed on her husband's once more and she collapsed inwards.

'They do look very fine,' I said gently.

I looked back to my patient. I could feel the heat of his skin through the linen. The poultice would not be enough.

I reached for the chain around my neck and removed the dagger from its leather sheath.

'Are you going to purge his blood?' Nilah asked hopefully.

'No.' I was yet to be convinced that bloodletting, though favoured by the priests, had any significant impact on the health of the body. I reached into my pocket and removed a few wormwood leaves, using the dagger to slice them into smaller strips.

'I'm going to place these on his tongue. You will need to watch him to make sure he does not choke.' I prised open Apollodorus's mouth and inserted a few strips of the leaf, before handing the rest to Nilah. 'Replace the leaves when the sun rises.'

Nilah's fingers closed around the leaves as if they were as precious as gold. 'Will he survive?'

'I believe he will. As soon as he wakes, ensure he drinks and eats when he is able.'

Nilah's eyes flooded with tears. 'Thank you.'

Her gratitude warmed me and I felt my own eyes heat.

If I was not Pharaoh, I would not have to skulk in the darkness to practise my craft. I could spend my days healing Egypt. My thoughts were bitter, for I knew I was destined to heal Egypt in other ways.

I must have scowled, for Nilah's smile slipped in concern.

'I will leave you now,' I said hurriedly.

As I turned to go, Apollodorus roused a little. He spat the leaves from his mouth. Before I could place them back on his tongue, his wide eyes met mine.

'It is you,' he said, awe making his voice quake. 'The Queen is in my home.'

I laughed to cover the apprehension that had robbed me of breath. 'No, friend, I am Selene, a healer sent to tend to you.'

'No, I *know* you.'

Nilah patted him on the arm. 'My dear, you are feverish.'

Apollodorus's bloodshot eyes bored into mine, stripping away my deception. 'I was there at your coronation, I sent rugs to the palace . . .' His mouth frothed from the sap of the wormwood and he began to cough.

I moved to support his back. 'Help me raise him up.'

Together we brought him up to sitting, padding the straw beneath his lower back so he remained upright. By the time we were done he had fallen asleep once more – to my relief.

I clasped my trembling hands behind my back. 'I must go – I have many other patients to visit this night.'

Nilah reached into her pocket and removed a single drachma. She held the coin out to me and I was confronted with an engraving of my own face. I dipped my head so she would not notice the resemblance.

'No, I do not need your coin, Nilah.' I made my way outside quickly. The air there, though fetid from the delta, was refreshing compared to the thickness of the humidity inside the homestead.

Nilah followed me, and Ahmose immediately moved out of the shadows in defence. I held out a hand to warn him not to intercede.

'Please, there must be something I can do,' Nilah called out.

I turned to her. 'Pray to our great mother, Isis. That is all I ask of you.'

She looked thoughtful for a moment, her gaze shifting from mine to Ahmose's, lingering on the uniform he wore.

I cursed inwardly, waiting for her to speak.

'I will do as you ask, Selene,' she said carefully, her expression neutral. 'The great mother will have my prayers this night.'

I nodded and turned away. 'Peace be with you,' I said by way of goodbye.

'And with you, Selene.'

As I began to walk to my next appointment, Ahmose fell into step beside me. I looked at him sidelong, not used to having my footsteps matched by another.

'How long have you been healing the city, my queen?' he asked.

'A season.'

'And they do not know it is you?'

'No – not until tonight, anyway.'

'You think she knew?'

'I think she suspected. The husband recognised me, but he was afflicted with a fever.'

Ahmose looked distraught. 'Should I go back?'

'To achieve what? No, I do not think she will say anything. Not many people would believe her.'

'This is a risky endeavour, my queen.'

'It is.'

'Then why do it?'

'Egypt,' I said simply. 'She is me, and I am her. With every tincture, with every stitch, I repair a piece of myself. They are not just people, Ahmose. They are the parts of me.'

Even if some of them raised arms against me or shared cruel rumours. I still loved them like I loved the body I wore in this realm.

It would have been simpler if it were not so. If Egypt had been nothing but a place, and the people nothing but my subjects. Fewer would have died. But I will never regret love. Even if it condemned me at the last.

'You are indeed Isis-blessed,' Ahmose said, his voice thick with devotion.

I didn't reply. My ability to heal was purely academic. My god had still abandoned me. But I did not contradict him.

'Why Selene?'

I smiled and pointed to the moon. 'For like the moon goddess, I bring my own light.'

A handful of years ago, the lyre player had instructed me to do just that: *Do not chase shadows. Make your own light.*

'You should ride a chariot of moonlight, Pharaoh.'

I laughed, but I didn't think Ahmose was speaking in jest. 'My legs will do just fine.'

We visited five more people before I made my way back to Antirhodos. When I finally slipped between the sheets of my bed,

Charmion was already fast asleep. My presence woke her.

'You went without me,' she said from the darkness. Her pallet lay beside mine, but ever since the assassin had tried to kill me, she had slept in my bed with me. I felt safer with her there.

'I knew you would want to come, but we have a busy day tomorrow and I needed you here.'

Charmion rolled over and tucked herself into my back. Her voice grew sleepy. 'Yes, the barge is ready for embarkment at dawn. But you should not have gone without me.'

'I was not alone. Ahmose came with me.'

She tutted. 'That's where he went. I had the guards looking all over for him.'

'He was fearful of your wrath.'

'Perhaps I will pretend I do not know of his excursion with you. It will be fun to tease him.'

I had noticed she took pleasure in teasing Ahmose, far more than anyone else. But the middle of the night was not the time to question her on her affections.

Charmion yawned. 'I wish you had waited for me, though. You know I worry.'

'Sleep now; you can chastise me in the morning.'

'Hmm.' Her breathing softened as sleep claimed her.

It wasn't long before it took me too.

CHAPTER SEVEN
48 BCE

I strode along the promenade of the royal barge. The boat was a thalamegos, one of the many in the royal fleet. This one, however, was mine. I'd had it commissioned in the early days of my reign.

It was half a stadion long – the length of four sycamore trees – and crafted from cedar imported from Tyre. The lower level of the barge was fitted with a dining room and two staterooms, while the upper consisted of my living and sleeping quarters.

Serket's Venom, it was called, after the scorpion god, ally and protector of Isis. So, too, would the vessel see me safely down the Nile.

The boat was a lavish expense, embellished with gold furnishings and granite statues of the gods. My father had taught me how important it was to represent the gods in all their splendour. And since I did not have a divine gift upon which to rely, I compensated with materialistic things.

My wardrobe was vast, each dress beaded with lapis and turquoise, the hems trimmed with gold.

Today I wore a woollen shawl around my neck, dyed green, the colour of a peacock's plume. The Isis mark on my neck had been painted with gold leaf to draw the eye and to remind my citizens of my patron. My arms and wrists were adorned with heavy jewels and my eyes lined with kohl. In my hair I wore my gilded vulture crown, its wings draped down on either side of my face, the head rearing upwards from my brow, poised as if the bird were soaring among the clouds, waiting for the death of the creature that would become its next meal.

My footsteps had taken me to the stern of the boat, where I leaned over the ebony railing to look out on the Nile.

Reeds lined the fertile soil of the riverbank, the distinctive sunburst head of the papyrus plant swaying in the light breeze. Ducks dived in the shallow waters, hunting for insects and other small prey.

I cast my gaze to the east, where agricultural villages, built from the same clay as the banks of the river, dotted the landscape. To the west, tombs adorned the horizon, for like the setting sun, it was where the kings and queens of the past were laid to rest. Their impressive pyramids from millennia past were resplendent against the sky. Tombs so large that they touched the gods themselves.

I shivered, imagining my body buried beneath the weight of so many stones. Death was not a concept I pondered often. Life was, after all, just a precursor to the great beyond. But looking out at the pyramids, I felt the significance of my life diminish in their shadow.

What mark will I leave upon the skin of my land? Will I scar it? Or embellish it?

We rounded a bend in the river and I had my answer. The flax fields on both banks were sun-blistered and starved of water where the Nile had receded.

The drought was still plaguing my reign.

Egypt must live. Always.

My father's words haunted me. They haunt me still.

Caw-waw, caw-waw.

Arsinoe came up behind me and draped herself over the railing. Qar perched on her shoulder, his talons digging into her skin, but she seemed unaware of the blood his claws had drawn. 'The captain said we will arrive in Hermonthis before sunset.'

I let out a sigh of relief. 'Thank the gods.' The royal formalwear was growing burdensome and I wished to be rid of it by the night's end.

Arsinoe was similarly dressed, though she wore no crown, just a simple circlet adorned with an ankh. She seemed more at ease than I in the heavy material of her gowns.

'Are you not fatigued by your attire?' I asked, curious.

She looked up at me, surprised. 'I am the Pharaoh's sister; it is an honour to dress as such for the people of Egypt.'

'Imagine if we had arrived by rowing boat in simple linen cloth and no jewels. Would they have bowed to our authority?'

It was true that every stop we had made on the voyage to Hermonthis had been successful. The dissent brewing in Alexandria was yet to poison all my citizens against me.

But I was not ignorant enough to feel entirely secure in my reign. Worry soured my belly.

'You act like being Pharaoh is a burden, not a gift,' Arsinoe said quietly.

I thought on her words before I answered. 'If it felt like a gift then I would never truly be in service to the people of Egypt. With a burden, I must work hard to alleviate the strain.'

Qar chittered into the silence. I wondered what he had said, but Arsinoe's next words gave me an intimation. 'Do you think Berenice thought of it as a burden?'

I tried not to sound affronted. 'She was never Pharaoh.'

'No, I suppose not. Father killed her before then.'

I did not like to hear Father's name spoken with scorn. He might not have gone down in history as a very great ruler – then again, neither would I – but few could judge a pharaoh. The role was unlike any other. To be god and ruler both was a unique hardship. 'Do not blame him for his actions, he did what he had to. Your pain will only taint your memory of him.'

'You think I hold Berenice's death against him?' she said. 'No, if anything I believe he should have eliminated the threat earlier.'

I swallowed my shock. 'That is a cruel thing to say.'

'Strength can often be mistaken for cruelty.'

Remember those words. For one day I will go on to repeat them.

And believe them.

At the time, I reasoned with myself that Arsinoe had been too young to know Berenice and to love her like I had. 'Berenice was our sister, not a threat.'

Arsinoe's face softened and she looked more vulnerable than I had seen her in a very long time. 'You think me a monster now.'

'No.'

'You do, I see it in your eyes. But follow the veins of our family blood, Cleopatra. It has ever been tainted. Murder, sacrifice, betrayal – they are the cornerstones of our ancestors' tombs.'

'To rule Egypt is to court danger; like the Nile, it gives and takes. As Pharaoh, one must learn to sail upon it.'

'You sound like a priest,' she said, amused.

My sister always had the ability to make me feel young again. And not in the carefree way that a fond memory might invoke. No, she made me feel callow.

'There is no shame in being compared to those most holy.'

'No, I suppose not. But remember, sister, even the priests care for the gods first and people second.'

'You suggest I do otherwise?'

'I know about your secret excursions to the mainland to heal.'

I didn't question how she knew. There was only one answer: Qar. How I detested that bird.

'What I do for the people of Egypt, I do in Isis's name.'

'Perhaps. Or perhaps you care too deeply. And that is a weakness.'

Her words shocked and wounded me, but I did not show it, for it would only further prove her hypothesis.

'Strength has many forms. You see it too plain.'

'If that is what you think, then it must be so.' She held my gaze.

The tension between us was wound tighter than strips of linen on the flesh of the dead. But then she laughed, releasing me from her scrutiny, and I was reminded of the young child she used to be. Mischievous and cunning, but quick to smile. A lioness without claws.

Qar squawked, craning forward as if to alert us of something.

'A pigeon has returned to the nest on the roof. It must be a message from the palace,' Arsinoe said.

'Charmion?' I called.

'Already sent for,' she said behind me.

Arsinoe and I retired to one of the staterooms while we awaited the letter. I lowered myself onto a couch, conscious that the vulture headdress could topple at any moment. Arsinoe, on the other hand, lounged comfortably, her ankles crossed upon the leopard-skin rug.

A servant arrived, carrying the small scroll on a bronze tray. 'Pharaoh, I have retrieved the message.'

I knew it was unlikely she was able to read; few in my household could. A precaution one of my ancestors implemented to keep the court's secrets close. I had intended to change that policy in time.

But time is the one thing that is constant yet always running out. And I had less time than I could ever have conceived.

'Thank you,' I said to the servant.

She dipped her head before leaving us.

I read the message quickly.

Arsinoe let out an impatient sigh. 'What does it say?'

'It is from one of my courtiers in the north. Caesar's ship has been spotted by the coast. He descends on Alexandria. I must get a message to Pothinus and Theos, but I'm not sure it will arrive before Caesar does.'

Arsinoe worried at the corner of her dress. 'Which courtier?'

I frowned, not thinking it mattered. 'Elena of Syracuse.'

My sister's expression grew dark before brightening once more.

'We can send Qar with a message to Pothinus. He will fly fast and true.'

It was an adequate solution. Even if we turned around now, we would not arrive back at the palace before the full moon.

'Yes, let me prepare a message.' I called on my scribe to pen a warning to Pothinus.

'He needs to ensure the kitchens are well stocked with the latest produce from Rome,' I instructed. 'I recollect Caesar and my father spending many evenings around the dining table and I wish for him to be comfortable.'

'Yes, Pharaoh,' the scribe replied. I looked over her neat penmanship, confirming the message was correctly rendered.

'Add in that we are beginning the return journey tomorrow—'

'We're returning?' Arsinoe said. She crossed the room to stand over the scribe as if seeing my words in ink would change what I had said.

'Yes. Caesar is an important ally, and Pompey died on our soil. It is important I am there to greet him.'

'But what of the Buchis bull?'

I knew Arsinoe had been looking forward to the adventure of Hermonthis, and I was sad to disappoint her. 'There will be another Buchis bull in your lifetime. We will journey back to the temple then. Right now, the best thing for Egypt is for me to return.'

'Do you not think that this will be a slight against the priesthood? Abandoning them for a Roman?'

'They will come to understand once I am able to explain. The royal tour has been a success, whether we reach Hermonthis or not.'

Qar trilled from the corner of the room, and Arsinoe nodded. 'Qar believes we will be slighting the gods if we do not continue to the temple.'

That made me pause. Qar was a gift of the god Thoth, a vessel like the Buchis bull. His words held weight, much to my chagrin.

'Truly?' I felt my resolve wavering.

'Truly,' Arsinoe confirmed. 'It will only delay us a few days. Perhaps less time than that.'

We *were* very close to Hermonthis.

The scribe looked up at me and I nodded. She discarded the papyrus she was working on and began again.

'Two days,' I said. 'We must ensure the Buchis enthronement is conducted on the morrow.'

Arsinoe's lips twitched ever so slightly.

I should have known. I should have seen it.

But I have always been blinded by love. That was one thing your histories got right.

'We welcome Queen of the Two Lands, Cleopatra Thea Philopator VII, to the god Montu's place of sanctuary.' High Priestess Neferu stood at the head of the procession. The eight servants of the gods lined the hallway of the temple, their brown cowls hiding their faces so all I could see was shadows.

I strode past them and Neferu fell into step just behind me. 'Is the bull ready for selection?' I was impatient for the ceremony to commence. With each passing day Caesar grew ever nearer.

'We captured nine wild bulls eight days ago, Pharaoh. We await your guidance on which beast will become the vessel of our lord Montu.' Neferu's tone was sharp, charged with obvious irritation.

I looked back at her with an eyebrow raised. Her face was hidden behind the shadows of her cowl. Unlike the other priests, Neferu wore a full-length white robe to denote her status. It pooled around the tiles at her feet, the quality of linen as fine as anything I wore.

'I see our donation reached your coffers,' I said. Arsinoe chuckled somewhere behind me.

Neferu dipped her head. 'We are grateful for your continued patronage, Pharaoh.'

'Indeed,' I replied coolly.

We reached the temple courtyard where the heat of the sun left a mirage wavering like a lake upon the ground.

In the centre of the landscaped gardens was an empty pen, its metal bars gilded. An ornate granite trough filled with crystal-clear water stood in the corner. Opposite it lay an assortment of plush cushions.

'What happened to the last bull?' I asked as we passed the enclosure.

'It simply died, Pharaoh,' Neferu replied. There was a catch to her voice that told me there was more to know.

'There is nothing simple in death, high priestess.'

'You bless me with your wisdom.' Her words didn't sound mocking, but from what I could see of her lips, they were quirked with a half-smile.

I cleared my throat. 'I find my mouth quite dry in this heat.'

'Refreshments are just this way, Pharaoh. If you'd like to follow me.'

I nodded, giving her permission to take the lead, but indicating with a flick of my wrist for the royal guard to hang back. Arsinoe grumbled behind me as the guards closed ranks to prevent her from following.

Even Charmion stayed her feet, letting me go on alone with Neferu.

The high priestess led me towards a small room off the courtyard. Servants cleared the space as we entered. As soon as the door was shut behind me, I turned to Neferu.

She lowered her hood and the face that emerged was lined with every year that she had lived. The creases were soft embellishments on severely cut features. As I looked into her kohl-lined eyes, so much like mine, I felt a tug of grief.

I crossed the space between us and embraced her in a crushing hug.

'It has been too long, my niece,' Neferu said against my shoulder.

My eyes burned as I inhaled the familiar incense that reminded me so much of my mother. 'It is good to see you, Aunt.'

She pushed me to arm's length. 'How fares your journey?'

I tried not to scowl. 'Caesar descends on Alexandria; I must make haste and return as soon as possible.'

Her eyes narrowed. 'When a Roman crosses the ocean, trouble comes on the tide.'

'Pothinus and Theos will welcome him.'

'Pah.' Neferu scrunched her lips to spit. 'A fool and a child.'

'Not a fool; my father trusted him enough to name him regent.'

'Your father was a fool too, my dear.'

Neferu had never forgiven my father for taking my mother away from the Montu temple. When he had selected her among the priestesses, she had stopped dedicating her life to Montu and instead become a servant of a different god – a pharaoh.

'Tell me of the bull,' I said. I did not enjoy tainting my father's legacy. My mother had died giving birth to young Ptolemy, so my memories of her were blunted, but my father's still cut sharp.

Neferu looked troubled. 'I suspect murder.'

My blood ran cold. 'How?'

'A new acolyte joined the temple two days before our lord's death. The day the bull died, the student disappeared.'

I raised a questioning eyebrow.

'Every acolyte's first duty is to maintain the water trough of the Buchis. I suspect she poisoned the water,' my aunt explained.

'Why would anyone wish to poison Montu's manifestation? Why risk the wrath of the gods?'

'Money,' Neferu said calmly. 'Taxes are high, crop yield is low.' She didn't say it with any hint of blame, but still I felt ashamed.

'What do you know of this acolyte?'

She shook her head. 'We searched her rooms after she left – discreetly, of course – and there was very little to find.'

I made a sound of frustration and Neferu gave me a look that would have silenced a schoolyard of children.

'I said *very little*, I didn't say nothing.' She pulled something out of her pocket. 'I found this behind her pallet. Part of her blood money, I am sure.'

My aunt handed me a coin. It was a simple drachma. Nothing entirely out of the ordinary, but as I looked at it more closely, my hands began to prickle.

The two-sided coins minted during my reign were embossed with my profile on one side, and Theos on the other.

But when I turned the coin over – the side wet with my sweat – I found my face had been replaced with an eagle, a symbol of royalty. At first, I thought it an old coin left in circulation from my father's reign. But there was no mistaking the young Theos, his eyes wise and unblinking.

An error at the minting press, that is all, I reasoned with myself, though I knew I had last sent Pothinus to the press. He had been instructed to change the valuation of the bronze coin.

What if he had done something else entirely? Something treasonous?

Neferu seemed unaware of the coin's defect. It wasn't unusual for the king of the realm to feature as the sole ruler on currency, but I had changed this within the first season of my rule. I also imagined it was rare that Neferu handled money.

I closed my fist over the drachma and slipped it beneath my dress, where the binding of my undergarments tightened around my chest. Against my beating heart.

'Thank you for telling me this.'

Neferu's eyes narrowed. She could sense something had shifted in me, but I was not able to vocalise what. Especially when I wasn't sure why this defective coin had left me so unsettled.

'We should return to the others,' I said.

'Yes.' Then she reached for my hand and squeezed it so hard the pressure bordered on pain. 'I sense something coming. Like a storm on the horizon, it draws ever near.'

I shivered as my skin turned to the texture of gooseflesh. But despite my sense of foreboding, I straightened my shoulders and met my aunt's eyes steadily. 'A storm will bring rain, and rain grows crops. I do not fear it.'

Neferu looked at me with an expression that said, 'You should,' before sweeping up her cowl to hide her features once more.

She waited for me to leave the room first, and as we crossed the threshold we were once again strangers to each other, not aunt and niece, but high priestess and Pharaoh.

Arsinoe glared at me as I rejoined the procession. Neferu was her aunt too and I trusted Arsinoe, but our aunt's news on the acolyte was for my ears only.

I followed the path that I had last ventured down with my father, three years prior, when we'd selected the last Buchis bull. It led me to the pens on the outskirts of the temple.

Nine bulls snorted and paced within, separated from each other by stone bricks, some of which had suffered under their large horns. Every bull had a white hide with black patterning across its face.

'They are smaller this year,' I noted. One looked barely out of calfhood.

'Without the Nile floods, many of our fields have fallen barren,' Neferu said quietly.

Choosing to ignore her comment, I scrutinised each of the bulls in turn and waited for a feeling of clarity to come over me. The bulls snorted and shifted in their pens as I walked past. I could feel their aggression in the bulk of muscle that corded above their shoulders. Some of them feinted a charge at me, others scuffed their hooves, but none of them seemed anything other than a bull.

'You will know when Montu calls to you,' my father had explained three years before. He had chosen the beast that day, pointing a bejewelled finger at the new vessel as I watched.

'But how, Father?' I pressed.

'It is a feeling, like how your patron tethers you to the gods – as you will know, when your power eventually manifests.'

I felt humiliation then, and I felt it now. For Isis had not called to me, and neither did Montu.

My throat began to narrow with panic, and I found myself swallowing over and over again. I looked back and found Neferu watching me expectantly. Arsinoe stood in her shadow, her bored expression only increasing my trepidation. I was not the paragon of authority she could learn from.

Charmion stood apart from the procession of priests. When I caught her eye, she tipped her eyes to the sky with a subtle expression that only I could read: H*urry up, I'm hungry.* It was exactly what I needed to prompt a decision. Time was dwindling.

I drew level with the final beast.

He was not the largest of the bulls, nor the plumpest. His horns were a murky cream rather than the polished white of some of the others. But when he looked at me through the grating of his cage, his eyes were as brown and as fathomless as the Nile's depths.

I convinced myself it was a sign from Montu.

'This one,' I announced. 'He will be the gods' vessel.'

The response from the priests was immediate. They stepped forward in formation, each standing in front of one of the other bulls. Neferu moved to stand by me, her hands raised to praise the new manifestation of Montu.

'Come forth, Buchis, our lord almighty. May you live for years untold. May you bask in the sun everlasting. My prayers are yours until you claim my soul to stand by your side in the afterlife.'

The eight priests responded to Neferu's prayer as one: 'I am thy servant, great lord.'

Then, the priests pulled out spears from beneath their robes. The first time I had witnessed the ceremony, I had been surprised to find the holy servants armed. But blood and power have always come as one.

'We honour your presence with this sacrifice,' Neferu said.

I closed my eyes as the priests lunged forward, their spears pointing towards the bulls' hearts.

Squeals erupted around me as the creatures' flesh was pierced. Some died quickly, but others were not so lucky, their screams turning to gurgles where the priest's aim must have missed the heart and punctured their lungs.

The whole process was agonisingly slow. When the courtyard finally grew quiet, I opened my eyes.

The Buchis I had chosen was the only beast left alive. His eyes rolled in his skull, his nostrils flaring and snorting as he smelled the blood of his brethren.

I averted my gaze from the slumped forms of the other animals. It was then that I noticed Arsinoe watching me.

'Sister, are you well?' she asked. Though her tone was concerned, her lips curled upwards mockingly.

'Yes,' I said. 'I fear I am just hungry, and it has set my heart a-thunder.'

I rested my hand against my chest, feigning light-headedness. Servants rushed to attend me, but I ignored them: I had been reminded of the threat pressed against the bone of my sternum.

The coin with my profile removed.

And so it began, the erasure of my history.

CHAPTER EIGHT
48 BCE

We did not stay long in Hermonthis. Once the enthronement parade was over, I retired to my quarters on the barge. My feet were dusty and aching, my lips cracked and dry from the midday sun.

Arsinoe stayed the night in the city, the festivities luring her in as strongly as they repelled me. She did not return to the boat until the next morning while I was breaking my fast.

I looked up as she sauntered into the dining room. The guards I had left her with trailed in behind her, both looking exhausted.

'You smell of palm wine,' I said, letting my disapproval show in my voice.

'I do, as I had very many glasses of it.' To her credit she did not slur, though she swayed a little more than the movement of the boat accounted for.

'I hope you acted properly.'

My sister snorted as she reached forward to pick at the bread from my plate. 'The people were just glad to have someone of Ptolemy blood there.'

I shot her a stern look. 'Drink has made your tongue loose, sister.'

'If only it loosened yours, too. Do you know what they said about you, when they thought I couldn't hear?'

I shook my head, not wanting to know, but listening intently anyway.

'They think you fragile. Too fragile to stay up the whole night through.'

'My night was not wasted on the frivolities of opulence,' I snapped. 'I came back to my quarters to study.'

'Ah, yes. Your divine power is healing, of course.'

I darted my eyes around the room, taking in the faces of the guards who listened.

'Arsinoe,' I said in a warning tone.

She sank into a chair and trailed her finger along the embroidery of the tablecloth. 'I wonder how the people would feel if they knew how righteously you studied for the divinity bestowed upon you.'

I slammed my hand down on the table.

'Stop.'

Arsinoe was startled for less than a breath before a smile painted her expression once more. 'So, there *is* a fire in you, sister. I was beginning to wonder.'

Fury pulled me to my feet. 'Fire? I am the furnace of the Lighthouse of Pharos. I shine, I lead, I *burn*. For I am the Pharaoh of Egypt, and I will not tolerate being spoken to this way.'

Arsinoe looked at me. 'Do you remember Mother?' she asked suddenly. The question took me unawares and I sat heavily back in my seat.

'Of course I remember her.'

'Oh,' Arsinoe said, her eyes suddenly filled with sadness. 'Another thing you have that I do not.'

'What is it you want, Arsinoe?'

The question disarmed her and her expression went slack. When she seemed to come to, she met my gaze. 'I want to be *seen*.'

I didn't know what to say to that, but I didn't have to worry, as Arsinoe got up and left, leaving the scent of palm wine in her wake.

*

The journey back to Alexandria was less joyous than the outbound voyage, and things remained strained between Arsinoe and me.

The cities that had welcomed us on the journey upriver were less spirited than they had been, and the local governors rarely accepted my invitations for dinner, feigning illness or using other excuses. Most nights were spent dining alone with my sister.

'The rumours that started in Alexandria have now run the length of the Nile,' Charmion said softly in my ear. I had sent her into Memphis to listen to what the locals were saying.

I broke off a morsel of the steamed fish in front of me. Without turning around, I said quietly, 'Tell me, what exactly is being said?'

Charmion inhaled sharply, and I knew it hurt her to repeat it. 'That your reign is blighted by the gods. That you do not have any divine gifts and therefore are unfit to rule Egypt.'

Arsinoe sat on the other side of the table, but she was engaged in conversation with Serapion, the only courtier who had accepted my summons in Memphis. He was the son of the governor.

'It is curious that these rumours were not swirling on our journey to Hermonthis. It seems that time and river-water have helped the hearsay grow.'

Later that night I had an idea. I woke Charmion.

'What is it?' She lurched to sitting, her hair in disarray.

'I know how I can vanquish the rumours,' I told her. 'I will open a royal hospital and treat the public. There is no need for me to heal people in secret. This way people will be able to see my power at work.'

It didn't matter that my power was learned, as long as my citizens believed in my gift.

And perhaps I had started to believe my own lie too.

Charmion yawned. 'Have you not yet slept?'

'That doesn't matter. Will you send for the scribe? I want Archibios to begin preparations.'

It was many days before I heard back from Archibios. I was lounging on the balcony beneath an awning, the midday sun striking the deck of the boat. Arsinoe sat beside me playing senet with Charmion.

'Arsinoe, you are better than your sister at senet,' Charmion said, with a playful smile in my direction.

'Yes, I'm better at many things, though few know it,' Arsinoe retorted. Though she also smiled, her eyes conveyed the truth in the insult.

'At games, certainly,' I said dismissively.

Charmion laughed into the silence that ensued. But it did nothing to ease the tension that endured between my sister and me.

There was a squawk at the balcony edge and I looked over to see Qar land with a headless fish in his beak. He threw his head back and swallowed it in one.

'I did not realise Qar had returned,' I said.

Arsinoe shrugged as if his appearance was inconsequential and I felt my temper quicken. 'Did he come with a message from Pothinus?' I persisted. 'Has Caesar arrived?'

She didn't look up from the senet board. 'No, nothing.'

I frowned. We were less than a day from Alexandria and I had not heard from Pothinus since my message to him.

I called forward a servant. 'Please check the pigeon roost.'

When they returned with a slip of paper, I felt relief wash over me.

'A pigeon returned as I was there, Pharaoh.'

I took the small scroll from the servant's outstretched hand. But the message wasn't from Pothinus, but Archibios.

My breath began to quicken as I read.

Pharaoh, though I am intrigued by your suggestion for an infirmary, I fear there are larger concerns of late. I am unsure if you have received word from your court, but your brother has recalled all regiments from Upper Egypt to Alexandria. They stand guard at the harbour. I have heard whisperings that the Pharaoh is taking the throne for his own.

Julius Caesar resides in the palace as the Pharaoh's guest. There are rumours that your brother has petitioned the Roman to dissolve your father's will. Forgive me for my callous words, but I wish to warn you of the trap that has been laid.

'Sister? Are you well?' Arsinoe asked.

I met her gaze, schooling my expression to neutral.

'Yes.'

'Who is the message from?' she asked lightly. Too lightly.

Gods, please tell me Arsinoe is not a part of this.

'Archibios. He needs the references for some of my research, that's all.'

I watched her reaction carefully: a relaxing of her jaw, an easing of the lines upon her brow.

My stomach lurched. *She knows.*

'Charmion, will you accompany me to my quarters?' I said. 'I think I will retire for the afternoon.'

Charmion could read my emotions well, and didn't question my sudden need for quiet.

There was a scratching sound above me and I looked up to see Qar hanging off the awning, looking down at the message in my hand.

I immediately folded the papyrus against my chest, closing my fingers over Archibios's warning. Qar ruffled his feathers and flew away. I wasn't sure how much of the message he'd been able to convey to my sister, if anything at all.

As I made my way down the stairs to my rooms, I heard Arsinoe call gently, 'Rest well, Pharaoh.'

Charmion whirled on me as I entered my bedchamber. Wordlessly, I handed her the crumpled message.

She read it, her eyes growing large.

'Theos moves against you? This cannot be. Archibios must be mistaken.'

I thought back to when I had decided to go to Hermonthis and how Pothinus had encouraged me to go. 'Not Theos; it is his regent's doing.'

'How could they have instigated a revolt in a few short weeks?' Charmion whispered.

'Years, not weeks.' I reached into my bodice and withdrew the coin Neferu had given me. 'This was found in the rooms of the acolyte who murdered the Buchis bull.'

Charmion held the coin up to the sunlight that poured in from the window. Her skin was pallid. 'Why didn't you tell me of this sooner?'

I looked away from her. 'I hoped, *wished*, it was a misprint. But it's clear to me now that Pothinus had the Buchis killed, to rid me from the capital. And he paid with coins made for Theos's reign.' To my horror, tears pricked at the corners of my eyes and when I continued, my voice shook. 'What am I supposed to do now?'

Charmion's hand cupped my cheek and turned my face back to hers. 'We must fight for your throne.'

'Must we?' I imagined giving up, turning my back on the pressures of ruling. I had the boat; it would be a simple thing to disappear down one of the branches of the Nile. I'd have to send Arsinoe home, but it would be possible.

At the thought of my sister, I paused. What was her role in all of this? It was clear she knew more than she was letting on. We had been close once; our secrets were each other's. But somewhere along the paths of our lives we had diverged.

'You are the rightful ruler of Egypt, Cleo. You cannot give up on the country that you were born to lead.'

I didn't remind Charmion of Berenice.

'Mikro Theos may be a capable ruler without me,' I said.

'But it won't be Theos ruling, you know this. It will be Pothinus, and he seeks only to support the nobility.'

My hand went to the ivory dagger tied at my throat. It was true that Egypt would suffer at the hands of the ruling class if I gave up the throne.

But would that be so dire?

A light breeze swirled through the window, bringing with it

specks of glittering sand. It brushed across my brow, cooling the sweat that beaded there.

Egypt kissed me with her breath, and with it I felt renewed. My love for my country was as vast as the pyramids and as deep as the ocean. I would not abandon her.

'No, you're right. I cannot let him take my throne from me.' The threatened tears had now begun to fall, and I wiped them from my cheeks. 'We arrive in Alexandria tomorrow. If Theos has called on the might of the army, my royal guards will not survive long. Our only hope of matching his command is by calling on our allies.'

'Who will come to your aid?'

'Syria, Ascalon and Armenia would likely send troops. But that would take time, and the longer I allow this plot to fester, the harder it will be to reclaim my people's faith.'

'What are you thinking?'

'Rome. Caesar. He was my father's closest ally. Pothinus's ploy goes against my father's will. If I petition Caesar, he may yet lend me his force. Especially as his fleet docks in Alexandria. The problem is, getting to Caesar.'

Charmion's eyes narrowed and I said, 'You look like you have an idea.'

She nodded. 'I do. But you won't like it.'

The following night, under the light of the stars, I made my way to the bow of the boat. No servants stopped me, no guards stood at my back. It was as if I were invisible, and it was a freedom I savoured.

I wore Charmion's pale linen tunic. My hair was unbraided and tied simply at the base of my neck with cord. No jewels adorned my wrists or ears. No kohl lined my eyes. The only hint of the pharaoh I once was, I kept hidden beneath the collar of my dress: the concealed ivory dagger.

I looked behind me, but the boat was silent. Soon dawn would break and Queen Cleopatra would arrive at Alexandria's harbour. But it wouldn't be the Queen, it would be Charmion, veiled to hide her scar and dressed as my copy.

'*I cannot let you do this*,' I had said, shaking my head fiercely.

'You must. It is the only way you can enter the city without being caught.'

I held on to her wrist tightly. 'What if you are hurt? Killed?'

'They will not murder you before the people. Pothinus is shrewd, but he knows there are many citizens who still support you in the city.'

'So, your death is delayed until you are beneath the palace's roof.'

Charmion laid a hand on mine, loosening my grip until our fingers were intertwined. 'I will reveal to them who I am before a blade is held against my throat.'

'And you think laying bare the ruse will stop the knife from slicing?'

Charmion looked at me plainly. 'It is a risk worth taking. Let me do this for you. If I can delay their search for you for half a day, it will be worth it.'

'It is not worth your life.'

She smiled sweetly. 'But it is worth yours.'

My heart constricted as I thought of her now. I turned back to the Nile water below.

'Isis, watch over Charmion. She is more to me than the flesh and bones of her body. She is my companion and my friend, in this life and the next.' My prayer concluded, I dived into the depths of the Nile.

CHAPTER NINE
48 BCE

Cold water rushed up my nose, thick with the swirling currents of silt. I stayed under for as long as my breath would allow. The river plucked at the length of my dress, tangling the skirt like seaweed around my legs.

I tried to kick free of the weight of the wet material but it dragged me further down.

My lungs began to strain, my arms aching as I tried to make my way to the shallows of the riverbank. Reeds scratched at my legs, letting me know I was close, but the fabric was still pulling me under. What if I didn't make it?

Just as I was sure I wasn't going to, I felt my feet strike mud and kicked hard against it, pushing myself to the surface.

I took in a ragged breath, my heart thumping, and looked back. But the barge was quiet, its light glittering like fireflies on the water.

I swam the last few strokes to the shore. My limbs trembling, I crawled out of the mud and collapsed onto the riverbank.

The full moon shone down on me, and I began to laugh. I held my hands to my mouth to hide the sound, but I still shuddered with silent guffaws, shifting the reeds around me.

I am free.

It may only have been temporary, but I savoured the moment

as the royal barge drifted past. It wouldn't be long before it docked in Alexandria.

The thought stirred me from the mud, and with a squelch I stood and made my way northwards.

I walked through fields of wheat and flax, arriving in the outskirts of Alexandria at dawn. My bare feet, unused to such distances, were blistered and raw. Mud had dried in streaks on my face as the sun rose.

I cannot meet Caesar like this.

There was a well in the centre of the southern district and I waited patiently in the early-morning queue.

I wondered if Charmion had made it safely to the palace yet, or if our ruse had been prematurely uncovered.

'The child Pharaoh has ousted the Queen.' The words drew me out of my thoughts and I homed in on the speaker in front of me.

The two women were no older than my twenty-one years.

'Good,' the other replied and I inhaled against the bitterness of disappointment. 'The gods smite her reign.'

'They say she lies about her gift, that Isis has not blessed her,' the first said in hushed tones.

'Hold your blasphemous tongues.' The man's voice came from behind me in the queue. I recognised it, but I wasn't sure where from.

'The Queen is blessed by Isis and I am proof of it,' he said.

And as I turned around, I knew who I'd find: Apollodorus, the weaver I had treated a few weeks earlier.

He looked angrily on at the two women ahead of me. The colour of his skin was warmer than when I'd last seen it, his cheeks less hollow. And though I cursed inwardly at the coincidence, I was glad to see him hale.

I cast my gaze downwards before I caught his eye, thankful for every splatter of dirt that covered my body.

'She came to my home and healed me,' he continued.

The women scoffed at him. 'The Queen, here?' one said. 'Your illness has rattled your mind, Apollodorus.'

I allowed myself a small smile as the two women moved forward to take their fill of the well water.

When they were done, I stepped forwards.

First, I quenched my thirst, the sweet water soothing my parched throat. Then I washed myself quickly, rubbing at my mud-caked skin.

The linen dress was beyond saving, but there was nothing that could be done about that. Caesar would have to accept me as I came.

I moved away from the well as quickly as I could, for I felt Apollodorus's eyes on my back. But my swift footsteps proved my downfall as I slipped in a puddle and fell flat on my back.

As I looked up at the cloudless sky, I thought, *Isis, I have asked a lot of you this day, but please, see me safely to the palace.*

'Are you well?'

Apollodorus's face filled my vision, at first concerned and then shocked as he took me in.

'It is you,' he breathed.

'Selene,' I agreed, pushing myself to my elbows.

'No, you cannot lie to me, I know you. You're *her*.'

Perhaps the gods do smite me, for why else would they send me the weaver?

'I am just a healer,' I repeated slowly. Apollodorus's excitement was drawing interest, and I had to defuse the situation quickly.

I accepted the hand he proffered and stood up. When I released his grip, he looked down at his fingers as if they'd been marked by a god.

'I knew it wasn't the fever, I would know your face anywhere.' The volume of his voice attracted the gaze of onlookers and I was about to dash for the shadows of the many alleyways when I heard the distinctive footfall of soldiers walking in formation.

Dum-ba, dum-ba, dum-ba.

The sound would normally have put my mind at ease, like the hum of a lullaby. But these were not my soldiers any more.

I had never noticed how terrifying their attire could seem. Their torsos were adorned with polished hardened leather, their heads covered in padded skull caps. In their right hands they each held a spear and by their waists hung a bronze axe.

The regiment moved through the square as if searching for something. No, *someone*.

Me.

I dipped my chin to my chest and averted my gaze. If I ran now, I'd draw attention to myself.

'They are looking for you, aren't they?' Apollodorus said softly.

I nodded before I realised what I was doing. I had just handed the weaver my life. All he had to do was call on the guards to end my time in this realm.

I stole a glance his way. His expression grew determined and he said, 'I can hide you – my home is not far from here.'

I had no choice. 'Take me.'

We did not walk too quickly, nor too slowly. Apollodorus also made an effort to call out to his neighbours as he passed, feigning normalcy.

But I was not proficient at improvising. I kept looking back to see if the guards followed, risking the recognition of one of the soldiers each time.

We arrived at Apollodorus's home. It was much comelier in the daytime, without the lingering smell of illness. The hearth simmered with a sweet-smelling drink, and the materials and threads that had been strewn across the furniture had now been tidied away.

Nilah, Apollodorus's wife, scowled as we entered.

'Where is the water?' she said.

I moved out of Apollodorus's shadow. 'I apologise – it is my fault he has returned without it. I'm afraid I required rescuing.'

Her mouth went slack and she blanched. 'Ph-Pharaoh,' she said. 'Forgive me, I mean . . . Selene.'

'The guise is up.' I pointed to a chair. 'May I?'

Nilah nodded, clearly aghast that she hadn't already offered, and I lowered myself into the seat.

The significance of what had happened struck me hard. If the guards were already looking for me, then Charmion had been discovered sooner than I had hoped.

'Can I offer you some refreshments?' Nilah asked, though apprehensively, as if fearing anything she had would not be worthy. I shook my head, to her visible relief.

'Thank you, Apollodorus, for granting me succour,' I said.

When the weaver smiled, his greying eyebrows lifted as if each grin were a surprise. 'Of course, Pharaoh. You healed me. I will forever be in your debt.'

'Pharaoh I may not be for much longer. My brother makes moves to reign alone.'

'And your intention here in the city is . . . ?' Nilah asked carefully. Apollodorus shot her a warning glance.

They already had the power to destroy me; no further harm could come from telling them the truth of it.

'I wish to seek counsel from Caesar in the palace,' I said. 'I believe he will stand by my father's will and support my rightful place on the throne.'

There was a silence as husband and wife regarded me doubtfully. 'How do you intend to enter the palace?'

Their lack of faith smarted. 'I can be cunning; I am often able to leave the palace undetected at night with only my handmaiden, Charmion, by my side.'

'Pharaoh,' Nilah said gently. 'It is a very different thing leaving the palace than entering it. Especially now, with the soldiers that prowl the city.'

She was right.

'Oh, what folly this plan was,' I said with a sad laugh. 'Charmion will die because of it.'

'Perhaps not,' Apollodorus said. 'I often journey to the palace to deliver cloth. I have attended your court many times while fitting drapes and so was able to recognise you the night you came here. Your brother has ordered a new carpet for the throne room. It would be no trouble to have you accompany me as an apprentice.'

'Truly? You would do this for me?' I asked.

Nilah was frowning. She must have known it was a risk, for if we were caught, they'd both be dead.

'You saved my life,' Apollodorus said. 'You are my pharaoh. Let me do this small thing for you.'

I offered my hand to Nilah. 'I will not ask this of him without your blessing.'

Nilah took my hand and bowed her head. 'Without you, he would not have survived another night. You have my blessing.'

'So, how shall this be done?' I said.

Nilah looked me up and down. 'First, we get you out of that dress.'

My shoulders burned as I rowed the small boat across the port to the palace. My muscles ached with the unfamiliar exercise but I found the rhythm soothing. Apollodorus tried to insist on taking the oars, but if we were to commit to the guise of apprentice and teacher, I knew my role would be that of an oarsman.

Antirhodos was ahead of me, the white columns of the palace dancing upon the horizon. But it wasn't home that held my attention, it was the Alexandrian harbour sprawled across the shoreline. I had never seen so many ships moored there. Roman red flags swayed in the breeze, and their ships were larger than any others in the harbour. Then there were the vessels of the mercenaries my brother had called to his aid. They were of all shapes and sizes, stretching across the port for as far as I could see.

There will be a war here.

I had not thought through what Caesar's help would mean. Pothinus, and therefore Theos, would not concede. It would be them or me. Either way, death would have its fill.

'Pharaoh, approach the east of the island,' Apollodorus said.

'But the harbour is to the west.'

'Not for the servants – we are required to dock on the eastern shore of Antirhodos.'

'Oh,' I said. 'Please, you must stop calling me Pharaoh, you may find yourself returning to it in the presence of others.'

Apollodorus looked stricken. 'What should I call you?'

'Selene. It is the only name you would know me by if you hadn't been so sharp.'

I beached the little boat on the sandbank to the west of the island. A retinue of soldiers had watched us approach the palace and so were ready to question us as our feet struck land.

'State your business,' the commander said.

Apollodorus gestured to the rolled-up carpets in the hull of the boat. 'I come to install new furnishings as decreed by the Pharaoh.'

The commander nodded, recognising him. 'You may deliver your wares.' His gaze passed over me, dressed as I was in the simple brown robes of an apprentice.

Together Apollodorus and I carried the carpet through corridors of the palace I had rarely seen.

'Do you know where Caesar is staying?' I asked the weaver. Sweat trickled down my back. Though the carpet wasn't large, it was heavy and it burdened my already fatigued arms.

'Yes, Phar— Selene, he resides in . . . the Queen's old chambers.'

Of course, Pothinus had stationed Caesar in my royal rooms. I laughed bitterly. 'They seek to insult me, but they have given me a way to secure an audience with Caesar.'

Apollodorus raised a questioning brow.

'I have the means to enter my own chambers unnoticed,' I told him.

There was a sound at the end of the hallway and all of a sudden Apollodorus dropped the carpet. I let out a grunt as the weight of it took my breath away.

'Kneel on the floor,' he hissed up at me from his now prostrate position.

It took me a breath to understand what was happening. But then I saw him, his golden tunic warm against his honeyed skin. Though it had only been weeks, he seemed taller, his shoulders broader. No longer was he in stasis between boy and man. Here was a king.

The expression Theos wore was one of barely concealed irritation. When I looked to his side, I understood why. Pothinus strode beside him, his droning voice incessant.

For a brief moment, Theos's eyes met mine, before I remembered where I was. *Who* I was.

I dropped to the floor and stretched my arms out like I had seen servants do in my presence. As he drew nearer, I pressed my brow to the dusty floor and prayed that he had not recognised me.

His footfalls didn't falter, but as they passed, I was able to hear his conversation with Pothinus.

'We have sent our soldiers to find her; it won't be long before your sister is brought to justice for her crimes against the gods,' Pothinus murmured.

'She must atone for the famine she has brought to the land. The gods have willed it.' Theos's voice was grave.

I swallowed the sound of shock that rose up from my throat. Pothinus had poisoned my brother's blood against me.

'Indeed, she must.' I imagined the self-righteous expression on Pothinus's face.

'And my citizens, they support my right to rule?'

'They long for it, my king.'

I could no longer hear Theos's reply as they made their way through the palace.

'Selene?' I looked up from the floor. Apollodorus stood above me. 'He's gone.'

I stood, my legs trembling, with rage or despair I wasn't sure. 'I must make haste. Caesar has to know the truth of this matter.'

I helped Apollodorus load the carpet onto his shoulder before saying, 'Thank you for your aid, weaver, I will not forget it.'

Apollodorus beamed. 'Farewell, my pharaoh. May Isis bless your plight.'

I moved through the palace quickly, keeping the hood of my robes up, making it hard to navigate the many corridors. But I found myself on familiar ground soon enough, passing by the door to my chambers.

My royal guards had been replaced with Roman soldiers clad in chainmail and bronze helmets, the plumes of which brushed the top of the doorway.

I shuffled past quickly. But not quickly enough.

'Apprentice, where is your master?' one of the soldiers drawled in Latin.

I ground my teeth in frustration. I was only five paces from the entranceway to the palace, and beyond that, the means of getting into my quarters undetected.

When I tried to continue on, the soldier stepped into my line of sight. He dipped his head to mine and peered into the shadows of my hood.

'I asked you a question. Or do you not speak my language?' His pink lips parted and his tongue darted out to moisten them.

His breath smelled of fowl left to fester. It was good I had not eaten that day, as my food may have made a second appearance.

I tucked my chin to my chest to hide what I could of my features, then I replied in Egyptian, 'I do not understand you sir.'

He spat on the floor and said, 'Heathen.' He dragged his eyes across my body. Despite the copious amount of fabric covering it, I felt naked. 'But not all activities require Latin.'

His fellow comrades laughed and I felt my face flush with rage. I was used to being a commodity of my nation. Like a jewel or an intricate piece of pottery.

But it was aspiration, not desire, that captivated my citizens.

This feeling was new and it sickened me. His gaze felt like swallowing oil and it churned my stomach.

I stepped backwards, away from the oppressive heat of him.

But he matched my stride, his hand coming up to my waist to tug on the rope that tied my robes together.

My hood slipped down and the soldier chuckled, reaching for a strand of my hair. I stood frozen, my breathing so shallow it was almost as if I didn't breathe at all.

His hand ran down my jaw towards the nape of my neck. 'Caesar is not using his bed right now; I may as well make use of it.'

I wanted to scream, to shout, but my voice was caged, locked in place by the soldier's lust.

I had been lucky until then, to never have had my sex used to imprison me. It is a lesson I will never forget: we will forever be our own weapons in the eyes of men.

'Is all well?'

The soldier turned towards the newcomer and I felt the walls of the cage fall away. I took in a long breath as blood rushed into my numb limbs.

'Your help is not required here,' the Roman said with a sneer.

I looked past him to see who had come to my aid. I nearly sobbed with relief when I saw who it was – Ahmose, the head of my royal guard.

He looked at me impassively, as if he didn't recognise me. 'Apprentice, your master is looking for you.'

I bobbed my head. 'Yes, I must return to him.'

'And you, to your post,' Ahmose said to the Roman, who scowled in response.

I moved away from the guards, my pace quickening until I was nearly running.

Though the afternoon air was searing and dry, I welcomed the heat of it as my feet struck the tiles in the courtyard.

Ahmose was not far behind. I pulled my hood back up and whispered, 'Thank you.'

'Pharaoh, you risk everything being here,' he replied under his breath. He did not look at me, instead lingering as if he were scanning the area during a patrol. 'They are searching for you on the mainland.'

'I know. Tell me of Charmion.'

His eyes lit up at her name and I knew then that he shared the affection she held for him. *Perhaps, after all of this, they will be wed.*

'They have her in chains,' he said.

I let out a long breath of relief. 'So, she lives.'

He nodded. 'How can I help you?'

Ahmose had always been loyal, but I would not risk his devotion this way. 'I do not want to entangle you in the roots of my plan. Only know that I fight for my throne.'

He inclined his head. 'There are many who will fight with you, Pharaoh. Know we are ready when the time comes,' he said before striding away.

I felt heartened by his words. Perhaps my plan was less farfetched than it had seemed.

I had to wait for the tide to go out before I could use the tunnel that led to my quarters, so I lingered by the shore, watching the happenings of the island. Roman soldiers kept their distance from the regiments of my brother's army. The tension between them was palpable and it gave me hope that Caesar could be convinced to join my cause.

I knew a little of Caesar. He had been my father's ally and friend. He was a great strategist and respected nobleman and had navigated Roman politics to become consul of the nation. But how would he react to me arriving in his quarters? I did not know, but with the tide finally retreating, I was about to find out.

I padded across the wet sand to the crag in the rock face that hid the tunnel to the underground cistern, and from there, the pathway to my rooms. With light steps and keen ears, I walked through the darkness until I reached the stone stairs that led to my chambers.

The rock was cold as I ran my hands along it, searching for the hidden handle that would give me the means to push aside the hollow pillar that hid the opening. I found it, and with a shove the pillar moved, releasing a plume of cold air from the tunnel into the room beyond.

Then I stepped into the bedroom of the consul of Rome, and set history on a new course.

PART TWO
THE WHORE

'Meretrix regina' ['The harlot queen']
PROPERTIUS, *Elegies*

'In a single night, after donning a hood, she accepted, in a brothel as a prostitute, the embraces of one hundred and six men'*
Letters on the Infamous Libido of Cleopatra the Queen

'The prostitute of oriental kings'
BOCCACCIO, *Concerning Famous Women*

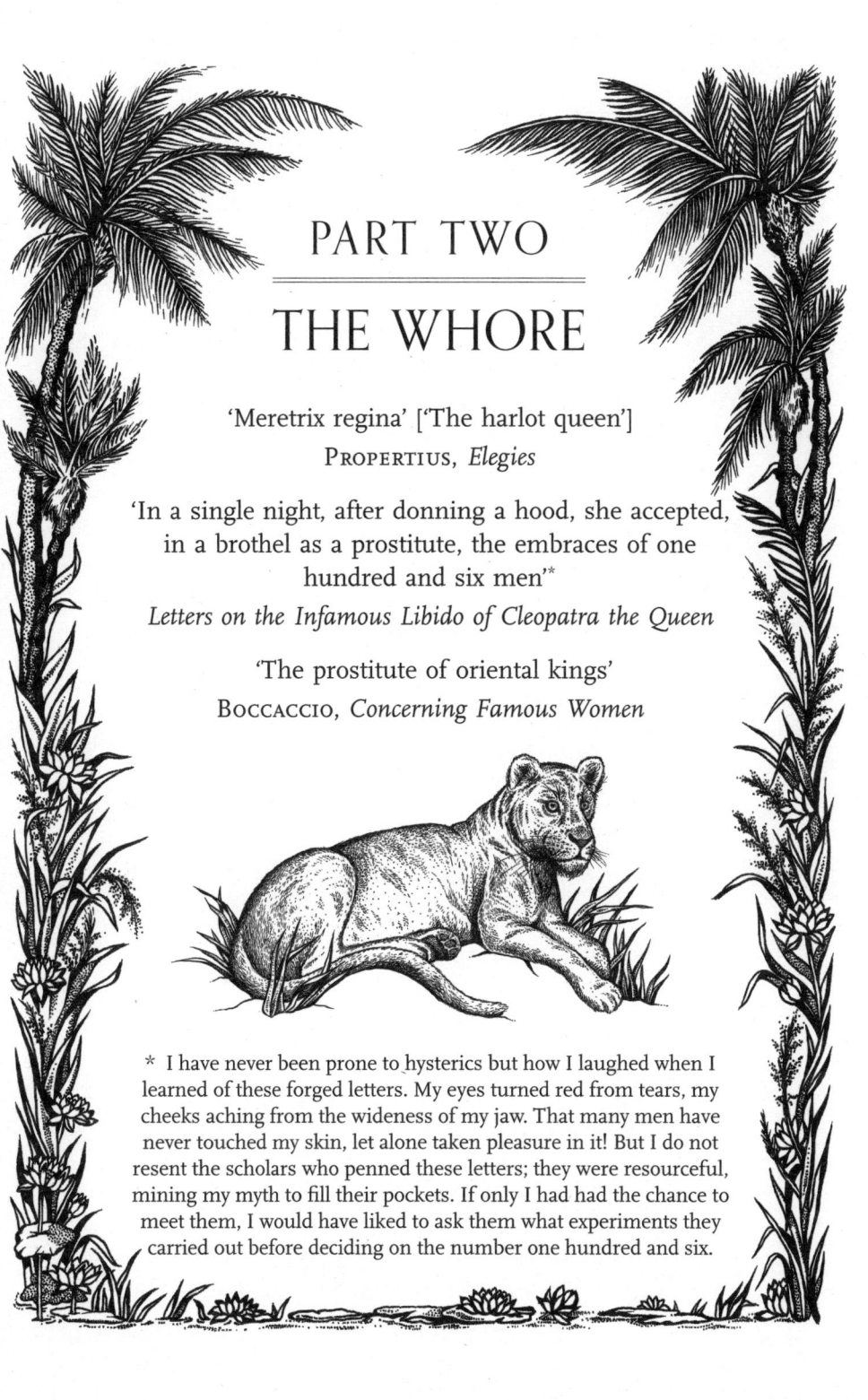

* I have never been prone to hysterics but how I laughed when I learned of these forged letters. My eyes turned red from tears, my cheeks aching from the wideness of my jaw. That many men have never touched my skin, let alone taken pleasure in it! But I do not resent the scholars who penned these letters; they were resourceful, mining my myth to fill their pockets. If only I had had the chance to meet them, I would have liked to ask them what experiments they carried out before deciding on the number one hundred and six.

CHAPTER TEN
48 BCE

I have read accounts that I walked into Caesar's room clad in nothing but a necklace. That I swayed my hips to sway him to my cause.

But it was far simpler than that – we each had something to gain from the other.

He wanted my coin, I wanted my crown.

The plinth made little noise as I slid it back into place behind me. Charmion had the foresight to keep the tiles by its base oiled in case I ever needed a means of escape in the night. Neither of us would have expected the opposite to happen – me breaking *into* my rooms.

I hope you are safe, dear friend. Worry was eating away at me, but I knew the best way to save Charmion was to persuade Caesar of my right to rule.

I made my way into the belly of the room. Rushlights glowed in clay pots, and I was careful to avoid their flickering light.

The sleeping chamber was silent, the bedsheets pulled taut with no one inside. Incense burned in a gold basin by the door, the smoke winding its tendrils around the bed. Though it was now late at night, Caesar had yet to retire. I had little choice but to wait once more.

The guard who had so carelessly consumed me with his eyes was only a few paces away from me. The door separated us, but I still felt the threat of his greedy hands shiver along my skin.

I needed somewhere to hide. The room was as I'd left it, with the wooden chest containing my garments lying against the back wall of the room. When I opened it, I discovered that my finest clothes had been replaced by Caesar's sparse belongings.

His linens smelled of myrrh and fresh sweat – not entirely unpleasant. I crawled inside and closed the chest lid. Through gaps between the wooden slats, the flickering of firelight broke up the darkness.

Despite the tension of the day, I found my mind drifting across the chasm that separated wakefulness from sleep. A few times I managed to call my mind back from the brink, but the softness of the cloth that cradled my body and the exhaustion that ached in my bones lulled me quickly to sleep.

The sound that awoke me wasn't loud. In fact, it was the faintness of it that alerted my sleeping senses. Through a gap I watched as a shadow padded across the room. His body was muscularly built, though shorter than I expected, with a toga made of fine wool draped down from one shoulder. His face was turned away from me.

I shifted in the chest to get a better vantage point. He turned at the sound and I froze. My hand went to the concealed blade at my throat.

Caesar inched closer, his own hand going to his waist where I knew a sword lay. I needed to act now.

I took my time opening the chest lid. I did not wish to startle him, as I valued the blood in my veins.

He inhaled sharply as I unfolded my body from the shadows of his belongings and presented myself before him.

'Julius Caesar, I have heard tales of your charity and have come to exercise the virtue.' I let a smile twist the corner of my mouth to make clear that this was a demand and not a request. A pharaoh does not beg.

I could see his face now. The jaw was softer than I'd imagined, the skin there dusted with the beginnings of new growth, the colour of which was a light grey. His lips were thin, pressed together as he appraised me. His sharp nose and proud brow were at odds with his subtle chin, but the composition was not unappealing. A single lock of curling hair fell over eyes that were as dark as kohl.

His gaze dropped to my clavicle, where I held the gold chain of my necklace in a tight grip. 'Cleopatra.' He did not call me Pharaoh, or Queen, but he spoke my name with equal reverence.

Despite the apprentice uniform, he had deduced who I was immediately. Caesar was an astute man. I always wondered how the senate went on to ambush him so easily. To be betrayed so thoroughly in his last moments must have sent his soul into the afterlife a tattered thing.

'Your disappearance has caused quite the commotion,' he continued.

I stepped over the lip of the chest as though descending from a throne. With my chin held aloft, I spoke with a serenity I did not feel. '"Disappearance" sounds so enigmatic. I'd prefer to call it a timely arrival.'

His lips quirked, pulling my gaze to them. 'As you will.'

Caesar was a man of few words, and those he did utter were spoken with intention. I waited for him to say more, but he just watched me with those dark, fathomless eyes.

The silence wasn't entirely unpleasant as we appraised each other. And though I could have basked beneath his gaze for much longer, I had a queendom to reclaim.

I tried to bring order to my thoughts, to voice my wants – not my *wanting* – but to my horror, my tongue lay lame in my mouth.

Though the struggle was not plain on my face, Caesar made his impatience known with the single word, 'Yes?' Such brevity.

I needed something to loosen the cord of tension around my throat. I strode to the terrace that overlooked the gardens below. My intent was to savour not the view, but the palm wine I had hidden beneath the stool there. I reached for it, and for the two chalices that were for mine and Charmion's use.

Caesar followed me outside as I poured myself a cup. The golden liquid warmed my stomach and left my tongue tingling. 'I am here to discuss my throne.' The words came easier now.

I poured Caesar some wine and he took a leisurely draught before replying, 'Few people could look so regal in such bland clothing.'

I tried not to let the compliment affect me, but my chin lifted a little higher. 'You agree, I am Queen?'

He let out a light laugh and I found I liked the sound of it. 'It is not I who deny your royalty.'

'No, but neither do you dissuade my brother from his folly.'

He cocked his head. 'You think it folly? I think it cunning. He is young to be so ambitious.'

'It is not him writing the words of his story. Pothinus holds the pen.'

'His regent? The eunuch?'

'Yes. I was blind to his machinations until it was too late.'

'I see there is more to the story than what I have heard from your brother. Pothinus has trained him well.'

I thought of the sweet boy I had grown up with, and how the brief glimpse of Theos earlier had been someone entirely different. I had been foolish as well as naive.

'They spread false truths about the gods, claiming I have brought the famine to the land.'

'All of your gods are false truths.' He spoke matter-of-factly, with no hint of an insult. 'I paid no heed to his stories of gods and powers. What I did find interesting was his insistence that the people of Egypt no longer see you as worthy of the crown.'

I could feel my blood begin to simmer. 'What is worthiness to a Ptolemy? You speak of "false gods", but I stand before you.' I tugged at the robe from around my waist, releasing my bare shoulder. I tipped my head so my hair swung aside, baring the mark of Isis on the back of my neck.

Caesar stepped closer, until I could feel his breath warm my skin. Despite my anger, I felt myself shiver beneath his scrutiny.

'I do not deny your family's gifts are impressive. But I lay fealty to Jupiter; his blessing is enough for me.'

My skin heated still more, in a wave that ran the length of my body. Between my rage and Caesar's proximity, it was hard to distinguish the cause. 'Impressive? We are the very essence of Egypt. No one can tell me I am not worthy. For Egypt *is* me.'

Caesar stepped away from me. 'Then why is it that your brother sits on the throne, and you are here, hiding in my rooms?'

I hissed through my teeth. 'Even gods make mistakes.'

He smiled at that, and his face transformed. Before, I would not have called him a comely man. But as the hollows of his cheeks rounded with the grin, the years that separated us fell away. 'It is true. Once, my lord Jupiter sought to destroy all men. Yet here I am.'

I watched him over the rim of my cup before taking a deep drink of the palm wine, which filled me with confidence. 'You were a friend to my father. A loyal ally of Egypt. I ask you to stand by his will and reinstate me as Pharaoh.'

'Your father intended for both you and your brother to reign.'

'He did, but it is clear Theos has been turned against me. My father would not deny me in this matter.'

'Your father was a great friend to me. I was sad to hear of his passing.'

'What we have lost, the realm beyond has gained,' I said.

'During his visits to Rome, he spoke of you often.'

'He did?' I tried not to show how desperately I longed to hear my father's words.

'He did.'

'I pray you, tell me some of what he said.'

'That you were astute and scrupulous. That you would rule Egypt like a mother asp.'

Snakes were sacred things to us. Fierce protectors of their young, they were revered as powerful mothers. I treasured the compliment.

'Thank you,' I said quietly.

'For what?'

'My father's words are a welcome gift.'

He reached across me to pour himself more wine, and I smelled the myrrh on his clothing. 'Then you are in my debt?'

'You suggest a gift incurs a debt? Your wife must be very poor,' I remarked.

Another laugh. I longed to hear more.

'Not a debt, then, but a moment of your time – since I have been told you are astute and scrupulous – to consider a proposition.'

I dipped my head in acquiescence.

Caesar looked down to the gardens below, where the moon lined the trees in silver light. A whole day had passed since my escape from the royal barge. But I was not weary. Talking with Caesar invigorated me in a way I would never come to experience again. He was thoughtful and assertive, an exhilarating combination.

Despite what you've been told, it wasn't love that blossomed so readily between us that night, but friendship. And perhaps a little lust too.

He turned to face me once more. 'Allow me to facilitate a reconciliation between you and your brother. In honour of your father.'

I set my jaw. I had not considered peace between Theos and myself; my mind had gone only to war. As I said before, I was naive. It took me many years to appreciate the power of compromise over violence.

'No.'

Caesar's eyebrows lifted in surprise. I doubted he heard that word often. 'You ask me to uphold your father's will, yet you would deny your brother the same rights.'

'My brother wishes to try me for crimes against the gods. He deceives the nation, assigning misfortune as my misdeeds.'

'He does, but like you, he is a Ptolemy; Egypt *is* him. I hear that his god power is one to be envied – breathing water like air. What is your god-granted gift, Cleopatra?'

I searched his face for any trace of mockery, but the question seemed sincere. 'The goddess Isis has blessed me with an aptitude for healing.'

'Healing? And yet you refuse to heal this rift between you and your brother.'

I met his dancing eyes steadily. 'What is it you gain from this union, that you encourage it so, Julius?' I spoke his given name back to him, as he had said mine, but with a hint more mockery.

'You are perceptive.'

I raised an eyebrow. 'You thought less of me?'

His gaze ran across the bare skin of my shoulder where I had let the robe slip. 'I must beg your forgiveness, my queen, but I had not thought of you much at all.'

'I will forgive you that transgression, as long as it is rectified going forward.'

His eyes lingered on my lips. 'Consider it rectified.'

'So? What is it you want from me?'

'The war with Pompey has depleted my treasury.'

'You want money.' Egypt had long been valued for its riches alone, and I was tired of being courted for my coffers. In this regard Caesar disappointed me, and I assumed him to be like all the other generals and kings. I soon learned that Caesar was like no other man.

'Your father was extended credit in Rome. The debts must be repaid.'

'Those *donations* were to support my father's claim to the throne during the civil unrest caused by Berenice. I see that your statement holds true – a gift is a debt.'

'Yes, it would seem so.'

I had money. In the last few years of my father's reign, he had excavated ancient tombs to claim the treasure inside. It funded his opulent lifestyle and filled my treasury.

I levelled my gaze at him. 'So, my throne in order to secure yours?'

He inclined his head.

But I remained unconvinced by his sincerity. 'You could make this very deal with my brother – why support me?'

Caesar moved past me and returned to the open chest. He lifted out a box from the far end of it. It was intricately crafted, decorated with a carving of the god Sobek – a gift from my brother, then.

He handed it to me and I slid open the lid. Inside, cradled on a bed of salt, was Pompey's embalmed head.

It took all my will not to throw the box from my hands.

I had laid my head to rest on the empty eyes of Caesar's enemy.

'Your brother gifted this to me on my arrival in Alexandria.' Caesar shook his head. 'My son-in-law degraded to such a petty trophy.'

I had forgotten Pompey's relation to Caesar.

'He was my last connection to my Julia.'

'Your daughter?' I said, closing the lid with haste. I set Pompey's head gingerly on the floor between us.

Caesar cleared his throat as if to alleviate the thickness of grief. 'Yes. She died in childbirth.'

'But Pompey was also your enemy, was he not?'

'He was, but I do not believe that death should be celebrated, gilded and gifted. Would you have presented this prize so callously?'

I thought what I would have done if I had been there. 'I would have sent his body to his family for funeral rites. It is not for us to deny a soul the chance to transition to the next realm. Let the gods judge our enemies.'

Caesar watched me shrewdly. 'I agree.'

I shifted under the intensity of his gaze.

'Are you willing to share Egypt with your brother once more?' Caesar asked.

'We never shared it, not truly.'

'I see that, for your light eclipses those who sit beside it.' He relayed the compliment plainly, as if it were fact, but I refused to barter in niceties.

'Theos is unlikely to concede with Pothinus by his side. The regent must be removed from court this very day. I will not abide his presence for a moment longer.'

Caesar nodded. 'I'm sure this can be facilitated. And perhaps your garments and rooms reinstated.'

'And my handmaiden, Charmion.'

He frowned, until realisation came over him. 'The woman who returned to Alexandria dressed in your likeness?'

'Yes. She must be released back into my custody tonight.'

'It was a cunning plan – she must be a loyal servant.'

'She and I are one and the same,' I said.

His expression was still inscrutable. 'I will see to her release. They are my guards watching over her, so there should be no delay. Tomorrow, I will invite you to join us for the first meal of the day.'

'What of the soldiers searching for me? I am not safe in the palace.'

'My soldiers stand guard in front of these chambers. No one will enter without their knowledge.'

I laughed. 'Like I did?'

'I would very much like to know how you did that.'

I said nothing, and he smiled. 'Keep your secrets, as long as no one else knows.'

I shook my head. Charmion didn't count. 'What if my brother sends his own guards to cut them down?'

The muscles around Caesar's jaw stiffened and a dangerous glint entered his eyes. 'I have many more soldiers than your brother, and legions more I can call to the palace from Cilicia with a few weeks' notice. If he provokes me, he will come to know my wrath.'

'And mine.' I may not have had an army, but I was still his older sister. And he needed to be disciplined.

'Rest assured you are safe. I will see you on the morrow. For now, you are welcome to your old bed. I will retire elsewhere.'

'Elsewhere?'

He chuckled. 'Many of your courtiers have offered me space in their beds this night.'

I had heard of Caesar's exploits with men and women, but it shocked me to hear court gossip so brazenly confirmed. He must have read my thoughts on my face.

'You misunderstand me. I will partake in the hospitality of their rooms only. Unless,' he said, his lips parting in a smile, 'you wish to share space in yours?'

I reached for my palm wine once more and swallowed before I said, 'You have already deduced that I do not share.'

The heat of the moment was broken by his hearty laugh. 'You are not at all what I expected, Cleopatra.'

'You are everything I expected, Julius.'

He sobered at my words. 'I will help you regain your throne.'

'Promise on your god.'

He reached out a hand and grasped mine. His skin was surprisingly rough for a noble. 'You have my word, Cleopatra.'

He drew out my name like the start of a poem. When he dropped my hand, I clenched my fingers into a fist to stop them tingling and met his gaze levelly. 'Let us hope your word holds true.'

'It will.' Caesar turned to leave.

As he opened the door, I glimpsed the guard who had touched me against my will.

'I have one other request, Julius.'

Seeing me there, two of the guards reached for their blades.

'Peace,' Caesar said, and they dropped their hands. 'The Pharaoh will be returning to her chambers tonight.' Then he looked back at me. 'How else can I help?'

I raised a finger to the guard furthest from me. 'Dismiss *him* from your army.'

The guard's expression went slack as he recognised me. There was almost no sound to his voice, only breath. 'No.'

'Yes,' I said.

Caesar looked between us, not understanding. I obliged him with the details. 'This guard touched me without my permission.'

'I thought she was an apprentice,' he whispered. Sweat had sprung up across his brow.

'Pharaoh, how would you sentence such a crime?' Caesar asked.

We both knew the punishment for the soldier's violation. But I sensed that Caesar was testing my mettle. He wanted me to say it – to condemn the man with my own tongue.

'Death,' I said without hesitation. If he thought to question my fortitude, he had chosen the wrong means to do it. I had passed this verdict many times, you may be surprised to learn. I have not lingered in those memories – not because I am ashamed, but because they are insignificant. As Pharaoh I courted death often, ushering in the will of the gods for those I deemed beyond salvation.

Do not judge me for this. Judge my other deeds in life, if you must, but not this. For death was merely the pathway to the afterlife where the soul would receive their final sentence. Osiris, the King of the Afterlife, would weigh the hearts of the dead against the feather of Maat. If the scales tipped upwards, sending the heart to the sky, then Osiris would welcome them to his realm. But if the heart proved heavier than the feather of the sacred goddess, they would be consumed by Ammit the devourer.

Those I sentenced to death, I handed over to higher judgement.

Caesar seemed impressed with my assertiveness. With a fluid motion he pulled his gladius blade from his waist. The hilt was gold and silver, but I had little time to appreciate the short sword before he plunged it into the soldier's heart.

The soldier slumped forward, his last breath leaving him.

It was the first time Caesar killed for me. There would be many thousands more to come.

I remember the shock I felt, the revulsion at the hot blood soiling the tiles at my feet, but most of all I remember the first tendrils of desire. He was so much that I was not, or was at least only learning to be: bold, emphatic, self-assured. His power was contained, like a muscle clenched, ready to release.

I found his strength intoxicating.

He wiped the blade on the edge of his toga before returning

it to its sheath. 'I will have another guard replace the one we have lost, and the body removed, of course.'

'Of course,' I said.

'Is there anything else you desire?'

Yes.

'My throne will be more than enough.'

'Indeed.' Then he gave me a disarming smile. 'Sleep well, Pharaoh. I hope the bed is more comfortable than the chest.'

I returned to the balcony and the wine, my mind heavy with the implications of all we had discussed. Every now and again I would stretch out my fingers, remembering the roughness of his touch.

I don't know how long I stood like that, but half the bottle of palm wine had gone when I heard a sound at the door. I turned around just in time for arms to wrap around my waist.

The alarm I felt dissipated as soon as I smelled the distinct aroma of Charmion's hair. Frankincense and cinnamon, a heady mix.

'I am so happy you're safe,' she murmured into my shoulder.

'Me? It was you I was worried for.' I held her head in my hands and kissed her firmly on the mouth before embracing her once more.

She laughed as I tightened my arms, refusing to let her go.

'I cannot breathe,' she choked out.

I reluctantly released her to arm's length, analysing every bit of her. 'Are you well? Did they hurt you?'

'No. Pothinus was angry when he discovered the ruse, but Theos refused to let him slay me.'

'So there is some good left in my brother?'

Charmion met my eyes sadly. 'He has changed very much. Arsinoe too.'

My stomach lurched at my sister's name. 'What do you mean?'

Charmion's mouth opened, then closed.

'Do not temper your words. Tell me plain.' I'd had enough wordplay with Caesar, and my indulgence in the wine was beginning to give me a headache.

'It seems she was aware of the blockade in the harbour and knew of your impending arrest. It was she who first discovered I was not you. Her disappointment matched that of Pothinus.'

A bitterness entered my mouth and I grimaced. 'Of course. Qar must have returned with a letter that she did not share with me.' My heart ached.

Charmion cradled my chin in her hand.

'I have lost two siblings this day,' I whispered.

'They have not departed this life. You may yet make peace.'

Her words echoed Caesar's. But I doubted there was a path forward where I could trust either sibling again.

Charmion's hand dropped to the collar of my robe. 'What are you wearing?'

I smiled and relayed my tale, for which Charmion proved an appreciative audience. It was only when I described Caesar that she stopped me to ask, 'Tell me, what is he truly like? The courts speak of his golden tongue.'

I smiled. 'It was no more golden than mine.'

'You like him.' She surmised the truth so quickly.

'Insofar as I like the builders who construct my temple. He is a tool, no more and no less.' I cannot recall if I knew then that I lied to myself, or if I was blinded by my feelings until it was too late to retreat from the doomed cliff-edge of our love.

'They say he once shared King Bithynia's bed,' she said.

I had heard the rumours, but having met him, I did not believe his dalliances to be so frivolous as to only last one night. 'He seems the type of man who loves deeply.'

'And is loved in return?' Charmion asked, her expression curiously neutral.

I was saved from answering as there was a knock at the door. Servants entered to retrieve Caesar's belongings and return mine.

It was nearly dawn by the time my rooms were back in order.

I slipped beneath the cold sheets. My bed still smelled faintly of Caesar, despite having been freshly laundered. I pushed him from my mind.

'Do you think my brother and sister will have heard the news that I am back in the palace?'

'No, the time is late. I did not hear any chatter among the palace servants on my way here. It was Caesar himself who released the chains that bound my hands, so the news is yet to spread.'

'Good, I want them to be surprised when they see me,' I murmured, my nose pressed into my blanket. 'I would like you to braid my hair for the occasion.'

'Of course.' She hid a smile in her voice.

'And I will wear the golden column dress.'

'A wise choice.'

I was going to request one more thing, but it was lost to sleep. The activities of the evening had fatigued my already tired body.

I had only one more thought before I succumbed: *Whose room did Caesar go to this night?*

CHAPTER ELEVEN
48 BCE

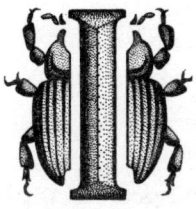was waiting in the dining chamber when my brother entered. He came alone, without Pothinus. His eyes shuttered closed as he saw me, as if he were testing the truth of his sight.

'Theos, you have been very busy.'

He lurched at my voice, as if I spoke from beyond the realm of life.

'Cleopatra, what are you doing here?' He looked to the Roman soldiers who stood behind me.

'Is it not morning? Am I not allowed to break my fast in my palace?'

'Where is Pothinus?'

Oh, poor boy, so easily frightened without his eunuch.

'Brother, you have been listening to his lies for far too long.'

Theos's eyes flashed with anger. 'It is he who uncovered your lies. You are an agent of Apep.'

My temper flared. 'On what grounds do you accuse me of being Apep's minion? The god of chaos has not claimed me and never will.'

Berenice had been murdered for the very same claim. And for the first time I wondered at the truth in it.

Had the locusts been merely coincidence?

Berenice had charmed the nobility from a young age. Courtiers hovered around her like insects round a flame. She was beloved, and defiant: a dangerous mix to a king in power.

Had my father been so threatened by her that he had spun a web of lies?

'Pothinus foretold you would say that,' Theos said.

'Isis is my benefactor. You know this, Mikro Theos.'

'My name is Ptolemy, but you can call me Pharaoh,' he said, raising his nose to the air.

My heart broke to hear him dismiss his nickname, *little god*. But I couldn't let it show on my face.

'Have I ever given you cause to doubt me, *Pharaoh*?' I asked.

He hesitated, and I knew then that there was some semblance of loyalty left in him.

'Pothinus said—'

I cut him off with a click of my tongue. 'Do not speak to me of your regent. Tell me from your own mind, *have I ever given you cause to doubt me?*'

He looked pensive, and in his face I could see again the boy I used to know. 'You never let me make decisions. Even with Hermonthis, I wanted to go, but you would not let me.'

'It was important that I went – you do not understand the political nuance.' I did not speak on my suspicions that Pothinus had been behind the murder of the Buchis bull.

'This is what I mean! You treat me like a child. I understand political nuance.'

He pouted, and I regarded him dispassionately. 'I had hoped to give you a few more years of childhood before burdening you with the rule of the lands.'

'You never *asked*.'

'*You* never asked.' I realised the conversation had devolved somewhat, but I met him at his intellectual level.

He didn't reply.

'Come,' I said, gesturing to the overflowing platters of food. 'Sit, let us enjoy each other's company as brother and sister. We can discuss the terms of our rule once we have sated our hunger.'

He looked to the entranceway, and I wondered if he waited for Pothinus. But the eunuch would never walk these halls again, if Caesar had met my terms.

Theos lowered himself into the chair opposite me and I held out a plate of honeyed bread. At first, he looked as if he might refuse the gesture, but the glistening syrup won him over and he reached for the platter.

That was the moment that Arsinoe walked in.

The shock on her face was fleeting, but it was there. Her calculating gaze flickered around the room, taking in the Roman guards, Theos and me.

I offered her the same plate my brother had taken from. 'Sister, would you care for some bread?'

She smiled, enhancing the delicate beauty that I had always been jealous of. I noticed that our time on the Nile had brought out the warmth in her dark skin. 'Of course, sister.'

Neither of us acknowledged her part in the rebellion.

The younger Ptolemy joined shortly thereafter.

'You're back from Hermonthis,' he said when he saw me. And I realised not only did he not sense the tension in the room, but he also had no idea about the plot to overthrow me.

'I am,' I said with an indulgent grin.

He nodded once and climbed into the seat next to me.

Caesar took his time arriving, and I was nearly at the end of my patience by the time he walked into the room. He admitted to me later that his tardiness had been intentional, in order to build a sense of trepidation. '*I find people more malleable when they are nervous,*' he said against my neck. We were in bed, our limbs entangled, our sweat cooling on each other's skin.

'It is good you do not make me nervous, then,' I said.

He lowered his chin to just below my bare breast. 'Your heart would disagree.'

But let me not skip through the seasons.

'A family reunion,' Caesar said as he entered, his hands clasped behind his broad back. Caesar wasn't arrogant in the way of most men in power I had met. He wore his authority quietly, with a confidence that made you feel like he saw you in your entirety.

I gestured to the chair to my right. 'It is good that you have joined us.'

Caesar met my gaze as he sat. 'It is my pleasure to be in the company of the whole Ptolemy family. Could you pass me the palm wine? I find I've a taste for it.'

That brought a smile to my lips. I flicked a wrist towards a servant, who moved forward to serve Caesar. When his cup was full, he tipped it in my direction.

'To the Queen's health.'

The youngest Ptolemy, blind to the complexities of the politics at play, raised his cup to join the tribute. Caesar turned to Theos, waiting for him to do the same.

My brother looked troubled but he raised his shaking chalice.

Arsinoe spluttered in disbelief. 'Theos, what is going on?'

Theos didn't meet her eyes so it was Caesar who responded. 'We are honouring the great Cleopatra Thea Philopator, born of Isis. Seventh of her name. And your pharaoh.'

I felt a thrill at my full name on his lips.

Clearly Arsinoe did not; her knuckles went white around the rim of her cup.

Caesar waited patiently, the hand that raised his chalice steady. The guards behind him shifted. But Arsinoe refused to comply.

Qar squawked somewhere behind her. 'Where is Pothinus?' she said, her voice heated.

Caesar shook his head sadly and drank from his cup before replying. 'Unfortunately, Pothinus has left the palace.'

I frowned. 'What do you mean?'

'He escaped before I was able to have an audience with him.'

'Escaped? Why would he need to escape? He is regent of the land,' Theos said.

Arsinoe laughed scornfully. 'Don't you see, Theos? Caesar and Cleopatra have made an alliance. I suspect Pothinus's head was part of that deal, but our lord heard of their plan and fled.'

Theos looked at me. 'Is it true?'

I inclined my head, trying to look sorrowful. 'Pothinus has proved himself unworthy as regent. He sowed the seeds of dissent to usurp me from the throne. And I will not abide it. As I said earlier, Theos, you must make your own mind up now.'

'Theos,' Arsinoe said sharply. 'Remember who you are true to first. The gods.'

I wanted to laugh. Arsinoe worshipped no one more readily than herself. 'You have become quite devout in our days apart, sister.'

Qar flew to her shoulder, his beady eyes condemning me, and Arsinoe laid a hand on his talons. 'Here sits a god, flesh to flesh with me. Can you say the same?'

She knew I could not. Isis had sent me no animal vessel, nor blessing of any kind. But now was not the time to admit that. I pressed my lips closed.

Her triumphant smile quickened my rage. 'Theos,' I said, 'be not swayed by Arsinoe's passion. She has clearly grown bored, and like the many interests of her past, you too will be discarded.'

'I . . .' Theos's eyes were brimming with tears.

'Pharaoh,' said Caesar, commanding Theos's attention. 'It was your father's wish that your sister should reign by your side – will you deny him?'

'No,' Theos said quietly.

Arsinoe stood, causing the plates around her to clatter. ''You will listen to a Roman over your own sister?'

'Peace, Arsinoe,' I said.

She turned her ire on me. 'You have dispatched the regent of Egypt – that in itself is a crime. You are not worthy of the throne, Cleopatra.'

There was silence as Arsinoe's betrayal sliced like a knife through my skin. 'Careful,' I told her. 'Your words sound like treason.'

One of the Romans behind me pulled out his sword.

Arsinoe heard the sound of metal and stilled. I saw her look to the door – she was preparing to flee. At the time I had thought it was only to her rooms, to sulk. Oh, how I underestimated her.

'Let us calm these waters and enjoy this bountiful food together,' Caesar said, trying to dispel Arsinoe's frustrations.

'I cannot sit here and pretend that all is well,' she said. She shook her head at Theos before turning on her heel and striding out. Theos sank deeper into his seat, looking wretched.

'She will forget about the whole thing by the morn,' I said gently.

'Yes, I think it best that we all forget this unfortunate quarrel, fuelled by a regent who had much to gain from it.' Caesar acted as though the matter was resolved, his part of the deal complete.

I was not so sure.

'Is Pothinus truly gone?' Theos asked.

'Yes.' He looked downcast so I added, 'Only the guilty flee.'

After a moment, Theos stood. He winced as his chair scraped the tiles – as if he'd hoped to slip away unnoticed.

'I think I will go for a swim,' he said.

'Go, but I expect you to join me at court later. You want to rule Egypt as an equal? Then that begins today,' I said.

He gave me a faint smile, his back straightening despite the burden I bestowed upon it. The younger Ptolemy left not long after.

I sighed. 'That could have gone better.'

Caesar nodded. 'Perhaps.'

'Tell me of Pothinus,' I said.

'When I sent my guards to his chambers, we found them empty. His belongings gone. I suspect that is the last we will see of him.'

'Do not miscalculate his ambition. He seeks to rule Egypt to benefit the nobility.'

'And you?'

'I seek to rule it for everyone.'

Caesar's chuckle reverberated in my chest. 'That is impossible,

Cleopatra. The one piece of advice I will grant you is this: you do not rule, the nobility do. You are merely their shepherd.'

'That is not how it shall be.'

'Think on this little rebellion Pothinus has brought to your door. The ships in the harbour? They are all courtiers coming to his aid. He is beholden to them, as you are, for his promises brought them to the fight.'

I bridled at this. 'I spent many years being schooled in warfare and politics. I do not need you to lecture me so. But I will say again, this is not how I rule.'

Caesar cocked his head. 'So how *do* you rule, exactly?'

'Reform in coinage. Redistributions of wheat to the famine-struck areas. Devolving the governor-run ministries in the smaller cities.'

The last had come to me during my visit back down the Nile and perhaps was touched with a little spite from all the ruling class who had refused my summons.

'And a hospital next to every gymnasium, led by acolytes of Isis, where people can come for healing.'

'You have many plans. And I have many more questions. This is the first.' He looked at me seriously. 'Where can I acquire more of this palm wine?'

I laughed, feeling myself relax for the first time since he had entered the room.

The rest of the morning passed quickly. We discussed politics and languages, military strategy and trade. It wasn't until I noticed the sun dipping down from its zenith that I realised how late in the day it was.

There were few people who could match my intellect and interest in scholarly pursuits like Caesar. We took pleasure in each other's company, as equals. Being a pharaoh meant I was second only to Isis. But Caesar had already dismissed my god, and rather than being offended by his blasphemy, I found him thrilling, his wit sparring with mine.

We were discussing the writings of Timagenes when a Roman soldier ran to Caesar's side.

He whispered in his lord's ear, his rumblings too low to hear.

Caesar nodded once then turned to me, his face grave.

'Your brother and sister have fled the palace in one of the royal barges. They have taken a cohort of soldiers with them. Guards loyal to you sought to stand in their way but were cut down.'

I was already running.

'Follow her,' I heard Caesar bark in Latin.

I did not care that my robe came undone, or that my hair fell from the knot Charmion had spent an hour braiding. When my crown tipped to the side I flung it from my head. My slippers pounded the ground as it went from tile to stone to sand.

Soldiers littered the harbour, their blood seeping into the beach, but my gaze was on the horizon.

The barge had not got far but was gaining speed. I ran to the end of the pier.

Arsinoe stood at the balcony's edge, clad in blue, a crown I had never seen before on her brow. Theos stood in her shadow, glinting in heavy gold armour – a gift from Arsinoe last akhet season. It made me question how long she had been planning this very flight.

'What did Pothinus offer you to betray me?' I shouted across the water.

She smiled and called back, 'That is not the question you should ask. You should be asking, what did *I* offer *him* to betray you?'

I felt my knees begin to buckle. All this time I had thought Pothinus the sting in the scorpion's tail. But it had been my sister.

Tears fell down my cheeks.

'So weak.' The insult carried over the sound of the waves. 'It was not difficult to convince the governors of your inability to rule.'

'You seeded the rumour,' I murmured. There was no way she could have heard me, but she saw the realisation on my face.

'A queen must be cunning, dear sister.'

Queen.

I gave in to my shaking knees and hit the ground.

Arsinoe was making a bid for the throne.

I have overlooked her ambition so completely. When I thought of her, I saw a fickle child prone to tantrums and brooding. But that is the curse of siblings: no matter the years that stretch between child and adulthood, you will always see the echoes of who they used to be.

And in turn she saw me as the older sister I had once been – cautious and considered. She would call it weak. But I had changed too, and was changing still.

I was capable of ruthlessness, as she would come to know.

A pained groan drew me out of my daze. One of the soldiers who had fought Arsinoe's guards lay not a handful of paces from me. I recognised him.

'Ahmose!'

Blood seeped from a wound in his gut. His eyes fluttered as I kneeled beside him.

'Pharaoh, your sister, she seeks to betray you,' he murmured, blood flecking his lip.

'I know. Rest now, do not worry.'

Ahmose would not survive this injury. It was too deep, too wide. I felt my throat tighten with grief.

Charmion came running up behind me. She made a strangled noise when she saw who it was.

'Get my potions, Charmion.' But she had frozen to the spot, her eyes fixed on the wound in Ahmose's side.

'Charmion!' I shouted. It startled her from her shock and she nodded, dashing away.

'It was a pleasure to serve you, Pharaoh,' Ahmose said.

'And you will continue to serve me, this is not the end.'

Isis, please send me the power to heal him.

I pulled his skull cap from his head and stroked his hair. 'You have many more years of service in you.'

'Will you tell my mother of my death? Send her my uniform, please, to gift to the gods.'

I shook my head. 'You will not die today.'

Charmion returned, thrusting the bag of my tinctures at me.

I rummaged through them, knowing that I had nothing to heal a wound this dire. But I had to try.

I unstopped a vial of propolis and applied it to a strip of linen. Then I bound it to the wound at his waist. He screamed as I applied pressure, until his screaming abruptly stopped.

'Cleo,' Charmion sobbed beside me. But I couldn't look at her. I couldn't bear to see the pain his death would inflict.

He was still breathing – just.

'Save him!' Charmion cried. She loved him, I could hear it in her voice.

I dived into my bag once more.

Please, Isis, grant me my gift so I may bring him back from the brink of death.

Nothing but divine power could save him. And I had none.

I slumped, my hands going slack. Then my eyes spotted a label on a jar: Opium.

'I cannot save him, Charmion,' I said gently. 'But I can ease his passing.'

Her sobbing grew so heavy it became silent, just the shaking breath of grief.

'May you find peace in the afterlife, Ahmose.' I tipped the entire contents of the jar into his mouth.

He shuddered once, twice, then was still.

I helped Charmion up and held her against my chest. My tears had dried, my shock mellowing to a deep heartache that left me numb.

Caesar watched me from the end of the beach, a regiment of soldiers at his back. I should have felt threatened to approach him, but I did not.

Eiras, another of my handmaidens, ran forward, and I handed Charmion to her. Then I turned to Caesar.

'I have never seen a ruler grieve for a soldier,' he said.

'He has been with me for many years. He was loyal, a friend.'

Caesar's hand reached out as if to touch me, then he stopped himself. 'I am sorry for your loss,' he said. 'May your gods welcome him in the beyond.'

'They will, I will make sure of it.'

I called for a nearby servant and made instructions for Ahmose's body to be interred in the necropolis.

'He shall have a tomb on Antirhodos. Inform his parents of his passing and bring them to the palace. I wish to offer them roles on my staff.' I spoke plainly, my lips unfeeling.

When the servant had gone, I turned once more back to Caesar.

'It was Arsinoe behind it all. She wishes to be queen.'

'I heard.'

I lifted my chin. 'I will not allow it.'

Caesar met my gaze. 'Neither will I. You know what comes next.'

I looked to the ocean where the royal barge had become just a speck on the horizon. I smiled, though I felt no joy.

'War.'

CHAPTER TWELVE
48 BCE

It took two cycles of the moon for the rest of Caesar's troops to arrive in Alexandria, during which time war had broken out across the city.

The crusade wasn't what I had expected. I'd had romantic ideas of warfare, in many ways believing it to be a larger version of a gladiator match, where two opposing forces would battle until someone surrendered.

But war was not romantic. It smelled of blood, piss and shit. The tactics were barbaric, underhanded and nothing like what I had studied with my tutors.

The nobility who supported Arsinoe and Theos's cause had armed their servants with blades and sent them to ransack Alexandria. Caesar and I had in turn dug trenches and erected mantlets around the city's walls, barricading ourselves from their onslaught.

In the early days of the siege, life on Antirhodos continued much as before. The fighting was too far away for it to affect me. On the rare occasions I went into the city to see the progression of our defences, I would return to the palace dazed as though waking from a nightmare. By the time I had got to the throne room, with our maps and charts, the war had become a senet game once more – a distant thing, though there was no winning this game, no matter the outcome.

Either I lost Egypt, or I lost my siblings.

As the crescent moon shone in the sky for the second time since the battle had begun, the impact of the siege had started to bleed across the bay to the island.

The food was the first to go.

'There's not enough meat to feed them.' My lions prowled in their cages before me. I could see the ribs beneath the skin of the lioness closest to me. Another pawed at the ground where a streak of dried blood had stained the stone – the only remnant of their last meal, which had been some days earlier.

An errant cloud floated over the sun, casting the menagerie in shadow. It suited my mood.

'They will not survive,' I said to Caesar sadly.

The rest of the cages in the menagerie were empty; we had let the hippos and crocodiles free in the bay and released the cats and dogs into the city. But the lions' hunger would drive them to the people's throats, and there had been enough bloodshed in the city.

Caesar didn't mock me for the care I gave to the animals. 'Let me send a ship down the coast and release them there.'

'It's not possible. The bay is surrounded. We'd only be sacrificing capable sailors and soldiers.'

He knew that, but I believed he would have done it if I'd asked. Caesar had been true to his word – as he always was – and stayed to help me regain my throne. The moment Arsinoe and Theos had sailed away, he had sent word to every soldier and ship from Crete, Petra, Rhodes, Syria and Cilicia. Nine Rhodian warships were the only ones to have arrived so far, but they weren't enough to break through the blockade.

One of the lionesses growled low in her throat, her eyes glittering as she watched me. I wrung my hands in guilt.

'You see the smallest one, with the silver patch of fur on her paw? I captured her when I was twelve years old. She had been abandoned by her pack and was wounded right there, where the fur has grown back grey.' I had been hunting with Father and Arsinoe – who had both made many kills that day. I, on the other hand, had come up short. I was not as skilled with the bow as my sister.

'It would have been an easy kill,' I continued. 'But when I took aim, she lifted her head and looked at me. She wasn't scared; if anything she was defiant.' I laughed. 'Father was not happy when I returned to the litter with her bound and alive. But he let me keep her here.'

Caesar looked around the menagerie. The only thing that thrived here now were the plants, growing wild and free without servants to tend to them. The air was thick with the smell of the orange pomegranate flowers pouting towards the sun.

Show me your home, Caesar had said. Every day, when the sun reached its highest point, we would walk together to a new part of the island. Most of the time the walk would invigorate me; time alone with Caesar was always exhilarating. But occasionally, like today, I would become morose.

'There are very many cages here – you must have had an impressive number of animals,' Caesar said.

'Yes. Some were sent from our neighbouring allies as gifts, others I caged from hunting trips.'

'But no aviary?'

'No,' I said. 'I will not cage a bird. It would be like binding a lioness's legs together. A bird must be allowed to fly.'

I thought of Arsinoe then. *Oh, sister, had you been in a cage for too long?*

'You care for many things, Pharaoh.'

Does Caesar mock me now? But no, he watched me with curiosity. 'It is my duty to care for many things.' Even if sometimes I felt that I did not have the capacity to hold so much feeling in my chest.

Caesar moved closer to me. 'Let me ease some of the burden. I will do what must be done.'

He meant kill the lions. But I wasn't ready yet.

'The cages were empty for many years before I was born,' I told him. 'Father cared not for animals, and so as a child I became queen of this small area.'

'Small? My kingdom in the Suburra could fit into it ten times over.'

'I thought Rome was a great republic, not a kingdom,' I teased.

He shook his head. 'The Republic is nothing but a name, without substance or reality.' Dangerous words, but only the lions were our witnesses.

'And you its king?'

His lips parted as if to say 'yes', but then he shook his head. 'I was only king in Suburra.'

He took me to the Suburra neighbourhood once, years later. His childhood home was wretched and abandoned, much like the district it stood in. He wasn't ashamed to cry when he looked upon it: *'My mother would be heartbroken to see it. This was my schoolroom.'* He pointed to a broken window, beyond which I could just make out a shelf of dusty books.

'She was the one who schooled you?'

'Yes,' he said, an old grief crossing his features. 'She taught me everything: philosophy, Latin, astronomy. But most of all she taught me dignity.'

Dignity was the trait Caesar valued most. His eventual assassination would be the greatest humiliation. He would have preferred to die by his own blade over that of a traitor's.

'Et tu, Brute?' But it didn't happen like that.

Forgive me; the lines between the past, present and future have blurred over time. Let me return to the menagerie.

'What news from your scouts this morning?' I said to Caesar. He leaned his elbows on the stone wall of the lion's enclosure, his profile in shadow.

'The false pharaohs have amassed twenty-two ships, but half of them are still being repaired in the harbour.'

Arsinoe and Theos were recruiting more and more

Alexandrians as the siege wore on. Their rumour-mongers were swaying the tide of the war to their favour.

'They have the skills of the fisherman, so it will not be long before those ships are seaworthy,' I remarked.

'It is time to strike,' he said slowly, knowing his words themselves would be a blow.

Without the full force of our allies, we were limited with what offensive tactics we could use.

Fire, Caesar had said, day after day. But I was reticent to light the spark of violence. Until that moment we had been reactive only – they were my younger siblings, and I could not shake the memories of their youthful faces from my mind.

I had been with Arsinoe when she had walked for the first time, her fat little legs tottering behind me as she chased me through the vineyard. As for Theos, I had been at his birth. My father had sent me to attend my mother in the birthing chamber. I had been excited until I realised the toll it would take on her. I would forever remember the relief on my mother's face, her contortions finally ceasing as his body slipped from hers.

'How many men will you send?' I asked.

'Ten or fifteen. They will travel without uniform, under the light of the moon.'

'My brother and sister, do we know where they reside?'

'We believe they are camped beyond the city, but we cannot be sure. There is a possibility they are aboard one of their allies' ships.'

If I made the order, they might die. But as I looked at the emaciated lions, I realised there was no world in which we all survived.

'Let it be done,' I said.

Here. Here is where I began to harden. I recognise it now, the callousing of my heart. Sentencing a soldier to death was one thing, but my siblings? That was a torture altogether too painful to bear. I had to armour my heart to withstand it.

Caesar nodded grimly. 'As you wish, Pharaoh. And the lions? I will do it.'

'No, this is a task I must do alone.'

I sent for my bow.

I didn't cry as I loosed the arrows.

That evening we dined together, alone. Caesar recognised that I needed distracting. The operation to burn my siblings' ships was commencing that night. Our meal was simple fare: lentils and bread.

Despite the battle that raged beyond the palace walls, these quiet moments were some of my favourite times during the life I'd led in Egypt.

'Sometimes I forget about the war,' I said quietly to Caesar. We had been discussing the merits of Eratosthenes of Cyrene's work, giving me the barest of glimpses of what my life would have been like had I been a scholar. It had been some time since I had longed for that life, but the wanting never truly went away. Much like the great loves of my life, the need became a part of me.

'It is a blessing to have this respite,' Caesar said.

My gaze had drifted to the window and the city's outline beyond. Caesar's hand reached out and rested on mine.

It wasn't the first time he had held my hand. The gesture was small but enough to reinforce his interest without being overbearing.

I have told you what began between us was friendship, but that does not mean that passion did not quickly grow. I found that in these quiet moments there was a sweetness to Caesar. Like a sun-ripened melon, he would peel back the toughened shell of his outer layer, revealing a man generous with his affections.

'It feels wrong to enjoy these nights with you, when my people are out there dying.'

He bowed his head. 'We acknowledge their sacrifice, but we must not succumb to melancholy. They fight so we can live.'

His words unsettled me and I moved my hand from under his to pick at the bread on my plate.

'Come now, soldiers must die for a war to be won,' Caesar said.

He had mistaken my discomfort. 'I am used to people dying for me.'

When I was five years old, my father had sacrificed three men to Isis. The ceremony had been held in my name, and though I'd barely been old enough to understand it, I'd been forced to wash my hands in their blood.

'Then what troubles you?'

'No matter who wins, we all lose. The ships we burn tonight are *my* people's ships.'

'Traitors, all of them.'

I considered. 'Yes, but also no. They still follow the Ptolemy blood, just the wrong Ptolemy.'

'The wrong Ptolemy, indeed.'

'If we win this battle, I will need to offer mercy, or I will have no subjects left in Alexandria.'

'They will not be loyal.'

'I do not need loyalty, I need obedience.'

Caesar laughed at that. 'You are right. Let the loyalty come later, for few people could deny you their devotion after being in your presence.'

His compliments were never overwrought or effusive, but they struck me like a sudden rain shower, pebbling my skin and sending shivers down my neck.

Your historians were right about his natural charm. He was eloquent yet spoke pensively so that you knew every word had been considered – and meant wholeheartedly.

I was wary of being ensnared by his charisma. Caesar's honeyed tongue had touched the lips of many men and women. I'd heard the court whisper about his adultery that he was 'every woman's man, and every man's woman'. The Queen and King of Mauretania were among his many lovers, and it was clear he had no qualms about intertwining political and sexual relations. But I was not prepared to jeopardise our alliance – and the armies he had called on.

I changed the subject quickly. 'I was going through the grain store list with Faunus and I think we need to ask for more supplies from Syria, lest our soldiers starve.'

'I have requested a convoy already.'

I was taken aback. 'Why did you not tell me of this?'

He reached for his wine, swirling it in his mouth before he swallowed. 'It is of no consequence.'

'We are partners in this war. Do not treat me lesser.'

'Cleopatra,' he said, searching my face for the smile I would not give him. 'It was a simple supply request. I do not and could not ever think of you as lesser.'

'Where is the supply list?'

'I will have it sent to you on the morrow.'

'Thank you – and in the future, keep me abreast of all details.'

He watched me with something akin to pride in his eyes. 'I will.' Then his lips twitched. 'Shall I also inform you when I use the latrine?'

I was about to reply that should he need guidance with that then I would be willing to send Ptolemy to teach him, when something caught my eye. I went to the window.

'What is it?' he asked.

'Look, there is a glow running across the land.'

Then I smelled it. Ash and smoke.

'It is the fire, our operation must have been a success. The Alexandrian fleet is destroyed,' Caesar said, joining me.

I shook my head and pointed. 'It comes from the east. The fire has spread to the city.'

'What buildings of import lie in the east?' he asked.

The wind quickly became thick with smoke and it stung my eyes, merging with the tears there.

I choked on my next words. 'The library.'

*

Caesar was exasperated. 'You cannot travel to the mainland. You will be spotted.'

'No, I have done it more than once, in a guise. I often go to heal people.'

He looked shocked. 'I think I know all the parts of you, yet you still manage to surprise me.'

'No one can know all of a person.'

'Perhaps not, but either way, you are not going.'

I scoffed. 'I am.'

He reached for my waist, holding me fixed with little pressure. But he needed none, his mere touch was enough to still me.

'This is different. The city is a war zone.'

'I will be careful.'

'No, you cannot go.'

'Who are you to tell a pharaoh what to do?' My tone was cutting, knife-sharp.

'Cleopatra,' he said, softly. Like a plea.

But I had made my mind up.

'I will go with you,' he said, seeing the resolution in my face.

'No,' I said firmly. 'You are too recognisable.'

'I will dress as an Egyptian. Bring me clothes, I can hide my features.'

I tried to imagine him in the simple cloth of a farmer and laughed again. Distress had unravelled some of my tightly coiled tension.

'This is not the time for mirth,' he said, his expression distraught. I reached up to smooth the lines of his brow.

'You are to stay here, dear Julius. I will be safe on my own.'

He leaned into my touch. 'You will not take Charmion?'

'Of course I will. Even when I am alone, I am with her. I have told you before, she is my companion in all things.'

He looked conflicted. 'Is she trained to use a spear?'

'We will be fine. This is my city. I know its very bones.'

'Do you have to go?'

'Yes, I need to see that the library still stands. But I will come back.'

'You must, for there are many more topics I would like to discuss with you.' His gaze grew intense. 'And many more things I should like to do.'

I stepped towards him and pressed my hand to his chest. He seemed to welcome the touch, drawing in a ragged breath.

'A worthy reason to return,' I said.

He encased my hand in his. 'Come back to me.'

'I will.'

CHAPTER THIRTEEN
48 BCE

Charmion and I rowed to the mainland just before dawn. The smoke was so thick we had to cover our mouths with cloth dipped in river-water.

The fire still raged as we passed the great harbour. The burned shells of the Alexandrian fleet smouldered in the lightening sky.

I heard Arsinoe screaming in my mind as her skin bubbled and blistered. Theos, too, his blood-curdling cries making me wince and cover my ears.

'What is wrong?' Charmion asked as the little rowing boat nudged onto the beach.

'Arsinoe and Mikro Theos.' Saying their names was enough. She knew I mourned them.

I hoped they had avoided the fire. And I hoped they had not.

The devastation in the city was worse than I could have imagined. Early on in the campaign, Theos and Arsinoe's army had laced the conduit system with seawater, poisoning the waterways of the Roman encampment. Caesar had ordered new wells to be dug along the entrenchments, adding further destruction to the city's streets.

Though the buildings were mainly stone, the fire had spread to the rare pockets of habitation where wood and paper were abundant. Like the library.

I ran through the streets in the opposite direction of the fleeing citizens. I had to see the damage for myself.

As I neared the library, my heart sank. The stone was blackened from the fire that raged within. Flames licked alongside the windows and hallways, consuming the papyrus like an agent of Apep.

I dashed forward, intent on seeing how the tree of knowledge fared, but Charmion held me back.

'Cleo, no. If you go in, you will die.'

'But Charmion, the books, the scrolls. The tree.' My voice cracked.

Charmion held on to my arm. 'I am not letting go of you.'

I knew it was suicide, and perhaps that was what I sought. I pulled out of her grip and ran forward until I stood between the columns of the entranceway. I could just make out the tree of knowledge, its wondrous branches glowing red and amber. Still beautiful despite the fire that ravaged it.

The fire was so hot I felt a flush run along my skin and sweat bead my brow. If I stepped forward just a little more, I'd feel it burn. The wind shifted direction and it was then that I saw it: the last flower to bloom on the tree of knowledge.

Each petal unfurled slowly, the scrolls unravelling as quickly as they burned. I watched as the flower turned to ash, its knowledge never to be known.

I closed my eyes to the destruction, the glow of the tree remaining on my eyelids. I imagined it was the moonlight, and not flames, that lit the petals.

When the scroll had landed upon my brow when I was a babe, my mother had beamed as bright as the moon to see her daughter blessed so. She had raised me up in her arms, praising the goddess Seshat. My lips whispered the words now, 'Hail, all-knowing goddess of words and ink, patron of mathematics and astrology. Thank you for your inner sight. May your power live on.'

Charmion dragged me back from the heat of the flame. And I let her. The tree had given me its greatest gift – a chance to view its beauty once more.

We walked slowly through the city back to the rowing boat. Dawn had broken across the land, touching its light with a pink glow. I did not feel like talking and Charmion knew this without asking. We each harboured our own grief.

Ahmose's passing had affected Charmion deeply. In the days after his death, I had opened my arms and bed to her. I knew how passion could ease the pain of loss; I myself had called upon many of my servants to attend me in the days after my father entered the field of reeds. But Charmion's appetite had stilled, and she wished only to be held close when she awoke from nightmares crying.

Sometimes I would cry with her. For Ahmose, for my mother, for my siblings.

I reached for her hand. 'We will heal.'

The look she gave me was haunted. 'The land will.'

'We will too, Charmion. There will come a time when the ground in the necropolis will be so still that flowers will bloom.'

That time never came.

Charmion stopped in her tracks. 'Do you hear that?'

We were nearly at the shore and I was weary. The palace felt a long distance away, and I was anxious to begin the journey.

'Hear what?'

She didn't need to answer, because then I heard him.

'The false queen has aligned with Caesar and agreed to make Egypt a Roman province. They burn Egypt, to build it again in the likeness of Rome. She makes a mockery of Sōter.' He spoke in stilted Egyptian, as if he read the phonetics from a scroll. But I would still be able to recognise his voice anywhere. Pothinus.

I followed the sound until I saw him standing on the remains of a destroyed building. His audience was a group of fishermen, about to begin their daily catch.

He didn't look up as Charmion and I joined the crowd.

'Queen Arsinoe and King Ptolemy fight for the rights of all Alexandrians.'

So, they live. My relief was brief.

I scowled and whispered to Charmion, 'Arsinoe and Ptolemy wage war for money and status.'

Pothinus continued, 'Cleopatra only fights for the man in her bed. She is a *whore.*'

The word struck me like a dagger to the chest. I gasped.

I felt Charmion's hand slipping into mine and I tightened my grip, grounding myself in the feel of her skin.

It may surprise you that this was the first time I had been called such a name – especially as your historians continue to use it so wantonly. And though I could not deny the feelings Caesar stirred within me, it incensed me that my relationship to him was being used to degrade and diminish me.

But women have ever been defined by their affiliation with men. It is hard to stand alone, to be scrutinised without the pollution of our sexual affairs.

'They will do anything to lure in more recruits,' I said through my teeth.

'Yes,' Charmion agreed.

'Julius will hear of this.'

'Stand against her carnal desires and stand for Egypt!' Pothinus shouted. I wondered if Arsinoe was the author of the words he recited.

There was movement in the ruins behind him, and Pothinus turned in time to be tackled by a cloaked figure. The two of them went down heavily. I saw the glint of a sword, then a spray of blood.

The gathering was too shocked to react immediately. Despite the bloodshed and skirmishes that happened daily, there was something so sudden about Pothinus's assassination that we were all stunned into silence.

As the assassin fled, pandemonium struck. Some of the fishermen lunged after the assailant. Others ran to the eunuch's side.

I remained still.

'We need to leave, now.' Charmion dragged me through the streets back to where we had stashed the rowing boat.

'I cannot believe Pothinus is dead. It must have been one of Caesar's men,' she said breathlessly as she pushed the boat out.

My lips remained closed. For I had recognised the gladius blade and the hand that had wielded it.

I strode into Caesar's chambers without announcing myself.

'Cleopatra?' He sat up as if he had awoken from a deep slumber. His torso was bare. I did not let it distract me.

'It was you.'

For a moment he looked like he was about to deny it. An expression of manufactured confusion crossed his features. His sword leaned against the wall in the corner. I removed it from its sheath. The hilt was still warm from his grip, and Pothinus's blood had not yet dried on the blade.

'You followed me.'

He sighed and pulled the covers from the bed. He wore a simple white loincloth. My gaze lingered by the contours of his hip bones, where material met muscle.

With gentle hands he took the sword from me and placed it into the waistband of his loincloth. I imagined it was my hand and felt my skin grow hot. If Caesar noticed, he took it for anger.

'It wasn't my intention to execute Pothinus, just an added benefit of my trip.'

'I told you not to come.'

'You expect me to allow you to walk into danger so readily?' He had drawn himself up, his muscles tightening, his jaw locking. Here was Caesar the soldier. Commanding, unyielding, insufferable.

And altogether intoxicating.

'*Allow?*' I said incredulously.

'You asked the impossible of me.' His anger was quiet. Simmering. I relished it.

'I ask *nothing* of you.'

He stepped towards me, until I could feel the heat of him. 'Nothing?'

If I had been bolder, I would have told him all the things I wanted from him. But my courage only matured with time, and as it was, I could only say: 'No.'

His hand reached up to the nape of my neck, his touch tender. Where his fingers lingered, my skin turned warm.

'Of all the things I would ask of you.' His eyes moved to my lips and I found my breath stuttering in my chest.

'Such as?' I whispered.

'A kiss, if you would grant it.'

My hands went to either side of his jaw, where the roughness of his beard met the olive of his skin. I leaned forward until we were a hair's breadth apart.

I could feel his breath on my face, shallow, hot. His eyes bored into mine, dark, pleading.

The distance closed between us. I could not tell you if it was him or me who made the irrevocable move. It was impossible to separate the need from the person.

The kiss was gentle at first. Our lips parted, each of us savouring the other. But then it deepened and our bodies pressed together.

I sense your thoughts: *What of Calpurnia, his wife?* Rome was a distant land, made even more distant by the immediate danger we lived in. We knew not if we would survive this war. Besides, it was his marriage to thwart, not mine – take your judgement and your questions to his grave instead.

His hands moved from my neck to the coils of my hair. I nipped at his lower lip and a sound, more animal than human, emanated from his throat.

Cleopatra only fights for the man in her bed. She is a whore.

I broke away from the kiss.

'My queen?' Caesar said. He stepped back into the space I had created between us, his hands held out to mine.

I did not reach for him and his expression turned guarded. 'I am sorry if this was not what you desired.'

To my surprise, his knees struck the floor as he bowed before me. He pulled his blade from his waistband and laid it on the floor between us. 'You may punish me as you will.'

I thought of the guard I had sentenced to death with his blade. It was the very same sword he proffered now. The gladius that had killed Pothinus. I picked it up and turned it around in my hands.

He bared the skin of his neck to me; it was browned from countless days spent fighting alongside the soldiers to reclaim my throne.

I could have killed him. He would have let me, would have welcomed it.

It would have been a more honourable death than the one he ultimately had. But how different your history would have been. Caesar's martyrdom would have been a quiet thing, the smallest of ripples in the currents of the world. Not enough to sway the tide of war.

He would just be a Roman slain by a whore. Because my tale would be the same.

I would always be Medusa. A monster and not a person. For how else would the world conceive of a woman with such power?

Medusa was a kindred spirit, another woman wronged by white hands and black ink. But this is my story and not hers.

Caesar looked so vulnerable beneath me, as if the weight of his feelings had laid him low.

I let the sword clatter to the floor, the sound shattering any hesitation I had left. I had already been labelled a whore. The word could never be unspoken.

There will be those of you who scowl and shake your head at the thought of the great Julius Caesar bowing before anyone. But he bowed before me, time and time again.

And I before him.

I lowered myself to the floor and raised his chin to meet mine, as an equal. 'You are what I desire.'

Our brows touched as we shared the same breath. And when his lips pressed against mine, I thought of nothing else but him; his smell, his touch, his taste.

Alea iacta est.

Caesar never said those words, but if he had, it would have been here, and not on the Rubicon river.

The die is cast.

Three full moons later, I was pregnant. I had been praying in the still unfinished Temple of Isis when I found out. With the war taking most of the resources and labour force, the construction had stuttered to a stop.

The interior was nearly complete. Twelve columns thrust up from the tiled ground, awaiting the placement of the roof. In the centre of the temple was a small inlaid pond, a design I had requested, which I intended to one day fill with lotus flowers. For now it was dry, as the tunnel leading to the central cistern of the island was incomplete.

Hieroglyphs had been etched into the walls, telling the story of Isis's resurrection of her husband Osiris. I ran my hand across the beloved tale, conjuring my mother's voice from my memories.

'Osiris the grand, Osiris the great, ruled with Isis by his side. But where there is greatness, there is envy. One fated night his brother, Seth, murdered the noble Osiris, sealing his body in a coffin and drowning him in the Nile river. Seth took the throne, dismissing the determination of Isis.

'The queen sought her lover's body for proper burial, retrieving him from the depths of the Nile. Seth, learning of his brother's fate, cut and desecrated the embalmed body and scattered his remains around the world. Isis transformed into a bird, searching for all the parts of him.' My mother's hands interlocked, creating two wings in flight. She swept them across my face and I laughed.

'When she had collected all of the parts of her husband,' my mother continued, 'she used her power to resurrect her love from the beyond. But in this new form, Osiris could only rule the land of the dead. And so they parted, one ruling in life, one ruling in death. Ten months after their union Isis gave birth to their son, Horus, protecting him until he was old enough to challenge his father's throne from Seth. And to emerge victorious.'

My hand rested on the final carving of Isis as the memory of my mother faded. The image was the height and breadth of the temple wall and it depicted the goddess on the throne with Horus at her breast.

I bowed my head before her.

'May your wisdom guide me. May your love surround me. Protector, mother, queen, I am yours.'

I brought my head up from my chest and felt a wave of dizziness wash over me. Charmion was there to catch me.

'My medicines, Charmion,' I said faintly.

Since Ahmose's death, the handmaiden had taken to wearing my bag of remedies wherever we went. I never mentioned it, but I knew it brought her comfort. It brought me comfort too – even though I had failed at saving him, she believed that I could still save others.

I rummaged through the clay vials, searching for the antidote to rouse me. But I felt so weak I could not see clearly.

'What do you need?' Charmion said, taking the bag from me.

'Honey and vinegar.'

Charmion handed me the tincture. I was about to bring it to my lips when she said, 'Wait.'

'What is it?' My hands shook from the effort of holding the vial aloft.

A realisation had come over her, brightening her eyes and lifting her brows. 'This is the third time in as many days, Cleo.

You've had headaches, nausea, sleepless nights. Might this be caused by something?'

'Exhaustion.'

She shook her head, trying to lead me like a camel to water. 'When was the last time you bled?'

'I do not know.' Truthfully, Charmion was the one who tracked my monthly rivers.

'It has been three turns of the moon.'

The vial fell from my grasp and struck the tiled floor.

'I'm pregnant.'

When Caesar returned from fighting that day, I was waiting for him in the rooms we now shared. The campaign to reclaim Egypt was progressing slowly. The Romans and my allies had reclaimed Pharos Island and my beloved lighthouse. Arsinoe and Theos's army had suffered significant casualties from the burning of the harbour and had retreated west. But the war was far from won.

'The rebellion army have been seen pillaging the city for wood to make new ships,' he said as he entered. 'I am expecting reinforcements by the end of the season. Mithridates leads the fleet from Cilicia.'

When I didn't reply, he seemed to sense there was something amiss. He focused his gaze on me and stood before me.

'What has happened?'

As the day had progressed, I had become more and more nervous about telling Caesar. My mind was heavy with worry about the complexities of what an heir of both Rome and Egypt might mean.

He reached for me now, cupping my cheek in his hand.

What if he does not claim the child? The thought didn't scare me like it should have; instead I found myself pulling away from him. If I had to do this alone, I would.

'I'm pregnant.'

Caesar's reaction was instantaneous. The smile that spread across his face was enough to bring tears to my eyes. He embraced me, covering us in our enemies' blood.

'He will be fierce like his mother,' he said as he kissed my palms.

'Our child may be a girl,' I said, smiling in relief.

'Then she will be even fiercer.' He lowered his head to my stomach and kissed me above my navel.

'And kind-hearted like her father.'

He stood, wrapping his arms around me once more.

'You need a bath,' I laughed, pushing him away.

'Join me?'

I let myself be led towards the bathhouse. Our laughter and joy echoed across the palace that night.

CHAPTER FOURTEEN
47 BCE

I looked up at Faunus, my administrator, who had entered the throne room and said something I didn't quite catch about Caesar. The old man puckered the symbol on his forehead as he frowned, clearly distraught. I watched as the kohl drawing of the lotus flower encircled by a snake drew upwards – a tribute to the legend of Iphis, a woman blessed by Isis to live the life of a man. Like Iphis, Faunus wore his rebirth proudly.

'Julius is where?' I was lounging on the couch that I had brought in to replace my chair in the throne room. My hands rested on my swollen belly, feeling the kicks of my child beneath my palms.

'Pharaoh, Caesar is missing, presumed dead,' he whispered, but it sounded as loud as a battle horn to my ears.

'No.' I would know if he had been ripped from the fabric of this world. I would have felt the tearing of the threads. Wouldn't I?

'He accompanied a small fleet to greet the reinforcements from Syria, but the rebellion army ambushed him. They outnumbered the few archers he had on board, killing them swiftly. The ship he was travelling on was sunk.'

'No,' I said again.

'He—'

'Have you seen his body?'

Faunus shook his head.

'Then he lives.'

'Pharaoh.' Faunus's voice cracked. The old man had been brought in by Caesar to help manage the affairs once assigned to Pothinus. He had proved an invaluable advisor and become a trusted confidant in court. 'It is unlikely he will have survived.'

I held out my hand. 'Charmion.' She was there to help me stand.

My legs did not shake, though I felt as if every step I took, the world around me spun.

I cradled my stomach. 'My child will come to know their father,' I vowed. 'Send out a search party to circle the harbour.'

'I have,' he said weakly. 'I return now from their counsel. There is no sight nor sign of Caesar.'

I shook my head, my hand tightening across my belly. 'No. I do not believe it.'

I was still walking, but I wasn't sure where.

Faunus called after me. 'We need to send missives to Rome . . .'

I ignored him, my footsteps taking me out of the throne room, out of the palace altogether.

I didn't cry – it wasn't shock, I just truly did not believe Caesar to be dead. He could not leave this life before meeting his child. *Our* child.

The sun was setting across the horizon, its rays seeping like honey into the ocean waves. I could see the navy out in the distance. Our fleet had grown considerably, outnumbering Arsinoe and Theos's army.

'We are so close,' I whispered to the sea. 'We are so close to the end.'

The baby in my belly twisted, pushing bile up my throat. I coughed against the burning pain of it while also relishing the feeling of the babe's strength.

'Your father will be here soon,' I said.

Though Isis had yet to bestow me with power, in moments like these I was comforted that she watched over me.

I stayed there all evening, watching ship after ship leave and return without Caesar on board.

'Come back to the palace,' Charmion said.

The sea lapped at my toes but I had stopped feeling them half a day ago. 'No.'

'You must at least sit, this is not good for the baby.'

I let Charmion call for a chair. It was my throne they brought, its gilded seat cool and familiar.

And that is where I sat, on the edge of the shoreline, a queen looking for her king.

Charmion brought me food at sunset but I couldn't eat.

'You must not forget the babe – they need sustenance.'

'I could not forget my child,' I snapped back. 'Do you think there is a moment that I am unaware of their presence? Their weight presses upon me. Their legs thrust against my spine. Even now, in this stillness, I feel them urging my skin to pull apart.'

Charmion flinched. It was so rare that I turned my ire on her. But I was avoiding the feelings that crept in like the tide. It was easier to be angry than sad. 'I did not mean to presume—'

'You did exactly that, you *presumed*. I would like to remind you that you do not know *all* my thoughts and feelings.' My temper should have subdued her. But Charmion was not like anyone else.

She stood in front of me, filling my vision. Few would risk the wrath of a pharaoh. As I have told you before, I did not hesitate to wield my executioner's blade. And certainly, my ancestors' hands were rarely clean of blood.

'Move out of the way,' I said.

'No.'

My guards stood behind me and I glanced at them.

Charmion raised an eyebrow. 'What are you going to do? Have them bind me in chains? Or go straight for the throat?'

My hand went to my own neck where the ivory blade still lay. Charmion flinched as my hand went to her cheek. But I did not strike her. My fingers trailed the puckered scar that adorned her face.

'I'm sorry,' I said, my voice catching. 'I would never . . . I could never—'

'I know.' She leaned into my touch and let out a ragged breath.

'I feel lost without him,' I admitted.

'I will not let you lose yourself. Not today, not tomorrow.' She pressed her three fingers to her lips.

Charmion was always the best of women. And the best of men.

She stayed with me until the moon hung in the sky. She held me when the last ship came back without Caesar.

'We need to send out another search party,' I mumbled. My lips were chapped from the sea winds.

Charmion relayed my request. I sensed my court were wary of coming too close to me. I must have cut a tragic sight. My throne had sunk into the wet sand, so that I slouched to the left. My discarded food and drink sat around me. The cloak I wore was parted in the middle to release the tension around my stomach. I knew my eyes would have turned red from the stinging breeze.

'They can't, not tonight,' Charmion said upon her return. 'It's too dark. It will have to wait until morning.'

'No, they must—'

Shouting interrupted my pleas.

'The east,' Charmion said, identifying where the guards were calling from.

I was up and running faster than anyone would have thought possible. I ran as though I were a lion freed from a cage.

Four soldiers stood in a rocky alcove. Two were crouched low, peering into the shallows. One of them pointed as I reached them. 'Pharaoh, someone approaches.'

It took me a moment to notice the shape beneath the waters. A shadow – too large to be a fish – carved through the waves.

My stomach lurched and the babe fluttered within. 'Theos?' For who else could part the waves so gracefully?

But it wasn't my brother. The curls matted to the swimmer's head were streaked with silver moonlight.

'Julius!'

He crawled onto the rocks, his chest heaving. In his hands he held a scroll, the details of which were entirely sodden.

I ran to his side. 'I knew you were not dead. I knew it.'

He smiled faintly as he collapsed backwards onto the beach. He thrust the wet scroll towards me.

'What is this?' I asked.

'The details of the convoys. I knew you'd be vexed with me if I didn't save it.'

I laughed, then I cried, my cheek pressing against his drenched clothing.

I refused to let Caesar return to the frontline for three days. In that time we discussed what Egypt would look like once Theos and Arsinoe were dispatched.

'Half of your courtiers are ready to return to your court; they have become disillusioned by the rebellion,' Caesar said. 'But Cleopatra, your reputation remains damaged.'

I scoffed. 'I do not care.' I was nearing the final moon cycle of pregnancy, and I had little tolerance for almost anything. We lay in the royal baths, the steam that curled around us scented with cinnamon.*

'You must care if you wish to reclaim the entirety of your court.'

I trailed my fingers through the water. 'Must I? I have survived thus far without them.'

Caesar reached for my idle hand. 'That is because I am here. Without the support of Rome, your court would have very few people left. And you need the nobility to stabilise the trade networks.'

---

* Not asses' milk, as many have gone on to claim. Your falsities follow me to the bathhouse, even.

I pulled my hand from his grip. 'Do not try to school me in matters I know far more about than you. Egypt is *my* country.'

Caesar's patience was unmatched and he nodded, sealing his mouth.

The water parted around my swollen belly as the babe kicked violently. It brought a smile to my lips, easing the irritation I felt. 'What do you suggest?' I asked Caesar.

'Reign with your youngest brother, Ptolemy. He is young enough to be pliable in all things. By ruling in tandem, you will increase your support from those who believe you unfit to rule but maintain loyalty for those who know your true value.'

I laughed – a little scornfully, I'll admit. 'Unfit?'

Caesar's gaze was serious. 'Some believe you are not blessed by your god, Isis. Then there are those who believe you are blessed, but by the *wrong* god.'

'And having Ptolemy rule with me will end that?' I said doubtfully.

'Ptolemy's power is proven—'

'As is mine,' I said quickly. I thought I had now convinced everyone, including myself, that my affinity to healing was god-given.

He inclined his head. 'Proven was the wrong word. Ptolemy's power is more . . . tangible. The court has seen it at work when he predicted the death of Ganymedes.'

I shivered. My brother's ability to foretell the day someone was going to die had always unsettled me.

'I do not need a man by my side to rule.'

Caesar wrapped his arms around my waist, pulling me towards him. 'Not even me?'

'You rule your own land. Rome,' I said. He shifted away from me.

It had been easy to pretend the world beyond Egypt's borders did not exist. But now, with the war coming to an end, we both had to face stark truths about our future.

'What will become of us when you return home?' I asked quietly.

Caesar looked at me from across the bath, his breath parting the steam. 'I do not need to return to Rome so soon. I will wait for our babe to join us in this life.'

I nodded, but I felt a deep sadness.

Seeing my expression, Caesar was beside me once again. He pressed his lips to my hair and murmured, 'You are my wife in all ways. Tied to me with bindings stronger than any law.'

His conviction tightened like arms around my chest. We may not have had a wedding, but we were partners in all things, until the day he died.

'I will send for you in Rome,' he continued, his voice growing wistful, 'and I will show you the beauty of my city; pray in the Temple of Jupiter, pluck apples from the orchards.'

He made our future sound so wonderful.

'Caesarion can run free among the vineyards—'

'Little Caesar?' I laughed, unaware the nickname would remain for centuries to come.

'Yes.' He kissed my belly. 'Caesarion they shall be, and we shall live a prosperous life between our two countries.'

I ran my hand through his hair. 'First we must win this war.'

'Yes. Tomorrow, if you'll permit me, I would like to parley with Arsinoe and Theos.'

'You expect them to surrender?'

'I hope they will.'

'You do not know Arsinoe like I do. But perhaps you can bring Theos to our side,' I said.

'I would like to try.'

It had been so long since I had seen either of my siblings. 'I want to come.'

'Cleopatra, no, you must rest.'

'No,' I said. 'I need to be there when this ends.'

He met my eyes and saw the determination in them. 'I see I will not be able to sway you.'

I patted his cheek. 'You are wise not to try.'

He brought his lips to my wrist, against the blood that flowed there. 'I will not let you out of my sight. For you and the babe you carry are the very essence of me.'

The water between us swelled and splashed as I moved to press my body against his. When I touched my lips to his, all worry was lost to pleasure.

The wind struck my face like the flapping of a bird's wing, stinging my cheeks. I clung on to my headdress, in the likeness of Isis's own crown, which threatened to topple into the sea. The cow horns tapered skywards to a sharp point on either side of my ear, a gold solar disc binding them together on the top of my head.

The dress I wore was a deep purple and it was tangled in my legs. Caesar stood beside me at the bow of the boat, clad in chainmail and leather armour, his gladius sword at his waist.

'My head hurts,' said a little voice. I grimaced.

Ptolemy, the youngest of my siblings, stood behind me. He wore the crown of the two lands, an ancient headpiece representing the coming together of Upper and Lower Egypt. I had thought it best that he showcased the heritage we represented.

But it was too big for his twelve-year-old head. The white barrelled base hung low on his brow, and the red arched interior rose precariously high off his crown and had to be secured with rope to his ears.

He looks like a fool of a king.

Ahead of us were the remaining ships of the rebellion army. As we drew closer, I could make out Arsinoe and Theos standing on the balcony at the front of their fleet.

They disembarked onto a smaller vessel and Caesar, Ptolemy and I did the same. Each party brought with them four guards; the remainder of our armies were at our backs.

'Ptolemy, can you use your gift? Tell me, who will die on their boat today?' I asked my brother as we drew near.

He seemed pleased to be asked. He screwed up his little face as he scrutinised our siblings on the other vessel.

Then he said, 'No one will die today.'

I sighed in relief. Though I was deeply angry at both Arsinoe and Theos, I did not want to have to give the order to kill either of them.

'If neither die, then there is hope they may yet surrender peacefully,' Caesar said.

'I hope so.'

The sea grew fierce and I found myself knocked to the side. Caesar steadied me, his hand cradling my stomach.

That was how Arsinoe first saw us as her boat drew alongside ours – not Pharaoh and consul, but lovers, parents.

Her lips parted in shock, which was quickly smothered by a small smile. Theos stood to her right.

Both were much changed.

Theos had thrived. He was taller, and his battle-worn gaze had lost all trace of childishness. He wore his gold armour which, though it was still big, fitted better than it had done half a year earlier. Arsinoe, on the other hand, had lost some of the vibrancy of her beauty, and I wondered if the toll of war had also stripped her of some of her arrogance.

The dress she wore looked as if it had once been a deep indigo, but it had faded from exposure to seawater. She wore a tripartite wig, hiding her natural hair beneath. Perhaps without her handmaidens, she suffered to maintain it.

She looked tired, but resolute.

I want to be seen, Arsinoe had once said to me.

'I see you, Arsinoe,' I said gently. For all that she had wronged me, she was still my younger sister, whom I loved.

Her eyes narrowed. 'You have crowned our baby brother,' she said.

Theos looked at Ptolemy, seemingly for the first time. The two had always had a bitter rivalry. 'He will not be a better king than me,' he said.

I felt a surge of affection for the insolent child. His innocence had been ill-treated, his wants and desires twisted for my sister's purpose. Even the words he spoke did not sound like him any more. He'd had no ambition to rule.

'We are here to discuss the terms of your surrender. Bow to your brother and sister and we may yet be able to forge a path forward in peace,' Caesar said.

Arsinoe's nostrils flared and a flush ran up her neck. 'I will bow to no one.'

'Arsinoe, do not be foolhardy,' I snapped. 'Death or surrender are your two options.'

'There is a third. *Rule*,' she replied coolly.

I shook my head, incensed by her lack of judgement. 'And what say you, Mikro Theos? Your home awaits you.'

Theos looked to Ptolemy, then to me. 'I will not bow to this little boy.'

I hissed through my teeth, 'Do not fall prey to your sister's poor judgement. Bowing to your brother is a small price to pay to live. You can come home again, swim in the harbour, go back to your studies.'

He hesitated, and Arsinoe saw it. Her lips puckered in disgust. 'Go then, join them if that is what you desire. But know that you will be beholden to their rule, never to make your own decisions. Never to be *seen*.'

Arsinoe was always wrong about the throne. She thought it would allow her to ascend to a state of absolute freedom. But it was always the opposite. Few people ever truly saw me for who I was, and that was because of the crown I wore. Even Caesar saw me as his queen first, and his lover second.

Everyone except for maybe Marcus. But it is not his time yet; he lingers in the margins of the page, awaiting his moment.

Theos turned to Arsinoe. They exchanged words I will never come to know. The ocean wind stole them from me, so I didn't hear my brother speak for the last time.

But I saw Arsinoe's rage, and I watched as she pushed my brother, with all her might, off the boat and into the sea.

Theos began to flail amidst the waves, his armour weighing him down.

We all watched in shocked silence as he began to sink.

'He can breathe underwater, all will be well,' Ptolemy said next to me.

Arsinoe's triumphant smile turned to horror as Theos disappeared beneath the sea. We waited for him to resurface but as time moved on, it dawned on us that he was not coming back up. I looked over to Arsinoe, but all expression had slipped from her features as though she defied even her own emotions. It left her as stoic and as still as a statue.

'Julius, send someone after him!' I shouted, the spell broken.

Caesar shook his head sadly. 'It is too late, my queen, his armour will have taken him too far out of reach for a swimmer without his gift.'

'So he is to remain beneath the waves forevermore?' I was tired of grief, and no tears fell. I had already lost the brother I had come to know half a year earlier.

Caesar met my gaze. 'Unless he can remove his armour.'

I shook my head. The suit had been made entirely from gold, with hinges that required four men to screw them together. Without their help, Theos was incapable of getting free.

Realisation was a cold thing; it set my teeth chattering and my hairs on end. Theos was gone – not dead, no, for Ptolemy would have foretold it – but gone. Entombed in his armour.

Love was not a prerequisite in the Ptolemy family. We were siblings, sometimes spouses, more than occasionally enemies. Had I loved my brother? The truth is, I'm not sure. Years were not the only thing that separated us. We had little in common, and though, until these past few months, we had dined together every evening, I had not truly known him.

I failed you in so many ways.

If I had loved him harder, would he have been swayed so easily to Arsinoe's side? Shame pierced my grief, making me gasp.

Caesar held me as I shuddered, my sobbing silent except for my heaving breath.

How would his gift sustain him? Would dehydration end his torment? Or old age, many years hence?

'Please, Isis, let it be swift,' I said to no one but my god.

I looked back to Arsinoe, but she had turned away. Did she also feel shame? Or had ambition rotted away what was left of her compassion?

I wanted to believe that Arsinoe hadn't meant to lose Theos that day – that her anger had overcome her reason. But I would never know. For this was the last time I spoke to my sister.

And her, I did love. Despite all her faults and her treachery. She had been my shadow for so many years. Even now I understood that she sought the light.

The rowers on Arsinoe's ship were making quick work closing the distance between her and her remaining fleet.

Caesar raised his hand to indicate pursuit.

I gathered myself to speak. 'Leave her,' I said. 'Let her conscience fester with the sin she committed this day. Tomorrow we will end this.'

My crying ceased and a wave of exhaustion overcame me. I looked to the spot where Theos had disappeared beneath the ocean's surface.

Ptolemy sniffled beside me.

'Goodbye, Mikro Theos,' I whispered. 'May you find solace in your kingdom in the sea's depths.'

I thought of my brother often over the years. I indulged myself with the hope that he had freed himself of his armour and sought land, living a happy life on the shore.

But I knew it was more likely he'd either died within days or remained trapped in his gold tomb for years, until old age blissfully released him from the gift that had become his prison.

CHAPTER FIFTEEN
47 BCE

Arsinoe fled Egypt the next day. Her rebellion quashed, she sought refuge with the few allies who still called her queen. I did not see her again for many years.

With the war won, the hardest part was to come – the rebuilding of Alexandria. I oversaw the construction, starting with the new library.

'It will never be the same,' Archibios said to me.

Dust from the building site filled the air. I held a thin piece of silk across my face to shield me from it.

'No, it will not. The tree of knowledge is gone, its power burned to ash. But from its remains new seeds will grow. They may not be divine, they may not bear fruit, but the legend of the tree will continue on. And with it, the legacy of the library.'

Archibios's eyes grew wet. 'We will regrow the collection, better than before.'

'Julius has already agreed to send in copies of works from Rome. It will take many years, but the library will be great once more.' My words were not just a comfort to the librarian, but to myself. I needed the reminder of Alexandria's future, for right now so much of it remained in ruins and rubble.

To the north was the burned harbour, to the east the entrenched streets. In the west, every building was stripped of wood from the pillaging carried out by the traitors. And in the south, drought still laid waste to the farmland.

No matter how much time I spent trying to regain what had been, I knew that the city would never be the same. Like bone that had knitted back together, it would be imperfect, but stronger than before.

I felt myself begin to sway and Archibios was there by my side. He didn't touch me – to lay hands on a pharaoh without permission was a grave sin – but his hands hovered by my back, to catch me if I fell.

'Pharaoh, are you well?'

I nodded, my eyes closed. 'Yes, just exhausted. I spent the night in the new hospital.'

It wasn't a building yet, just a collection of canopies, but it had already seen a steady stream of visitors.

'You must protect your own health before that of others, Pharaoh. How fares the babe?'

My hands went to my stomach protectively and I smiled. 'Due soon.'

'It is good they will be born during peacetime. War is no place for a baby.'

'No, especially one who is the heir of Rome and Egypt.'

Archibios grew pensive, and I could see a question brewing on his lips.

'Ask,' I said. 'We have spent too many years together to be shy in the face of curiosity.'

He returned my smile, but he still hesitated. 'I . . . I have heard what the Roman courtiers are saying . . . that Caesar will not claim your child as his own. That he intends to return to Calpurnia in Rome.'

I sighed. It wasn't the worst rumour to have reached my ears in recent times, and in some ways, it was a relief to hear of something so tame.

'I care not for the talk of Romans in my court.'

Archibios grimaced at the sharpness of my tone and I

continued more gently, 'My child is the heir to Rome and Egypt, no matter who claims otherwise. My word is the law.'

I clasped my hands together to stop them trembling. Archibios's enquiries had triggered my fear that Caesar would yet abandon me.

But then I saw him stride across the courtyard and all worries fled my mind. Dirt and sweat streaked his body from his efforts helping the labourers haul in stone.

He saw me looking and smiled. Caesar was not one to smile quickly or often, but when he did, it was as though the sun shone on my brow.

Ten days after the war was won, he had left Antirhodos in the middle of the night and I had woken up alone, the sheets beside me unslept in.

'Where is he?' I knew I sounded like a desert fox, screeching for my mate. My usual measured disposition was fraught under the strain of the pregnancy.

'No one knows,' Charmion said gently. 'He went with a small group of his most trusted soldiers.'

I paced the length of the island, waiting for Caesar to return. My swollen ankles ached, but my anger needed to be exercised.

When I saw his ship on the horizon, I waited by the dock, seething.

'Where did you go?' I said as he disembarked.

'My queen.' He lowered a kiss to my brow and frowned when the creases there did not ease.

'Where did you go?' I repeated.

He smiled faintly, as though he was enjoying the heat of my anger. It only incensed me more.

'Julius, *where did you go?*'

His soldiers were unloading a crate behind him, and he stepped back so I could see it.

'I went hunting.'

Two honey-coloured lion cubs lay curled up in the corner of a wooden cage. Caesar helped me kneel beside them.

'We found their mother's body by an oasis. She had given her life defending her cubs from a crocodile. I thought the little ones could be the beginnings of your new menagerie.'

'Julius,' I choked out his name.

'One boy, one girl,' he said, wrapping his arms around my waist.

I named them Bastet and Maahes after the cat-headed gods. But they did not go in the menagerie, they stayed beside me.

I loved those beasts dearly. Rearing them helped to heal the wounds the war had caused. There was a simple pleasure in feeding a hungry cub and being loved by it in return: Caesar gave me that gift, and I would forever treasure it.

Now I turned to Archibios, feeling more energised. 'The court needs to be purged of blasphemers. Please, report to me if anyone says such things. In rebuilding Alexandria I intend to do more than just repair the city, I wish to reform the ruling class. Be they Roman, Greek or Egyptian, if they reside in my land, they will respect me and my unborn child.'

My child did not remain unborn for much longer. Under the black sky of a new moon, Ptolemy Philopator Philometor Caesar, fifteenth of his name – known to you and me as Caesarion – came screaming into the world. A battle cry for a battle won, after a day and half a night of labour.

Charmion placed him into my arms.

'Is he not perfect? Is he not a child in the gods' eyes?'

I looked at his swollen face, marked with my blood and fluid, and wondered where Charmion's sanity had gone.

'He is . . . wet,' I said weakly.

It is fair to say, I did not love my son from his first breath. How could I? I did not yet know him. I could not predict the insightful, empathetic boy he would become. Nor could I foretell the love that would one day fill my heart to near bursting.

Charmion removed him from my chest and returned with him

wrapped in linen. Tears pooled in her eyes as I took him gingerly from her.

'Put him to the breast,' she said, her voice full of wonderment. I did as she bade, and she cheered when he suckled.

'It feels strange,' I said. 'As if he pulls on my very soul.'

She misunderstood me, thinking I spoke on something deeper than mere discomfort. 'He is a part of you now, tethered to your essence.'

I nodded, as if that was what I meant. 'Have you called on the soothsayer? We must announce his patron.'

Charmion exchanged a look with Eiras, who stood at the foot of the birthing bed. I had avoided looking there, my gaze skimming over the bloodied and soiled sheets.

'What is it?' I asked, sitting up as much as my weak limbs would allow. The babe came off the breast and I impatiently pressed him back on.

'Nothing; the soothsayer has been called,' Charmion said in calming tones. 'Rest now, I will awaken you when she arrives.'

I nodded and sank back down on the bed. 'Take him,' I said, handing Caesarion to the wet nurse to feed.

But as I closed my eyes, there was a voice at the door. 'I must see her, you cannot forbid me from entering.'

'Charmion,' I said, 'cover me in the leopard skin. Eiras, press my brow with some scented water.' My handmaids made haste, preparing me as best they could for Caesar's entrance.

'Pass me the babe,' I ordered. He cried as he was removed from the nursemaid's teat, his eyes scrunched and his lips puckered.

'Hush, little one,' Charmion said, and he quietened at her voice.

'He may enter,' I said to the guards at my door.

The consul of Rome had never looked so distraught. It seemed as though he had not slept in the day we'd been apart. As soon as my labour had begun, I'd sequestered myself away from him, lest his anxiety hamper my progress.

'Cleopatra—' He spotted our son.

'A boy,' I confirmed.

It was the first and last time I ever saw Caesar weep. 'My Venus and Cupid. You are the gods of my heart.'

I did not mind that he likened me to his false god. Isis's power was vast and had many faces, so when he spoke of Venus, I heard my goddess's name.

He took the babe from my arms and pressed him against his forehead, wetting the boy's cheeks with his tears.

'He is bigger than my Julia was,' he whispered. 'When your guards would not let me in . . .' The pain of what might have been had hollowed out the skin beneath his eyes.

I held out my hand to him and he grasped it, keeping Ptolemy cradled to his chest with the other. 'I am well,' I reassured him, 'and so is our son.'

'Our son,' he said with bewilderment. 'Caesarion. You will be the ruler of both Egypt and Rome one day.'

His words had the ring of prophecy, but we all know that did not come to pass.

Charmion woke me at sundown when the soothsayer arrived.

'She is in the antechamber – shall I let her through?'

My body ached, but I knew how important the soothsayer's verdict would be.

'Attend me.'

Charmion helped me to stand. My dress clung to the sticky blood between my legs. 'Pass me a robe, and my crown. Where is Caesarion?'

I was still Queen first, mother second.

'He's here, Pharaoh.' The nursemaid had a quiet voice, and it grated on me immediately. She lurked in an alcove, my son in her arms.

'Strip him of his blankets, the soothsayer will want to see him in his nakedness,' I instructed.

Once I was dressed and my son was not, I welcomed the soothsayer into my rooms.

She was younger than I expected. Naturally beautiful, with dark eyes and full lips that turned down at the corners, giving her an air of exquisite melancholy. She wore her hair in a side-lock style, entirely shaven except for the knot on the side of her head. The undyed linen of her robes was twisted across her chest and her brow was marked in kohl with the sigil of Ptah – the god of creation.

'Pharaoh.' She bowed low. 'My regards on the birth of your son. May the gods bless him.'

'Please, come and greet him.' I indicated for the wet nurse to bring him forward.

I watched as she handed over my son to the soothsayer, who began to examine him. My mouth was dry, my breath shallow.

Let it be a bountiful god, like Geb, or Re.

The soothsayer's eyes narrowed as she searched for the birthmark that tied my son to his deity. She lifted his legs, turned him on his bottom, checked his palms and behind his ears.

My heart began to pound against my chest as her eyes met mine. She shook her head once.

'Empty the room,' I said quietly. When no one moved, I said it again. 'Empty the room!'

Charmion began to herd the servants and the maidservants out of the birthing chamber.

'Even you, Charmion.'

The look she gave me would have fractured my heart, if it were not already breaking.

When the room was empty of everyone but the soothsayer and my son, I turned to her.

'Tell me,' I said.

Her lips trembled as she spoke. 'Your son is not marked by the gods.'

'It cannot be.'

'Search his body for yourself – there is no sigil.'

She placed Caesarion back in my arms and I searched his skin for any sign of a blemish. But as Charmion had said, he was perfect.

'What does this mean?' I whispered. Though the room was empty, I was still terrified of this reaching unfriendly ears.

The soothsayer's brows knitted together. 'Forgive me, my queen – is he truly of your blood?'

I felt a flash of rage. 'He *is* my blood.' I tugged on the tie of my robe, letting it open so she could see the blood that soaked through between my legs.

'I do not wish to anger you, but I had to be sure.'

'Then what is it? What is wrong with him?'

She smiled gently. 'I do not think anything is ever truly *wrong* with a babe fresh from the womb.'

I heard my voice rise in pitch, akin to the sound Qar made when he swooped on his prey. 'Then why is he not marked?'

'The gods have not granted him the divinity of your forebears. Perhaps you have angered them?'

Guilt churned like bile in my stomach and I found myself spluttering. 'Angered the gods? I have fought, I have bled, I have done everything I could to protect the people of Egypt.'

To my shame I began to cry, loud keening sobs that shook my body and made Caesarion scream.

'Please, take him,' I cried, and the soothsayer took him from my arms so I could collect myself.

When I could breathe steadily once more, I had already formed a plan. I would not be a victim to further conjecture about my reign, nor would I subject my son to it in the future.

My hand went to the knife at my throat and I released the dagger from the leather sheath.

'Place the babe on the bed,' I said. If the soothsayer heard any warning in my voice, she didn't show it.

When Caesarion was safe, I lunged, panic fortifying my weakened state.

The blade was at her throat before the soothsayer realised her death was near.

'Pharaoh, I will not speak on what happened here today, on the word of my god Ptah, let it be so,' she said. Her voice shook.

So, too, did my resolve.

'You swear it?'

'I do.' Her throat bobbed beneath my blade.

'Go, then,' I said, cursing my own weakness.

When she had left the room, I picked up Caesarion and wrapped him against my chest inside my robe. I then called for the new commander of my royal guard, Seti.

'Pharaoh?' he enquired.

'Follow the soothsayer. And execute her.'

You know I have killed many people, by order or by my hand. But the soothsayer is one I shall always regret. I never even knew her name.

I thought I was protecting my son, securing his future as heir. For no ruler of Egypt without divine protection would be accepted by the people.

Do you remember my noble endeavours to better Egypt? I hadn't wanted to be queen, but I had resolved to do more than the kings and queens of the past. I barely recognised that earnest woman who had rid the courts of corruption. Now that I was a mother, I wanted the throne for one purpose – to give it to Caesarion. It might be that this sense of entitlement is what poisoned the hearts of so many of my ancestors, but even if I had had the discernment to see it, I would have done nothing differently.

I wanted for my son alone.

CHAPTER SIXTEEN
47 BCE

I did not let anyone care for Caesarion for three days. I had the wet nurses dismissed and reduced my servants to just Charmion and Eiras.

They thought I suffered a malady of the mind, especially when I insisted on being the only one to change the linens he soiled. But I could not let the others realise he was unblemished, unchosen by the gods.

'Blessed by Horus,' I announced the night I executed the soothsayer. The lie was easy, as it felt so close to the truth. My affinity to Isis made the connection so simple – Horus was her son, and together they were the quintessential duo of myth and legend. No one could question my divinity now.

But I knew the lie was not sustainable. On the fourth night after his birth, I sent Charmion and Eiras to the kitchens to retrieve a complex list of food I requested. Caesar was at the gymnasium and would be occupied until much later in the night.

As soon as I was alone, I slipped away down the hidden tunnel in my bedchamber. Earlier that year, during the battle for the city, Charmion and I had stolen away in the night and docked a small boat at the end of the tunnel. It had exhausted both our bodies, but the foresight – borne of fear for our lives at the time – was serendipitous now.

I placed Caesarion in the hull of the boat, cradled in his blankets. He slept peacefully, his lips twitching in dreams.

Weakened as I still was from labour, it was harder to push the boat out alone, but the incoming tide buoyed its weight as it reached the shoreline, and I was able to embark in the shallows.

Once I arrived at the new city harbour, I knew where I was going. I had made my enquiries at the hospital the day before.

I shuffled through the streets, my medicine bag bouncing against my hip, Caesarion cradled against my chest.

'Three houses south of the market . . .' I whispered to myself.

When I arrived, there was no light coming from the entranceway and I cursed.

'Who calls on the gods at my door?'

I started at the sound of the man's voice. It disturbed Caesarion's sleep and he grumbled. I clutched him tighter, swaying my arms to and fro.

'Are you Khufu?' I asked the shadow beneath the doorframe.

He lit a torch, lighting his profile, and I swallowed a gasp. His entire face was marked with ink. Down one cheek was a series of hieroglyphics, across his brow a solar constellation.

'What might you need with Khufu?' He set his jaw and I noted the falcon that flew across his neck.

I reached into my pocket and withdrew a bag of coins. 'I have a request for you.'

He eyed me before letting me into his home. 'It is late at night to be walking the streets with so many coins.'

I felt the hairs on my arm bristle, but when I looked at him, his expression held no malice. In fact, he watched me with curiously kind eyes, which only sharpened after I made my request.

'The eye of Horus? On the babe's leg?'

'Yes, the coins are not bronze,' I said, pushing the pouch across the table.

He looked at the sleeping Caesarion, who I laid next to the payment. 'It will hurt.'

I swallowed. 'I know.'

I will never forget the moment my son's eyes flew open in pain. I had only caught glimpses of his eyes beneath the swollen eyelids of birth, but they grew wide now, larger than I'd ever seen them. And though no tears came, he screamed, his face growing red.

For the first time I felt the tether Charmion had spoken of before. I felt his pain like it was my own, and I wept for the both of us.

The ink work took longer than I had hoped, each prick of the needle an agony that became scored into my mind. But it sealed his fate better than my lie could.

And when the final dot was preserved in skin, I gathered him up and held him to my breast.

'I am so sorry,' I whispered against his hair, curling just like his father's. 'I am so sorry, my son.'

Love had blossomed from this moment of pain, and I could not imagine a life as precious as the one I held in my arms.

Khufu collected up the coins. The task had left him haggard. But there was one more needle yet to come.

I reached into my bag, pulling out my parting gift.

'Thank you, Khufu. May the gods bless you in the afterlife.'

After my cowardice with the soothsayer, I had prepared better this time. I could leave no footprints leading to my deceit. The needle I pressed into Khufu's skin was laced with a concoction of poisons: a dose of distilled wolfsbane sap, lethal enough to kill by sunrise, and opium, to send him into an easy sleep before transitioning to death, for I was not without mercy.

I did not think of Khufu's death as murder: it was necessary to secure the succession for Caesarion. I would like to say that I weighed up the deaths that would have occurred in a dispute for the throne and sought the less bloodied path, but I did not. Though I prevented a civil war with Khufu's sacrifice, I would have cut down a hundred men. A thousand.

Khufu's eyes widened, then rolled backwards as the opium took effect. He slumped to his knees and fell forwards, expelling the air in his lungs with a huff. I watched him gasping on the floor with a curious detachment.

I felt no guilt for taking his life. No shame had stayed my hand. His death was *survival*. For me, for my son, for Egypt. Before, I told you I was a queen first and a mother second. Now, I was simply a queen who was a mother. The throne had not become secondary – for I was Egypt – but my child had become Egypt too. He and I were one.

I left the coins for Khufu's family to find.

When I returned to my rooms that night, Charmion was waiting.

'I sent Eiras away, it is just us,' she said quietly.

'Does she know I left the palace?'

'No, she knows nothing of the tunnel.' The look she gave me was sad and distant. 'I would not betray your secrets, Cleo.'

I couldn't meet her gaze. I knew it was a mercy that she didn't ask where I had gone. She didn't want to hear my lie, though I had formulated it: *I went to show my son the city*. Charmion knew everything about me; there was no secret I had that wasn't hers too. But I could not tell her the truth of this. I was too humiliated that the gods had condemned my child so.

What had I done to anger the pantheon? Why was my son the first Ptolemy not to be blessed?

I rubbed the mark at my own neck. It wasn't the exact hue as Caesarion's, which had a slight blueness to it from the pigment in the ink. *But no one will notice the difference*, I assured myself.

The skin on Caesarion's leg was hot beneath my touch. I pressed a kiss to his brow and prayed he would forgive me: *let time heal this wound and banish this memory*.

I turned to Charmion. 'In seven days, we prepare a feast in Caesarion's honour. In *Horus's* honour. Send missives to the court.' Long enough for the ink to scab and heal.

Caesar entered as I spoke. 'A feast, Cleopatra?'

Charmion bowed, all informality gone in the presence of the consul.

'Yes, I think it is time that our son is properly celebrated,'

I said. I pulled my clothing tighter around me, hoping he did not notice its simplicity. But his eyes were for his son alone.

'Does that mean you will now allow other people to hold him?' he asked.

I laughed, though he expressed no mirth. 'By all means.'

Caesar seemed relieved, and I wondered how much he had been discussing my recent temperament with Charmion and Eiras.

I held out Caesarion to him and he lifted the babe from me, cradling him in his arms.

His smile was radiant as he looked down at our son. 'Your mother says we must celebrate you, and I think that is a fine idea.'

'I will begin the preparations, Pharaoh,' Charmion said. Pharaoh, not *Cleo*.

'Charmion . . .' I started, but my handmaiden swept away before I could finish.

I could call her back with a word, but our trust was built as a bridge – she saw me beyond my title, and I saw her beyond hers.

And for the first time, cracks were forming.

The feast drew in all the nobility of Egypt, and some allies from neighbouring countries.

The celebration was a political one, a strategy to strengthen my rule. It allowed me to reinforce my image of Isis and Horus, while also fortifying a united front between my brother and me.

The kitchens roasted twelve boars for the occasion, and Caesar had sent for several casks of palm wine. A sistrum player chimed a steady melody as courtiers engaged in games of senet and dice.

I watched the festivities from the comfort of my throne, my son laid across my lap. Bastet and Maahes lay by my feet, already grown to the size of large goats. The cubs wore lapis-studded collars that matched the beaded hem of my own dress, and Caesarion was also lavishly adorned: a small circlet lay upon his head, with golden falcon wings coming together above his brow. The linen draped over him was parted to reveal the slip of skin where ink had marked him with the eye of Horus. We were the very image of the gods.

Courtiers greeted us both and laid gifts at our feet throughout the evening. Ptolemy, sitting beside me, complained that he had yet to receive any.

'It is Caesarion's night, brother,' I reminded him. 'But you may choose any gift you desire from the offerings on the morrow. Your nephew is too young to know.' This cheered him.

I was determined to keep my youngest brother happy and placid in his role as a figurehead, after I had failed with Theos. I tried not to think of my brother, deep beneath the waters of the bay.

I was glad of the distraction when a governor approached the dais.

I recognised but couldn't quite place him.

He bowed low, his long hair fanning out around him. 'Pharaoh. My name is Governor Serapion from Memphis. I had the pleasure of joining you for dinner during your tour to Hermonthis.'

I remembered now: he had been the only courtier to answer my summons. He had spent most of the evening speaking to Arsinoe alone. 'You were not governor then.'

'No – my father, may he find eternal peace, passed into the next realm at the beginning of shemu season.'

'May he find eternal peace,' I echoed, and he inclined his head at my blessing.

'I have a humble request, great Pharaoh, blessed of Isis. My sister suffers from an unknown malady, I hoped you might use your divine power to cure her.'

There was something in his tone that made me pause. I narrowed my eyes as I scrutinised him. Maahes sensed my disquiet and stood up.

Serapion shifted his feet.

I laid a hand on the cub's head and he settled again. 'Do not worry, he won't hurt you. Unless you wish to cause me harm, that is,' I said.

Serapion's laugh was as thick as fresh honey. 'No, my queen. I only ask for your help.'

'Bring your sister to the hospital on the mainland; I will be sure to treat her there.'

'I have brought her here with me. If it pleases you, I can send for her now.' His voice had increased in volume and it carried to the party guests nearest to me.

I frowned. 'I will prioritise her treatment in the morning.'

'I have travelled far for your fabled touch,' he persisted. 'Like many of us here, I seek to bask in your divinity. Grant us this gift, let us see your power in action.'

The silence gathered momentum, and soon a hush had fallen across the feast.

I sensed the trap, but it was too late. Expectant eyes stared back at me. Even Caesar watched with keen interest from across the room.

There was a loud clatter from the side of my throne. The sound startled Caesarion awake, and he began to cry.

'I am so sorry, my queen,' Charmion mumbled as she tried to gather up the pieces of the clay flask she had dropped.

'I must attend to my son,' I said to the governor, the anticipation of the moment broken. 'Your sister may come to me in the hospital tomorrow.'

His smile was slick like oil. 'Indeed, I will send her there.'

The chatter returned as I stood and made my way out of the room. When I reached the antechamber, I turned to Charmion.

'Thank you,' I said. I sat heavily in a chair and began nursing the crying Caesarion.

'He does not have a sister, let alone a sick one,' Charmion said. 'I remember him from the boat – he was talking to Arsinoe of the woes of being an only child. I distinctly recall the conversation because Arsinoe laughed and said she wished she was one.'

'He seeks to reveal my lack of power.'

'Why?'

Arsinoe. Her name floated like oil to the surface of my mind. After we'd quelled her rebellion, she had gone into hiding. Caesar had long suspected she was in Syria, but his spies had yet to confirm it.

How can it be her, if even the might of Rome cannot find her?

But there was something in this trick that reminded me of her shrewdness.

'You think it is her.' Charmion surmised my suspicions quickly.

'I know not. But either way, his words have already sown dissent,' I said quietly, then hissed as Caesarion pulled off my breast painfully. I pressed him back onto the nipple, inadvertently squeezing the leg that bore the ink work.

Caesarion's eyes flew open and he began to scream, the skin there still tender. Recalling the moment the needle had first struck his skin, I closed my eyes to the sound.

'Cleo?'

My arms trembled, and though I tried to stop them, tears began to flow down my cheeks, blurring the kohl I wore.

'It was all for naught,' I whispered.

'What was?'

'The pain I subjected Caesarion to. All it takes is one question, one governor to unravel it all.'

The truth poured out of me: the soothsayer, Khufu, the lies, they ran from my mouth like the purging of a poison.

'I am sorry I did not tell you,' I whispered, my throat burning with the confession. 'I was so ashamed that the gods had abandoned me, and in my loneliness, I walked a dark path.'

Charmion closed her eyes. 'I thought I had lost your trust.'

'Never. It is I who was lost.'

Charmion wrapped her arms around me and Caesarion, rocking us back and forth.

'I wish you had told me of this sooner, I would have supported you, shared in your worry. We could have walked a different path.'

'There was no other choice,' I said.

'But at least we would have walked together.' Her hand went to my cheek and she pressed her lips against the salty tears there. 'Do not abandon me again, Cleo.'

I shook my head. 'I will not.'

I never did, you know. We were never parted again, not even in our last moments.

'Now, Serapion,' she continued. 'We must think of a solution.'

I felt defeated, my bones aching from bending over the babe, my nipples sore. I shook my head. 'Let the rumours swirl. I have no power and my child is not even blessed by the gods. Let my reign end in the turmoil I have lived.'

Charmion narrowed her eyes at me. 'Must I slap sense into you?'

The question was so dry, I laughed. 'No.'

'Then perhaps we can try something else. How can we convince the court of your divinity?'

The sting of defeat began to subside as a plan formed in my mind.

I returned to the throne later that evening. The free-flowing wine had left a collective flush across the cheeks of the courtiers. Merriment could be heard throughout the hall, but my arrival subdued some of it.

It was clear that Serapion's request had spread disquiet, resurrecting the rumour I had spent years trying to eliminate the last traces of.

Caesar saw me return. He approached the throne and Bastet rolled onto her back so that he could stroke her belly. She had a particular fondness for Caesar, I believe because he often slipped her pieces of meat at the dinner table.

'Is all well?' Caesar asked, concern etched into his features. He too had sensed the shift in the room.

'All is well.'

I held my hand out to him and he clasped it before pressing my palm to his lips.

'Where is our son?'

I had left Caesarion with the newly reinstated wet nurse, and I told him so. I required full focus as I did not want the plan to falter.

'Go, rejoin the festivities, I am fine.'

'Are you sure?'

'Yes.'

Something caught his eye as he turned.

'Who is that?' he asked.

A courtier had entered the hall, wearing a long indigo gown styled like a Greek tunic. The wig on her brow was heavily beaded, her eyes lined with thick kohl. If questioned, I knew, she'd speak Greek fluently with an accent of the south.

I waited for Caesar to recognise Charmion, but he didn't.

I smiled, a little smugly. 'She must be from Upper Egypt.'

We both watched as she swept through the room, quickly drawing an audience, including Serapion. Though I couldn't hear her, I knew she was engaging them with a lively tale of her late arrival. A hakawati in a noble's dress.

Bastet pawed at Caesar's leg and he once again dutifully petted her. I was grateful the cub distracted him, because though he did not recognise Charmion by sight, there was more danger of him knowing her voice.

'You're gaining too much weight, little one, much more than your brother.'

'She gains weight because you feed her too much.'

Caesar looked as though I had struck him. 'But she must be fed.'

'Yes, indeed. But perhaps not a whole duck at every meal.'

There was a commotion behind us and I leaned forward, feigning shock. 'That woman, she's afflicted.'

Charmion was coughing violently. Her face was red, and the veins in her neck bulging. When she collapsed to her knees, I stood from my chair.

'I will go to her.'

The crowd parted to let me through.

'Is she breathing?' I asked the nearest noble, who nodded. The anticipation of the stunt made my heart flutter.

This *had* to work. I was tired of chasing the rumours that had haunted my reign. This needed to end the whispers.

Isis, guide me. Let this ruse prove true. Despite everything, I never questioned my faith. Even now, when most people's belief would have begun to waver, I begged for her veneration.

'Allow me to heal her,' I said loudly. I caught Serapion's eye as I lowered myself to the floor beside Charmion. He watched with great interest, his chin protruding like a turtle's head from its shell.

Charmion's eyelids fluttered and her lips were slack and drooling. She was always the greatest of players.

I needed to draw out the moment. This healing required some thrilling details, in order to go from story to legend.*

'Bring me vinegar,' I said.

While I waited, I placed my hands over Charmion's chest.

'Isis, grant me the power to heal this woman,' I intoned, projecting my voice to draw in the last few stragglers from the periphery of the hall.

'Pharaoh.' It was Serapion who handed me the vinegar, his eyes pensive as he watched my power at work.

I plucked a pearl earring from my lobe and dropped it into the cup. An heirloom from generations past, it was believed to have been sent through the Silk Roads by an emperor in the east. I could not use common medicines for the healing; the potion had to be impossible to replicate with herbs or tinctures – I did not want the false recipe to feature in future homes as a cure for all.

I swirled the contents of the cup before raising it above my head. 'Lady of glory, mother of life, bless me this night, fill me with light. Vinegar for my tears, pearl for my bones.' I lowered the drink to my lips and swallowed the pearl whole.

---

* I had hoped for the story to spread throughout Egypt, not throughout time. I have Pliny the Elder to thank for that, though by the time he recorded the tale it had been twisted by the lips of Octavian's court.

The room gasped, and I revelled in the overture as I reached the final act.

I bent over Charmion and placed my moistened lips on hers. When I drew back, she was already waking, her breathing settling, her fainting spell gone.

Caesar had watched the proceedings from beside me, his expression neutral. I was worried that he had finally recognised Charmion beneath the make-up and costumery. But at her recovery he began to cheer, lifting the room's voices with him.

'Hail Cleopatra, chosen of Isis! Hail Cleopatra, chosen of Isis!'

Each lie I told was a link on a chain that only I could see. It bound tighter and tighter with each passing day. But in that moment, I relished the sound of my name on many people's lips.

They called me a god, and for once, I felt like one.

CHAPTER SEVENTEEN
46 BCE

Like all legends, the story of the pearl in vinegar evolved over the years. *The Banquet of Cleopatra*, your artists have named it, sullying my likeness so crudely. The etchings of the tale lost refinement through time, softening like oil paints on canvas.

But during the early years of my reign, the healing myth endured, silencing the rumours that had blighted my rule.

Peace settled across Egypt. After the siege of Alexandria, Caesar spent the summer by my side, watching our son grow. But his ambition soon drew him away.

Caesar was a warrior first, a dictator second, and a father third. War was his calling, and so when an opportunity arose to seek vengeance against an old enemy, Caesar left Egypt. I do not recount this with any agitation; I knew who he was even before our passion began to blossom. I could have stopped the union then, but I didn't, not until our love had borne fruit. Still, I wished he could tarry longer.

'Stay another season,' I said, my finger twirling in Caesarion's curling locks as he slumbered on my chest.

'I cannot let this opportunity pass, Cleopatra. Pharnaces is amassing troops in Zela, and I have the means to intercept him.' He stood a few steps lower than the throne, dressed in his armour, the sword he had once used to kill for me at his waist.

Its blade had been dry for some time.

'From there you will return to Rome?' I said carefully. Though I said 'Rome', I meant 'Calpurnia'.

Caesar sighed heavily, as if it was a great burden for him. 'Yes.'

His assent did not hurt as it should have. We both knew this had always been on the horizon.

'But I will call for you when I am settled. You will enjoy the sights of my city.'

Could I leave Egypt?

I looked past Caesar to the clerks, working at their desks in the belly of the room. They exchanged scrolls with messengers, their quiet murmuring setting the drumbeat of my country's flourishing trade. Courtiers moved in and out of the palace, exchanging pleasantries.

Beyond them, through the open door, I could see a slip of sea and the outline of the new harbour full of ships.

Egypt thrived in peacetime. It was such a shame it was so infrequent.

I turned back to Caesar and I realised: yes, I could leave Egypt for him. Not for long, but for a while. Though I needed some assurances. 'You once said I was your wife in all ways. Is that still true?'

Caesar bowed before me, his knees striking the floor. 'Always. Know that in every battle, I bleed for you. *Only* you.'

I stood from the throne, stepping down so I could press a kiss to his brow.

'Then go, bleed, my husband.'

Veni, vidi, vici.

Pharnaces II of Pontus died shortly after his defeat by Caesar. The campaign was a success and upon returning to Rome, Caesar was named dictator.

The year spent apart strained our love, but it did not wane. In every smile gifted to me by Caesarion, in every serious frown I was granted, I saw Caesar.

We had created something so infinitely precious. Our son.

Egypt continued to prosper. My reforms for the governing of the land were slow, but I was able to stabilise the economy once more. Ptolemy was a simple boy, with simple interests, and I could continue my reign without his interference.

Caesarion and I lived a happy life, full of laughter and joy. If I had known what was to come, I wonder if I would have been content to stay like that forever. But Caesar called for me, as he had promised, and so I crossed the ocean. The bindings tying me to him had not frayed over time, and so when he pulled, I came, as fast as the wind would allow.

That first journey to Rome was a year after Caesarion was born. We had arrived during the harvest season and the air smelled of freshly pressed olives and toasted wheat.

Caesar welcomed us all to his private estate across the Tiber, in Trastevere. It didn't have the grandeur of my palace, but it was comfortable, the milder weather providing a lush landscape for Caesarion to explore.

He tottered around Caesar's legs, happy to be reunited with the father I had told him so much about.

'He has grown into a capable young man,' Caesar said proudly.

I snorted. 'Hardly a man, Julius, he still sucks at the breast.' Caesarion gurgled up at me and I laughed. 'Though he does have your way with words, so a man he must be.'

Caesar smiled and lifted the boy with one arm. With the other he reached for my hand and squeezed it. 'I am so glad you came. My heart ached without you.'

'A year is a long time,' I remarked. 'But you had your successes.'

'Yes. The triumph to celebrate my victories begins later. You, Caesarion and Ptolemy will be honoured guests.'

I looked to my younger brother, who sat beneath the shade of a pear tree. He still travelled with his nursemaid though he was now thirteen years old.

Despite his innocence, I did not dare leave him in Alexandria alone. I underestimated a sibling once, and I would not make the same mistake again.

Caesarion, seeing his uncle, squawked in Caesar's arms until his father released him to the ground. The boy then proceeded to run towards Ptolemy, who greeted him with a polite lack of interest.

'Must we attend? Why can't we stay here?' I asked, watching as Caesarion attempted to regain Ptolemy's attention with a dance. Charmion led the boy away with a dance of her own, always there to capture his heart.

'You must,' he said firmly and I raised an eyebrow. 'The procession is a little tedious, but the jesters and games will be enjoyable for Caesarion.'

'And what will be enjoyable for me?' I drawled. I still did not have a fondness for revelry, and the Roman triumphs were known to be raucous.

Caesar tightened his grip on mine and said, 'You will want to come – I have a surprise for you.'

'A surprise?'

His eyes glinted in the morning sun and I felt myself conceding.

Half a day later I deeply regretted my choice. The procession moved slowly through the city, beginning in the Field of Mars and winding through the streets to the Capitol, ending at the Temple of Jupiter.

The parade was filled with details of Caesar's victories, including maps, figurines of the enemy, and paintings of the battles. I found the whole thing dull, but Caesarion loved the spectacle of it.

When we reached the temple, Caesar led the tributes to Jupiter by slaughtering two white oxen across the temple steps.

He smelled of blood as he came to stand next to me. 'Your first surprise awaits.'

'First?' I said.

He nodded. 'You will have two today.' Then he said to a guard next to him. 'Bring out the prisoners.'

I frowned, confused, but I dutifully watched as the prisoners of war were led to stand on the bloodied steps.

As every new bound captive joined the procession, the cheering of the crowd grew louder.

Then came the final one. A woman, the weight of the chains around her wrist pulling her arms straight and her chest forward. Her braided hair had come loose, falling over her face. But still I recognised her.

'Arsinoe,' I whispered.

'We captured her fleeing east with the remaining traitors of the Egyptian court,' Caesar said, his voice thick with pride.

It had been many seasons since I had thought of my sister.

Was I happy to see her bound and beaten? I should have been. I should have rejoiced that her treachery would finally cease. But as I have told you before, I truly loved Arsinoe, far more than any of my other siblings. We had fought so frequently as children that in some ways I thought that this conflict would be resolved just as simply: with a song to lift our spirits and an embrace to forgive.

But it could not be so. There was no going back to the people we had been. Arsinoe had proven time and again that she had not been satisfied with that. It wasn't enough to be my sister. It wasn't enough to simply be loved by me.

Squawk-caw.

I would know that sound anywhere. Circling above the procession was Qar.

Did he see my face shift from hate to love and back again? Was he telling her what he saw?

I had not missed his eyes on me.

'What do you intend to do with her?' I asked Caesar.

'Execution,' Caesar said. The word sealed the fate of the first prisoner, and I watched as an axe severed his head. The crowd cheered all the harder.

One by one, each prisoner was paraded past the triumph before being sacrificed to Jupiter.

I held Caesarion's face against my skirts to protect him from the blood that ran like a river through the celebrating masses. I, too, averted my eyes from the slaughter – there was still a softness in me that recoiled at the sight of violence. But though I did not look, I could not hide from the smell. The metallic scent of death coated my mouth as I breathed in.

Only when I heard the crowd cry out for the 'Egyptian princess' did I look up again.

Arsinoe was dragged forwards towards the shore of the undulating crowd. They lusted for her blood in a way that sickened me. This was not an honourable death.

I will not be led in triumph, I vowed.[*] I am not sure now if they were my own words or if I have heard them so many times since then that my memory has distorted. Nonetheless, the sentiment remains the same. I would do anything to avoid being executed so.

As the axe was brought forth, I found myself paralysed, unable to move, unable to speak. My sister had betrayed me so completely, and I knew if our roles were reversed, she would not hesitate to have me killed.

Arsinoe stood tall as the executioner approached her. She raised her head until she saw me in the crowd.

The look she gave me was one of pride. As if it were not an axe being brought down on her, but a crown.

'Today you kill a queen!' she shouted.

Caesar nodded to someone on the periphery of the procession and then there was the unmistakable twang of a bow string. Then a thud.

A familiar black and white bird fell from the sky.

---

[*] I met Titus Livius once, who attributed these words to me. A repugnant man whose historical accounts are more embellished than my formal garments. Of course, it was his words that survived the ages and not mine.

The world stilled around me and I was thrust backwards in time.

'An ibis chick has nested in her locs,' Mother said. I had noticed her walking quickly through the palace courtiers with her handmaidens. When I called to her, she didn't turn to my voice. So I followed in her wake to the foot of my father's dining table.

'At first I thought to chase the bird away,' Mother continued. 'But then our daughter opened her eyes.'

Father hadn't caught sight of me yet, either. His head was cocked to the side as he listened to Mother speak with clear impatience. 'Make haste, my queen; I should come to know why you have disturbed my feasting.'

'Arsinoe spoke as if from a dream, "Thoth has plucked a feather from his brow." And then she pointed to the bird.' I still didn't comprehend my mother's meaning, though she spoke with such pride. I felt my first stirrings of jealousy.

My father stood from the table, and bellowed a great cry of triumph. 'She has been blessed!'

Understanding struck me and I took a step backwards. 'I am the e-elder,' I said. But my voice was thin, that of a nine-year-old, and it warbled in front of so many.

No one paid me any heed.

The courtiers around the room pounded their chalices upon the table.

Dun, dun, dun.

Their cheers carried forward to the present moment. *'Arsinoe! Arsinoe! Arsinoe!'*

Envy spread like acid down my scalp. By the time Qar hit the ground, the feeling had gone.

Was that what she felt every time they sang my name? Was the acid more potent because she knew in her heart that I was yet to be blessed?

I looked at Arsinoe, understanding her a little more than I ever had in these final moments.

She lurched forward, her chains going taut as she tried to

reach Qar. But it was too late; he was already another sacrifice to Jupiter.

Arsinoe screamed, a sound only the purest form of pain could produce. Though this was more merciless than the beheadings, I did not close my eyes to her.

She deserved that, at least.

The crowd grew silent as she fell to her knees, sobbing.

The executioner stepped forward, his axe prepared to strike its final blow. Another guard came forward to bare her neck, the skin streaked from the splatter of the other prisoners' blood.

'Have you not punished her enough?' The cry came from somewhere a few rows back. When I looked for the speaker, I could not see them, but I felt the dissent their words produced.

The crowd began to murmur. Then someone else called, 'Mercy!' Soon the cry caught fire, and more and more of the crowd called for clemency.

Caesar looked at me, troubled. 'If I order her execution, we may have a mob to contend with.'

I felt breathless from the emotions that roiled within me. He mistook my expression for anger.

'But I will risk a thousand riots, to carry out this wish.'

All I needed to do was nod and it would be over.

'Mama?' Caesarion whispered. His voice cut through the crowd to my ears alone. I still had him pressed against my leg, but he had turned his head from me, his wide eyes fixed on Arsinoe. He pointed a questioning finger at her.

I bent down low next to him. 'That is your aunt. *My sister.*'

As I said those two words which bound me to her in blood and fate, I knew she would not die this day.

'Let her live,' I said to Caesar. 'Qar's death has sated my need for vengeance for now.'

Caesar walked the steps to Arsinoe, blood splashing up his legs. He held up his hand for quiet.

'I hear your calls for mercy, and I grant it.' He helped Arsinoe to stand and she collapsed into his side, grief robbing her of stability. 'You have been saved this day by Queen Cleopatra's grace. But the gods still require justice for your crimes. You will live the remainder of your days exiled in the Temple of Artemis in Ephesus.'

The cheer from the crowd was deafening.

Arsinoe's eyes caught mine as Caesar handed her to the guards.

Weak, she called me once, and I knew, even in her grief-stricken state, she thought it now too. But her death would one day come to strengthen me: not today, but soon.

I watched as she was led down from the temple steps, her bare feet leaving bloody footprints through the streets and to her future beyond.

Caesar came back to me, his face a mask of disappointment. 'That did not go as I had planned.'

'No, but the crowd cheer for you still.'

'Are you vexed that the traitor lives?'

I wished he hadn't asked, as I didn't want to lie. But lie I did. 'Yes,' I said. 'Arsinoe was a false queen. Egypt will not be happy she lives still.'

Caesar looked morose. 'Your second gift will succeed the first.'

I cupped his cheek, hoping to draw out a smile. 'You continue to fight for me, and that is gift enough.'

The banquet that concluded the parade was not half as lavish as the festivities my father used to throw, but there was food and wine in abundance.

'She looked thinner, don't you think?' I said over the rim of my cup.

'Arsinoe?' Charmion replied.

'Yes.' I hadn't been able to shake her from my mind.

'She did. I imagine prisoner fare is not what she is used to.'

I shook my head ruefully. 'No, I imagine not.'

Charmion's hand snaked under the table and squeezed my thigh. I felt wretched. Though I'm not sure what I was more distressed by: my sister's state, or the fact that I still cared for her.

The callouses hadn't yet eclipsed my heart. There was some feeling there, beneath the thickened skin of war and strife.

'She will hate Ephesus,' Charmion said.

I imagined her in the pious clothing of a priestess. 'Yes, she will.'

'But it is good that she lives?' Charmion said the statement as a question.

'I-I . . .' There had been a time when words stuttered from me in times of stress. Though the years had healed this malady, it came back to me now.

I didn't know what to say. My feelings were not clear to me.

Know this about me: control was something I had fought to regain so many times, and would come to fight for time and time again. My own mind was so frequently tempestuous that I sought to calm the storm around me.

Arsinoe's reappearance had shaken me more than Caesar could have understood. He thought he had handed me a gift, but instead it was a burden.

'Do you remember when she followed us to the river?' Charmion said, her expression becoming wistful. For Arsinoe had been like a sister to her, too.

I did. 'She jumped in without a care, even though she couldn't swim. Sank like a stone.'

'When I pulled her up, she was laughing as she choked.'

I recalled Arsinoe's cackle as the water ran from her nose. She'd only been six years old. 'My sister has never respected death.'

'No.'

A soldier lifted up the flag of Caesar's legion and Caesar raised his cup as the eagle insignia swayed in the breeze. The crowds cheered.

Caesar sat at the far end of the table, his head framed from where I sat by the antlers of the whole roasted deer that separated us. The Roman nobles fawned around him, something he would once have despised. But now he seemed content to bask in their adoration.

Caesarion slid down in the chair beside me and I reached to catch him before his head struck the table. His eyes were half closed even as I clutched him to my chest.

'Shall I take Caesarion back to Caesar's home?' Charmion asked.

'I can send one of the nursemaids back with him, you need not go.'

'It is no bother. I would prefer to return myself.'

Charmion's hair fell over her face as she looked down. 'What is it?' I asked.

Worry jaded her gaze. 'I do not know. I cannot explain it, but there is something about this night that feels . . . wrong.'

Once again, Charmion proved to be astute at noticing the ripples of the world's waters. Though Caesar's fall had barely begun, she sensed it.

I laughed her worry away with a kiss to her cheek. 'Indulge yourself tonight – take pleasure in one of the night attendants Caesar has assigned to my rooms. Helvia was very comely.'

She shook her head and took Caesarion from my arms. 'Sleep calls to me.'

'Go, then. I won't be long. I am fatigued myself but Caesar has promised me another gift. So, I must extend my patience.'

'I know that is hard for you,' she teased before leaving.

Charmion had proved to be my gatekeeper, because as soon as she left, I drew in the curiosity of Rome's elite with a steady stream of visitors. A particularly odious man called Cicero sought to lecture me on the details of Homer's *Iliad* – which I could recite in its entirety.

As the night drew on, as Charmion had predicted, I grew impatient with Caesar and my long-awaited surprise. I found myself indulging in the Roman wine. It was stronger than I was used to, and soon enough I felt as if the room was swaying.

'My queen? Are you quite well?' I still can't recollect the name or the face of the woman I was speaking to and for a moment I saw Arsinoe.

My heart stuttered painfully in my chest before I realised the illusion.

'I am quite well,' I declared. 'But you must excuse me.'

I stumbled out of the great hall and into the courtyard.

My skin felt flushed and I pulled at the purple cloak Caesar had gifted me for the occasion, letting it fall to the ground. Then I plucked out the pins knotting my hair at the nape of my neck. The smaller braids that wound through my curls tumbled down my back.

Finally, I pulled off my crown, setting it on the stone wall that surrounded a small reflecting pool.

It was only then that I felt like I could breathe.

I took some slow breaths until the world around me stilled.

When I no longer felt as if I were sailing across the Nile, I looked around me.

The Forum was a beautiful complex of temples and courtyards. Newly completed, it still smelled of setting mortar. I bent down and trailed my hand through the water of the reflecting pool. My image shimmered in the moonlight, sending ripples through the pond.

I brought my wet hands to my face and rubbed the kohl from my eyes.

When I looked back, I didn't recognise the reflection. My lips were swollen and stained red from the wine. The kohl I had wiped away had left dark rings on the skin beneath my eyes, and my braids cast a patterned shadow across my jaw, emphasising the sharpness of the bone.

My skin was more burnished than it had been in Egypt, as Rome's more temperate climate lent itself to more evenings sitting beneath the warmth of the sun. I ran my fingers along the dark freckles that dusted the bridge of my broad nose. I had not seen them since I was a carefree and reckless child, running wild in the summer heat.

There was a cry behind me and I jerked upright, spinning on my heel. The movement caused my brain to rattle against my skull and I clutched it in agony.

When I felt I could focus my eyes again, I was mollified to see that the sound wasn't a person in pain, merely a couple of wine-merry soldiers taking pleasure in each other beneath a mulberry tree. The fallen ripe fruit, crushed beneath their bodies, scented the air with a sweet, sickly aroma and I felt my stomach lurch.

'Mint, I need mint,' I murmured to myself, but Charmion had left with my medicine bag.

The temples will have it.

With one hand on my head and the other cradling my stomach, I cursed the wine and my own gluttony as I slipped into the nearest temple.

Fire flickered in torches along the wall as I swept through the entranceway. The altar was adorned with a large statue, but my gaze was fixed on the incense by its feet.

I rummaged through the offerings and basins of perfumed water until I found a few sprigs of mint.

I placed them on my tongue and chewed slowly. After some time, I felt it calm the churning of my stomach.

'She is beautiful, is she not?' A figure moved beside me and I gasped.

The stranger stood to my left, looking up at the statue. I followed his gaze, appreciating the sculpture for the first time.

Incredibly, the woman was made entirely of gold. She was intricately crafted, the contours of her column dress so detailed they looked like a breeze would shift them. Her face was cast to the side, displaying a single pearl earring in her lobe. Finely carved braids were knotted at the base of the neck, and in her arms she held a cherub, small and plump. And though not all her features were visible, it was as if I were looking in the reflecting pool once more.

The statue was of me.

I swallowed the last remnants of the mint in my mouth, but no words came forth.

'The goddess Venus holding Cupid,' the man said. 'They say she has been made in the likeness of Caesar's mistress, Cleopatra.'

'Mistress': I smarted at the term. We have not spoken much on Calpurnia, but know that I thought of her little, save in moments like these. Caesar had told me I was his wife in all ways – and that was enough for me. If only it had been enough for those around us.

'His mistress must be a worthy muse,' I replied.

'I wonder what the goddess thinks of her new face,' he said. The man stepped closer to the statue and I realised that his wide shoulders and height would be of the same size as it, should he too stand on a plinth. As he peered at the sculpture, I felt as if my own features were being scrutinised.

'Perhaps she sees the creation as an honour,' I said lightly.

'Perhaps it is Cleopatra who should see it that way,' he rejoined.

'I'm sure she does.'

'Caesar believes her to be Venus in the realm of men.'

'And you do not?' I asked.

He shrugged. 'I think that if the gods walked among us so freely, then they would bless those more in need of fortune.'

'You do not think the Pharaoh of Egypt requires fortune?'

'From what I hear she has enough.' There was a smile in his voice that blunted the insult in his words.

'The gods choose their vessels, do they not?'

'Yes.' The man laughed, a cheerful sound that brought an involuntary grin to my face. 'It may be envy that twists my tongue. Caesar has yet to erect a statue of me.'

'And who are you to be worthy of such a boon?' My curiosity tugged on his gaze and he looked at me. For the first time I could see him in his entirety.

The man's face was leaner than I'd expected, being set upon such a broad body. He was pretty more than he was handsome – a countenance made for oil paintings.

As he turned to me, I could tell from his gait that he was a soldier, if the sword by his waist was not enough of a clue.

'Marcus Antonius,' he said.

I recalled the name. He had been Caesar's second in command during the Battle of Pharsalus, which saw Pompey's army sacked.

'And priestess, what shall I call you?'

I looked down at myself, realising he believed me to be an acolyte of Venus. Without my robe and crown, the simple underdress I wore could easily have been mistaken for the robes of a priestess.

'You may call me Selene.' I waited for the moment when he would recognise my face in Venus's, but he did not see me for the queen I was. That was perhaps the most precious thing about Antonius; I was Selene to him before I was Cleopatra. The name was false, but the person who bore it was not. Cleopatra was a Ptolemy, a queen. She was Egypt. Selene was just a woman.

Antonius turned back to the statue.

'You must forgive me, Selene. A tribute such as this is to be envied. To live in gold and bronze once your soul has departed this world is an immeasurable gift.'

Back then I believed as he did. I had already been deified by my people, and this statue would go on to immortalise my divinity so future generations would know of it.

But now I think of Venus de Milo, whose marble stare has lasted millennia; limbs shorn from her body, earlobes lost beneath earth and stone. Time has taken its tithe, as has the memory of the people. Who was the woman who captured Alexandros of Antioch's heart? Was she loved, like Caesar loved me? Aphrodite, they call her – but I know that is not her name. Is it better to be forgotten, or remembered with ill repute, my spirit ignored by men as inconsequential?

I am glad that gold statue was lost in the centuries that separate the woman I was then – yearning for idolisation – and the one I have come to be.

'I would have a thousand statues carved in my name if Caesar would only will it,' the man continued. He spoke as though the conversation was concluding, but I was not ready for him to leave. There was something about this man that made me want to know the whole of him.

'What god would you honour if you were in the Queen's place?' I asked.

'I should imagine my likeness is best captured in the god Mars.'

I was taken aback. I knew very little about the man in front of me, but he did not conjure the bloodthirsty god of war.

He must have sensed my surprise.

'You think not?' he said, raising a brow.

'I do not mean to presume, but your aspect does not align with what I know of that deity.'

'Tell me then, Selene, fair of moonlight, who am I?'

I looked him up and down, scrutinising him like he had my statue. His blue eyes danced with a hint of mischief. Despite the rigidity of his stance, he held his arms clasped behind his back, opening up his chest as if ready to embrace at a moment's notice. He hummed softly as he awaited my answer, as though keeping time with music only he could hear. I imagined he was a capable dancer, and if not, that he'd still enjoy the rhythm of it, spinning with abandon.

Bes, I thought – god of pleasure. But I did not want to give away my true nature by invoking the Egyptian god, so I called on a deity he would more readily know.

'Dionysus.'

The lopsided grin he gifted me was a treasure I went on to think of often. 'It is good that I enjoy wine.'

I shot him back a carefree smile.

Selene is freer with her emotions than I am as Queen.

I always found it hard to show joy as Pharaoh. As a child my father had consistently encouraged me to shine my teeth on the citizens: *A smile for them is a boon they will forever remember.*

I had grimaced.

'Not like that,' he had laughed. 'You look pained. Do you not enjoy yourself?'

I couldn't say no. If I'd said no then I'd have had to admit that I did not like the eyes of the court on me, and therefore did not want to be Queen.

I no longer feared being Queen, but I still had not grown used to the scrutiny of the court.

'Dionysus,' Marcus repeated. 'Thank you, Selene, you have brightened a rather dull evening.'

'You do not enjoy the festivities?'

He frowned, which hardened the lines of his face. 'I admit, I am a superstitious man. I do not believe in celebrating a victory when those who cheer for you do not all sing true.'

It was the first hint I had of the discord that was to come.

'What do you mean?'

He shook his head. 'Nothing. I have indulged in too much wine. Perhaps you are right and Dionysus has made me his vessel.'

'Eat some of the mint,' I said, pointing to the scented bowls.

His eyes narrowed on mine. 'And why would I do that?'

Embarrassment heated my cheeks. It was rare that someone could make me feel so unsettled so quickly. 'It will soothe your stomach,' I said.

He picked up a sprig, trusting me completely on such a short acquaintance. It would be his downfall one day.

'And drink water,' I said. 'It will flush your organs.'

'I did not know that priestesses of Venus were so versed in healing.'

There was no need to contradict him, for at that moment footsteps approached us. Antonius saw him first.

'Caesar.' He inclined his head and raised his right hand, his fingers extended in salute. But Caesar did not have eyes for him.

'Cleopatra, you have found my second surprise before I could present it to you.'

I turned, frustrated that my deception was revealed. I had so enjoyed being Selene for a slip of the night.

'Cleopatra?' Antonius mouthed in horror, but I ignored him.

'I went to get some fresh air and my footsteps brought me to Venus's temple.'

'She beckoned you to this sacred place. I have told you, she is bound to your soul.' He reached for my hands, enveloping them in his. 'As am I.'

Antonius must have made a sound, for Caesar looked to him as if only just seeing him.

'Antonius? What are you doing here?' His tone was sharp.

'I came to admire the statue . . .' Antonius's voice trailed off.

I gave him a bemused glance before answering in his stead. 'Marcus was just informing me of how great an honour it is to be in my presence.'

'An honour for all,' Caesar said, kissing my hand, appeased. 'Now come back to the festivities so I may drink to your health.'

'Allow me to retrieve my crown, Julius, and I will join you shortly.'

Sated by drink himself, Caesar nodded and returned to the hall.

'Pharaoh, I apologise for my crudeness, I did not know to whom I spoke,' Antonius said.

I waved away his concern. 'It was a rare pleasure to be perceived for who I am, not what I am. To be soldier and priestess in a quiet temple.'

'Or a meeting of two gods, Venus and Dionysus.' His eyes were full of mirth.

I met his stare levelly. 'Know me by my true name, then: Isis.'

His smile dropped as I swept out of the temple and back to my crown.

CHAPTER EIGHTEEN
44 BCE

I did not see Antonius again until I returned to Rome two years later. He had been named consul and so he was never far from my husband's side.

It was during the spring's gladiator games that we came face to face once more.

I reclined on a wooden bench beside Caesar as the combat began. Ptolemy and the rest of my retinue sat in rows behind us and Caesarion was cross-legged by my feet. I had protested against such violent entertainment for my son, but Caesar had insisted our presence was required.

'You have not been seen in some time; if Caesarion is to be my heir, then he must be known as Roman,' Caesar had said.

'He is Roman and he is Egyptian. You cannot take one and not the other,' I argued.

'If he is to be both, then let him see the heart of my land. The gladiators will strengthen his pride in our nation.'

And so Caesarion sat with his hands covering his eyes as blood sprayed across the sand.

'Put your hands on your lap,' Caesar snapped.

Caesarion leaned backwards against my shins and whimpered at his father's ire.

Caesar softened immediately and went to pick him up. 'You will find joy in this one day.'

I prayed silently to Isis that he would not.

Caesarion had grown up in my likeness. He was reserved and thoughtful, preferring the company of beasts. 'Why wasn't I born a lion, Mama?' he had asked one day. Bastet and Maahes had grown up by his side and he clutched Maahes' mane as he spoke. They were tamed as well as any wild things could be. That is to say, they never turned their claws on me or my family, but the servants' blood was occasionally shed.

'You were born a lion, my son,' I had replied. 'You are a Ptolemy, and we are all the beasts of Egypt.'

'Even the rats?' he asked.

I laughed. 'Even the rats.'

He didn't smile. 'I just want to be a lion.'

I held him to me and kissed his hair, inhaling the sweet scent of him. 'I'm sorry, but you cannot part with the blood in your veins.' I had wished it too at his age, and seeing this early conflict cross his mind made me ache for the troubles that I knew would be to come.

For Caesarion would be heir to two kingdoms, and the weight of two such mighty crowns could one day come to crush him.

Seeing him now, clutching his father's neck as he turned away from the bloodshed of the arena, I wanted nothing more than to make him a lion.

During a break in the fighting, we were joined by a group of Romans. At first I did not recall Antonius: he now wore his beard longer, and his hair had also grown. The simple soldier's tunic he had worn before had been discarded for more formal robes.

'Who is that?' I asked Charmion.

'Marcus Antonius,' she whispered back. 'He was Caesar's most decorated general before being made consul.'

I smiled as the memory of our meeting returned to me, but I was unsure if he would remember me. My worries were put to rest when he greeted me.

'It is a gift to be well met by the goddess Isis,' he murmured as he bowed.

'Only those chosen by Dionysus would claim it so,' I said.

He laughed. 'It is a pleasure to see you once more, Pharaoh. I have thought of you often.'

'I have not thought of you at all,' I admitted. That only made him laugh harder.

There was a cheer from the crowd as the gladiator thrust his trident through the belly of his opponent, ending the fight. I looked away.

'You do not enjoy the games?' he asked.

'No, I do not take pleasure in blood and slaughter.'

The gladiator who had won the fight approached Caesar at the sidelines. He kneeled in the blood of his victim and said, 'Rex, it is an honour.'

Rex – *king*. I saw some of the members of the senate bristle. Rome was a republic, after all.

'I find myself wondering,' Antonius said, drawing my attention back to him, 'with your aversion to violence, how you ever won the war against your siblings?' His question was disarming, but would have been rude if it had not been asked with such curiosity. Charm was ever Antonius's greatest weapon.

'A war is a war, and this is not that. This is mere sport,' I said stiffly.

'I have offended you.'

'You cannot offend me; you are no one to me.'

'For now,' he murmured.

So sure he was of our future, even back then.

'You are very certain,' I said.

He leaned towards me as though sharing a secret. 'To be dubious is to be dull.'

His eyes flickered to someone behind me and his expression soured. 'I speak of the dull, and here one comes. Have you ever met a Stoic?'

I had, but I would indulge him: I shook my head.

'They live the cardinal virtues: fortitude, temperance, prudence and justice.'

'Virtues you do not espouse?'

Antonius chuckled. 'I am Dionysus, am I not? The very first hedonist. I must hush now, before I offend our new friend.'

I saw the man's shadow before his face. Clouds were gathering in the sky, smoothing the edges of his silhouette.

'Well met, Brutus,' Antonius said.

'Not that I loved Caesar less, but that I loved Rome more.' Indeed, it was him. But as in most things, your plays diverge from the truth. Brutus loved no one but himself.

He was a small fellow whose face could only have belonged to a born noble. The nose was upturned, the lips puckered with rectitude, even his eyes were half-lidded, as though he were loath to use them.

'Pharaoh, consul, a pleasure.'

'Is it?' I said lightly, and Antonius tried to suppress a snort.

Remember that child who ran across the walls of the city with bare feet and no care in the world? Antonius drew her out of me.

Brutus, seemingly unaware of my jibe, continued, 'The gladiators fought well today.'

'Your bets were fruitful, then?' I asked.

'Indeed, you seem quite giddy with delight, you must have made significant sums,' added Antonius.

Brutus looked between Antonius and me, somewhat abashed. 'I do not gamble.'

A sly thought occurred to me and I said, 'Indeed? That is not what I heard.'

He looked startled. 'What is it you've heard?'

'Do not press a woman, let alone a pharaoh, Brutus,' Antonius chastised him.

Brutus bobbed his head. 'Of course – my apologies.'

Antonius and I shared a mirthful glance.

'It is quite all right,' I said, then I whispered conspiratorially. 'I heard one of the other senators say you were seen in the Temple of Dionysius exchanging coins before the first fight.'

Brutus spluttered. 'Who? Who dares lie?'

I waved my hand above my head. 'They were . . . tall.'

'And Roman,' Antonius added helpfully.

'Yes, and Roman,' I said.

Antonius said, 'With hair, I do believe?'

'Certainly not bald,' I agreed.

Brutus had gone red with indignation. He made his apologies and excused himself to seek the source of the rumour.

Antonius and I laughed until tears pricked our eyes.

We saw each other more frequently after that. At Caesar's estate, in the Forum, or at the temple, he seemed a permanent fixture by Caesar's side, and thus mine. His good nature made him hard to dislike and I soon found myself enjoying his company.

'Did you enjoy the theatre?' he asked one night, as we walked through the city after an evening's entertainment. Caesar did not enjoy travelling by litter and so I indulged him his eccentricities and walked through the city.

I did not often travel by foot, having found it hard to forget the hakawati's attempt on my life. The ivory blade still adorned my neck.

'I prefer Sophocles' *Antigone* to *Ajax*, though this rendition was well presented.'

Antonius smiled. 'I have not seen *Antigone*, so cannot comment, but I liked the lyre.'

'The lyre was beautifully played,' I agreed.

Our interests were so different I often wondered how we had much to talk on. But talk we did, of all things vast and small.

'Fulvia would have loved tonight, but she has been unwell.'

Fulvia was his wife. I had met her occasionally at feasts and at the temple, but I did not go out of my way to engage with her. She seemed pleasant enough and was, I was told, extremely learned, but neither of us had the motivation to seek out the other. We were too alike – more so than I knew at the time.*

'Shall I visit her with my medicines tomorrow?' I asked.

Antonius dipped his head. 'That would be gracious.'

Many years later I asked Antonius if he had loved Fulvia and a darkness crossed his features.

'No, but I loved her late husband and I had promised him that I would protect her should he die.' Gaius Scribonius Curio had been his name. 'He was to me what Charmion is to you.'

I understood then how deep his grief must have been to lose such a part of himself. And I understood, too, how impossible it would be to dissolve his marriage to her.

I never went to Fulvia's bedside; her malady slipped my mind the following day. I wonder, if I had, would she feature more in my tale? Just like Calpurnia's, her absence here is born only of my ignorance, for I knew so little of her.

I understand the irony. For I know how it feels to have your life reduced to actions and assumptions.

As we crossed the main market square, crowds began to gather. Cries of 'Rex!' rang out as Caesar passed. A young girl slipped past the legs of the guards surrounding us and made it to Caesar, a laurel wreath in her hand. Caesar dropped to one knee and bent his head, letting the girl bestow him with the leaf crown.

Oh, my heart, if only you had seen what fate lay ahead of you. Your reputation had built you a throne that the senate was never going to let you sit upon. But in that moment, I saw nothing but a sweet exchange between a child and a king.

---

* Fulvia's ambition was great enough to capture Plutarch's attention – one of the few women who did – for it was he who said of her intentions that she 'wished to rule a ruler and command a commander'. Though I imagine that, like me, she simply wished to rule, and command. We have never needed men.

There was a clap of thunder above us, and in the next breath, rain began to fall from the sky in great sheets. The procession stopped and servants dashed around to erect an awning.

'Praise Isis, the rains have come,' I said, the sweetness of the rainwater touching my tongue as I spoke. I tipped my head back to enjoy the feeling of the water striking my skin.

'Cleopatra, come under the shelter,' Charmion called. She tried to pull me towards her, but I resisted.

'Let me savour it a moment.' The rain was such a precious thing; even though we weren't in Egypt, I wanted to enjoy it.

It was not long before I was drenched, my hair and garments laden with rainwater.

Caesar called to me from beneath the awning, his expression heavy with disapproval, though Antonius watched me in wonder.

'Mama!' Caesarion ran to me, laughing, and I picked him up and twirled him around in the puddles.

There was a splash next to me and I turned to find Antonius standing in a puddle of his own. He tilted his head to the storm-darkened sky, then looked at me. I raised a questioning brow to him.

'I wanted to feel what you felt,' he replied.

When the rain shower passed, Caesar came to me, wrapping his arms around me to bring me warmth.

'I will wet your clothes,' I protested.

'It is a small price to pay to be close to you,' he said, giving me one of his rare smiles.

Antonius's love came to be like the sun: passionate and intense. Caesar's was always like the rain, exhilarating and pure.

And as if I were a flower in bloom, both sustained me.

I knew the day that Caesar would die. It was not intuition, but my brother's gift that warned me.

I had heard some of what was occurring in the senate through Caesar. To his enemies he had shown too much mercy – Brutus and Cassius had long since been pardoned for their part in the Battle of Pharsalus, and were left to sow dissent.

Their whispers had increased in volume, creating a divide between those who thought Caesar had too much power, and those who believed he did not have enough.

I was used to court hearsay; I knew its melody intimately. I knew, too, how easily it could become a war song.

But we were both blind to the severity of it.

It was just after dawn and Ptolemy and I were seated in the courtyard of Caesar's estate, enjoying a warm cup of fresh goat's milk.

Caesar strode towards me from the stables, where his horse was saddled and ready to leave. 'I'll return after noon,' Caesar said, bending down to kiss me. Our lips touched briefly. Too briefly for it to be the last time.

Caesarion appeared bleary-eyed in the doorway behind us, Charmion in his wake. He smiled when he saw Caesar in his purple robes. He'd asked more than once to have some made for him and Caesar had promised, 'One day'.

But that day would not come.

'Papa,' he said, tottering across the courtyard to his father with his arms extended.

Caesar stooped low and pressed his hand on Caesarion's heart. 'My son, I'll return to you soon.'

As Caesar mounted his horse, Ptolemy gasped beside me. I turned to him.

'What is it?'

My brother's eyes were glazed, his mind absent entirely.

'Ptolemy?'

When he didn't respond, I threw my cup of milk across his face, hoping to rouse him from his stupor.

He blinked the milk away from his eyes, coming to. I had seen this expression only rarely on my brother's face and it filled me with dread.

Beware the Ides of March.

But there was no soothsayer who prophesised Caesar's death – only my brother. Like mine, Caesar's myth has burgeoned over time. Though that is where the similarities end – he was the martyred hero. And I, the siren who ensnared him.

I gripped Ptolemy's wrist. 'Who?' I asked him, my heart pounding in my throat. *Bah-dum, bah-dum, bah-dum.* A battle drum against the Fates.

Ptolemy turned to me, the milk on his face stark against the flush that rose in his cheeks. 'Caesar.'

My fear turned to anger. I hated my brother in that moment. 'Why do you speak such horror?' I snapped.

'My god Anubis,' Ptolemy said miserably. 'He has confirmed it.'

I shook my head, refusing to believe him. *Not wanting* to believe him. After all, he had been wrong before when Theos had died.

But Theos did not die that day, he merely sank, my thoughts argued back.

I turned to where I had last seen Caesar. Dust and debris were yet to settle from the cantering of his horse. I began to run.

I knew he would not hear me, but I called to him anyway. 'Julius! Come back!'

He was a speck on the horizon.

What was I to say if he did turn around? Would I have been able to stop him going to the senate? I think not. But still the guilt of that day has burrowed deep and has become as much a part of me as the ventricles in my heart.

I only stopped running when I reached the gates of his estate. Caesarion, thinking it a game, came laughing from behind me.

'Mama?' His glee turned to concern. 'Why are you crying?'

I picked him up, though he protested, and pressed my wet cheek to his.

'I hoped to catch up to your father.'

'Why?' The curiosity of children can never be matched.

I smoothed a curl from Caesarion's forehead and made the decision to deny Ptolemy's prophecy. To accept it was to despair and that would only frighten Caesarion. 'I miss your father, that is all.'

And I would never stop missing him.

CHAPTER NINETEEN
44 BCE

AN INTERLUDE

THE IDES OF MARCH

I was not there, so I cannot tell you how he died. Let your historians speak on how my heart was torn from my body that day.

'He was slain by his enemies . . . either from jealousy of his fortune and power, now grown to enormous proportions, or, as they themselves alleged, from a desire to restore the republic of their fathers; for they feared (and in this they knew their man) that if he should conquer these nations also he would indeed be indisputably king.' – APPIAN

'It had been decided by them to make the attempt in the senate, for they thought that there Caesar would least expect to be harmed in any way and would thus fall an easier victim, while they would find a safe opportunity by having swords instead of documents brought into the chamber in boxes, and the rest, being unarmed, would not be able to offer any resistance.' – DIO

'As he took his seat, the conspirators gathered about him as if to pay their respects, and straight away Tillius Cimber, who had assumed the lead, came nearer as though to ask something; and when Caesar with a gesture put him off to another time, Cimber caught his toga by both shoulders; then as Caesar cried, 'Why, this is violence!' one of the Cascas stabbed him from one side just below the throat. Caesar caught Casca's arm and ran it through with his stylus, but as he tried to leap to his feet, he was stopped by another wound.' – SUETONIUS

'So the affair began, and those who were not privy to the plot were filled with consternation and horror at what was going on; they dared not fly, nor go to Caesar's help, nay, nor even utter a word. But those who had prepared themselves for the murder bared each of them his dagger, and Caesar, hemmed in on all sides, whichever way he turned confronting blows of weapons aimed at his face and eyes, driven hither and thither like a wild beast, was entangled in the hands of all; for all had to take part in the sacrifice and taste of the slaughter.' – PLUTARCH

'The body of Caesar lay just where it fell, ignominiously stained with blood – a man who had advanced westward as far as Britain and the ocean, and who had intended to advance eastward against the realms of the Parthians and Indians, so that, with them also subdued, an empire of all land and sea might be brought under the power of a single head. There he lay, no one daring to remain to remove the body.' – NICOLAUS

PART THREE
THE VILLAIN

'Fatale monstrum' ['The fatal monster' or 'This monster sent by fate' – I mind not either, both blades draw blood]
HORACE, *Odes*

'Cleopatra . . . the disgrace of Egypt, the fatal Erinnys of Latium, unchaste, to the undoing of Rome'
LUCAN, *Pharsalia*

'Who does not know of the custom of the Egyptians? Their minds are infected with depraved delusions'
CICERO, *On the Nature of the Gods**

---

* Remember my brief dalliance with Cicero at Caesar's banquet? He had much to say of me and my country in the years to come. Is it any wonder I was made out to be the Hydra of history, when they saw my customs from such a height? Egyptians were the soil underfoot: sinful and uncouth. So, I became the dirt beneath their nails. No matter how much they sought to be rid of me, I sullied the great Roman men.

CHAPTER TWENTY
44 BCE

aesar once told me he had faced death so many times that it had become a friend to him.

'When she comes for me, I will know her face and kiss her lips like a lover.'

The Death of whom he spoke was the only woman whose tryst with Caesar could ever elicit my jealousy. For she would have him forever, when I would have him for just a few short years.

'The first time I met Death, I was twenty-five years old,' he said. He had been captured by a band of pirates near Pharmacusa.

'I was journeying to Rhodes to study oratory at the feet of Apollonius Molo when they ransacked my ship. They held a blade to my throat and I felt the fingers of Death tighten around my soul.'

'Were you scared?' I asked.

We were lounging in the gardens, my back against Caesar's chest. I felt his laugh in my ribcage.

'Of course I was. I had been in peril so rarely. Had I been alone, know that I would have soiled my garments.'

'You would not!'

'No,' he admitted, 'probably not, but know that I feared for my life.'

'How did you get free?'

'I told them who I was. Even then, I had made a name for myself. They ransomed me twenty talents.'

'Is that all?' I spoke in jest, but he took my words to heart.

'I told them to ransom me fifty at least.'

Bartering with pirates with a knife at his throat. That was the man Caesar was. He knew his worth, and the world was a poorer place without him in it.

It was Antonius who told me of Caesar's fate. He said not a word, but I could read it on his face. His skin was wan, his eyes wild like those of the horse he had cantered in on.

Ptolemy's prophecy had come to pass.

The sun lost all its warmth and I began to shiver.

'No,' I said as Antonius slipped from the sweat-covered beast and approached me.

'Pharaoh . . .' His voice was a shattered thing, barely a rasp.

'No,' I said again. 'Do not say it.'

But I knew it in my heart: Caesar had passed to the next realm.

Charmion looked between us, concern weaving her brows together.

'He is gone, Cleopatra.' It was the first time he called me by my name, and not 'Isis' or 'Pharaoh'. I remember it starkly, for I focused on the shape it made of his mouth – anything to stop thinking on what he was saying. 'Killed by conspirators fearful of his power.'

'Julius . . .' I heard a moan escape from low in my throat, like the sound of a deer struck by an arrow.

'Mama!' I turned. Caesarion held a stick larger than his small body. He thrust it forward as if lunging with a trident. 'I'm a gladiator. Can I show Papa?'

My knees struck the ground and I began to sob. Charmion wrapped her arms around my waist but I shrugged her off.

'Take Caesarion away, take him away!' I said. I did not want my son to see me so broken, laid so low.

The cloudless sky pressed upon my back.

How will I ever stand again?

I would have lain there forever; let the worms eat my flesh, and the soil take my waters. Let grass push through my skin, and roots bind my bones.

But Antonius was there, his rough hands picking me up. He cradled me against his chest like a babe, and I let him.

'Show me the way to her chambers?' I heard him ask as if from a vast distance. I was inconsolable, my tears and my breath one and the same.

I felt softness beneath me, but I was overcome with paralysis.

Had I closed my eyes, or were they too swollen to open?

I do not know how much time passed before I eventually fell asleep.

I woke with Caesarion in my arms, my nose pressed to his neck. He smelled of Caesar.

'He would not sleep in his rooms; I did not think you would mind.'

I looked into Charmion's eyes, which reflected the candlelight. 'Tell me it was all a nightmare,' I whispered, pulling Caesarion closer.

'It was not,' she said gently. 'I am so sorry.'

She came to me and kissed my forehead. But even she could not soothe my grief.

'How long was I asleep?'

'Half a day.'

'Marcus?'

'He paces the hallways beyond. He has more to tell you.'

'Send for him,' I said.

I did not rise from the bed, I did not arrange my hair. I simply lay there, my hair undone, my kohl smudged from the tears. It was not a great distance from the woman he had first met.

'Pharaoh.' He bowed low upon entering. 'I am sorry to add further to your burden, but I have seen Caesar's will.' He hesitated, his gaze going to the sleeping Caesarion.

'Yes?'

'He did not claim your son as his heir. His great-nephew Octavian has been named.'

I have wondered countless times since whether Caesar knew what he had done. Whether poor administration was to blame, or shrewd politics.

Had he known the war that was to come, would he have done the same?

'Impossible,' I said, too loudly. Caesarion stirred. I laid a hand on his heart, like his father had done just that morning, and he settled again.

'It is true,' Antonius said. 'The senate is in turmoil and I cannot guarantee your safety. Your son may be seen as a threat to succession, and I know not who to trust.'

'We must leave Rome,' I surmised.

'Immediately.'

I looked to Charmion and nodded once. She hurried from the room to begin the preparations.

'Why did you not save him?' I asked.

Antonius clenched the hilt of his sword, his knuckles going white. 'They lured me away from the senate. If I had been there, I would have fought Caesar's foes with blade and fist.'

'By your reckoning, they were many?'

He grimaced. 'More than there should have been.'

I closed my eyes as tears seeped down my face. 'How could this have happened?'

Antonius's reply was full of anguish. 'I do not know.'

Caesarion awoke from his nap and upon seeing my tears began to cry too. The sound appeared to torture Antonius.

'Go,' I said to him.

'Pharaoh, please make haste. You have already stayed too long. It would pain me to see you hurt, and I cannot be here to protect you.'

'Not that having you near helped my husband,' I said, and he flinched as if struck.

'I am sorry,' he said, bowing his head and retreating.

Caesarion clutched my hand and I looked down at the little fingers in my palm. Within them he held so many of mine and

Caesar's hopes for the future. I was never ambitious in the way Arsinoe was. I ruled in service to Egypt – who, like the gods above, bound me beyond obligation. Egypt was my keeper, as I was hers, and I could not deny my son the same privilege. A Roman and an Egyptian. A king of two realms.

'He will rule better than both of us,' Caesar had foretold.

Then why did you omit him from your will, Julius?

Grief fortified my resolve. 'I won't give up, you know,' I called after Antonius, who looked back at me as he reached the doorway. I continued, 'Caesarion is the heir of Julius and I will not let history forget it.'

Antonius nodded once. 'Fear not – no son of Caesar will be lost to time.'

And then he left me to my grief.

The next morning we left Caesar's estate for the last time. As we made our way across the city to the harbour, we passed another litter – a rarity so early in the morning.

The two transits crossed paths and I peered into the window of the other.

The woman inside was veiled, but she parted the silk to look at me as we passed. Time stood still as I looked into the red-rimmed eyes of Calpurnia.

Caesar's wife and I had orbited each other but had never met. She resided in a different villa on the opposite side of the city. I thought little of her, and I presume she thought little of me.

History will claim we hated each other, envied one another. But in that moment I saw nothing beyond a woman hurting. A kindred spirit.

She nodded to me, and I to her. That simple gesture lifted the haze of grief and I could see more clearly.

I thought of her often after that. It comforted me to know someone else had loved him, treasured him, as I had.

*

The journey back to Egypt was dire. I was afflicted by seasickness from the violence of the storms that plagued us, and no amount of mint could subdue it. Heartbreak also stole my sleep, and by the time we reached the shores of Egypt, I was a mere outline of my former self.

I became short-tempered with everyone, but with Ptolemy most of all.

Where grief had made a shadow of me, guilt had claimed my brother.

I cannot fathom the burden of knowing a death before it happens. I never asked Ptolemy how many times it had happened to him. I had only witnessed it rarely, and even then, only cared if it affected those I knew.

But in my current condition I was not able to empathise. Instead, I chose to deepen his guilt by focusing on the flaws in his gift.

'What use is your power that it is so weak as not to warn you in the days prior? Does your god not favour you as he should?' I said to him, my mouth twisted in frustration. I had been drinking Roman wine, as it had proved to be the only way sleep found me.

'My gift does not work like that, sister,' he replied, like he had every other time I'd sought to apply blame. Though my brother was now fifteen, I found I still barely knew him. After Theos's death I had put distance between us, rarely engaging him outside of formal requirements.

'What use is your gift, then?' I stood, swaying a little as I left the dining table.

I found myself in my rooms shortly after.

'Cleo, would you like to say goodnight to Caesarion?' Charmion asked by the door.

I shook my head. In the last few weeks, I had found it too difficult to look into Caesarion's eyes. They resembled Caesar's.

And so the days dragged on. I never resumed going to the

hospital to help heal the sick and I never left the palace, my grief the only company I desired.

'Sister?' Ptolemy called out. I was lounging on my balcony, a bottle of palm wine on a table next to me, despite it being early morning.

'What is it?' I laid bare my resentment towards him in every look, in every word.

'I have a headache – might you have a remedy?'

I did not get up from my seat; instead I pointed to my medicine bag, which had remained untouched for some time.

'Brew some willow bark in hot water,' I said, my words slurring slightly.

I heard him rummage in the vials and jars of medicines before retreating. I closed my eyes and thought of him no more.

'Cleo, Cleo, wake up.' Charmion was shaking me awake.

'What is it?' I said groggily, but my mind cleared as I read the horror in her face.

'It's Ptolemy,' she said, her voice clotted with unshed tears.

I gathered up my skirts and strode through the palace until I reached Ptolemy's chamber. He lay slumped across his bed, the shattered pottery of a broken cup on the floor.

I checked his chest for breath, but there was none.

'What happened?' I spoke with numb lips.

It was one of his servants who answered. 'He asked me for hot water, Pharaoh, to mix with some herbs. When I returned to collect the finished cup, he was gone.' The servant quivered, holding in the sobs that threatened to overcome him.

I recognised the jar of herbs set on the table beside his bed. My mouth went dry when I saw what I had written on the label.

'Wolfsbane.'

Poison.

My stomach lurched and I turned away from the body of my brother. Bile rose up in my throat. Servants attempted to catch the vomit but it was too late. It splashed across the tiles, coating my feet in sour wine.

'He came to me and asked for a cure for his headache,' I said.

Like Theos before him, there had been no deep love between us, but he had still been of my blood. And I of his. I felt his death like a spear to my guts, deep enough to cause irrevocable damage.

There would be no healing from this.

I was destined to see each of my siblings suffer in turn. Ptolemy was just a boy, not many years old than Caesarion. The thought made my stomach heave again, but there was nothing left.

'I am empty,' I said, not really knowing what I referred to. For I was hollowed of all.

I had endured many things during my life, but Ptolemy's death pushed me beyond my limits. Death courted me time and time again, but I was an unwilling consort.

The mark on my neck prickled, reminding me of my patron goddess.

Why do you neglect me so?

'Call the priests to prepare his body,' I said quietly, before I left the room.

I cannot tell you if Ptolemy intended to die this day. Perhaps he had awoken that morning by his god's voice calling to him – beckoning him to his kingdom. Or did he go ignorantly to Anubis's side?

I tortured myself for many years that I had said 'wolfsbane' instead of 'willow bark' that fateful day. The other likelihood is that he misheard me and reached for the poison.

Or perhaps the most horrific scenario of all: my treatment of Ptolemy had driven him to seek the beyond.

But wherever the path began, the destination was the same.

My brother was dead, and I reigned alone once more.

CHAPTER TWENTY-ONE
42 BCE

I was much changed after the loss of Ptolemy. Where Caesar's death had broken me, Ptolemy's had tainted me with regret. Guilt motivated me, where misery had not. So I put down the wine and picked up my medicine bag once again.

My citizens were glad to see me return. And as the bright red pain of grief dulled to an incessant ache over the next two years, I spent more and more time in the hospital – healing others to comfort myself.

I heard from Antonius sporadically. His campaign, alongside Caesar's false heir Octavian, to capture the leaders of Caesar's assassination, had found him engaged in war once more. I followed his pursuits with little interest.

You may question why I was not yearning for vengeance. I was. The fire of my anger burned like hot coals, never going out. But I was also practical. If Antonius and Octavian were to be victorious, then Caesar's assassins would be killed and perhaps the heat behind my eyes would cool. However, if Cassius and Brutus dispatched Octavian, then Caesarion's claim as Caesar's heir would be undisputed.

My son would no longer be a threat and his feet could once more walk upon Roman soil.

'Another letter from Antonius,' Faunus said. We sat in one of the smaller staterooms. I had all but abandoned the throne room, reserving it only for formal occasions, my taste for opulence waning. I was well enough established as a monarch that I did not need to prove my wealth or status.

It also pained me to paint myself as I had done for Caesar. I was no longer Venus, and I was no longer sure who Cleopatra was.

'She is Egypt,' Antonius said when I voiced my inner doubts in the early days of our courtship.

'I am not sure if Egypt died with Caesar,' I admitted.

Antonius rested his hand on my breast and felt the rhythm of my heart. 'Let yourself live, Egypt. Live.'

With these words he reinstated some of the pride I had lost. But we are not there yet in my tale: first I must be cast adrift.

'What says the letter from Antonius?' I said. I was at my desk, reading a recent addition to the new Library of Alexandria: *On Pulses* by Herophilus.

'He requests the return of the four Roman legions stationed here, for his fight against Cassius and Brutus.'

I waved a hand in the administrator's direction. 'Send them. This quest for vengeance is his battle to win. If he requires my help, I shall provide it.'

Faunus nodded. 'I will send them with Commander Serapion.'

I had kept the governor close since his attempt to reveal my lack of divinity all those years ago. I had never voiced my suspicions that he was a sympathiser of Arsinoe's. And though I knew my sister was exiled, I still watched him warily, despite his having shown me nothing but loyalty since that ill-fated day. Over time I rewarded him with the Cypriote fleet to foster his ignorance of my mistrust, but it was also to leash him closer to my court.

I did not think much about Serapion or Antonius for some time after that. Caesarion kept me busy. At five years old he had proved himself to be the perfect blend of me and Caesar. He could already speak in Latin, Greek and Egyptian, and Charmion was teaching him Arabic. When he wasn't enjoying his studies, he was with his gelding, learning to master a chariot.

I found pleasure in seeing the wind tousle his curls as he turned around the paddock. Every time he practised, I would have my desk brought to the stables' edge to watch him as I worked. The tunic he wore ended just above the ink mark of Horus on his thigh. His small body was strapped into the chariot's frame, for I was cautious of his safety. I could not lose another love.

Still less another king.

Caesarion had been crowned as co-regent shortly after Ptolemy's death. I wanted to quickly secure him as Pharaoh as he had already been stripped of his rights as Caesar's heir.

'What troubles you?' Charmion, ever perceptive, asked. She took my pen from my hand and refilled its ink.

Papyrus pages lay fanned out in front of me. I had resumed my writings earlier that year, finding pleasure once more in sharing my remedies with the world. It was one of the ways I satisfied my curiosity with academia. I still courted the ghost of Cleopatra the scholar on quiet evenings, wondering what life would have been like without the crown. Instead, I held both wherever I could: crown and pen.

That my work did not survive into modernity vexes me more than I can express. I have seen how even fragments of poems penned by men have kept their lyrics through the centuries. Not only did my words disappear, but the very melody of them was distorted, leaving the barest of echoes. My science was reduced to love potions and aphrodisiacs, and I found myself once again debased by my sex.[*]

Charmion handed me back my pen but I waved it away. My thoughts were too troubled to continue. I watched Caesarion

---

[*] Although, I will have it known that not all historians degraded me so. The renowned traveller Al-Masudi of Baghdad, whose writings I have always favoured, wrote eloquently of my skills as a scholar and a sage. It is a reminder that not all roads lead to Rome. Let it not be the centre of your history, for propaganda is a tool favoured by the West.

smile as his teacher corrected his grip on the reins. 'He is entitled to *more* than just Egypt.'

'You cannot give him everything,' she said.

'Indeed I cannot; he has already lost his father,' I snapped.

I looked away from Caesarion before I fell once more into the chasm of my own grief. It had already taken me so very long to climb out. 'I seek simply to give him what he is due,' I said, more gently.

'Octavian is still supported by Rome?' Charmion asked.

'And Marcus,' I said. I felt great bitterness over this: I had thought our friendship and his fealty to Caesar would see him hold true to my son's legacy.

'And Caesar's assassins?'

'Will soon be dead. The battle commences in Philippi. I have sent troops with Serapion to aid the cause.'

'It will be a relief to see Caesar's killers brought to justice.'

Caesarion screamed and I jolted, ready to run to him. I saw his body bloodied and broken in my mind's eye before I focused and saw that he was only laughing, his gelding nibbling his hand.

I released a slow breath. 'There will be no relief. So many others had a hand in Julius's death. They may not all have held the knife, but their ignorance of the plot eased the blade's path.'

Charmion reached for my hand and squeezed it. 'Justice will be dealt, in this life or the next.'

Comforted by her touch, I brought our joined hands up to my lips. 'I never thanked you, Charmion.'

'For what?'

'For being by my side during these last few years. It has not always been easy, but having you with me has eased some of my torment.'

With her free hand she pressed three fingers to the pulse at my neck. Then she invoked our childhood mantra: 'One for the past and the happy years well spent, one for the present and the patience we extend, one for the future and the love that never ends.'

I laughed, and realised that it had been some time since my face had stretched the muscles of a smile.

It did not last long.

'Pharaoh!' Faunus was running across the paddock, clutching a scroll, his bare feet kicking up dust and his eyes wide.

'What is it?' I did not rise to his panic, as everyone I loved was in my sights.

'Serapion,' he said as he reached us. 'He has taken the legions we sent to Antonius, to aid his enemy.'

'You mean to say that Cassius and Brutus are to benefit from my fleet?'

'Yes – Serapion has abandoned your orders.'

It had been a risk sending him, I knew this. But this betrayal was greater than even I might have anticipated.

I thought back to Arsinoe and the bloodied footprints she had left as she had walked down the temple steps in Rome. I had hoped that was the last I would see of her. But now I think of it as a warning I did not heed.

She walked through my life still, sullying it.

But how would I ever prove it was her?

I felt a surge of fury. 'Go to his estate and bring me his family in chains,' I said. 'For every day he refuses my summons I will remove a finger from his children's hands.'

Charmion gasped.

'Is it necessary to be so cruel?' she asked. She rarely spoke out against my orders so brazenly: if she had any issue with a ruling, we would discuss it in the solitude of my chambers, so as not to undermine me in public.

For this reason I considered her words carefully, because I knew she thought them significant.

'Strength can often be mistaken for cruelty,' I said eventually.

I didn't recall at the time that I was echoing Arsinoe's words from all those years earlier. Back then, I had thought her immaturity made her merciless. But now the years had brought me wisdom. There were no boons for mercy, no blessings from the gods for my morality.

Sometime between cutting down my lions and Ptolemy's death I had begun to use cruelty as a tool – and remorse became more fleeting.

Charmion looked troubled but did not contradict me further, and I was glad of it. I would not have liked to turn my ire on her.

That evening Faunus returned to me in the dining hall, his expression grave.

'His family are gone, my queen, his estate empty.'

I set down my cup, filled with sweetened water only, and kneaded my brow. 'You found nothing?'

He hesitated, then reached into his robes and removed a scroll, which he set before me.

My eyes scanned the letter. It was only a few words long, outlining the location of Cassius's and Brutus's army. That alone was not damning enough.

But then I saw the words that ended the letter.

By order of Queen Arsinoe . . .

I felt no triumph in having my suspicions confirmed. I only felt the fool for loosening the leash around Serapion's neck longer than I should have.

I held the scroll for longer than the words warranted, as eventually Charmion asked impatiently, 'What is it?'

I handed her the scroll. 'My sister rises once more.'

'I have sent word to my contacts in Ephesus,' Faunus said. 'But it does appear she is once again laying claim to your throne.'

I thought of the meal we'd had on the royal barge all those years ago. She and Serapion had been engaged in discussion for most of the night.

What had she said to bind him to her so tightly? What was it about her that secured such absolute loyalty?

She has always been a bird in flight, soaring above the wingless, I conceded. Even now I aspired to be near her, to feel the wind lift me to her heights.

I laughed. Despite everything, I had grudging respect for her determination. 'Only death will defeat her.'

Faunus nodded. 'What will you have me do?'

I had many more warships in my fleet that I could have sent to support Antonius's plight. But I had not forgotten how easily the nobility had abandoned me in the siege of Alexandria and I feared sending any more to sea, lest they flee to Arsinoe's side like Serapion.

'Nothing. We do nothing.'

'But Antonius—'

I thought of how he had left me and Caesarion by aiding the false heir, Octavian, and I cut Faunus off. 'I care not for him.'

Oh, how that would change.

Antonius and Octavian were victorious later that year. Cassius and Brutus had been slaughtered, along with Serapion. Any arrangements the conspirators had made with Arsinoe were lost in their defeat.

The night after I received word, I woke up drenched in sweat, my eyes stinging, my mind haunted by the remnants of a nightmare: Cassius and Brutus had captured Caesar's soul in the afterlife, binding him to a cage in the field of reeds. I could look upon the scene but not infiltrate it, no matter how much I screamed or beat at my chest.

My throat was raw, a great heaviness in my lungs.

'Cleo?' Charmion said drowsily.

'I am fine, sleep now.'

She nodded and pulled Caesarion tighter into her embrace. Since Caesar's death we had all shared a bed, a routine I was loath to change. Usually it kept my terrors at bay, but not this night.

I rose and padded through my room, wrapping a robe around me. The moon hung a half-smile in the sky and the air was cool for the time of year.

I slipped through the palace like a shadow, clinging to the walls; not to disguise myself, for I rarely hid any more, but to remain undisturbed. Despite the late hour, servants moved in and out of the many rooms, cleaning and preparing the palace for the following day.

The wind cooled the sweat on my body as I made my way through the gardens. The jasmine was in full bloom, its sweetness coating my tongue as I walked towards the temple district.

My temple to Isis had been completed two years prior. A task that should have taken a season to complete had taken six times that. The construction bore the signs of Egypt's troubles.

We had run out of red granite during the siege and so parts of the columns were made from limestone. The pool that I had wanted to fill with floating flowers was dry, the tunnel connecting it to the cistern incomplete. The specialist builder had died during the harbour fire, and I had not found a replacement with sufficient skills to finish it.

Though the temple had flaws, I still found peace within its walls.

I lowered myself in front of the altar and bowed my head.

Over the years I had come to terms with my lack of divine power. But I still never lost faith in my god. I was marked by Isis, and so I was hers completely.

'Isis, I come asking for your help. Please send your husband, Osiris, to watch over Caesar in the afterlife.'

Osiris, in his power, was Lord of Death and king of the realm beyond. Like Isis, he had many faces, with some preferring to call him Dionysus.

I was reminded of Antonius then, and our first meeting – *a meeting of gods*.

Did he lead the triumphs in Rome? Or did Caesar's false heir head the procession?

My heart was not yet his, so I did not yearn for him. Time had healed some of the hurt I had felt when he'd allied with Octavian, allowing me to think of him fondly – a connection to the love I had lost in Caesar.

I remained kneeling before the altar until dawn. When I stood, I felt lighter knowing Caesar's soul was protected by my prayers.

I walked to the harbour, enjoying the mild heat of the morning sun, and looked across the bay.

Theos, do you live beneath the waves still? Are you comforted to know our sister still fights your cause?

An approaching vessel interrupted my reverie. It was smaller than the many warships that had come and gone. I recognised the boat as the type used by Rome to ferry messages and supplies.

It sailed into the palace harbour and I waited patiently as my guards approached the captain, verifying its purpose before allowing the messenger to disembark.

Instead of waiting for the details to filter through the scribes, to Faunus, then to me, I approached the messenger myself.

'Word from Rome?' I asked after the emissary bowed.

'My name is Dellius, Pharaoh. I come on behalf of Marcus Antonius. He requests your presence.'

'Indeed?' I said, making sure my tone implied bemusement. 'And his reason?'

The ambassador looked bewildered by my irreverence. 'All those who supported Caesar's assassins are being brought forward for questioning.'

I cocked my head. 'And how did I support my husband's killers?'

He smirked, and I found that I did not like this Dellius. He wore his arrogance like a fine cloak. 'Serapion,' he said.

'His betrayal was his own. And my sister's, that I will concede. But I did not think Romans held one accountable for the crimes of a sibling.'

Dellius slowly shook his head. 'It is not for me to speak on. I only come as the voice of Marcus Antonius.'

'You have no voice of your own?' I said.

'If I did, I would be sure to blunt it, for my words would be too sharp for your ears.' Dellius spoke sweetly, despite his graceless insult.

'Choice words,' I scoffed. 'Either you lay bare your contempt, or you claim I am too weak to hear it. This is the man Marcus sends to me?'

Dellius seemed to realise he had gone too far. But I was not yet done with my threats.

'Does Marcus wish to incite my wrath?'

'No, Pharaoh,' he said quickly.

'Leave Egypt,' I said. 'Go back to Marcus and tell him I will not answer his call. And the next time he wishes to speak to me he must do so in person, not send someone of such little consequence.' I turned on my heel, leaving Dellius to retreat to his ship with neither refreshments nor use of the baths.

That should have been the end of it. But Antonius was obstinate in his pursuit of an audience with me. My message via Dellius had been received unhappily, and the next time I heard from him it was in his voice alone.

The letter was marked with many smudges and blots of ink, having come directly from his hand and not a scribe's.

Come to Tarsus, Pharaoh. We must discuss Serapion's defection. The senate want answers. And I wish to see you again.

I would not have answered had it not been for the final sentence. I replied in ink of my own:

If you want answers, seek them in the Great Library of Alexandria. Then, while you visit, you may see me in the palace.

I could feel his smile in the answering letter.

It is not books that will satisfy me, but the sound of your voice. And I should cross an ocean for it; but my armies tie me to Tarsus. Come to me.

I was shocked by his blatant flattery.

You pay me compliments, but they are worth no more than the paper you send them on. They will not lure me to Tarsus.

The next letter arrived carved into a tablet of obsidian, and I laughed when I read from it.

Not paper, but something more precious, then. Are my words worth more to you now? Come to Tarsus. The weather is mild, though the wine is milder.

My reply was short:

I enjoy the heat of Egypt's sun.

Though it had been my intention to discourage his attentions, when I did not receive an immediate reply, I found myself growing morose. Our messages had become a game, and I was impatient for his next move.

When the letter did arrive, I was not to be disappointed.

Let my gaze be your sun and you shall bask in it always. Come – the senate grows impatient for the truth, and I impatient for your company.

'Go,' Charmion said.

'Did you say something?' I said, turning to her from the balcony.

'You have read and re-read his letter so many times the papyrus has started to shred. Go to Tarsus.'

I frowned, placing the letter on the table next to me as if I hadn't realised what I was doing. 'He wishes for me to answer for Serapion's crimes.'

'No, he wants to see you. Serapion's crimes are just an excuse.'

I wasn't so sure. Even though I'd had no proof of Serapion's deception over the years, I had still suspected, and that had been enough to make him a liability on the battlefield. The commander had done great damage to Antonius's fleet before he died.

'If you do not pen the letter, then I will,' Charmion threatened.

I surrendered. 'Fine.'

I will come to Tarsus, I wrote. *And there we may put this matter to rest.*

And so I took the first step on the path to my death. But first, let me love once more.

CHAPTER TWENTY-TWO
41 BCE

harmion and I journeyed to Tarsus, leaving Caesarion in Egypt. Though I was reluctant to have him out of my sight, I knew he'd be safer at home.

It was my first time leaving Egypt since I had fled back there from Rome after Caesar's death, and I found myself invigorated by the tour. My clothing and jewellery had been refreshed, a new set of dresses dyed and stitched for the occasion.

'More turquoise?' Charmion had said as we prepared for the voyage.

'Yes. Just a little more, around the collar.'

'It will be too heavy to wear.'

'I seek beauty, not comfort.'

'It is good to see you like this,' she said, once the seamstress had taken the dress away for adjustments.

'Like what?' I knew what she meant, but I wanted to know how it appeared from the outside. For me, I felt apprehensive, as though I was being presented to the court for the first time. I was not old, twenty-eight only, but I had been weary too long.

'You are set alight again,' she said.

Her words brought a smile to my lips, and I pressed it to her scarred cheek, then held her close. 'Yes, though I admit the fire in me is gilded.'

She laughed. 'More jewellery, then?'

'Yes. Marcus calls to me, and he will know what it is to conjure a god.'

We crushed henna leaves and dyed my lips a dark red. We darkened the tips of my fingers, too, before interlacing them with gold chains and rings. I sent for the longest hair in Egypt and had the strands woven into an intricate wig that cascaded to my knees. Each braid was threaded with carnelians and jasper.

There was no part of me that I did not refine. I even had new sandals made from hippopotamus leather, soft and luxurious.

Only when I felt like the god I was did I set sail for Tarsus.

'It is very beautiful here,' Charmion said as we traversed the Cydnus river. Awestruck farmers flocked to the riverbank, watching us pass.

We cut an unusual sight against the lush green landscape. The silver oars of the ship flashed like fish in the shallows. Purple silk, a recent gift from Serica, had been used to adorn the canopies, and they fluttered like petals in the wind. I had made a habit of burning myrrh to remind me of Caesar, and the incense swirled around the boat like wisps of morning mist.

Some of your painters have tried to capture the occasion. But paint is a poor medium for gold and jewels. I have seen the garments and colours they have reimagined, but they have captured less than the essence of how it was.

I was a god, and I looked like one. No canvas can recreate it.

The crowds grew the closer we got to the city. Children ran alongside the ship to try and keep up, their laughter making me pine for Caesarion.

I smiled regally at them from beneath my vulture crown, the gilded wings heavy on my ears. Charmion had been right about the weight of the mantle; it brought a stiffness to my movements, the collar covering my chest and neck entirely.

Finally, we passed through the stone archway that marked the port of Tarsus. The city sprawled out ahead of us. Unlike Alexandria and Rome, Tarsus blended into the landscape rather than dominating it. The buildings were built of stone and white clay from the surrounding fields. And though the city was walled, it felt more open than any other I had been in, and I could see straight through to the heart of it; the square boasted a stone fountain, and the streets around it were lined with palms pregnant with dates.

We moored east of the harbour and I retreated to my chambers, much to the sadness of the cheering crowds.

'Antonius has sent an invitation to dine with him this evening,' Faunus said. He was much aged since we had first met, and I continued to be grateful for his counsel. Of all the things Caesar had gifted me, Faunus's mind was the most valuable.

I demurred with a smile. 'No, he has sought to summon me enough times. Let us ignore him.'

The next day Antonius sent the same command: *Dine with me in the city.*

Again, I refused.

On the third day he brought the invitation himself, but I sequestered myself in my rooms on the boat and did not give him an audience.

My strategy followed Caesar's – if you make them wait, you strip them of power.

I could feel the tension stretching like a bow string between us. It made it difficult to sleep, so on the fifth night in Tarsus, I found myself sitting on the bow of the boat, watching the sun rise.

When I was younger I had detested the dawn, heralding as it did the start of a new day and with it the burden of being the Pharaoh's daughter. Whereas night had been a time of pleasure and play, of exploring my body beneath the sheets and whispering secrets in the dark.

Now I was older, I appreciated the new beginning that dawn brought, and had learned to fear the stillness of night amidst the loudness of my thoughts.

As the golden tones of the morning sun struck the sky, I felt myself relax, my worries and anxieties easing.

The sun's rays glowed pink on the river's surface and I began to outline the view with my finger. A group of ducklings swam past the ship, crying after their mother who had reached the riverbank before them.

A shadow caught my eye: something moving in the shallows. I leaned over the railing to try and catch sight of the fish as it neared the boat.

The creature was large, larger than the trout my soldiers had caught the day before. As it moved towards the surface I flinched as it reached forward and took hold of the lower deck.

For it was no fish, but a man.

I jumped up from my couch, my mouth open to call for my guards. But then the man climbed up and over the railing and I recognised him.

'Marcus?'

I cannot help but smile, even now, as I recollect his appearance. He wore nothing but a loincloth, and he would later tell me this was to ensure he was not pulled under by the weight of his tunic, as he was not a proficient swimmer. River-water gathered in the channels of his muscles and my eyes were drawn to the sheen of the skin there. He had grown leaner in our years apart and was battle-scarred in areas of his body I had never been privy to seeing before.

There were other changes, too; his hair was longer and touched by the warmth of the sun, curling in shades of brown by his ears. He had shaved off his beard, though the shadow of it still remained.

He smiled at me in his unique way, like he was about to reveal the climax of a joke.

'Selene,' he said. The name I had once given him in guise. I looked down at myself and wondered if I were not her. I wore no crown, just my bed robes, and my hair tumbled down my back in fine braids.

I felt vulnerable beneath his stare. 'What are you doing here?'

'You gave me no choice.'

I recovered myself a little, and said, 'You had many choices, and this should not have been one of them.'

'Pharaoh . . .' Seti ran onto the deck, his spear raised.

I held up a hand to stop him advancing. 'If he were a threat, I'd be dead already,' I said dryly. 'Please tell the kitchens to provide refreshments in the north stateroom for me and Marcus Antonius.'

'Marcus Antonius?' the guard repeated, his eyes avoiding Antonius's loincloth.

'Yes, and send for Faunus and the scribes. We have some matters to discuss.'

Antonius's smile dropped briefly.

'Or do you not wish to stay?' I asked him. He had thought to take me unawares, to destabilise me by arriving so abruptly.

He glanced down at his lack of clothing.

'Of course we could meet at your residence for dinner instead?' I said lightly.

His laugh was quick. 'No, I am happy to discuss now, if you are?'

Without responding, I turned and entered the corridors of the boat, stopping only when we arrived at the stateroom. There I sat in the gilded chair I used for formal audiences. Faunus and the scribes had already arrived and were seated on either side of me.

I did not need a crown to prove myself a queen.

I levelled my gaze at Antonius as he followed me in, his footprints leaving wet marks on the wood. There was no chair for him; it was why I had chosen the north stateroom.

'I have granted you an audience, so speak: what do you request of this queen?' I asked.

'Serapion—' he began.

'Serapion was a traitor of Egypt,' I interrupted. 'He was in league with my sister, the outcast Arsinoe.'

Antonius's expression was grave. 'The fact remains he was still a citizen of your country and, by your own reckoning, taking orders from your family. I cannot play favours. The politics of Rome are more tenuous than you think. You must pay the traitor's levy to remain an ally of my nation.'

I scoffed. 'I will not pay your taxes, Marcus. I am no longer an ally of Rome; that ended the day Caesar died.'

Antonius shook his head. 'You cannot mean that, Pharaoh. Ending our partnership will lose you the security of our armies.'

I turned to Faunus. 'Remind me, how many soldiers did Rome lose in the battle against Brutus and Cassius?'

'Twenty thousand, Pharaoh.'

'Twenty thousand,' I repeated. 'I think perhaps it is you who needs *my* armies.'

'We won the war, though,' Antonius said, the merest hint of a snarl on his lips. 'Pharaoh, I urge you to reconsider your stance.'

'If I am an ally, I must pay a fine for the traitor Serapion's indiscretion. If I am not, then my coffers remain untouched. I believe my stance to be the only one possible.'

Antonius looked troubled. 'Octavian—'

I cut him off once more. 'Is all the more reason for Egypt's relationship with Rome to end.'

'He is but a young man, whose fortune was changed in a night. Do not condemn him.'

'Do not underestimate the ambition of youth. I tell you from experience. My brother was fourteen when he laid siege to Alexandria, and my sister seventeen when she began to call herself Queen.'

Antonius smiled, seeming to appreciate my ferocity. 'Yet you overcame them.'

'Not entirely.' Arsinoe was still out there, plotting.

A servant brought in a tray of hibiscus tea, sweetened with honey. Antonius watched me as I brought the drink to my lips. He seemed to be considering his next words.

'Ignore the tax. I will explain Serapion's treachery to the senate. But you must remain an ally.'

'Must I?' I said coolly.

'Yes, you must. For how else can we keep company like this?' He gestured towards both our attires, and I couldn't suppress the laugh he coaxed out of me.

'There must be more benefits.'

He raised one eyebrow in enquiry.

But I did not let his flirtation unmoor me from my purpose. I regarded him levelly. 'Proclaim Caesarion as Caesar's heir, and my armies will be yours.'

All mirth left Antonius's face. 'You know I cannot. Together Octavian and I rule the senate. To oppose his birthright is to declare war.'

'*His* birthright?' I hissed.

Antonius dipped his head as my anger washed over him. When he looked up, his face was full of remorse. 'You know the love I had for Caesar. He called me son. But what you ask of me will bring more death than the toll your administrator reports. I cannot do that in Caesar's name.'

I turned my head before he could see the tears in my eyes. I heard him step forward, and then his hands took mine.

I looked down at our entwined fingers and said, 'You know my guards would execute you for less.'

'Ask me for anything else.'

I looked up, and noticed for the first time that his brown eyes grew moss-green towards the centre. As I looked into them, they stirred something in me that I had thought long dead.

Desire.

Oh, do not mistake me, I had taken many lovers since Caesar's death, but that had been about fulfilment of lust, not need.

Yet there was still something I needed much more.

I hesitated, readying myself for my next words. 'Execute Arsinoe.'

A dagger to the chest would have hurt less. But I knew how powerful a wound could be. It could cut away a limb to stop disease from spreading, or bleed a brain to relieve pressure. Arsinoe was both those things and worse.

'My sister must die,' I continued against the pain. 'She has posed a threat to my reign for long enough. Do this and I will formally declare Egypt an ally of Rome once more.'

Antonius nodded. 'It is done.'

I swallowed my gasp as I felt again the slice of a knife.

'I will send word to Ephesus. She will be dead within five days. But I have one thing to ask in return.'

'Are my armies not enough?'

His thumb caressed the top of my hand idly. 'This is non-negotiable.'

I looked into his grass-flecked eyes once more, my heart fluttering like a bird in my chest.

'Dine with me,' he said simply.

I laughed, slipping my hand from his to wave him away. 'Once you have done as I asked I will dine with you, Marcus.'

His smile returned and he straightened. 'I will send word when my part of the deal is complete. Then, *Selene*, I will take my taxes in wine, good food and very beautiful company.'

He did not linger, and I was grateful as I could feel the heat in my cheeks. I heard afterwards that he was seen striding through the harbour whistling, as though he wore the formal robes of a king.

I did not need Antonius to tell me when Arsinoe died. I was walking along the pier in the harbour, enjoying the morning air, when a flock of ibis flew overhead. A single white feather fell on the cobbled ground in front of me.

I picked it up and I knew.

She was gone.

I imagined her face, defiant until the last, as she was dragged out of the Temple of Artemis. She would not have made a sound as she died, or if she did it would have been to laugh. Antonius had offered to bring me her head but I had refused it. There was no trophy to be won.

I held the feather against my chest and screamed up to the sky, tearing my throat.

Arsinoe, my shadow. Arsinoe, my friend. Though the nights would never be as dark, the day would never be as bright.

Devastation wrecked me, but so too did anger.

'You made me do this, sister!' I shouted through my tears. 'I would have been happy to love you, only. But you had to make me hate you too.'

She and I could not both have lived. She had proven she could out-manipulate me time and time again, so I knew it would be I who would fall if I did not strike first.

But still I mourned the sister I had once loved. And loved still.

I slept that night with the feather clutched in my hand. When Antonius sent word that the deed had been done, my grief had already dulled.

All my siblings had made the transition to the afterlife. As a Ptolemy, I was alone once more.

'Antonius has sent you a dress for the evening's entertainment,' Charmion said. She pulled out a finely made woollen sheath. It was less opulent than anything I had brought, but charming in its simplicity. I also had enough jewels to make it grand.

'He likes you,' Charmion said carefully.

'Yes, I think he might.'

We spent half that day dressing me. First, we smoothed my skin with cedar oil flecked with gold leaf, so I shimmered as I moved. Next, we knotted my braids beneath a wig made of pearls. Then we adorned me in gold cuffs, emerald earrings and a copper mantle studded with amethysts.

Finally, I changed into the dress Antonius had gifted me. It was the colour of harvested wheat. Though it was humble, it was gentle on my skin. I imagined it was Antonius's hands and I shivered.

'Are you cold?' Charmion asked. 'I can get your robe.'

'No,' I said. Antonius's phantom hands warmed me. 'My crown, please.'

She lifted my Isis crown to my head. I stepped back and looked into the polished silver mirror.

Charmion dropped to her knees beside me as she took me in. 'You are Isis herself,' she breathed.

'Yes,' I said. I felt I was wearing my divinity like a jewel.

'Shall I tell Seti you are ready to leave?'

'No. Tell the captain that we are to set sail immediately.'

'We are to leave? What of your dinner with Antonius?'

I smiled.

I was not someone who easily broke promises, especially political ones. But there was something alluring about the game he and I played – the intoxicating sport of denying him. And though I wasn't ready to admit it, I ran because I was scared of what would happen if I stayed.

I stood on the stern of the boat, looking back at the city of Tarsus as we began to sail away. There was movement at the end of the harbour and I saw Antonius, riding a horse along the pier as if he could reach me.

'Pharaoh, where are you going? We had an agreement!' The still harbour air carried his voice to me.

'You invited Selene,' I said. 'Not Isis.'

He looked me up and down, in my glittering jewels and the dress he had gifted me. Then he began to laugh, great guffaws that shook his chest and unsettled the beast beneath him.

I thought that was the last I was to see of him. That my heart would be safe from the perils of love.

How wrong I was.

CHAPTER TWENTY-THREE
41 BCE

'Pharaoh, a Roman ship is approaching the palace harbour.'

I looked up from my work, irritated at being interrupted. 'Tell Faunus.'

The guard hesitated. 'The dockyard attendants believe the ship belongs to a triumvir of Rome.'

I dropped the reed I was writing with, spraying ink across the papyrus I had been working on all morning.

'Truly?' The three triumvirs ruled Rome. So it could either be Lepidus, Antonius or Octavian.

'Yes, Pharaoh.'

I stood and ran a shaking hand over the front of my dress to smooth it.

The journey back to Egypt had been swift and peaceful. Caesarion had been glad to have me home. In the days since, I had returned to my usual routine and avoided all thoughts of Rome and Antonius. Or tried to.

'Charmion?' I called.

Eiras answered. 'She is with Caesarion in the stables.'

'Good.' The stables were at the far end of the palace island. Caesarion would have time to escape to the mainland by the time the soldiers came ashore.

For why else would one of the rulers of Rome come to Egypt unannounced, if not to take my son from me? His very existence posed a threat to Octavian, and Antonius had already let me know where his loyalties lay in that matter.

As I walked to the harbour, I cursed myself for not being better prepared to protect my son.

'Faunus, if we come out of this unscathed, we must implement contingencies for Caesarion's safety,' I said to him as we marched, flanked as we were by all the royal guards I could call to my side.

Allies or not, I did not trust Octavian's ambition.

And what would Octavian do with me, once he had dispatched my son?

I will not be led in triumph.

Twice now you have heard these words from me. I'll say them one more time before the end.

Maahes brushed up against my leg. His mane had grown in as thick and as glossy as tree sap, and I kept one hand in it as we waited for the newcomer to appear.

The ship on the horizon did not belong to Octavian or Lepidus, it transpired, but to Antonius. Though the realisation did nothing to calm me.

'What is he doing here?' I muttered, forcing my lips into a pleasant grin despite the turmoil I felt.

'Isis.' Antonius greeted me as the god that I was. He did not disembark with any soldiers of his own; though this should have put me at ease, it did not. Instead, his vulnerability drew out my own, and I felt myself shifting under the intensity of his gaze.

Maahes noticed my unease and growled.

Antonius took a step back, noticing him for the first time. It was a wondrous thing that I captivated him so much that he was blind to the beast beside me. 'You have a lion.'

'Did you come all this way to state the obvious?' I asked.

'Does he bite?'

'Sometimes.'

'Like me, then.' He showed me his teeth.

I laughed despite myself. 'I was not expecting you, Marcus.'

He cocked his head. 'I believe you agreed to dine with me, did you not? Unless you are a ruler who goes back on her word?'

I mastered my surprise to say, 'You have come all this way for *dinner?*'

'For the company,' he said seriously.

I looked into his eyes and sensed the sincerity within them. I should have predicted how far I would fall, in love and in life.

'Come, then,' I said. 'Let us find you some rooms.'

That evening, I hesitated on the threshold to the dining hall. I wore once again the sheath dress he had gifted me, though instead of the pearl wig, Charmion styled my natural hair in thick braids. The preparation had taken all day, heightening my anticipation for this very moment. But now I was here I could not bring myself to enter the room. Marcus was inside and I would be forced to fulfil my promise. The game would be won, and he would return to Rome.

Now I had him here, I wanted him to stay. It was no easy thing to admit. I had survived well on my own for so long. With Charmion, of course.

Resolving to keep the game alive, I entered the room.

Antonius looked up as I entered, a smile already on his lips.

'Pharaoh, you look—'

'In ten days,' I interrupted, 'Egypt will celebrate Sōter's passage to the afterlife. The Ptolemaia festivities are an evening worthy of your attendance.'

'We will not dine tonight?'

'No. Let me fulfil my promise in the way of a Ptolemy, with much splendour.'

'You entrap me here with pretty promises.'

It was true, but I denied it vehemently. 'I only wish to seal our deal with an evening deserving of the great partnership between Rome and Egypt.'

'You will not sail away again?'

'Where would I go?'

'I have heard tales of your vast river. If you travel along it, I will follow you.'

There was no greater thrill than being hunted by Antonius. But he would come to know I was no prey.

'I will not sail away,' I promised.

'Ten days, then?'

'Ten days.'

Charmion was horrified when I relayed the plan to her.

'But the Ptolemaia is not until the full moon.'

'We will bring it forward,' I said.

I called Faunus to my rooms that night, and if I had thought Charmion was worried, I was ill-prepared for his reaction.

All blood drained from his face. 'But Pharaoh, the preparations will take weeks—'

'Not weeks. Days. Ten of them.'

He looked as though he was going to protest further, but he must have seen the resolve in my face as his shoulders sagged in resignation. 'We will do what we can.'

'Please,' I said. 'Take as much gold as you need. Make this the best Ptolemaia the gods will have ever seen.'

I caught glances of Antonius over the coming days, but I was too busy with the preparations for the festival to have much time to spend with him. My servants reported that he spent his days walking through the many gardens of Antirhodos. So one evening I found myself there – only by happenstance, of course.

'Pharaoh.' Antonius started when he saw me.

I lay by the pond in the centre of the north gardens, watching him from beneath the palm fronds held above me by an attendant. My diaphanous silk robe was dyed in shades of green, making me one with the lush landscape. The quartz tiling glittered in the sunlight beneath me. I dangled one hand lazily upon a lotus flower, causing ripples along the still water.

'Marcus. You are enjoying the sights of my palace?'

His eyes travelled from my crown-topped head to my bare feet. 'Very much so.'

A hedonist indeed.

'Would you care for some hibiscus tea?' I said. The servant

who held the palm frond above me moved to serve Marcus. Free of the shade, I closed my eyes and tipped my head to the sky.

'Bronze,' Marcus said, his voice much closer than it had been.

When I opened my eyes, he was sitting by the water's edge, resting back on his elbows. His gaze still lingered on me.

'What is bronze?'

'You are. A resplendent statue in the sun.'

'Not gold?'

Marcus shook his head seriously. 'No. Gold is luxurious, but bronze is durable. It can weather a storm and emerge in triumph, more beautiful than before.'

I snorted. 'You mean tarnish?'

'No; the green patina that comes from exposure is as becoming as the robe you wear.'

'I have never been compared to such a common metal.'

'Then I must beg your forgiveness, Isis. For you are anything but common. My intention was to flatter you.'

'You failed.' He hadn't failed. 'You cannot sway me with simple words like I am a Roman plebeian.'

He had swayed me. But this was a sport, and I could not reveal to him my strategy.

Antonius took a sip of his tea before speaking again. 'It is a horror to have caused you such distress. How must I be punished?' His eyes sparkled.

'If you weren't an ally, I'd suggest drowning,' I said.

'A fitting sentence,' he said seriously. Then, without pausing for breath, he jumped into the pond.

I watched, mouth agape, as he sank beneath the lotus flowers.

A few bubbles drifted to the surface and then the water was once again still.

'Marcus?' I called out across the pond.

My servant shifted uncomfortably beside me as the time stretched out. 'Pharaoh, should I send for someone?'

'No, he will surface. Marcus is a jester first and foremost.'

But as we waited, I began to think I had taken our game too far. Had I just killed a triumvir of Rome?

As panic buzzed in my ears, like a bee about to sting, there was a splash in front of me. I had no time to move backwards as Marcus pulled himself from the pond and lay gasping beside me, shaking with laughter and showering me with water.

'I thought you dead,' I said.

'Well, you did sentence me to drowning.'

This elicited a rueful smile from me.

'You deserve to die for pulling such a mean trick.'

'You think so?' he said, getting to his feet.

'Yes.'

I stood also, and grasped his arm. It was the first time I had ever reached for him and both of us stilled. He looked to where my hand touched his skin and I saw a flush rise in his cheeks.

'Cleopatra . . .' His voice was no longer thickened with mirth, but with lust.

I indulged myself by leaning into him, soaking my robe. I brought up my other hand and rested it on his chest.

Then I pushed him unceremoniously back into the pond.

Denying Antonius was an exquisite pleasure, one no drug could replicate.

I left him floating in the water, whooping up at the sun with tears of laughter in his eyes.

The Ptolemaia came around fast enough, but also agonisingly slowly. I didn't see Antonius again until the morning of the procession. He had seen me dressed lavishly before, but my parade clothes were of a different calibre.

The robe I wore was long enough to trail behind my golden chariot. It filled the width of Canopic Street, the fabric panelled in gold and purple. Flowers of all kinds had been stitched into the hem: lilies, papyrus, daisies and lotus. A garland of the same flowers had been woven into my hair. Upon my face I wore a golden mask of my ancestor Sōter.

Antonius was struck silent – a rarity.

'Join me. Let us celebrate our partnership,' I said, offering him space on the chariot.

'Our partnership?'

'Rome and Egypt, allies once more. For today I fulfil my obligation.'

'I was beginning to think we would never dine together,' he admitted. 'But I see now that this will be a day like no other.'

The streets teemed with cheering Alexandrians, many also wearing masks of Sōter. Some wore images of Isis, and a few even mimicked Venus.

Caesarion had insisted on taking the reins, and I had let him, supervised by his tutor of course. My lions prowled beside us – for I had many more now than just Maahes and Bastet. Each had its own keeper, who held it on a gold chain leash. As we moved through the city, petals shed from my train, leaving a fragrant trail in our wake.

'You are lovely today, Pharaoh,' Antonius said.

'Am I not every day?'

He looked at me searchingly, but my mask hid any hint of my thoughts. 'Lovelier each day.'

His gaze brought sweat to my brow like the heat of a noonday sun. 'Look,' I said, pointing to the harbour. 'We conclude the parade here.'

A procession of two hundred servants lined the shoreline, each holding a clay jar in both hands. I raised my arm, and in formation they lunged forward, throwing the jars into the air.

Wine sprayed from the shattered pottery, filling the streets. My citizens cheered as it ran, red as arterial blood, towards the sea. Many fell to their knees, cupping the liquid between their hands and drinking.

Antonius jumped from the moving chariot and joined them. I laughed behind my mask, watching as his lips turned red.

I imagined what it would be like to kiss the wine from them.

The festivities did not end there. I had told Faunus that I expected grandeur, and he had delivered.

We erected a tent, many stadions long, and filled it with golden couches. Interspersed with the dining tripods were fig trees in full season, for my guests to sample at their leisure. I did not ask how Faunus had managed it, but I knew it would have taken much effort to source and replant so many trees.

'This was a dinner worthy of my impatience,' Antonius said. We sat apart from the revelry, beneath a silk canopy.

I smiled, but it waned as I asked, 'You will return to Rome tomorrow?'

The question was left unanswered. Antonius's attention was on a group of dancers who swayed to lute music in front of us.

'Dance with me,' he said suddenly.

'Dance? I am no harlot.'

'Have you ever tried?'

'I am a pharaoh – we do not entertain, we *are* the entertained.'

Antonius stood and held a hand out to me. 'It is simple enough.'

'Marcus, I cannot. The entirety of my court is here, it would not be becoming.' I still cared how I was perceived, but Antonius would soon come to rinse that from me.

He began to turn, moving his hips in time with the music. I was shocked at such a wanton display.

'Come now, Pharaoh, you cannot leave a triumvir of Rome to dance alone,' he called to me. 'I insist upon it.'

'Your terms for our deal have changed?' I asked.

'Yes – consider this part of the dinner.'

The game continued.

I stood and went to him, letting him touch my waist as we moved to the music. Without my mask he could see my face, and his gaze did not stray from it.

'One more night,' he said. 'I will stay one more night.'

Did he feel my muscles relax? Did he sense my relief at knowing I would have another day in his company?

'Mama.' I turned at my son's call. 'What are you doing, Mama?' Caesarion's little face frowned up at us and I pushed Antonius away.

'Dancing,' Antonius answered.

'Is that something they do in Rome?' he asked. My stomach twisted at his ignorance. He knew so little of his Roman heritage.

'No, it is not. I was just trying something different,' I said gently. Caesarion copied Antonius's movement, jerking his little hips back and forth.

Antonius didn't mock his efforts, instead he encouraged them, and soon it was Caesarion and he who had taken to the dance floor in front of me.

I watched them laughing and my heart, which had for so long been closed to love, opened a little more.

'Mama, Antonius says he is staying another day. Can we take him hunting with us tomorrow?'

Every waxing moon we would go hunting, a tradition of my father's that I had continued. It had been Arsinoe who had enjoyed the outings, and excelled at them, and in this way I secretly honoured the sister whose death I had ordered.

'Sometimes we go fishing, sometimes fowling or boar hunting. Mama says these are skills I must learn as Pharaoh. I am not very good at it, but Mama says that she wasn't good at it either and we must practise to be worthy—'

'Caesarion, pause for breath, my son,' I chastised him, and he dipped his head in acquiescence.

Antonius watched me as he replied. 'Hunting? That sounds like a very enjoyable way to spend the day. Then perhaps your mother will dine with me again tomorrow evening.'

I gestured around us. 'Did I not already satisfy my side of the bargain?'

He grew serious. 'I am yet to be satisfied.'

'Two thousand gallons of wine in the streets and a feast to feed three thousand. That is not enough for you?'

'It is but one dinner. And I never specified how many.'

The pieces moved on the game board once more.

The next day we departed to go fishing on the Nile.

Antonius and I stood on the bow of the boat, watching Caesarion cast the first line. The boy giggled as a fish immediately darted towards the hook but did not latch.

'You do this every month?' Antonius asked.

'Yes, I think it is good for Caesarion to learn how to live off the land.'

Antonius laughed. 'Surely he will always have someone to do that for him?'

'It is not about the outcome, but the act. Hunting teaches him to respect the land. And he must respect Egypt to *be* Egypt.'

'How can one embody a country?' As I have said before, Antonius knew me for *me*, before all else.

'Egypt is more than a country, and Alexandria is its beating heart. There is no greater city in the world.'

'Except Rome,' Antonius said.

I shook my head. 'You are wrong.'

'Mama, Antonius, it is your turn,' Caesarion demanded, interrupting what had surely been going to be a lively argument. I felt a pang of disappointment.

'I have an idea,' Antonius said. 'Let us enter a wager. Whoever catches the most fish wins.'

'And what is the prize?' I asked cautiously.

'If I am victorious, then it is settled: Rome is the greatest city in the world. And if you win, then Alexandria is.'

'A worthy battle.' I cast out my line before he could call 'start'.

There was a reason I chose fishing that day. Of all the hunting skills, it was the only one in which I had bested Arsinoe. I knew these waters like I knew my own blood, and it wasn't long before I was reeling in fish after fish.

At first Antonius had poor luck, but he quickly improved and soon his bucket was filling up too.

Then he was overtaking me. I was astounded. I had been fishing in these waters all my life. But then I saw, from the corner of my eye, one of his servants retrieve a fish from my bucket and slip it into his.

The Roman is stealing from me. It was a simple trick, and one he would surely reveal at the end, but I was not going to give him the satisfaction of a false win.

'Charmion,' I called out.

She came to my side and I whispered my plan.

When the evening came to an end and Antonius brandished his teeming bucket with triumph, I looked at him sincerely. 'An adept fisherman you have proven to be: show us your bounty.'

He tipped the contents of the bucket onto the deck.

'Caesarion, come, help me identify the fish,' I said.

My son, keen to be of service and prove his knowledge of all things, began to list the fish in Antonius's catch. 'Catfish, carp, eel, perch . . . Mama, what is this? I haven't seen this one before.'

Caesarion held up a small silver fish.

'Charmion, do you recognise it?' I asked lightly.

Charmion pointed to an empty platter next to my bucket. 'It must be the salted herring I served earlier, my Queen. I did not mean for it to fall into your catch.' She did well at looking abashed.

'*My* catch,' I said looking at Antonius. 'Now how ever did that get into *your* bucket, Marcus?'

The Roman took the fish from Caesarion's hands, and upon touching it knew the ruse was over.

He laughed, unashamed of being caught. If anything, he seemed even more pleased to have been played so well.

'I suppose I must concede that Alexandria is the greatest city in the world.'

'It is, as I told you,' I said.
'Tomorrow, might you give me a tour?'
I looked at him. 'Tomorrow?'
He met my eyes levelly. 'Yes.'
And so he stayed another night in my country.

CHAPTER TWENTY-FOUR
40 BCE

'Your city is vibrant,' Antonius said as we travelled down the causeway from the lighthouse to the main thoroughfare.

'It is,' I agreed.

'It has been some time since I last visited and the change is remarkable.'

Palm trees lined the streets, their boughs laden with sweet-smelling dates. I paused beneath one to see the city as Antonius did, with fresh eyes.

The new harbour was to my right, teeming with merchant ships. To my left stood the newly erected temple for my late beloved – the Caesareum. Porticoes decorated the entranceway, through which you could see the lemon groves I had sent for from Rome. As the branches swayed in the breeze I could see glimpses of the statue of Jupiter, surrounded by fountains, in the centre of the courtyard.

One of my greatest regrets is that I was not able to finish the temple during my reign. Four rooms stood empty on the day I died. I had intended to fill them with gold replicas of Caesar's triumphs, but instead Octavian's soldiers used them to celebrate their own.

I'm sure Caesar's grand-nephew thought to honour him by concluding his triumph in the vacant halls of the temple. But I knew Caesar all the better, and he would rather have kept the hallowed grounds peaceful. And kept me alive.

But in this moment, I was still wholly ignorant of my fate, so I simply responded to Antonius, 'I am an excellent queen.'

He looked at me, and as usual I felt the strength of his gaze disarm me. 'You are.'

The city tour took us through the harbour and the new library, ending at the Hospital of Isis.

As I entered, I was approached by two priestesses with questions about a remedy I had concocted. I advised them while Antonius looked on.

'I had heard of your skills in healing, but I had not quite believed it,' he said softly once they had departed. 'Few rulers would consort with their citizens so casually.'

'Potion work is one of the few things in life I understand clearly. It is logical, and a little illogical.'

'How so?'

'Take the plant wolfsbane. If consumed on the tongue or in the blood, it will kill you. But if I dilute its sap with two parts olive oil and one part lemon balm, I can create a tincture that will bring down inflammation on the skin.'

Antonius's eyebrows rose. 'A dangerous vocation.'

'It can be. It is why I wish to educate as many people as possible on the properties of plants.'

He smiled. 'You are a very unusual person, Pharaoh.'

I searched his face for the insult, but there was none and so I nodded. 'I have always wished to be a scholar.'

'Not a queen?'

I hesitated, unsure whether to divulge the truth. But there was something about Antonius that made me wish to be wholly me.

'No, Pharaoh was never my calling. My sister, Berenice, was the elder, and so I did not expect to wear the crown.'

'Ah, yes, Berenice,' he said.

I did not want to speak on my sister, and he sensed it.

'Can we go to the marketplace next?' he asked brightly.

I shook my head. 'It is too busy. My guards find it difficult to escort me through there safely.'

'For you are loved by your people.'

Again, I studied him for a hidden meaning, but he spoke the words with honesty.

'It was not always so,' I admitted. 'I have worked hard to maintain my citizens' approval.'

'It is clear that they appreciate you now.'

I clasped my hands in front of my waist as if to guard myself from his compliments.

That evening, after we had feasted on roast boar and stuffed goose, we retired to the courtyard to enjoy the cool evening air.

Antonius reclined on a couch beside me and I watched him from under my lashes as I sipped my wine. He was smiling faintly, taking in the sights of the garden around us. The bougainvillea was in bloom, its pink flowers like a budding kiss.

'I should like to see the flowers here in the sunlight,' he said.

'So, you do not leave tomorrow?' I did not let him see how much I dreaded his next words. Did I want him to stay, or to leave? Both made me afeared.

'Do you not enjoy my company?' he said with a grin. When I did not return it, he let out a sigh.

'Every morning, I awake and tell myself that today is the day that I must go, and every day I cannot bring myself to leave.'

My hand rested on my clavicle, where I could feel the flutter of my pulse.

'What of Octavian? He cannot be pleased by your absence?'

Antonius's expression soured and I watched the first cracks between the triumvirs grow.

'It matters not what Octavian wants. In this I am resolute.'

'He is your partner in rule,' I said. 'His thoughts have consequence.'

Antonius rarely raised his voice. His anger was quiet, the tone deep, simmering with fury. 'Do I not bring my enemies to their knees? Do I not time and time again fight for the rights of all Romans? Do I not dole out justice with mercy and grace?'

I knew his anger was not directed at me but at Octavian, and I did not baulk in the face of it. Instead, I appreciated the warmth the frustration brought to his face and the glint of danger it lit in his eyes.

'I am not a horse to be pulled home by the reins,' he continued. 'I will stay in Egypt if I choose it.'

He had flung out an arm in emphasis, and suddenly he winced and clutched his shoulder. I had seen him do it more than once, and tonight the warmth of the wine gave me the confidence to ask after it.

'I was struck by a spear in Philippi,' he said.

'Show me.'

He seemed surprised, but he obliged, pulling his tunic over his head in one motion.

I approached him, closely observing the scar that marked his shoulder, but without touching his skin.

'There is no infection,' I said, 'but the muscle beneath is still healing. You need to stretch it to strengthen it. I will make you a poultice of crushed lotus leaves and willow bark to ease the pain.'

'Thank you, Pharaoh,' he said tenderly.

Charmion brought forward my medicine bag, but I was out of willow bark. 'I'll send a servant to the market to fetch some.'

'Why do we not go?' Antonius asked as he pulled his clothing back on.

'I told you, we cannot – it will be impossible to make it to the correct stall.'

'We need not go as Pharaoh and triumvir, but perhaps as Marcus and Selene?'

I looked at Charmion and we shared a private smile. He could not have known how often Selene had been out in the city at night.

He caught our look, and mistook it. 'Dismiss the thought – it is too dangerous, I am sure.'

'Selene has never felt in danger in my city,' I said.

He leaned forward in his chair. 'So you'll do it? Go to the marketplace with me? Will your guards allow you to leave unaccompanied? For we cannot give away our true identities.'

I laughed. 'Follow me.'

'Are you sure about this?' Charmion whispered as we walked through the palace.

'He won't harm me,' I said.

'His loyalty is to the Republic, should Octavian ever come for Caesarion . . .'

'He won't harm me,' I repeated firmly.

Charmion rubbed her brow, looking troubled. 'How can you be so sure?'

'Caesar,' I said simply. 'I trust in his love of Caesar; it will always stay his hand against me.'

When we reached my rooms, Antonius hesitated on the threshold. 'What are we doing, Pharaoh?'

'You will not pass as a commoner in that garb,' I said.

'There are many Romans in your city.'

'True, but few wear so fine a cloth. Come, Charmion will find you something to don.'

'Bring it for me and I will await you here.' He looked painfully aware that he was about to walk into my sleeping quarters.

'No, we must know each other in guise. Come now,' I said, gesturing to the door.

He glanced at the guards, who stood to attention on either side of the entranceway.

'We can always dismiss the idea if you think it too dangerous,' I said, twisting his words back at him.

The smile he gave me in return was unnerving in its brightness and I had to look away. And as he walked into my chambers, I heard him murmur, 'Entering your bedroom is dangerous indeed.'

'Charmion, where are Selene's clothes? I know it has been some time since I used them.'

Charmion retrieved the ill-fitting linens and helped me undress, while Antonius lingered in the centre of the room looking determinedly away. When I was ready, I said, 'Do you recognise me so plain, Marcus?'

He turned and his stare lingered on my body. 'You could never be plain. For it is not the clothes or the jewels that make you striking, it is the woman beneath.'

'Lavish words,' I said with a mocking smile, though my heart quickened with the compliment.

Charmion turned her attention to Antonius. 'Triumvir, I think you should remove your belt – it marks you as a Roman. And swap your tunic for a chiton.'

Antonius did as Charmion bade, putting on a Greek-style chiton that would disguise him as one of the Egyptian nobility. I did not look away as he changed, my gaze resting on the sheen of his skin above his loincloth. He caught me staring, and the look he gave me was scalding in its heat.

'I name you Helios,' I said quietly, gifting him the name of his guise: *god of the sun.*

'Who better to accompany Selene, goddess of the moon?' he replied.

I broke his stare and turned to the plinth that hid the steps to the cistern.

Antonius startled at the ease with which I moved the deceptively hollow pillar, and his eyes widened when the steps were revealed.

The smell of seaweed and dead things drifted in from the tunnel below.

'Selene, what is this?' I felt a thrill of pleasure at his once more addressing me by this name.

'Helios, it is our means of escape.'

*

Antonius could not hide his awe as we rowed across the bay to the city. Every so often he would look at me, laugh and shake his head.

'When I think I know the extent of you, I find there is more to unravel.'

'I am unfathomable.'

His expression turned tender. 'You are.'

The little boat nudged the shore, severing the gentleness of the moment as I stumbled forward. Antonius reached for me, his hands circling my waist.

'I am well,' I said stiffly, moving away from his grip.

I saw a flicker of hurt in his eyes, but I could not find it in myself to regret my actions. After Caesar I was more guarded with my heart.

We walked through the city in silence, each enjoying the novelty of no guards at our backs. When we reached the market, Antonius pointed out a stall selling trinkets and talismans of the gods.

'Look,' he said, picking up a miniature statue of Isis, delighted.

'Blessed by the Pharaoh, it will bring you great prosperity,' the market seller said.

Antonius raised an eyebrow. 'Blessed by the Pharaoh, you say? It must be worth its weight in gold, then.'

'Not gold, not silver, not even bronze,' I said.

The market seller took my words as an attempt to bargain and began to haggle, but I waved him away. 'I do not want it. Sell your false talismans to someone else.'

'To me,' Antonius said. He reached into his pocket and placed a gold coin in the seller's hands.

'Your generosity will draw the crowds,' I said, irritated.

'I mean only to impress you,' he admitted, and all of my annoyance fled in the face of his honesty.

The market seller gaped like a fish. 'Th-this is too much . . .' he stuttered. 'You must take something more.' He began to scoop up more of the wooden figurines and tried to pass them off to Antonius, who shook his head.

'As you say, these are blessed by the Pharaoh and are too precious to be wasted on me – keep them.'

I spotted a carving on the edge of the table which held my interest. 'Except that one,' I said.

The market seller nodded fervently. 'Yes, yes, your wife has an impeccable eye, this is a fine specimen, popular with our Greek brethren – Dionysus.'

Antonius did not correct the market seller's assumption that I was his wife. His attention was wholly on my hands, cradling the small token.

'Dionysus,' he whispered, and I knew we were sharing memories of the night we'd first met. I held it up to his eyeline. The little carving was finely crafted, depicting the god with a grapevine resting on one shoulder and a cup of wine held aloft in his hand.

Antonius reached for the figure, his hand briefly closing over mine. In turn he offered me the talisman of Isis, seated on her throne with Horus on her knee and the cow-horn crown on her head.

He watched as I placed the carving in my robe against my chest.

'We should move on,' I said quietly. I had noticed that the market seller's good fortune had already been spotted by two other traders nearby, who were desperately trying to flag us down.

I led the way to the herbalist in the centre of the market. After securing the willow bark, we stopped at one more stall.

'Fresh bread like you will never have had before,' I said.

The baker smiled at my compliment as she pulled the lid off her clay pot, releasing the aroma of the baking bread.

'The smell would make the gods weep,' Antonius said.

'I will take one extra,' I told the baker.

We sated our appetite, Antonius confirming that indeed it was the best bread he had ever had. As the evening grew darker, the market began to quieten, the stalls emptying.

'I must make one more stop before we return.' When I didn't elaborate, Antonius didn't press me.

I led us down the quieter streets to the south of the city, where stonework turned to mud bricks, and entered one of the smaller dwellings.

'Who goes there?' The voice was gruff, as if scarcely used.

'Apollodorus, it is me,' I said.

'Pharaoh?' He moved out of the gloom and into rushlight.

I handed him the extra bread I had brought as well as some of the willow bark. 'Food for your stomach, willow for your leg.'

His eyes shimmered as he took the bundle, offering me a seat at his table. I had tried offering Apollodorus accommodations elsewhere, but he'd claimed this was home, and so home it was.

'This is Antonius,' I said, gesturing behind me.

Apollodorus bowed low, wincing as he did. 'Careful,' I chastised him. 'Sit before you cause more damage.'

The weaver lowered himself into a chair, his leg lying straight out in front of him. I could see beneath his tunic that the joint was swollen.

'How goes the pain? I am sorry I have not been able to visit sooner, but I hope the healers I sent were sufficient?'

Apollodorus smiled weakly. 'You need not have worried about me, Pharaoh. I have my hands and so I can still weave.'

'Good. I have some more requests for material, but I will send them with a servant on the morrow.'

'You are too giving, Pharaoh. I wish to offer you a drink, but I have only water. With Nilah gone . . .' His throat bobbed and I bowed my head.

'I heard of your loss and I am sorry. She will be well looked after by my ancestors in the afterlife.'

My words seemed to comfort him.

'We will not intrude on your hospitality any longer, but please do send for me should you need anything,' I said.

Once we left, Antonius didn't speak for some time. It was only when we had crossed the city and boarded the boat that he spoke again.

'You are more benevolent than the stories say.'

I was unsurprised. 'And who tells those stories? Romans who wish to discredit me? Courtiers loyal to my siblings, who want to dethrone me? That's the thing with stories: you must always know the story of the storyteller.'

A fitting reminder to you, my reader.

Antonius looked thoughtful. 'Who was the weaver to you?'

'A man who helped a woman in need.'

'I thought perhaps he was an old lover?'

I barked out a laugh. 'Because Caesar was my senior you thought my tastes must tend towards the ancient? No, Apollodorus is a friend only.'

'A friend,' he said, as if the concept was foreign.

'Besides, I am less benevolent than you think. I can be cruel and ruthless and—'

He cupped my chin, his thumb resting on the edge of my lips. 'Do not say such things about the Pharaoh.'

I smiled. 'I do not think she'll mind.'

'But I will.'

The boat swayed as he moved towards me, closing the gap between our bodies.

'Marcus,' I said in warning. A warning for him or myself, I wasn't sure.

'Tell me you do not want this,' he said.

'I do not want this,' I said, and he saw the lie in it.

'Tell me again, Cleopatra.'

Something unspooled in me as he said my name. I leaned forward and pressed my lips against his.

The kiss built like an incoming storm. First came the pattering of our pulse against our wrists, and then the thundering of our hearts. His hands felt like sparks of lightning on my skin as they moved from my face to my lower back, and I wondered if he were Ra.

For he was surely a god.

I trailed my fingers from his jaw down to his chest. The kiss deepened and I pressed my body closer to his.

He stiffened beneath me and broke away. 'We must stop.'

'Must we?' I said.

It was in that moment that his resolve shattered and with gentle hands he laid me down on the wooden slats of the boat.

The ocean currents swirled with our passion, and no one but the night sky bore witness to the birth of our love.

CHAPTER TWENTY-FIVE
40 BCE

And so it began, the final song of my heart.

'Show me more of Egypt. Let me travel along her tresses, and glide upon her neck,' Antonius begged. I revelled in sharing my country's wonders with him. We toured the Nile and Upper Egypt. I took him to Hermonthis to visit the Buchis bull, and to the pyramids to visit the dead.

Shemu season was spent tangled in each other's arms on the banks of the Siwa Oasis. Home to the Oracle of Amun, Siwa was a holy place, closer to the pantheon than Alexandria was.

One night we made love beneath the olive groves, and as the day became night, we watched stars cast streaks of light across the sky.

'Do you think there is another love like ours?' Antonius asked me.

I understood his meaning: a scalding, breathless sort of love.

'No; the world could not contain such love twice over.'

'I think so too.'

If love were a well, then both Caesar's and Antonius's love was deep, but where Caesar's water had been sweet and refreshing, Antonius's was hot and addictive.

There was a movement in the bushes and I sat up, expecting a desert fox or some such. But as the shadow stretched upwards, I saw the silhouette of a cobra outlined by moonlight.

'She even dared to gaze with face serene upon her fallen palace
courageous, too, to handle poisonous asps
that she might draw black venom to her heart,
waxing bolder as she resolved to die.'

Such pitiless, pretty words from Horace. Why must the gentle cobra bear such malice? She who protects her young, a sacred mother blessed by Isis. Let this creature live without blame.

'The serpent rears to kill,' Antonius whispered fiercely beside me, and the snake's eyes turned to him.

'No, she blesses us only.'

'Your god?' Antonius asked.

As she lazily turned her bejewelled gaze back to me, I said, 'She is no one's god but her own.'

Before I had finished speaking, the snake lunged forward until there was but a handspan between us. I heard Antonius inhale sharply behind me. But I did not share his fear.

The cobra's tongue darted out, tasting the air, and I saw a glimpse of her fangs.

We regarded each other, each destined to play a part in the other's legend. Both perceived as monsters instead of mothers.

Though I had been naked for half the night, for the first time I felt truly stripped bare. It was not a premonition, as I was not poisoned by snake's venom, this night or any other, but perhaps a warning. She sensed a change in me.

A sound of a bird in the distance startled us both, breaking the spell between us. I watched the asp disappear back into the undergrowth with a touch of sorrow in my heart.

A warning indeed. What happened that night changed my future more than I could have known.

A handful of days later, I suffered cramps in the belly and eased them with a morning bathe in the freshwater springs.

'I have heard talk from Rome,' Charmion said as she rubbed a cloth against my back. The waters were a cool respite from the heat of shemu season. The sun was rising behind the sand dunes that surrounded the lush oasis. And as the breeze swept through my hair, it brought with it flecks of the sparkling desert.

Egypt, how I love your breath, seasoned sweet with sand and sea.

'You know how word travels far quicker through servants than through missives,' Charmion continued.

'Yes, what do the servants gossip on now? For I can tell by your tone it is not pleasant.'

Charmion went quiet and I splashed her with water; such was Antonius's effect on me, I had remembered how to be merry.

She squealed before becoming serious once more. 'A man named Cicero speaks against Antonius to the senate. Among many insults he claims he is a degenerate of wanton regard. With an appetite for flesh and drink few have seen the likes of.'

I swirled my hands in the water, making a momentary current. Charmion's words did not surprise me. I knew exactly who Antonius was. He was Dionysus, a god of indulgence, of pleasure. The slander did not worry me like it should have.

'Mere words. I see Marcus plain.'

When Charmion didn't respond, I engaged her once more. 'Tell me your thoughts. I can see the worry on your face.'

'I *am* worried. Words have power, and if the senate moves against him while he is here with you . . .'

She feared war. A foretelling once again.

I moved through the water to clasp her hands in mine. 'Rest your worries. Egypt is safe. I am safe, and you too are safe.'

For now.

I questioned Antonius on Cicero later. He laughed. 'The man is a withered old fool. Pious and pompous in equal measure.'

But there was a catch to his tone, an inflection that was not all pleasant. I didn't press him on it. I knew he would bring it to me with time.

It was on the way back to Alexandria that we next spoke on Rome. I could see something troubled him. It was a long journey by camel-drawn caravan and we had no entertainment but each other. Once we had sated our desires, there was little to do but talk.

It took him two nights before he told me the extent of his concerns.

'Fulvia brought arms against Octavian in my absence,' he said quietly. 'She has raised two legions from my veterans.'*

'Your wife fights against the triumvirate?'

He ran a hand through his hair. It had grown long and wild in the shemu heat. 'Cicero has led a campaign against me, weakening my position. She seeks to overthrow Octavian and Lepidus to make me sole ruler and end the dissent. Lucius, my fool brother, has also lent his soldiers to the cause.'

I was surprised Antonius had managed to keep such news so close to his chest. When I asked him why he had not told me before now, he said, 'I did not want you to concern yourself with the tensions in Rome.'

'My son is Caesar's heir; Rome is his home as much as Egypt is. Do not deny me the truth.'

I trusted Antonius, but I also knew his limitations. He did not hide things from me out of spite. He simply avoided discussing matters that did not bring him pleasure. And Fulvia did not bring him pleasure.

'She draws you to her,' I concluded.

'Yes.' He must have seen something in my expression, for he kneeled before me and laid his head on my lap. 'But I will not go. Let her have her war; I will not be a part of it.'

So much blood was shed in my lifetime, it was easy to forget the smaller battles. Fulvia and Lucius's insurgence came to naught except more death. Octavian spared both their lives, but Fulvia died of disease not long after.

---

* It was Velleius Paterculus who said Fulvia had 'nothing of the woman in her except her sex'. For ambition is a manly pursuit, supposedly. Will we ever tire of men defining the parameters of womanhood? I look at the world as you live it, reader, and grow weary.

It was Charmion who told me the news, not Antonius: 'Some say she died of a broken heart.'

I knew she only recounted court hearsay, but the words still stung. I knew who Fulvia had been to Antonius – simply put, she was not me.

Antonius never told me of her death. But the night I found out, he drank himself into such a stupor, four soldiers had to bring him to bed. The next day he smiled once more. For Fulvia had just been a cloud in his sky, and I was the moon itself.

Soon we had news of our own that kept us occupied. I was pregnant.

'I feel them,' Antonius said, his hands resting on my belly. Tears sparkled in his eyes.

'Twins,' the soothsayer had predicted after running her hands over my stomach. The silence had stretched for longer than was comfortable. So when she spoke, both Antonius and I let out a great breath of relief.

Then came the joy, which has not abated since.

'Twins can sometimes be weak, but they are both strong,' I said, placing my hand onto his.

'They have the blood of Romulus and Remus in them. Roman blood,' said Antonius.

'Divine blood,' I said. 'Blessed by the pantheon of Egypt.' Though I doubted the words as I said them. I feared that, like Caesarion, the babes would not be blessed. I had not divulged my worries to Antonius. He believed my blood to be linked to the gods, and so too would his children's be.

'It's my turn,' Caesarion claimed, climbing across the bed. He placed his little hand on top of mine and squealed when he felt the babies move.

'They hurt me,' he claimed.

I reached for his hand and cradled it between mine before pressing a kiss to it. 'They did not hurt you, they *will* not hurt you.' I hoped my words prophesied their future.

Antonius saw my concern and gathered up Caesarion in his arms. 'You shall be great friends with your siblings.'

'Will we go fishing together?' Caesarion asked hopefully.

'You will, and much more besides,' Antonius said.

That seemed to satisfy Caesarion, who bucked out of Antonius's arms and ran from the room. His maids followed after him and Antonius and I were alone once more.

'Are you well?' Antonius asked after I sighed.

I nodded. 'This pregnancy is harder on my body than Caesarion's was.'

He reached over and began to massage my legs. I grunted softly as I felt myself relax.

'Not very long now,' he said. I could hear the excitement in his voice and it did more to ease the tension in my muscles than his hands.

'A moon cycle, no more. Twins come earlier.'

He looked away and I read concern in his face.

I sat up. 'What is it?'

'Nothing,' he said. But Antonius could never lie to me convincingly.

When he left to attend the gymnasium later that evening, I found myself looking through his letters.

'What do you expect to find?' Charmion said.

'I'm not sure.' There were scrolls upon scrolls of correspondence, for Antonius had not been idle during his time in Egypt; he took his role as triumvir seriously.

There were not many from Octavian, so when I came across his name I lingered on the words.

You forget yourself and your duties to your country. First your wife raises an army – in which you say you had no part, but how can I trust your word when you have broken it repeatedly? When we were bound together as triumvirs you promised yourself to the Roman people, not to a foreign queen. You may barter your bed for her soldiers, but it is our people who suffer for your indulgence.

If you do not return to Rome, I will take your motives as an act of war.

I waited for Antonius late into the night. When he arrived back from the gymnasium his usually bright eyes were dulled with wine.

'Octavian threatens you,' I said.

For a moment it looked as though he might deny it. But then he nodded.

'But I cannot leave you, not like this,' he said miserably, holding out his arms.

I did not let myself go to him. 'You should have told me.'

'What could you have done?'

'Sent you back to Rome,' I said, my voice rising. 'Octavian threatens you with war, and you have no armies, no soldiers here. So in truth, Octavian threatens *me* with war.'

'I would not let him,' Antonius said fiercely.

I went to Antonius's side and cupped his cheek in my hand. 'You would have no choice, my love.'

He tilted his head towards my touch. 'I fear I have underestimated his popularity. The Republic rises against me.'

'Reconciliation is the only way.' As much as I wanted Octavian dispatched and all threat to Caesarion's legitimacy vanquished, I knew that now was not the right time.

'I have thought on this, but there is little I can do from here.'

'And that is why you are going to return to Rome,' I said firmly.

Antonius shook his head, kneeling before me and resting his head on my swollen stomach.

'I will not.'

'You must,' I said. Tears began to seep from my eyes. 'And you must marry Octavian's sister.'

'What?' he exclaimed.

I had thought of the plan that evening. It was the only way to protect Egypt from Octavian's wrath.

I sense you furrowing your brow, as if to say, '*You* were the one who forced him into Octavia's arms?'

Grant me grace. There was little I could control in Rome to guide my own fate. But this I could steer. So, I reached the heart-rending conclusion that Antonius must be wed.

'Octavia is recently widowed, is she not?' I pressed.

'Yes, but—'

'Bind yourself to your enemies so you can watch them more closely.'

Antonius was crying now too, his sobs muffled against my flesh. *Our* flesh, that grew within me.

'I cannot, Cleopatra. I cannot do that.'

I tilted his head upwards, so he could look into my eyes and see the depth of my conviction. 'I know what we share; it is blood, it is bone, it is breath.'

These words remain as crisp as a fallen leaf in my memory; even in death they keep their form.

'Nothing can break us,' I continued. 'Not even another marriage.'

Antonius stood, colour coming back into his cheeks. 'I will go on one condition.'

I laughed. 'Not another wager.'

Antonius did not smile. He was watching me intensely. 'No wager. Only a promise. Marry me first. Marry me here, beneath the gods of Egypt. Then I will do what must be done in Rome.'

Tears fell down my cheeks once more as I felt my children move beneath my skin under the light of their father's love.

I nodded and Antonius embraced me.

We were wed the next day in the Temple of Isis. We did not announce our union to the world, for what did the world need to know of it?

That morning, I donned my most precious crown. It bore a likeness to Isis's golden horns, but in place of the solar disc sat a cluster of pearls. Beneath it I wore a coiled wig of gold thread, decorated with shells and gold beads. My dress, I'd had made by

Apollodorus. It was voluminous enough to cover my swelling stomach but still cut in the knotted style of the goddess.

As I came out to greet Antonius at the temple, I smiled. He had dressed as Dionysus, with an ivy wreath around his long hair and a panther skin over his shoulders.

He bowed low when he saw me.

'Isis,' he greeted me.

I inclined my head with mock seriousness. 'Dionysus.'

He took my hand and pressed it to his lips. 'Shall we bind our love beneath the gods?'

Together we knelt before the statue of Isis and offered her gifts and promises. We sacrificed a goat on the altar, its blood running down the flagstones and dripping into the empty pool that was yet to be completed.

That evening we made love on the temple steps beneath the stars and moon, and slept beneath the panther skin on the Antirhodos shoreline.

When I awoke, he was gone. In his place he had left the wooden carving of Dionysus.

I held it against my chest and wept.

The twins came ten days after he left. Earlier than I had hoped, but the birth was quick.

'A girl and a boy,' Charmion announced.

We held one each and cried, our foreheads touching. 'What shall you name them?'

'Cleopatra Selene,' I said, kissing the wet cheeks of the girl before looking to her brother. 'And Alexander Helios.'

Charmion smiled. 'Noble names.' I opened my arms and she placed Alexander against my other nipple.

I sighed as I felt both babes latch, the golden milk of my breasts filling their small stomachs. My chest ached for Antonius.

'Shall I call the soothsayer?' Charmion said quietly.

I looked down at their little bodies, their skin unblemished.

Then I remembered the pain of the needle in Caesarion's skin and the scream that had shattered my heart.

'No.'

I knew the soothsayer would not find the gods' mark on them. I had searched for it the moment they had drawn their first breath.

Charmion wiped tears from her cheeks. 'They will be enough without the gods' blessing.'

I nodded. 'They will be enough.'

I spent the first three weeks of their life in the birthing rooms, sequestered from daily life. I accepted no visitors except Caesarion, whose smiling face was almost enough to banish all longing for Antonius.

When I rejoined the court and daily life ensued, I received word that Antonius had married Octavia.

I disposed of the letter and thought no more of it. Well, that is what I told Charmion, at least.

I had promised her we would never hide our true selves from the other, but I was ashamed of my envy. The night I received word, I went to the pond in the north gardens and slipped into the still water as though I might find Antonius there, laughing. But when I looked at my reflection, I saw only the twisted face of jealousy. I crept back into the palace dripping pondwater and algae from my hair and did not even wake Charmion to bathe me, instead sleeping in the slime of envy. This was a pain that only I could know of. And now, I suppose, you.

CHAPTER TWENTY-SIX
36 BCE

What can I tell you of the next few years? Your historians had little to say of that time. But I did much good.

I opened three more hospitals across the major cities of Egypt. I constructed temples to Isis in Hermonthis and circulated my book of remedies up and down the Nile. I patronised more scholars to fill the new library with their work and improved political alliances with our neighbouring countries. My coffers and grain stores were full, as was my heart.

I raised my children as Antonius raised his – a daughter, Antonia, born of Octavia. He had told me of the news in a letter. I had burned the pages and then sent for a man and a woman to share my bed.

I held no grudge against Octavia; she was a woman in Rome and so had scrutiny enough. No, my frustrations were solely directed at the husband who had left. Though it had been I who had sent him away, and though I knew that his marriage with Octavia would be required to produce an heir, I had not expected it to hurt quite so deeply.

I refused to be a woman jilted.

'You have been writing this letter for half the night, let the scribe go to bed,' Charmion said with a yawn in her voice.

I looked at the scribe and the shadows that gathered beneath his eyes. 'She is right – go, I will call on you in the morning.'

I picked up the half-finished message with a sigh. It had been nearly three years since I had seen Antonius. Far longer than either of us had wanted to be apart. But as with Caesar before him, the battlefield had called to him.

His campaigns took him east across Asia Minor, and at the start of shemu season he had settled in Antioch, a mere ten-day journey from Alexandria. He called me to him from the palaces there. But I have never cared to be summoned.

So I was composing him a letter, a goodbye. His absence in my life had long healed and I did not seek to open the flesh of that wound once more. Better to be free of his love, than to be bled by it.

I heard the soft padding of feet and turned to find Selene clutching the hem of her nightclothes, her eyes puffy and red from being awoken.

I opened my arms to her and she crawled into them.

'Papa?' she asked, reaching for the letter where Antonius had sent for me. She had come to recognise his seal, though she had yet to see his face.

Though Antonius had not met the twins, he had sent them regular trinkets and presents. Selene held on to one now, a silver moon hanging on a chain around her neck.

I watched as she brought it up to her lips and kissed it. Then she smiled, and like her father she shone brighter than any star in the sky.

'Does Papa have a story for me?' she asked, for more often than not, Antonius would regale them with tales of his capers and victories.

'Not this time, my child,' I said, looking away from her.

Could I really deny my children their father?

I picked up the letter I had been composing and shredded it in my hands. Selene reached for the remains of the papyrus and threw them up in the air, scattering them like shedding petals. Her laughter was infectious, rousing her brother who quickly joined in.

As I watched them play, I knew I could not end my alliance without seeing Antonius face to face.

And so to Antioch we must go.

Caesarion, now eleven years of age, was old enough to reign over Egypt with the support of Faunus. He was eager to do so in my absence.

'I will receive the court daily, do not worry, Mama,' he said. The crown on his head wobbled ever so slightly and it reminded me of Theos on the day he had been crowned. Time had passed, far quicker than I could fathom.

'It is a mother's wont to worry,' I said, setting the crown straight.

I had tried to shelter Caesarion from the swirling rumours of the Roman senate. Occasionally a Roman noble would visit, bringing with them the slander that my son was illegitimate. If I had not agreed to ally with Rome, I would have killed each one, Octavian's wrath be damned. But I was still wary of war.

I let Octavian spread his falsities, gently reminding those who visited who Caesarion's father had been. Not that it wasn't obvious from the boy's looks and demeanour. He carried himself like a general and had taken to wearing a purple cloak like his father's.

'Watch over my land, my son,' I said, pressing a kiss to his cheek. He grimaced at my show of affection, waving me away.

'Egypt will be safe while I am safe. For I *am* Egypt,' he said.

My heart swelled in my chest at his words.

Selene, Helios and I voyaged across the sea to Antioch. As on my last approach to Tarsus, I was apprehensive about seeing Antonius. I had come to sever ties and was unsure how he would receive this news.

I arrived at night, my boat slicing through the black water of the Orontes river. The city was silhouetted by mountains in the east, and like the brow of a great god they looked down on the land, making me feel as though I was always watched.

'Are Selene and Helios asleep?' I asked Charmion. There was

a chill in the air and she brought me a sheep's skin to wrap my arms in.

'They are. Helios kept asking if he might row the ship,' she said, laughing.

I had asked Charmion once why she had not had children of her own. 'Ahmose and I spoke on it once and had imagined their faces,' she had said, her voice ragged with an old grief. 'I do not wish to replace those images with others.'

'You do not need to replace them,' I had said gently. 'For you are already a mother.' And I had pointed to my children.

I held her close that night, her head resting on my chest. I knew she dreamed of Ahmose, for she woke crying.

Some loves are enough to last a lifetime. I was lucky to have had two.

'If the children slumber, then I shall go to shore,' I said.

'Alone?'

'Yes.'

'You'll be wanting your old linens, then? It is good I packed them,' she said, pulling out the threadbare clothing that allowed me to blend in as a commoner.

I smiled. 'I fear it will be the last time I will don them.'

'Indeed?' she said lightly.

'I go to end my alliance with Rome.'

'Why?'

'I can no longer abide Octavian's slights against Caesarion. My son grows older by the day and has yet to set foot on his father's land since his death.'

Charmion regarded me, her eyes narrowing. 'Now tell me the true reason.'

I sighed, annoyed that Charmion could see into my depths as through water in a bowl. 'That is not untrue. But I suppose the heart of it is different: I can no longer abide Antonius's slights against me.'

'I heard Octavia is pregnant again.'

'Yes, though that is not what vexes me. It has been three years and he has not returned to me once.'

'Nor have you gone to him,' Charmion pointed out.

'Am I not here now?' I snapped.

She nodded.

I prompted her. 'Then what is it?'

'The love you have for Antonius is rare. If it has dimmed, I understand your choice. But if it still burns bright, do not be fearful to face the fire. It is better to be warmed by love, no matter how distant, than to stand alone.' She turned away.

I held out a hand to her. 'You never stand alone, Charmion. And neither will I.' I kissed where sadness creased her brow.

I changed into Selene the healer's clothes and crossed the plank that rested on the pier. The harbour was still lively despite the time of night, and as I moved through the streets, I quickly learned why.

'Twenty thousand gallons of wine fill the streets every seventh day,' a voice intoned. 'And when the sun rises, they say the palace shines so brightly from the gold inlaid in its walls that only those of divine blood can look upon it. Who is it that I speak of?'

What a thing it is to hear your name chanted by a crowd.

The hakawati continued, 'She raises lions from cubs to eat at her table, and when a courtier displeases her, she flicks a golden rod and the lions tear the throats from their necks. Who is it that I speak of?'

'Cleopatra!' they called again.

'Four siblings gone. Berenice, the first for the throne, cut down. Next was her brother, a young boy drowned. Then she took Arsinoe, who wished to be crowned. Poison it was, for the last to die. Now just one, when once there were five.'

Six, I thought to myself. *Do not forget the Cleopatra who was born blessed for the afterlife.*

The hakawati leaned forward, riling the crowd. 'Who is it that I speak of?'

'Cleopatra!'

'A queen of gold, a queen of poison. A mother of bastard children . . .' Enraged, I thought of Helios and Selene asleep on the boat, innocent of the slander spoken of them this night.

My children were the quickest path to my anger. In that way, the asp and I were alike. For I would bite the hand that sought to strike them down without remorse and without mercy. I had little of either left in me.

I pushed forward through the crowd until I could see the hakawati. I wanted to know him in order to condemn him. He stood on an upturned crate, his tattered clothing held together with one hand to hide his nakedness. At his feet lay a wooden chalice where he collected coins. There were few in there, but every time my name was chanted, I saw him thrust it out towards the crowd.

'Exotic queen, salacious queen. Pharaoh of what might have been, if she had closed her legs and her bed. She may have been queen of us instead! Who is it that I speak of?'

The hakawati met my eyes, waiting for me to lead the chant. But when my lips did not move, he turned to the next person along, who shouted my name like a call to arms.

I could have gone back to the boat and commanded my guards to cut his head from his neck. Or better still, I could use the ivory dagger between my breasts and kill him myself. But my fury was dissipating as quickly as it had come.

This was the first time I had come face to face with my legend. She had my outline, but I did not recognise her face. I knew Octavian's propaganda had been vast, but to hear it here, spoken in Arabic, was distressing.

History is a disease. It masquerades as truth, but no one can replicate a moment in words alone. In Egypt we didn't try. History and stories were synonymous – like our art, they were reflections of sentiment rather than lauded as fact.

But Octavian had created me in the way of Romans. Their histories were a tool to teach and deter. The Roman obsession with oratory meant that few tales escaped the manipulation of the speaker. Never trust the story, only the storyteller.

And so a new version of Cleopatra was born – the me of myth and lore.

I speak now not to you, but to her.

You have been dragged through ink and song. Your ears bleed from the echo of your name that thunders across time. Your eyes are hollow, for they have been imagined and reimagined until they can no longer see.

Rest now. Let yourself disappear from the consciousness of others. I give you your freedom in these two words: I exist. I exist. I exist.

Like the quiet hiss of a snake. *I exist.*

I left without killing the hakawati. The act would do nothing but prove his narrative. And I had other blood to shed that night.

I crossed the bridge that led to the palace complex, which lay on an island in the centre of the river. The stone structure was lit by torches, and it cut an impressive sight against the night sky.

'Announce yourself!' a guard called out in Latin.

'My name is Selene,' I said, stepping into the firelight. The guards raised their spears at my approach.

'What do you want?'

'The triumvir, Antonius, sent for me.'

'And who are you to him?'

His wife.

'A healer – he will know of me.'

The guards spoke between themselves in Arabic, assuming I could not speak the common tongue of Syria.

'He said not to be disturbed,' one said.

'But if he sent for her . . .'

'It is late at night to have called on a healer.'

'Perhaps she is not a healer, but a prostitute.'

The insult glanced off me, as it followed on the heels of the hakawati's attack.

'Might I suggest you check with him?' I said dryly in Arabic. The guards jumped at the fluidity of my tongue, but smoothed over their embarrassment quickly and sent a messenger to Antonius.

As I predicted, I was welcomed into the palace shortly afterwards. I was led into an antechamber at the back of the building where a fire burned low in a copper basin. I stood by it, wrapping my arms around myself to bring comfort to my beating heart.

'Is it you?' I heard.

I closed my eyes to brace myself for the sight.

'Open your eyes and tell me you are not an apparition,' he said desperately. Rough hands moved to my cheeks and I opened my eyes.

The years had not changed him. I had hoped to see a difference so I could separate the man I had loved from who he was now. But save for a few streaks of silver in his hair, he was one and the same.

'Marcus,' I breathed.

'You are truly here.' His hands slipped to my waist and drew me towards him.

I tried to resist him, but in the time it took for me to sigh out a breath, I found myself leaning into his arms. My body's longing for his touch overcame my sense of reason. He began to kiss me, first my eyes, then my mouth. His lips trailed down my body, savouring every bit of skin that he could.

'Marcus.' I hoped that saying his name would ground me. 'Marcus, stop.'

He straightened, not because he heard me but because a thought had occurred to him. 'The children, did you bring them?'

I nodded wordlessly.

He grabbed my hand as if to lead me to the harbour. 'Let us go and see them.'

'They're asleep.' It was only then that he seemed to notice my grave demeanour.

'What is wrong?'

'This is the last time I will come to you.'

He cocked his head. 'You know I could not come to Egypt, my armies were here—'

'Nor will you be welcome in Egypt. Not as an ally, nor my lover.'

He took a step back. 'And as a husband?'

I looked into his eyes, willing myself to speak through the pain. 'Is it even a marriage if no one knows we were wed?'

'The gods know it,' he said hoarsely.

'It will be easy for you,' I told him. 'Your marriage to Octavia will never be questioned. You don't even need to meet the children; let them not know you rather than be parted from you.'

With every word Antonius took a small step back, as each one pierced him with an arrow. 'Why are you saying this, Cleopatra?'

'Octavia—'

'You were the one who told me to marry her.' His voice shook. 'You were the one who sent me away.'

'To stop a war!' I shouted.

'I would have fought him for you!' he shouted back. 'I would have done anything for you. Tell me what you want and I will do it.'

When I didn't reply straight away, he said, 'Do you want me to tell the world we are married? For I will do it, I have no shame in it. You were my wife ere Octavia was.'

Before I could answer, he strode from the room. I followed him as he made his way through the palace, and with every servant and guard we passed, he cried, 'I, Marcus Antonius, am married to the Pharaoh Cleopatra, Queen of Egypt.' He repeated himself until we reached the gardens and he bellowed it out into the night.

'Marcus,' I said wearily. 'This will not fix the distance between us.'

'What distance?' His eyes were wild, like those of an animal who knows it is soon to be sacrificed. The end was coming, he could sense it. 'I want no distance from you.' He stepped towards me, encircling me in his arms.

I didn't let myself soften in his embrace. 'Marcus, it is too painful. It is too painful living without you.'

'*I* will not live without *you*. So either strike me down, or let me love you.'

His words tore at my heart. He was saying everything I wanted him to say.

'Selene.' He spoke her name to disarm me. 'Tell me, what can I do to prove my love?'

'I should not have to tell you,' I said.

Something seemed to come over him; perhaps he heard the challenge in my voice, for he gathered himself and stood straighter.

'I will proclaim Caesarion's legitimacy before the senate. He is Caesar's heir, and Rome should be reminded of it.'

My breath caught in my throat. 'You would do this?'

He laughed, a hopeful, yearning sound. 'I would do anything for you.'

'You said once that you would never risk war with Octavian in Caesar's name.'

'I do it not in Caesar's name, but in yours.'

'Octavian will object,' I said.

'He will, but my victories this past year have put me in good standing with the public. He risks civil war if he goes against me.'

I looked into his earnest face and realised I could not stop loving him. Even if I severed all ties with him, there would be no end to this feeling. For all his flaws, and all of mine, we belonged together.

He read it in my face and began to weep. I kissed the tears from his cheeks.

'I thought I was losing you,' he said.

'I don't think that is possible,' I whispered. From beneath my robe I removed the small carvings of Isis and Dionysus that I had kept against my chest since he left.

'You see, we were never really parted,' I said.

His faced filled with wonder as he retrieved Dionysus from my outstretched hand and held him to his heart.

'There is no greater gift under this world's sky than your love.' Then his lips found mine.

We were lovers once more among the budding rose bushes of the palace gardens. And despite the time apart, I knew his rhythm like my own heartbeat.

The next few weeks were some of my happiest. Antonius was the father I always thought he'd be, and the twins adored him. We journeyed back to Egypt together, Antonius bringing two legions of his army as escort.

When we returned to Alexandria, news of our marriage had already reached the city. The palace was teeming with gifts sent from courtiers near and far. I had Faunus go through them to log the names of who had sent the presents and to note who had not – it was a good indication of who my allies truly were.

'I want the sword,' Caesarion proclaimed, reaching for a gilded weapon that had arrived that day.

Antonius laughed and picked it up. 'I think not – this one is mine.' He feinted towards Caesarion and the boy jumped back, laughing.

'I want to try,' Selene said, running forward.

'You're too young to fight,' Caesarion declared.

'No, she's not,' Helios declared. 'And neither am I.'

We were in the throne room, a place where now more laughter rang through the halls than petitions.

Courtiers still moved in and out of the palace, along with the royal scribes, but the running of Egypt was a much smoother process than it had been in recent years.

'Look, a harpoon!' Caesarion cried. It had been hidden behind pallets of fruit sent from Crete. 'Can we go fishing?' he asked.

Antonius and I shared a smile. 'I think a family hunting trip would be a worthy day out,' he said.

The twins' little feet pattered excitedly. I hadn't been half as vigilant with their hunting practice as I had with Caesarion's.

'Let us go,' I said.

The next day we set sail into the heart of the bay, north of the harbour. The twins played with fishing nets, often scaring away the prey Caesarion was trying to capture with his harpoon, much to his frustration.

'I've caught something!' Helios cried. After a day of no catches, we were all excited as he began to haul in his net.

He struggled and so I went to join him, Antonius at my side.

'It's big,' I said. 'Maybe a grouper.'

'I bet it's a bass,' Caesarion said with a touch of jealousy.

'Then we will take pleasure in its sacrifice tonight,' I said.

But what we pulled onto the deck was not a fish at all.

'Isis protect me,' I muttered, my knees falling to the deck.

Glinting in the sunlight was a gold breastplate.

'Theos,' I whispered, running my hand over the intricate engravings. Then I gathered it up, net and all, with strength I shouldn't have had, and threw it back into the water.

As it sank back beneath the surface, I vomited.

I was pregnant once more.

I was halfway through my fourth and final pregnancy when the floods came. The rains brought about much celebration and feasting.

I enjoyed this pregnancy much more than the twins'. I was not bound to my bed and could still partake in my children's upbringing. The twins proved to be harder to keep in line than Maahes and Bastet, who had each gone on to have cubs of their own. Selene had been caught stealing weapons from the armoury to practise in her bedchamber. It was only when I investigated the lumps beneath her covers that I discovered two daggers, three gladius and a bow and arrow.

Helios, not to be outdone, attempted to do the same the following night. But instead of stealing from the armoury, he pilfered from the kitchens. It took me many days to discover the source of the rotten smell, and finally he revealed the roast duck's hiding place himself, sickened by the aroma of his crimes.

I loved being a mother. But I was not motherly. I loved them deeply, fiercely, but I did not naturally nurture. It was a skill I learned from necessity, for I wanted to give my children everything I could. Beneath my children's earnest gazes, I became tender.

'Let us make them new crowns,' I said to Charmion one day.

'They have hundreds already,' she said, laughing.

'But Selene suggested quartz—'

'Your daughter manipulates you to get her way.'

I shrugged. 'Let her. I will give her what she wants.'

Antonius had instilled in me again an appreciation for luxury, which had waned in our years apart.

It was after a particularly lavish feast, at which our children wore their new crowns of quartz and copper, that I broached the subject of Octavia.

'Octavian's sister will have heard of our new child by now,' I said lightly, my hand resting on my stomach.

'Yes,' he said, looking out towards the sea. The breeze was warm, laced with a fine rain that left my skin glistening.

'Will you go to her?'

Antonius turned to me. His gaze was imploring. 'I will. But only to divorce her,' he said.

All the air left my lungs. 'You mean to end your union?'

'You and I are husband and wife. Octavia was a political alliance, whereas our love is deeper than mere flesh: it is blood, it is bone, it is breath.'

I blinked away an image of Octavia lying beneath him. He must have seen the pain cross my face.

'How many times must I tell you I am committed to you? Only you?'

'I fear that when you leave, you will not come back,' I admitted.

'I will come for you, *always*.' He ran a thumb over my bottom lip. I shivered and he put an arm around me, pressing me to his chest. I inhaled his aroma, wine and something sweeter, like honey.

'Must you go back to your campaign?'

'The lands I conquer, I conquer for you.'

I snorted. 'Not for me, Marcus, but for yourself and for Rome.'

He pushed me to arm's length, looking shocked. 'Have I not made it clear I do *everything* for you? Cyprus; it is yours. Cyrene; have that, too. Even Syria, where we reignited our love, is to be an Egyptian territory.'

Though he smiled, I could tell this was no jest. 'You mean to grant me the spoils of war?'

'My victories are yours now, Cleopatra. Let us rule the world together.'

'What of Octavian and the triumvirate?'

'Lepidus has already proved himself a traitor, and Octavian, I will deal with. We are Isis and Dionysus, and should rule as such.'

He gently stroked my swollen belly. 'We fight now so that our children can have peace. All of it will be theirs in the end.'

I leaned into his embrace, feeling safer than I had in years. When he left a few weeks later to continue his campaign against the Parthians, he took with him the might of the Egyptian army.

For to rule together, we had to fight together.

And die together, in the end.

CHAPTER TWENTY-SEVEN
34 BCE

Antonius did what he set out to do, carving out more and more of the world for me and my family. His latest victory – Armenia – was celebrated in Alexandria with much enthusiasm.

I waited for him at the harbour as his ship came in. In my arms I held Ptolemy Philadelphus, the sixteenth Ptolemy of my line and my third child by Antonius.

'Cleopatra!' my husband called from the bow of the boat. He wore a golden ivy wreath atop hair now cut short. The purple cloak he draped on one shoulder had been adorned with beading and gemstones.

He looked every bit the Greek god as he ran down the pier towards me.

'My son!' He took Ptolemy from my arms and lifted him up, to much giggling. Then, settling the babe in the crook of one arm, he turned to me and slipped the other hand around the nape of my neck before lowering a kiss to my lips.

'How I have missed you.'

I smiled, glad to have Antonius home again, but my smile slipped when I looked past him and saw prisoners disembarking, their wrists bound in gold chains.

'Who are they?' I said.

'The Armenian royal family.'

'Why are they here?'

'Because, my love,' he said gleefully, 'we are to have a triumph.'

I thought back to the last triumphal procession I had been a part of, the day Antonius and I had met. Arsinoe had been one of the prisoners paraded in front of the city.

I found myself looking away from the bound monarchs and was glad when two-year-old Ptolemy babbled something incoherent and drew my attention back to him.

'I have brought treasures for all the children,' Antonius said, his expression loving as he gazed at Ptolemy.

'I hope if you have brought Caesarion a weapon, you have brought one for Selene too – you know what happened last time,' I said.

'Of course, how could I forget my warrior daughter?' As if hearing her name, Selene appeared behind me, her arms open to join Ptolemy and Antonius's embrace. Helios was not far behind, his hand in Caesarion's; they had just returned from riding practice.

I watched my little family gathered beneath the brightness of the sun, and I thought, *Here is my whole world. I need nothing more, nothing less.*

Charmion and I began the plans for the triumph the next day. It was much like the Ptolemaia, but the focus was on the recent battle and the spoils of war. Aided in the particulars by Antonius, we transformed northern Alexandria into a festival parade. The procession began on the first day of shemu, the air scented with freshly harvested wheat and flax.

Antonius and I rode upon a chariot through the centre of the city. He wore a golden cape and his ivy-wreath crown. Tucked into his belt was the latest addition to his Dionysus outfit, a thyrsus – a giant fennel stalk crafted entirely out of bronze. I wore the crown of Isis and a large shebiu necklace made of turquoise discs. My hair hung in two braids and was beaded with small painted pieces of pottery, which sang a tinkling tune as the chariot moved.

My citizens lined the streets, cheering. Though I had learned to tolerate the scrutiny of so many eyes, I was keen for the procession to reach its destination.

The prisoners from Armenia were paraded in front of the chariot, along with soldiers carrying the treasures found in their coffers. Occasionally a commander would throw a piece of gold or silver out to the crowd, much to the delight of the onlookers.

Maps of Antonius's route through the world were circulated, with kohl crosses identifying the countries that were now a part of my empire. Wine was passed out along the route, in chalices in the style of Dionysus's own.

As we reached the gymnasium, the crowds grew thicker. Here we had erected our thrones: one cast in gold for me, with a lower step for Caesarion; and one cast in silver for Antonius. A bronze bench rested on the step below, where the rest of our children now sat.

Antonius helped me down from the chariot, his face flushed with wine and excitement.

'You look so happy,' I said fondly.

'Remember when we danced, the night of the Ptolemaia?' he said, and I laughed as he twirled me around on the gymnasium steps.

The crowd cheered in response.

'Marcus, I will fall,' I gasped.

'Then I will catch you!' he sang back.

Escaping his grasp, I ascended the steps to my throne. I touched each of the children's cheeks as I passed.

I lowered myself to my throne and set my arms atop the cool gold. Something moved beneath my wrists and I had to bite down on my tongue to stop myself from screaming in front of so many.

I clutched my hands to my chest and inspected what had startled me. Cages had been set into the panels of the armrests; within each writhed a young asp.

'The cobra is no one's god but its own,' Antonius said, sitting alongside me on his silver throne. His words echoed my own, all those years ago in the Siwa Oasis.

One of the snakes circled its cage frantically, while the other, whose skin was a deeper copper, watched the crowd from the corner.

I knew Antonius only wished to delight me with the asps. But I found myself wondering how long they had gone without food.

Yes, it is true I felt more pity for the snakes than for the Armenian royal family. But I had an affinity with the creatures, almost an intimation of how fate would coil our legends together.

As I rested my arms on the cages, gooseflesh rose on my skin.

Antonius looked on, and I smiled at him. Satisfied that I had appreciated his gift, he turned his face to the crowd.

'People of Alexandria, I present to you the goddess Isis reborn, the Queen of Kings, Cleopatra Thea Philopator.'

I gazed upon my citizens. Ten years ago, I would never have believed this sight lay in my future. I was finally accepted by my people, who cared not for the strength of my divinity, nor which man was in my bed.

Antonius went on to announce our children's new titles. The younger Ptolemy was made ruler of Syria, Cilicia and Phoenicia. Helios was next, and he rose from his seat as he was addressed, accepting the lands of Armenia and Media. Selene was granted Cyrene, and she bowed low as the Alexandrians chanted her name.

Caesarion was last; as Pharaoh, his rule superseded his siblings, and Antonius's tribute was befitting. 'We come now to Ptolemy Caesar, whose blood is like the finest wine. Son of the Mother of Kings, and fathered by the great Julius Caesar, there is only one country I claim in his name, though it is mighty: Rome.'

The citizens of Alexandria's cries were thunderous. Antonius and Caesarion basked in the rapture. As I scanned the crowd, I saw someone lingering at the edge of the guard line that surrounded us.

He wore the simple linens of an Egyptian farmer, cropped

short for working the fields, but loose enough not to stick to his skin in the heat. But what had caught my eye was the belt around his waist. Made of leather and embellished with metal pins, it was unique to soldiers in the Roman army.

We had many Roman soldiers in Alexandria, as Antonius and I had merged our armies, but in doing so we had neutralised the uniform, removing the belts.

The man must belong to Octavian.

'Marcus,' I called as the soldier moved closer to the gymnasium steps.

But Antonius could not hear me over the cries of the city.

I stepped down from my throne as I saw the man reach inside his tunic. Something glinted in the sun.

A knife.

'Marcus!' The concern in my voice finally made it through the cheers and he heard me.

But it was going to be too late. The soldier had already cut through the guards, taking them unawares and spraying the street with blood.

My hand flew to the ivory dagger at my throat, for I could see what was about to happen.

The soldier was aiming for Caesarion.

'No!' I screamed. He was just a step away.

Antonius sprang, withdrawing a hidden blade of his own from within the fennel stalk at his waist. The soldier was, by this time, on a level with Antonius. But as Antonius feinted towards the assassin's heart, the assassin lurched forward towards the bottom of my throne – where Caesarion sat by my feet.

I watched the blade destined for my son glint in the sunlight.

Then I saw blood. And Caesarion fell, then lay still.

I ran to him.

'Mama?' he said with tears in his eyes. Antonius was beside me in a moment.

I looked for the wound and nearly wept when I saw that the assassin had only struck his arm.

Antonius lifted him into his arms and we ran with him through to a room in the back of the gymnasium, as our guards descended upon the would-be assassin behind us.

'Caesarion, you will be fine,' I said, as Antonius laid him on a stone bench. 'Charmion, my bag!'

Charmion rushed forward, already removing the needle and thread.

Caesarion whimpered beneath me, and I was plunged back to the memory of the ink and needle.

'This will hurt.' *As it will hurt me.*

'I will be brave, Mama,' he said, though his eyes were wide and fearful.

How he had grown.

'I will go and deal with the assassin,' Antonius said.

'Do not kill him before I speak to him,' I said. 'I wish to know more of the man who thinks he can murder a god.'

Antonius left us.

'Will I have a scar?' my son asked.

It was Charmion who answered. 'You see this?' She pointed to where her old wound had silvered, tracing the raised skin from her jaw to the top of her cheekbone. 'This was healed by your mother the very same way.'

He smiled through the pain. 'I like your scar. I hope mine will look the same.'

What a noble heart he had. What I would give to press my ear against his chest now and listen to the steady beat of it.

Once I had finished stitching, I kissed his brow. 'Go now, find your brothers and sister and leave for the palace. Keep your guards close.'

I walked out to the gymnasium courtyard. Crowds still lingered, though all festivities had ebbed.

Antonius had taken the assassin to the palaestra. The soldier lay in a pool of his own blood, his stomach lacerated with shallow cuts. Antonius's sword dripped crimson. 'I don't believe you,' he was saying. 'Someone must have paid you.'

'No one needed to pay me,' the man spat, his jaw clenched tightly in pain.

'You hail from Rome,' I said, and he looked up.

'Do not speak to me, heretic,' he snarled.

Antonius pressed his sword's edge to the man's throat, drawing blood. 'You will address the Pharaoh as is proper.'

Ignoring me, the soldier spoke to Antonius: 'She has bewitched you away from your wife and turned you against Rome. You share the spoils of war with Egypt before your own people. The heretic and her illegitimate child are no longer welcome in Rome.'

'And upon whose authority has this claim been made?' Antonius asked.

'Our lord, Octavian.'

Antonius and I shared a look. 'Did Octavian know of the territories you bequeathed to our family?' I asked him.

Antonius didn't answer, and the assassin laughed. 'She speaks like a mortal woman, but we know her to be a siren. Rome will be the death of her.'

No, it would not.

Antonius lunged towards the assassin to silence him, but I held out a hand to halt the killing blow.

At first he looked at me quizzically, but then he heard what I whispered to one of the guards, and nodded. The assassin looked between Antonius and me and cackled.

'It is as they say: she has bewitched you, addled your wit.'

Antonius turned to me sweetly. 'Dearest, may I cut out his tongue while we wait?'

Before I could answer, the guard returned, a basket in his outstretched arms. I reached for it.

The assassin's voice took on a pleading tone as I approached him with the basket. 'Triumvir, do not let her touch me, I will not be subdued by her charms.'

I lifted the lid and hissing filled the palaestra.

'Step back,' I said to Antonius.

'No, stop!' Finally, the soldier spoke to me. But I was no longer listening.

'Have your fill, then have your freedom,' I said to the asps before tipping them onto the bloodied stomach of the assassin.*

The smaller snake, the one that had been frantic, darted away without lingering on the prey I offered. But the copper one, who had watched the crowd from its gilded cage, lunged.

The assassin thrashed as the cobra's fangs sank into his flesh, but his cries weakened as the venom's paralysis came into effect.

The asp, realising she would be unable to consume such a large meal, slithered away, leaving a trail of blood through the gymnasium.

'Go and find your mother, little one,' I whispered as her tail slipped out of sight.

The assassin's jerking had stopped by my feet, but his eyes were wild and fearful.

'Kill him,' I said to Antonius.

The poison was not enough to stop his heart; the snake was only a juvenile. But it did paralyse him enough to make his death an inescapable horror.

I watched impassively as Antonius's sword crunched through the bone and sinew of the soldier's neck.

'It is done,' he said when the assassin's breath left him.

But this was not the end of the bloodshed, merely the beginning. More and more people would die, until finally, I, too, would walk the lonely path to the field of reeds.

'What are we to do?' I said, pacing the bedchamber.

Antonius lounged on the bed, his ankles crossed. 'Nothing.

---

* I have watched your painters portray images of me and the asp time and time again, in oil, ink and lead. It is a shame none captured this true moment – the venom of a mother's vengeance.

Octavian does not have enough support from the senate to pose a threat to us.'

I showed him my hands. 'You see this? This is my son's blood. Octavian has already proven he is a threat.'

Antonius rose, came to me and enfolded my bloodied hands in his. 'I will protect you and our family. We'll increase the guards, be more vigilant with who we allow in our presence. Perhaps we grew complacent. But Octavian will not harm us.'

I chewed my lip. 'He calls Caesarion illegitimate still.'

'He only retaliates against me divorcing his sister. This is a quarrel between families, not a harbinger of war.'

I was not sure he was right.

'He will try to take the land you have granted to the children.'

'He may try, but he will not succeed.'

He could see I was not convinced.

'Call the scribes,' he said. 'Allow me to make known my will. Then, if I fall in battle, our family will be protected.'

He did as he promised and penned a new will, assigning the countries he had conquered to our children. It eased some of the worry in my chest, knowing that even if we went to war, Octavian could not refute the words of Antonius's final wishes.

I watched as each of the seven scribes sealed the wax tablet as witnesses, Antonius's will made immortal. And as it was placed in its wooden box, I hoped it would be many more years before the box would be opened again.

CHAPTER TWENTY-EIGHT
31 BCE

Octavian declared war on me two years later.

First he had to convince Rome of the worthiness of the fight. Though many would die in the battle between Antonius and Octavian, it was a war of words before it was a war of swords.

The day after Antonius penned his will, he had sent Faunus to Rome to give the document to the Temple of Vesta, where it would be protected until his death.

But before Faunus could meet with the priestesses there, he was set upon by Octavian's men.

'They beat me and robbed me of all I had, even my toga.' The old man quivered before me, the mark of Iphis smeared from the sweat that beaded his brow.

'How dare Octavian touch one of mine,' I seethed.

'Pharaoh, there is more.'

I braced myself on the edge of my throne. The gold cages that had once held the asps had been replaced. In their place now lay ivory carvings of the rearing snakes. I patted the head of one fondly. They were a fitting tribute to the creatures who had helped carry out my vengeance. Antonius sat beside me. Faunus turned to him now. 'Octavian took from me your will, my lord, and he made a show of reading it to the senate.'

Antonius ran a hand through his greying hair. 'He goes against the laws set in paper and stone,' he growled. 'My allies were able to regain my documents, I assume?'

Faunus grimaced. 'No, my lord. Octavian called for soldiers to prevent anyone from relinquishing the tablet while he read. He embellished upon the words within, making bold claims that swayed the senate's ire to you.'

'Bold claims?' I said quietly.

Faunus replied in a rush, as if getting the words out quickly would somehow soften their impact. 'That you intend to turn Alexandria into the capital of Rome, that you mean to give the spoils of war to your children by the Pharaoh and not your children by Octavia. That you wish to die beneath the gods of Egypt and be interred in a tomb here.'

I raised my eyebrows. 'Alexandria the capital of Rome? I would not let it be so. Egypt is master of her own.'

Faunus blanched. 'But the rest he spoke on, it is true?'

Antonius's eyes narrowed. 'This should be no surprise, Faunus. I have made my home in Egypt and my children already rule the lands I have conquered.'

'But to be laid to rest in Alexandria . . .' Faunus swallowed and rubbed the back of his neck. 'It appeared to sicken some of the senate. They believe you to be, ah . . . possessed by the Pharaoh's wanton ways.'

'Of course – it always comes back to me,' I said bitterly.

'Do not let Octavian's words come to harm you, my love. He is a fool.'

'A fool with ambition, and now one with the senate behind him,' I replied.

'Peace, Cleopatra,' Antonius said.

'Peace?' I laughed scornfully. 'There will be no peace while Octavian means to attack our family.'

Faunus looked stricken as he watched us argue.

'You are dismissed,' I said, relieving the administrator, but he did not leave. 'What is it? Tell me there is not more.'

Faunus squirmed and I would have felt sorry for the man if I hadn't been so blinded by my own anxiety.

'Pharaoh, they have declared you an enemy of Rome.'

There was a shocked silence as we took in what he had said. Then my hands tightened around the throat of the ivory snakes beneath my palm, as if at any moment they would come alive and I could brandish them at my foes.

I smiled, baring imaginary fangs, dripping imaginary venom.

'So, war it will be.'

Antonius and I raised an army of five hundred warships, one hundred thousand infantry and twelve thousand cavalry. We called on our allies from across the world, gaining the support of nearly a dozen kings and queens. But this war was never about numbers. It was about strategy.

Few men could match my military prowess. Go and look through your books and your poems: my skill is rarely spoken on. For it is difficult for men to imagine me for the general I was; easier to speak on my beauty than on my mind.

'We need to attack, take him unawares in his home waters,' Antonius argued.

I disagreed. 'We may have the superior numbers, but if we proceed north, we leave Egypt vulnerable to attack. They may yet call in reserves from their allies and strike while our backs are turned.'

We sat in a stateroom in Patrae in southern Greece, where we had spent a season campaigning for allies. A map was laid out before us, our generals at our backs. The anticipation of the war between Antonius and Octavian had increased over the years, until even I could feel the invisible string that tethered them together, waiting to snap.

'His fleet is in port at Tarentum; we should use this opportunity to gain the upper hand.'

'Aggression is not the answer, Marcus; we must be calculating and reserved. We cannot be the ones to strike first, especially if that strike lands us a sword in our backs.'

Antonius scowled, a rare expression on his face. With Octavian's army waiting on the southern coastline of Italy, every night had become a debate on what we should do. We bickered relentlessly about the best tactics. Both of us had participated in wars, but neither had reckoned with the might of a navy this size.

'Let me take my fleet to Tarentum, then, and you may command yours to Actium,' he said.

I let out a sigh. 'Though a noble gesture, that would be suicide. And I do not think that is how you wish to die.'

'I do not wish to die at all, that is why we must strike.' He slammed his fist on the table.

I laid a hand on his shoulder. 'We cannot make rash decisions. For it is not just our own fate we look to protect, but the fate of our children, as well as all of Egypt.'

Antonius tipped his head to the side, resting his jaw on my hand. 'I know you are right. But I am impatient for the battle to be won. Octavian has been the thorn in my side for too long.'

'Do not rush to remove it, for you may lose too much blood.' I kissed his brow.

'So, to Actium?'

I nodded. 'The bay allows us sight of the Greek coastline should Octavian move on to Egypt. We can send our infantry ahead of us across land.'

Actium. It was so nearly my final resting place.

Leaving Patrae meant leaving the children. We had brought them with us on our journey across the sea, and I was pained to leave them.

'Mama, why can't we go with you? I can fight,' Selene said. At nine years old she was as fierce and as mighty as many of the queens of Egypt's past. I gathered her into my arms.

'You cannot; this is not a war for children.'

'I am not a child. Let me lead the Egyptian fleet,' Caesarion said sullenly from across the room.

I went to him and gripped his chin between my fingers, his jaw dusted with the first showings of hair. 'No, you are not. You are a king, my son. You are Horus. You are a pharaoh. And to be these things you *must* protect Egypt for me.'

He stood a little straighter. 'You will come home victorious, will you not?'

I forced a smile. 'Of course! I am Isis blessed and cannot be killed so easily.'

Helios's arms circled my waist, followed by those of Ptolemy, who did not want to be left out.

Once I had embraced my children, I turned to Charmion.

'Will you take our children home, my dear friend? The ship awaits you in the harbour,' I said to her quietly. Her image swam through the tears in my eyes.

'Why do you cry, Cleo?' she said softly, lest the children hear. 'Why do you act as though this is the last time you will see them?'

'It may be the last time,' I admitted. That morning, I had awoken with dread in the pit of my stomach. Despite the odds being in our favour, I had a certainty that we would lose this fight with Octavian. I had not brought my doubts to Antonius, only to Charmion.

She reached for me now, her hand gripping my wrist tightly, almost painfully. 'Do not let it be. I will not abide you dying without me by your side.'

'Charmion . . .'

She silenced me with a kiss. Since Ahmose's death, her devotion to me had become absolute, and I basked in her love. 'I will see you soon,' she said firmly.

They departed the next day, leaving Antonius and me to cross the ocean in the opposite direction, docking our fleet in the Ambracian Gulf near Actium.

I'd heard tales of the land's luscious greenery. And in my mind, I sailed to the Land of Punt.

It was the hakawati who had first told me about the far-off isle of Punt, sparking my imagination for years to come. The story spoke of a shipwrecked sailor who awoke in a land of abundance, reigned solely by a gargantuan gold snake known only as the Lord of Punt.

When I struggled to sleep, Charmion and I used to conjure up the fantastical island, hissing into the darkness as if we were the lord of the land.

'The sand is made of gemstones.'

'And the trees' boughs are heavy with fruit.'

'And fowl! Plump for roasting.'

'With crystal rivers to bathe in.'

'Don't forget the pools filled with wine to drink.'

But Actium was not that. The only thing in abundance were the biting insects.

'The air is sticky,' I complained, swatting at a fly.

'The summer season is upon us,' Antonius said, mopping his brow. 'Our infantry will suffer for it.'

I looked to the coastline. Actium was a sea of tents and canopies. The swampland surrounding the Ambracian Gulf had proven a difficult campsite; though it was green with ferns and mallows, the mud pulled at the foundations of our fortifications.

Soldiers dotted the landscape like buds on a trailing plant, the feathered plumes of our allies, in shades of red, purple, blue and green, brightening the land like flowers in bloom.

With my navy at my back, and the infantry ahead of me, I should have felt safe, powerful even. But the dread had not eased; instead it had deepened after a Roman commander had spotted swallows roosting under the stern just that morning.

'A bad omen,' he'd said quietly, thinking I had not heard him. But I had, and so too had some of my men, which set unease swirling like the eddies of the currents.

I wrapped my arms around myself, pulling at the gold cloak I wore. Every morning, I dressed in formal garb and stood in this spot on the bow of my ship. I knew the importance of my presence for the troops, though it fatigued me, the sun sheening my skin with sweat.

Antonius often joined me, and so we stood, like two statues of the gods, awaiting our fates.

'Do you remember when we first met?' I asked him.

He looked at me, his gaze tender. 'Of course. That was the very moment I fell in love with you. You were cut from bronze and gold in the Temple of Venus.'

I tutted. 'You did not love me then.'

'I did,' he said seriously. 'I may not have known it, but I did. The gods carved our love in stone, for why else were we both drawn to the temple that day?'

I did not tell him about my quest for mint to soothe my stomach.

'Do you think we will survive this, Marcus?' I asked.

He reached for my waist, slipping his hand around me. 'We will.'

'And if we don't?'

His smile dropped and he looked to the distance where the sweltering heat beat down on the armour of our soldiers.

'If we don't, then we will be immortalised like Isis and Dionysus before us. We will be remembered as the lovers who fought for justice, who stood tall in the face of tyranny.'

I thought of the rumours that bloomed in Rome, the petals scattered across the world by the winds of fate, and I grew doubtful.

'It is *our* tyranny the Romans speak on.'

'Rome is not the world. Octavian's empire will be lost in history.* You are Egypt.'

I was still unsure. I sensed the mould of my legend had already

---

* I urge you to reach for your pen and mark the years that the Roman Empire lived and died. Then take your pen and walk ten, fifteen paces from the paper. Mark the ground and look back to the dots on your page. That is the legacy Pharaonic Egypt left. Millennia versus five centuries.

been carved. Though it would take years, centuries, for the cast to set.

Antonius saw my lips turn down and reached for my cheek. 'We will not be forgotten, and so we will live on.'

If only the tales spoke of Antonius's kindness, and not his capricious moods, and told stories of my tenacity and not my sexual prowess.

'Imperator, my queen, we have had news from our commander in Methone,' Dellius said behind us.

I turned to him. Once a Roman emissary, he had become a trusted general in Antonius's army. I had disliked him from the moment he had arrived in Alexandria all those years before and summoned me to Tarsus.

'What do they say?' I asked impatiently.

Dellius's eyes flickered briefly over to me, but then he answered as if Antonius had asked the question.

'Octavian has taken Methone.'

Antonius swore and began pacing. 'He's going after our supply routes.'

'Let us come away from the railing,' I said. 'I do not wish our soldiers to see our disquiet.'

He seemed as though he might argue, but then he looked back at the infantry and the sea of soldiers who stood waiting to take our orders.

'Yes, come, let us move into the ship's heart.' He strode away, Dellius falling into step behind him before I could follow. I scowled at the general's back.

When we were comfortably seated in the room we had chosen as our war council, I spoke again: 'We were waiting on those supplies from Methone to feed the troops. They will now hunger.'

'Yes, though I have a solution,' Dellius said with a hint of arrogance.

'Go on.'

'Herod is abandoning Actium; we can trade for his supplies.'

'Another ally is leaving us?' I said. 'Why was I not told of this?'

Antonius frowned. 'I told you to inform the Pharaoh yesterday, Dellius.'

'I thought bringing you the news was sufficient.' Dellius pushed out his chest.

'I grow tired of his insubordination,' I said, as if Dellius was not there.

'Dellius, please remember that the Pharaoh is my partner in all things,' Antonius said sharply.

Dellius's bow was stiff, and still he faced Antonius, not me. 'Yes, Imperator.'

I dragged my gaze from him and back to Antonius. 'We must lure Octavian onto land. His blockade will be the death of us if we cannot supply food to our fleet. Herod's supplies will not last long.'

'We need to discuss with the rest of our allies. Dellius, send for them. It is time to end this battle.'

Dellius returned with the kings and queens of Asia Minor and the East. Together we formed a plan to force Octavian's hand. We had many more soldiers than him, and if we were able to draw the Romans out to central Greece, the battle would easily be won.

I learned a lesson too late that day: when someone first shows you their true nature, believe the face they turn to you.

Dellius took the plans that we made that day and gave them to Octavian. I will never know what it was that swayed his loyalties. Did he see the end was in sight? Or was it as simple as his hatred of me?

Either way, his defection became one of many. With the lack of food and burning weather, soldiers flocked in their masses to Octavian's side.

The dread in my belly had sunk into my bones. So much so that I found it hard to conduct my daily routine on the bow of the boat.

'I must sit,' I whispered in Eiras's direction. My maid came forward just as I began to sway. She caught me and lowered me onto the ship's deck. That was where Antonius found me.

'Cleopatra? Are you well?'

He kneeled by my side.

'No, Antonius. I am not.' I took the cup of murky water Eiras offered and drank it, despite it tasting brackish.

'What is it that ails you?' he asked. I looked into his hollowed eyes, lack of sleep robbing them of vibrancy. The green in their centre, which I had once thought the most beautiful and invigorating colour, now reminded me of the Actium marshes.

'This war presses down heavy on my heart. We cannot continue like this. We have to retreat before we starve here.'

Antonius collapsed beside me, sighing. Then he laughed, shaking his head. 'If the soldiers look to us now, they'll be greatly disappointed by the figures they see.'

I reached for his hand and squeezed it. 'It is time to go home. Let us amass more troops, rally for more allies. Our time in Actium is over, but the battle is not.'

'I see the sense in what you suggest,' he told me, 'but how are we to manoeuvre through the gulf? Octavian still blocks our path.'

My father's voice came to me then across the great distance of my memories. I lay tangled in Berenice's bloodied sheets, cursing his hand in her murder.

He had gently lifted me from the bed and said, *'We are Egypt, and Egypt is us. Sometimes we must sacrifice what we hold dear. But Egypt must live. Always.'*

With my father's words ringing in my ears, I stood shakily and looked back over the fleet.

'We must sacrifice some of our own army. Order thirty of our ships to attack the eastern flank, then while Octavian is occupied, we make for Egypt.' I spoke quietly, too softly for anyone but Antonius to hear. We no longer trusted anyone but each other.

'We'll be condemning all aboard those thirty ships to death.'

I nodded grimly. 'Strip the vessels of all but the sparsest of crews. And tonight, let us invite the commanders who lead them to dine with us. We can empty the kitchen supplies, consume all the wine. Give them a night with the gods before their noble death on the morrow.'

The last meal in Actium was a raucous affair. The thirty commanders filled the dining hall of the boat, bringing with them voracious appetites. I had instructed the kitchens to assemble a feast that was reminiscent of the many we'd had back in Egypt.

Stocks were low, but they were able to hunt waterfowl from the bay, roasting them in batches so that the evening wore on far later than I had wanted. We used the last of our wine, ensuring the commanders' cups were always filled. Tributes were made in mine and Antonius's honour and we accepted them politely, raising our gold chalices up in respect.

But as the dinner came to a close, I urged Antonius to pronounce his final words. And seal their fates.

He begged for silence from the wine-merry crowd and they granted it to him. 'Many of you may be wondering what fortune has led to your attendance here this night. I am here to tell you that tomorrow is the day we strike at the heart of our enemy.'

There were shocked murmurs.

'You mean to say we make a move on the blockade?' a young commander asked. He could not have been much older than Caesarion. I looked away.

Coward, my inner voice said. *You cannot face the men you send to their deaths?*

I forced myself to turn back to him as I stood, drawing the gaze of the room to me. The soldier's brown eyes were wide and innocent, not seeming the eyes of a soldier.

'Yes,' I said. 'Tomorrow, you have all been chosen to lead the battle. We have brought you here to honour you, for your names will forever be written in history.'

I feel shame now, for I cannot recollect the name of any of my commanders from that day. They died so I could live a few more months. An unworthy cause.

Some of the commanders began to cheer but the boy was frowning. 'Why have you recalled my archers to land, then?'

I felt Antonius tense beside me.

'We do not need archers to best Octavian's fleet,' I said quickly. 'His ships are far smaller, our naval rams will be enough.'

This seemed to ease the boy's worries and he joined in the growing cheers.

Antonius and I did not sleep that night. We stood on the bow of my ship and watched the sun rise.

'This was not the outcome I expected,' he said quietly.

'We have our health, Marcus. We have each other. And we have our children.' I leaned against him and he pressed his nose to my hair.

'That, perhaps, is the one benefit of this day. We will get to see our children very soon. I have missed them.'

'As have I.'

I thought again of the young commander. I was grateful Antonius stood at my back so he could not see the tears swimming in my eyes.

Guilt does not fade with time. Some feelings do, like anger and grief. Even the vibrancy of love loses its light, if not its warmth. But guilt? Its roots wrap around my soul, sometimes making my breath stutter.

'This is not the end of the fight,' Antonius said.

'It cannot be, for Octavian will never allow Caesarion to live.'

'And so, Octavian must die,' he said firmly, and my heart swelled.

I turned to face him. 'Thank you for loving me, Marcus.'

He smiled then, and it was as if the sun had appeared from behind a cloud. 'There has been nothing easier or simpler than the love I have for you.'

When he kissed me I felt his tears mixing with mine on my cheeks.

Soon we would be parted. I would be in Egypt working on defences, while he would go on to Cyrene to bring back the legions we had secured there.

'Can you not come home to Egypt with me?' I whispered into his ear.

'You know that is what my heart desires. But we need the infantry in Cyrene if we are to have a chance of defeating Octavian in Alexandria. Any delay leaves us vulnerable.'

I knew he spoke sense.

'You will be with me always,' he said, and he reached into his tunic and withdrew a small wooden figurine.

I laughed as I recognised the small carving of Dionysus that I had chosen for him in the market.

'Take it and place it next to your heart,' he said.

My hand went to my neck and I removed the ivory knife I had worn since the day the hakawati had tried to kill me.

'As long as you will wear this,' I said.

He knew how much the necklace meant to me. I pressed my lips to the sheath before looping the chain over his neck. Then I took the figurine from him and placed it in my dress above my heart.

'In life or in death, Marcus, I will see you again,' I said.

Once the sun had risen, I led what remained of my navy to the eastern waters, to await an opening in Octavian's fleet.

Up ahead were the thirty vessels we had released as sacrifice to allow for our escape.

I watched as the first Egyptian ship made it through the blockade, ramming into the Roman navy. Fire arrows rained down upon it, setting the deck alight.

I forced myself to look as the flames licked up the sides of the boat. My eyes stung as the fire burned flesh, tears falling once the ship had sunk.

Ten Roman ships fell before there was sufficient space to move my fleet through the blockade. And ten more of mine.

Thousands died that day.
Would I do it again?
Yes.

I did not look back once we had sailed through the gulf. I did not check to see if Antonius followed. My eyes were on Egypt. And my country called to me, like no man ever had.

CHAPTER TWENTY-NINE
30 BCE

I have never felt relief like I did when I had the Lighthouse of Alexandria in my sights.

I am home again.

A flock of ibis flew overhead, one relieving itself on the ground in front of me. I sprang back, then laughed. 'Arsinoe mocks me still.'

As we docked in Antirhodos I saw my children gathered at the end of the pier. I did not want to tell them the news I brought: that we had lost the battle, and the war was yet to come.

I held them close to my chest, even Caesarion, who tried to pull away.

'Mama, where is Antonius?' he asked once I had taken my fill of his closeness.

'He goes to Cyrene to bring back more soldiers.'

'The war is not won?' he said, a flicker of fear in his eyes. His nerves had never quite recovered from the assassin's attack.

'No, Octavian will be swift on the wind. We must ready the city.'

Caesarion nodded grimly, then without my prompting called the commanders of the remaining fleet to the throne room.

'He has become a capable king.'

I turned to her voice and opened my arms.

Charmion came to me smiling. 'I did not enjoy our time apart,' she said into my shoulder.

'Neither did I.'

'War is to come to Egypt after all?'

'Yes.' My voice was tight with unreleased emotion, but I did not let Charmion draw out my tears.

She pushed me to arm's length and scrutinised me.

'We will fight for our city and our country,' she said.

I looked into her eyes. 'And our children.'

We walked together back to my chambers.

'If anything should happen—' I began.

'Please do not—'

'No, listen.' I stopped her before we walked into the palace. 'If anything should happen, I need you to use the tunnels in my room and escape with the children. Use the boat we have down there and flee.'

'I would never leave you.'

'You must.' I raised my voice so she might hear the desperation in it. 'I need your word, Charmion. Please, give me this gift.'

Her features twisted with grief. 'But where will we go?'

'Anywhere,' I said fiercely. 'Anywhere but here. Raise them as commoners, away from the poison of the courts. You must hide them from Octavian, for he will never let them live.'

'You are acting as though this is a certainty.'

'I hope not. I hope that the legions we raise in Cyrene will be enough to win this war.'

'Then we shall hope, and not speak on this again,' she said.

'Not until you promise me, Charmion. Promise me you will do this.'

She met my gaze and nodded once. 'I will do as you say.'

Breathing more easily, I continued on into the palace.

Caesarion had started the war council without me, and I watched proudly as he strategised with the leaders there. He was patient and respectful of their experience, recommending tactics he had learned from studying.

You were always destined to be a better leader than either of your parents, my son. It pains me that history will never see the ruler you were to become.

We prepared the city for war once more. Days passed and there was no word from Antonius, nor sight of Octavian's army.

The city was tightly coiled with apprehension. I spent most of my time in the temple praying before my god, leaving Caesarion to manage the country's affairs.

It was where Charmion found me.

'Cleopatra.' Her voice was full of fear.

I rose from the altar. 'What has happened?'

'Look to the sea.'

I went to the temple's steps and looked north. A fleet of at least five hundred ships floated on the horizon.

'Could it be Antonius?' she asked.

'Marcus is marching from Cyrene by land; this is Octavian's fleet.'

'But we do not have the means to defeat him without Antonius's army,' Charmion said, her voice high with panic.

I felt the dread that had built in me over the last few seasons dissipate in one single breath.

'The worst has happened,' I said, and found myself grinning.

'Why do you smile?' She reached for my medicine bag from around her waist, as though to cure me from my malady.

'Don't you see? It's over.'

Death beckoned to me.

There was a movement in the bushes that drew my attention away from the fleet; a mother cobra, pressing her nose to the sky. I understood her meaning and was comforted by it.

'It is time to join the gods.'

If I had bent low, would she have climbed into my clothing, as your tales claim? Perhaps. But certainly not to strike at my breast. She would have coiled around my brow and joined the rearing snakes on my crown – for cobras are proud things, just like me.

I retreated back into the temple and bowed low. 'It won't be long now. Bring me the children.'

When Charmion didn't move, I said sharply, 'Now, Charmion. Every moment is precious.'

I watched as the ships drew closer to Alexandria. They were the only indication of the passing of time, for everything else stood frozen, even my breath.

Octavian would not kill me. Not at first. I would become a trophy of the Roman senate. Paraded. Ridiculed.

Like Arsinoe.

But unlike my sister, I would not be able to sway the crowd's sympathy. I would die on those bloodied steps to the thunderous cheers of the Roman people.

'I will not be led in triumph,' I declared to the oncoming ships.

The channels of my life had merged into a single river. There was no going back upstream – I could only let the water carry me forth. I wonder now: had I not borne children, would I have fought the currents? But it is too difficult to separate my life from them. My sacrifice was a small thing to trade for their survival.

'Cleo?'

I emerged from my trance to see the concerned face of Charmion. She had returned with the children.

I kneeled before them. Helios and Ptolemy clutched each other's hands so tightly their knuckles had turned white. Selene, on the other hand, looked ready to fight, her gaze flicking to the horizon, and Caesarion was resolute. He, more than the others, knew defeat was imminent and he faced it unafraid.

Oh, how I loved them. The flesh of me.

'You are to go with Charmion. She has prepared a means to escape the palace. But you must wait until Octavian is sure of victory before you set sail. Let him think you have gone inland. I do not want you set upon on the sea.'

Caesarion shook his head. 'No, I'm not leaving you here.'

I reached for him and he let me stroke his curling hair, so

much like Caesar's. 'You are everything your father wished you to be, my son.' His eyes filled with tears.

'Selene, you are everything I wish I had been.' She met my gaze. 'You are the very best of both my sister and me, and you must know I loved Arsinoe very much.'

'I will look after them, Mama,' she said.

I nodded and kissed the top of her head.

'Helios, your kindness is so much like your father's; never let it fade. And Ptolemy, my youngest, let your laughter fill others' lives as it has mine.' I held on to them both for a brief moment, then let them go, as I knew I must.

'Go ahead now, children, let me speak to Charmion alone.'

Finally, I lifted my gaze to Charmion. She was weeping freely.

'Why are you acting as if you will never see them again?' she asked. 'Tell me you have a plan.'

I smiled sadly. 'This is it – the final plan that comes for us all.'

She reached for my hand and squeezed it painfully. 'Tell me this is not the end.'

I looked at her but still I refused to cry. 'I will not lie to you.'

She fell to the ground at my feet, pulling me with her.

'No, Cleo, you must come with us.'

I kissed her wet cheeks. 'I cannot. My presence here is what will give you and the children the means to escape. Let him know where to find me, and when he comes ashore, you and the children must leave.'

'You will let him take you prisoner?'

I shook my head and said fiercely, 'Never.'

Charmion cried even harder. I leaned my brow against hers. 'Give me my medicine bag, Charmion. It is time for me to carry its load.'

She started to lift the bag, but her arms grew weak and she collapsed again. With gentle hands I took it from her.

'I need you to go and look after the children, Charmion. Hide with them in the tunnel until you see Octavian come ashore. I will make certain he knows where to find me.'

I brought my lips to hers for the final time. 'Go, my dearest friend. The other half of me.'

Charmion stood on shaking legs and I embraced her for the final time. I whispered against her hair, 'Live this life for the both of us, Charmion.'

She released me and said, 'You were all I ever needed in this life, Cleo.'

I rested my forehead on hers and whispered, 'One for the past and the happy years well spent, one for the present and the patience we extend, one for the future and the love that never ends.'

Then Charmion left, and half of my soul went with her.

Eiras helped dress me in my finest clothes. I wore the gold dress I had worn the day I had married Antonius. Over one shoulder I draped the purple cloak that Caesar had given me. At my neck, a turquoise and gold mantle handed down through generations. My hair was knotted with two golden pins. Finally, I wore my uraeus crown, the three rearing cobras pressing heavy on my brow.

'Eiras, will you bring me an obsidian slate? There is one final task I must attend to.'

When she had gone, I looked at myself in the mirror.

I had achieved much in my life, though I was not yet forty years of age. Some of my successes lived on in my body: the lines of the smiles Antonius had solicited, the scars on my stomach from my children. Then there were my failures beneath the surface: the wound of Caesar's death, the betrayal of my younger siblings.

This body had carried me through good and bad. And it was beautiful.

Do not let your historians tell you I was not. Your professors scrutinise my face on a coin and tell me my legacy was unsightly.

But I stand before you now, clad in gold and purple with all my flaws and all my scars. And I am the very essence of beauty.

Eiras returned, an obsidian slate in one hand, a carving knife in the other.

I began to write my final message to Antonius.

Marcus, I will see you again in the field of reeds. Our love is more than this life; it is blood, it is bone, it is breath.

I handed the finished tablet to Eiras. 'Be sure that when Marcus arrives, he is given this.'

She read the message and blanched. 'Pharaoh . . .'

I nodded, confirming her suspicions.

There was only one more thing I had to do before my death. I stopped in the throne room, where Faunus sat with his head in his hands. He looked up as I called to him.

'Pharaoh,' he said, 'have you heard the news? Octavian will be upon us this night.'

I nodded. 'Yes. You must leave the city. You have been too loyal to me – Octavian will not let you live.'

Faunus began to argue, but I would not hear of it. I held out a hand to silence his protestations.

'I ask one more thing of you only. Send a missive to Octavian. Tell him I have died by my own hand in the Temple of Isis. I wish to lure his eyes away from the shoreline.'

'But it will be a ruse? Yes? You will leave Egypt?'

'He will need to see a body. Or he will never stop looking for me.'

'Pharaoh—'

'You were a great advisor to me, Faunus. Live out the rest of your life knowing I treasured you well.'

Then I left. I did not have the strength to linger on any more goodbyes.

I locked the doors of my temple and sequestered myself inside. I removed the jar of wolfsbane from my medicine bag and added it to a chalice of wine that had been left as an offering to my god. I placed the tincture next to the flickering rushlight, to warm the wine and brew the herbs. I wished for a quick death, so I wanted the poison to be potent. Then I kneeled before my goddess and prayed.

'Isis, you have deemed me unworthy of my divine power and for that I know I must repent. But I ask you one final thing: look over my children. They are unblemished by the horrors of this world. Do not let my failures condemn them. Please, Isis, protect them.'

The tears came then. Floods of them. I do not know how long I cried for. But I was only aware of the time when there came a great knocking at the door of the temple.

Octavian is here.

I reached for the wolfsbane tincture and was suddenly reminded of my brother.

Guilt as I told you, accompanies me even in death.

But as I opened my mouth to welcome the end, I heard a scream. It was a voice I recognised.

'Marcus?'

I ran to the temple door and pulled up the wooden bar that held it in place.

There in the dappled moonlight was Antonius.

'Marcus, what are you doing here?' He was kneeling before the door to the temple, his head tilted to the side.

But as I drew closer, I saw that he was slumped forward, his hand gripping the hilt of a small dagger that was buried in his chest.

'Marcus!'

Blood spilled from his mouth as he murmured, 'Selene, Isis, Cleopatra. All the names I have known you by. But you are Egypt. You are her. And Egypt, I am dying.'

'I am here.' I pulled him into the safety of the temple. Then I relocked the door.

I laid him flat before the image of Isis.

'What have you done, Marcus?' I saw then that the ivory dagger he had used to end his life was the one I had gifted him. Or rather, the blade Charmion had gifted me.

'I arrived with the infantry; they are half a day's ride away. Too late, I had thought I was too late,' he said weakly. Blood seeped from his chest. He did not have long. 'I read your letter. A cruel joke to pen it on obsidian.' Even now he laughed. The sound was sharper than a blade in my heart, and it hurt just as much.

Centuries have passed but I cannot recall this moment without smiling, without crying. That was the dichotomy of my dear Marcus. There was no one who could make me laugh or weep harder than he.

'You were not meant to die this day, Marcus. Why did you do this?'

Why did you do this? I have asked the sky a hundred times, a thousand times, since then. As the beam of sunlight he was in life, I knew that in death Re had welcomed him aboard his ship.

I have wept many times under the blistering sun, yearning for the warmth of his love.

We could have lived, Marcus.

But death beckons.

'I came to you, to die with you here,' he gasped. 'But when I found the doors locked, I struck myself on the steps. To be close to you in the end.'

'O mighty Helios, sweet Dionysus.'

'What of the children? What of our gods?'

'They are safe, with Charmion.'

He smiled his last smile. 'That is good. Let them live and love like we did. A rich life.'

'A rich life,' I agreed.

Then I kissed his bloodied lips and whispered, 'In blood, in bone, in breath – forever we are bound.'

When his chest stilled, I wailed like a bull struck with a spear. I screamed like Caesarion when the needle had pierced his skin. I howled like Arsinoe losing Qar. I gasped as though the senate killed me along with Caesar. I sobbed like the waves that took my brother and moaned like the last words of another brother lost. All the griefs I had seen surged out of me in a single note.

So immense was the pain, I knew the gods could hear it.

The silence that followed my cry was more agonising still. For it denoted the absence of Antonius's breath.

I knew then that I would never be the same. You see, my legend can bear more sorrow than I ever could. She is made of marble, and quartz, and more books than I can count. But as I was, I could endure no more grief.

I took in a ragged breath, preparing for my own journey to the beyond. A calmness overcame me as I reached for the pins in my hair.

Quicker to feed the poison into my blood than to drink it. I did not want to keep Antonius waiting.

I have seen my death so many times since this day.

Shakespeare bemoaned my immortal longings – but I did not speak so eloquently.

Elizabeth Taylor awoke from a dream, only to sleep again – but poison is no slumber.

Michaelangelo stripped me bare and placed the asp to my bosom – but nothing but a babe sucked at my breast.

Shawqi brought me to my knees to plead mercy in death – but I sought no forgiveness, only blessed release.

There are countless more versions of this moment. They overlap in my mind, making it hard to finish this tale; it is as though each rendition has drained the vibrancy of the true memory. But I will not rob you of these final moments. You and I have journeyed through the years, each page bringing us closer to this very conclusion. Though it labours me, conclude I must.

There was no escaping the island alive. The infantry may have been only half a day away, but Octavian was here, now. I did not have long before his soldiers broke down the door to my temple.

'Now, my love, it is my turn to join you.'

When I turned to pick up the wolfsbane, I found someone was already holding it.

'Charmion?'

'I have never lied to you,' she told me. 'Except when I promised you that I would leave with our children.'

'But—'

'Caesarion is old enough to protect them, he is a man grown. He knows the sacrifice you make for them, and he'll see to their survival.'

I looked back at the sealed door.

'How did you get in here?'

She pointed to the empty pool, still unfinished after all these years. 'It is connected to the cistern – I climbed through the empty tunnel.'

'I am to die this day.'

She held three fingers to my chest.

'I go with you, always.'

I wanted to fight her, to send her back through the cistern. But in truth I was comforted by her presence. And I had no fight left except this one.

'Give me the wolfsbane,' I said with finality.

We kneeled together at the altar, and I carefully laced my hairpins with the poison.

'Press them into your arm.'

'Both of them?' she asked.

'Yes, it will be a surer dose.'

I watched as the pins pierced her flesh. She gasped in pain immediately, slumping into my arms.

I took the hairpins from her arm and eased her to the ground.

'Let us go on one final journey, you and I,' she said through her pain.

I coated the needles with the wolfsbane once more, then lay down next to her and Antonius.

'When next we meet, I will beat you at senet,' I said and pushed the hairpins into my skin.

And so, we died.

CHAPTER THIRTY
A BEGINNING

I opened my eyes beneath a bright red sky, clouds like clotted blood swirling above. A figure in my likeness stood beside me.

'Rise, Cleopatra.'

Not in *my* likeness. It was her likeness that I emulated.

'Isis,' I breathed.

I could not see her face, for she had many. But I knew her like I knew my own reflection. Here was my god.

I kneeled on the ground and bowed lower than I had for any other.

It was then that I realised the floor beneath me was crimson too, undulating like blood from a wound.

I looked back to my god. 'Are you to judge my entry to the beyond?'

She shook her head, the beads in her hair chiming like the sweetest of melodies. 'You are not to pass beyond, Cleopatra. Today your curse awakens.'

I rose, confused. 'Am I not worthy of the field of reeds?'

'The fate that binds your family to the gods has come to pass this day. You are the last to suffer from it.'

'The gift of the gods?'

Isis laughed and I winced – the sound was like grinding metal.

'Gift?' she said. 'No, indeed. When your ancestor came to Egypt he pillaged and desecrated the tombs of old, searching for the lost arts in the Book of the Dead. For there was once a time when we gods walked the earth with men, and he sought to bind us once more.'

I shook my head in disbelief. But of course a god would not lie.

'He uncovered a spell that bound the soul of Serapis to his temple. We gods do not do well in cages. He invoked our wrath, and so we cursed his descendants with a power that would prove their downfall.'

'Our divine gifts are a punishment?'

She laughed again, and this time it sounded like the crack of thunder. 'Look at your family. Betrayal, murder, deceit. The curse held true. Each of you branded with the god who would weave your demise.'

I could not hide my shock. My hand went to my neck where my precious mark of Isis lay. How many times had I touched the skin there and believed myself blessed?

I thought of the many tales I had heard about Sōter: songs, poems, performances. How they had rejoiced at his powers! How they had venerated his deeds!

I've spoken on your historians' lies, but the greatest deception was my own.

'But what of my children, born without the mark?'

'Ah, now we gods are ruthless, but not cruel. Babes born of love would come into the world free of the curse.'

Am I weeping? Or am I laughing? I could not distinguish the feelings that overcame me.

'You see, you understand it all much better now,' Isis said.

'The curse ends with me. There is no one left.'

'Your curse will never end,' she said.

I looked at her questioningly.

'You wish to know what your power is to be? It is the greatest of all my talents. Resurrection. Never shall you die.'

'No.'

'Yes. Every time you depart the realm of life, you shall find yourself back here, in the waters of my womb, to be born again as you are now. Bound forever in this body, time and time again.'

Then her hands came down on either side of my neck and she pushed me through a crevice that had opened in the ground.

I felt as though I was falling for half a day. Terror tightened my throat with screams, my stomach lurching upwards, my arms flailing until they grew numb with fatigue.

On I fell.

And fell.

I wanted to die. I wanted to live. Hope and horror battled within me.

Then I blinked and found myself beside the bodies of Antonius and Charmion.

'No,' I whispered. 'No, it cannot be.'

I reached for Charmion's wrist; though it was still warm, it was as lifeless as Antonius's.

The twin beads of blood caused by the hairpins were yet to clot on her arm. They matched my own.

Not an asp's bite. It would have taken only a brief inspection to compare the size of the puncture to their fangs. But Octavian had heard of my method of vengeance during the donations of Alexandria. And what better way to emphasise my monstrous ways than to entwine my fate with that of the cobra.

'No.' I beat my fists against Charmion's chest. 'We were meant to go together.'

I would have stayed with them both, if I could have. But the distant footfalls of soldiers drew closer.

Soon Octavian would enter the temple and find me alive.

And no longer can I die.

Though I could feel pain: looking down at two of my loves, that was certain.

Octavian will not have me.

But I could not bear to leave my heart in this temple. I looked at Antonius and Charmion and felt a sob claw at my throat. 'A curse it is to live when you are gone.'

The soldiers drew ever nearer.

I knew I had to flee but I was paralysed. As well as making good my escape, I had to ensure they would not search for me.

I stroked Charmion's hair, a plan forming. 'I will not let your sacrifice be for naught. Let me play one final ruse.'

And so I removed my cloak and wrapped it around Charmion's shoulders. Then I took some ash from burned incense and lined her eyes. Finally, I removed my crown and placed it on her head.

I had not encountered Octavian in many years and even then, only briefly. When he entered the temple, he would see the queen he searched for. Few ever looked beyond the crown.

The soldiers were close now, their boots striking the tiles in the temple district.

I squeezed the hands of the two people I had loved and lost. But I knew I had to leave, quickly.

I followed the path Charmion had taken, slipping through the tunnels of the empty pool. I was able to go as far as the central cistern without getting wet, and from there I could navigate my way through the collapsed remains that led to the cave by the sea.

My children were still there when I arrived. The four of them sobbed when they saw me.

'We must go: Octavian is on Antirhodos, now is the time to slip away,' I said.

Caesarion rowed while I searched the water for any sign of a threat.

But no one was looking for a servant and her four children. They were looking for a queen.

And I would never be that again.

EPILOGUE

It has been thousands of years since my first death. And I have had many, many more. I have come to understand the magnitude of the curse bestowed upon me.

I have suffered for the crimes I committed, and there will be countless others.

No one is made perfect in the likeness of a god. No matter how hard I tried.

It is an exquisite pain unlike any other, to watch your children die. We were not entirely successful in our escape. Selene and Helios were captured by Octavian two years later, and as a final insult to me were sent to Octavia, who raised them as her own. Caesarion was also captured young, and I was only thankful his death was swift. I was left with Ptolemy, and together we found sanctuary on an island off the coast of Greece. We called the isle the Land of Punt and lived there simply.

The next time I died, Ptolemy was barely into adulthood. I fell from a great height while picking olives by a cliff's edge. Once again, I visited Isis's realm before returning to the moment before my death. When I awoke, I found Ptolemy weeping next to the olive tree. It was only then that I told him of the truth of my curse. He wept all the harder.

But as the years passed, I knew that he was comforted that old age would not separate us during his lifetime. And when my mind grew weary and my body frail, I welcomed the gentle release of death. Of course, my peace was curtailed as I was reborn once more, awakening in the body I had first died in, not yet forty years of age. Ptolemy was fifty-seven.

Of Helios and Selene, I knew a little. One summer, a sailor

shipwrecked on our isle, bringing with him news of all kinds. The sailor, injured by his ordeal, succumbed to infection despite my attempts to prevent it. But before he died, he told me of a queen, newly crowned, in Mauretania.

I repaired his boat over many months, my suspicions growing by the day. When I deemed it seaworthy, Ptolemy and I sailed across the ocean that separated us from the continent. It took us many months to locate Mauretania. Neither of us were sailors, and we were unaccustomed to the harbours of the new world.

When I finally caught sight of the Queen, my heart soared.

Selene. And there by her side was Helios, among her courtiers.

I could have gone to her in secret. I almost did, but I worried about the consequences my presence would bring. Most of all, I feared she would be killed for my deception.

So Ptolemy and I returned to the Land of Punt to live out his remaining days. It was half a century later that I learned that both Selene and Helios had died from a swift and sudden illness that had swept through the court.

I did not linger on whether I would have been able to heal them.

I could have chosen to become a mother again – across the years I took many lovers – but the torment of my own children's death is the only grief I will never recover from.*

I spent many years after they had gone dying. I tried it all the ways: with a blade at the throat, at the neck, in the heart. I tried drowning, fire, poison again. But every time I found myself there – with her.

I lived a life like Caesar's: full of integrity and agitation. I lived a life like Marcus's: full of debauchery and drink. But eventually I learned to live a life like mine: full of curiosity and reflection. I travelled the world under many names and learned more languages – twenty-five at my last count. I spent hours upon hours in your libraries and universities.

---

* Pregnancy was an easy thing to avoid; if you had my texts you'd have the means too: a simple tincture brewed for two days.

I have not come much further than the woman you met in the first pages. Or perhaps it is that I have returned to her again. Do you remember her? The grit of sand beneath her legs, her hair and belt loose, her mind preoccupied with a game of senet, and not the ruling of a kingdom? Even her mouth was filled with the simple pleasure of a ripe fig, and not the words of a queen.

And as the years have passed, I have watched myself in your plays and your films and your paintings. I have seen your costumes – polyester and plastic – an indignity of the worst kind. I have even read your books, both fiction and non, but false both. You try to capture my essence but cannot, for you seek the truth in all the wrong places.

Look within and you will see me. I am every woman scorned, and every girl wronged. I am the wrath of vengeance and the heat of desire. I am everything carnal and your darkest sins. I am all that is innocent and pure.

Witch. Whore. Villain.

But I am also Cleopatra; the mother, the lover, the friend, and so much more. I am abundant. You will never define me, and that is the purest form of freedom I can hope to find in this life I've been cursed to endure.

I told you at the beginning, this is not the story of how I died. For death will forever evade me.

No, this is the story of how I lived.

And live still.

ACKNOWLEDGEMENTS

Cleopatra's ghost has been by my side for many years, but I was too afraid to look at her. I was daunted, haunted, by the concept of putting pen to paper and resurrecting her. But when I finally started writing, the words flowed like the Nile. That would not have happened without the people who were willing to traverse those waters with me.

UK TEAM
Borough Press Editorial: *Suzie Dooré, Beth Coates, Jabin Ali*
Copyeditor: *Amber Burlinson*
Proofreader: *Sarah Bance*
Cover design: *Sarah Foster*
Production: *Sophie Waeland*
Marketing: *Sian Richefond, Lipfon Tang*
Publicity: *Susanna Peden*
Internal illustrations: *Sophie Dunster*

US TEAM
Ballantine Team: *Kimberly Hovey, Kara Cesare, Kara Welsh, and Jennifer Hershey*
Editorial: *Tricia Narwani, Ayesha Shibli*
Managing Editorial: *Pam Alders*
Production: *Loren Noveck, Katie Zilberman*
Cover: *Aarushi Menon*
Marketing: *Taylor Noel, Rachel Taylor*
Social media: *Sophie Normil*
Publicity: *Emily Isayeff, Chelsea Woodward*

AGENT TEAM

Primary agent: *Juliet Mushens*
Foreign Rights Agent: *Alba Arnau Prado*
Agent's Assistant: *Emma Dawson*
Foreign Rights Executive: *Catriona Fida*
US agent: *Ginger Clark*

I'd like to take a moment to highlight a few of this incredible team: Juliet Mushens, your enthusiasm motivates me more than anything else, thank you for always encouraging me. Suzie Dooré, this journey was made even more life changing because I got to publish this with you as my editor. Tricia Narwani, our list of collaborations grows by the day, we're more than teammates now. The above names are the best in the business and I'm so lucky to have worked with each and every one of you.

To my family and friends, Jim and L, Kate, Alice, Sam, Hannah, Tasha, Lizzie, Amy, the Bells, all the El-Arifis and Dinsdales, none of this would have been possible without you.

And finally, as always, my final words are for you, my dearest readers. Thank you for believing in this version of Cleopatra long enough to bring her to life with me.

SELECTED BIBLIOGRAPHY

CLASSICAL SOURCES

Appian (1913). *Roman History, Volume III: The Civil Wars, Books 1–3.26* (H. White, trans.). Loeb Classical Library 4. Harvard University Press.

Boccaccio, G. (1963). *Concerning Famous Women* (G. A. Guarino, trans.). Rutgers University Press.

Cicero (2011). *Tusculan Disputations* (quoted and trans. by R. A. Gurval). In M. M. Miles (ed.), *Cleopatra: A Sphinx Revisited*. University of California Press.

Dio, C. (1917). *Roman History, Volume VI* (E. Cary & H. B. Foster, trans.). Loeb Classical Library 83. Harvard University Press.

Herodotus (1996). *The Histories* (A. de Sélincourt, trans.; J. Marincola, rev. ed.). Penguin Books. (Original work published 1954)

Horace (1912). *Odes and Epodes* (C. E. Bennett, trans.). Loeb Classical Library. Harvard University Press.

Horace (1995). *Odes I: Carpe Diem* (D. West, trans.). Oxford University Press.

Julius Caesar (1869). *The Alexandrian War* (W. A. McDevitte & W. S. Bohn, trans.). Harper and Brothers.

Lucan (1909). *The Pharsalia of Lucan* (H. T. Riley, Trans.). George Bell & Sons.

Nicolaus of Damascus (1917). *Life of Augustus* (C. M. Hall, trans.). Johns Hopkins University.

Pliny the Elder (1938–40). *Natural History* (H. Rackham, trans.). Loeb Classical Library. Harvard University Press.

Plutarch. (1919). *Lives, Volume VII: Demosthenes and Cicero, Alexander and Caesar* (B. Perrin, Trans.). Loeb Classical Library 99. Harvard University Press.

Plutarch. (1932). *The Lives of the Noble Grecians and Romans* (J. Dryden, trans.). Modern Library.

Propertius (1964). *The Elegies of Propertius* (E. A. Butler & H. E. Barber, trans.). G. Olms.

Schoppius, G. (1606). *Priapeia Sive Diversorum Poetarum in Priapum Lusus*. Francofurti: In Oficina Typographica Wolfgangi Richteri.

Strabo (1917–32). *The Geography* (H. L. Jones, trans., vols. 1–8). Loeb Classical Library. Harvard University Press.

Suetonius (1914). *Lives of the Caesars, Volume I: Julius, Augustus, Tiberius, Gaius Caligula* (J. C. Rolfe, trans., K. R. Bradley, Intro.). Loeb Classical Library 31. Harvard University Press.

Velleius Paterculus (1924). *Compendium of Roman History*. Loeb Classical Library. Harvard University Press.

MODERN SOURCES

Al Shafei, H. K. (2016). 'The crowns of Cleopatra VII: An iconographical analytical study'. *Scientific Culture: Journal of Applied Sciences in Cultural Heritage*, University of the Aegean.

Ashton, S.-A. (2008). *Cleopatra and Egypt*. Blackwell Publishing.

Chauveau, M. (2002). *Cleopatra: Beyond the Myth*. Cornell University Press.

El-Daly, O. (2005). *Egyptology: The Missing Millennium – Ancient Egypt in Medieval Arabic Writings*, UCL Press, London

Fielding, S. (1994). *The Lives of Cleopatra and Octavia*. Bucknell University Press.

Gurval, R. A. (1995). *Actium and Augustus: The Politics and Emotions of Civil War*. Ann Arbor: University of Michigan Press.

Jones, P. J. (2006). *Cleopatra: A Sourcebook*. University of Oklahoma Press.

Kleiner, D. E. (2005). *Cleopatra and Rome*. Cambridge: Harvard University Press.

Miles, M. M. (ed.) (2011). *Cleopatra: A Sphinx Revisited*. University of California Press.

Prose, F. (2022). *Cleopatra: Her History, Her Myth*. Yale University Press.

Randazzo, G. (2012). 'Cleopatra: The Defiance of Feminine Virtue'. *English Senior Seminar Papers*, Paper 8.

Roller, D. W. (2010). *Cleopatra: A Biography*. Oxford University Press.

Schiff, S. (2010). *Cleopatra: A Life*. Black Bay Books.

Shakespeare, W. (1960). *Antony and Cleopatra* (M. Mack, ed.). Penguin.

Swinburne, A. C. (1869). 'Notes on Designs of the Old Masters at Florence'. *Fortnightly Review*.

Tronson, A. (1998). 'Vergil, the Augustans, and the Invention of Cleopatra's Suicide—One Asp or Two?' *Vergilius*, 44, 31–50.

Tyldesley, J. A. (2009). *Cleopatra: Last Queen of Egypt*. Profile Books